Selling Air

Daniel D. Herchenroether

Front cover graphics and website by Greg Herchenroether
Back cover graphics by Lee Ann Heltzel

ISBN 0-9754224-0-5

PUBLISHED BY:
***DDH MEDIA,* PITTSBURGH, PA**

WWW.SELLINGAIR.COM

Printed in the United States of America

Published April 2004

To
Wendy, Ben and Amy
and
All my friends and colleagues from
Active Software

Acknowledgements

I couldn't have written this tome without the help and encouragement of many friends, mentors and advisors. I am blessed to have worked with and for some of the best in the software business and they have provided unfailing support and encouragement in the writing of this book.

Foremost among these are Tom Looney, who taught me everything I know about software sales - and a lot about life; Mike "Mr. Hands On" Ping, who likes to "cherry pick the low hanging fruit"; Jim Green, one of the few CEOs or managers I was – and still am – willing to run through walls for; marketing wizard, Zack "Valley of the Geeks" Urlocker; and Andy Ostrowski, my good friend and business idol in the UK.

Several other "early adopters" reviewed the manuscript (or at least parts) and provided very valuable feedback: Elisa Cafferky, Bob Barnett, Nader Nafissi (one of the best SEs there ever was), Anne MacDonald, Pat and Sue Stewart and Gary Limongello. Thanks to all who endured the rough early releases.

In addition to Zack's expert advice on how to market this work, Peter Park deserves tremendous credit for passing along a wealth of knowledge about marketing on the Web.

Special thanks to Tom and Pam Chickness who introduced me to an extraordinary editor, Gina Hillier. This manuscript was a total mess when Gina first reviewed it and patiently helped me craft a real novel.

Kudos to Greg Herchenroether who did an outstanding job on the front cover and www.sellingair.com website designs. Likewise, Lee Ann Heltzel did an exceptional job redesigning the back cover.

I also need to acknowledge Rich Karlgaard of *Forbes* for the best, most concise description of what the Business Development function is in the software business (see chapter 3 and the *Forbes* 12/26/2000 issue). Also, credit to Chris Halligan for "fat bear" philosophy.

Finally, I'm grateful beyond words to my wife, Wendy, who has allowed me to indulge in my dream of writing books. It has been painful for her at times as I manically bounced back and forth between euphoria and despair. Thanks for your love and patience: It was not in vain. I love you.

Chapter 1 Reboot

Wayne Angelis hunkered down in his black Saab 93, reluctant to get out and enter his Scarsdale, New York home. He didn't want to face his wife just yet, as it would be one of those "I told you so" moments and he wasn't going to rush it.

As sales manager for a New York software startup, he had dedicated most of 1997 to the task of building a sales team in anticipation of a major sales push in 1998, perhaps resulting in an initial public stock offering. For the second time in three years, however, his career-defining goal of riding a software startup to IPO would elude him. He would, yet again, have to justify to his wife his feverish allegiance to the crazed world of software in the 90's: constant contract negotiations, obscene sales quotas – "the Number" – but also technology's great promise to change the course of human evolution. Or something close.

Finally, he raised his towering frame out of the car and retrieved two boxes of office belongings from the trunk, including his prized Rolodex of contacts – now reduced to his Palm Pilot – numerous sales award plaques and other tokens from the last two years at Interframe as well as Wang, IBM and a couple of no-name companies in the decade before that. Wayne snuck slowly into his house via the kitchen door hoping that he could slip into his home office unobserved to compose his thoughts.

He didn't get past the sink.

"Owww, owww, rowl, rowl!"

Unfortunately for Wayne, his beagle, Charlie, greeted him with his full throated, blood curdling wailing and howling. Helen, weighted down with a basket of freshly laundered polo shirts, responded to Charlie's yelps by detouring through the kitchen.

"Hey, Redford! What are you doing back?" she asked, using her pet name for Wayne. She liked to tease him that he was a Robert Redford look-alike with his boyish, freckled face and sandy hair with a bit of gray at the temples, hinting that he was well over forty. "Didn't you just leave an hour ago?"

Wayne smiled but Helen recognized phony happiness when she saw it. She also noticed the box of office items on the counter and suspected the worst.

"Okay, what's going on?" she asked, flicking some stray hairs from his face.

"We got bought today."

"Not again! By who?"

"IBM. They simply handed us severance checks…" he said, tossing his check on the kitchen table, "… and shook our hands. Our stuff was already boxed up."

"Are they trying to buy everyone these days?"

"Anything web-related."

"And your stock options?"

Wayne shook his head. "The founders got their share for sure. The rest of us? Jack shit."

Helen crossed her arms across her chest and tried to restrain herself, but it came out anyway.

"I TOLD YOU…"

"…ah, here it comes…" Wayne said, covering his ears.

"…we should have stayed at Star Micro…"

"DAMN IT, HELEN! Don't kick me when I'm down!"

"…I guess I better cancel the BMW upgrade…"

Even though he expected this kind of exchange, Wayne was always shocked at his wife's priorities. They weren't in the poor house having built up a sizable investment portfolio from his sales winnings through the 80's and earlier 90's. Even so, it was never enough for Helen.

"Look," Wayne said, "Interframe should have gone big. The web server market is exploding and this software could have been a standard. These guys simply took the money and ran. We could have been an independent winner."

"Winning. You keep chasing this dream about 'winning', which you define as taking a company public. I applaud your persistence…" Helen said, frowning in disappointment as she examined the severance check. "… but isn't it better to be at a stable place like IBM?"

"They left a lot of money on the table, and IBM doesn't want us for sales anyway."

"Oh, give me a break. This isn't about money with you – unfortunately. This instability drives me nuts."

"Instability? You know damn well we can afford that beemer. Hell, let's get one from each series, all different colors if you want. You can finally impress all your tennis friends."

"It's 'bimmer' not *'beemer'*. A 'beemer' would be a motorcycle…"

Wayne stood back up, shook his head and headed to the refrigerator for a soda. He really didn't care about proper slang for a car. He wanted to get Helen to understand his goal in life.

"It's about helping to build a company starting with nothing but an idea. I want to be part of that. I can sell ideas." He turned to see Helen staring at him with a blank expression. "You just don't get it, do you?"

"Well, it's not for lack of trying," Helen replied. She selected her own soda and followed Wayne into his home office, a Spartan existence by Helen's standards with simple Ikea trestle tables and bookcases. She would have outfitted the space with mahogany or at least cherry.

"I'm not comfortable about you 'selling ideas'," Helen said. "Sounds like selling air to me. How is a company going to make money on your 'ideas'? I'd like to see something tangible. Something I can touch, drive maybe."

"See? You really *don't* get it. What do you think software is? It *is* the tangible expression of mental activity…"

"Oh, please!" Helen said, rolling her eyes."

"…and it is certainly tangible in the customer's bottom line."

"Oh, and all that bitching about *stupid* customers? I guess they don't 'get it' either. Of course, you were still paid on those sales even when they didn't get your promised results."

"At least I did it with full disclosure of the cost and benefits."

"As *you* saw it. I recall how the message always got stretched toward the end of the quarter."

Wayne was stung, offended by Helen's tone. "I resent your implications. You know I'm an honest advocate. Unlike some."

"I don't suppose you'd consider something safe like Realtime Analytics again?"

"You can't be serious! I'd rather drink acid. Most of those snakes at Realtime would sell their grandmother for a quarter. See, that's what I'm talking about; they made claims that never could have held up. You certainly remember that scum bag, Tom Gatto, right? How he never let the truth stand in the way of a deal?"

"Of course I remember. You spent more time trying to protect your turf from him than selling. But at least Realtime is public, profitable and growing. And Gatto isn't still there, right?"

Wayne smiled weakly, recalling that he had a hand in Gatto's departure. "No, he's not. I don't know where he is and I couldn't care less."

He started to pace his office. "I had a call a week or so ago from my headhunter friend, Harry, wanting to recruit me into a company called 'InUnison'. They do integration software, which is actually kind of cool…"

"Do they sell something tangible, like computers?" Helen asked.

He turned to Helen and raised an eyebrow. "No. They 'sell air'. Software."

"Don't do it! I don't care if it cures cancer."

"Harry said InUnison was a real straight, high-integrity company. No bullshit."

"Haven't I heard this before? Pardon my cynicism, but I think this whole tech frenzy has sent everyone over to the *dark side,*" Helen said, doing her best Darth Vader imitation and clenching her fist in the air. "The force, my dear, *the force!*"

"Not funny. Anyway, maybe I should look into it."

Helen looked at Wayne, shaking her head incredulously. She decided to try a different tack.

"If you're really serious about this, shouldn't we be in Silicon Valley?"

"That's the last thing I would do. I'm a New Yorker; not some surfer dude," Wayne said, leaning on the back of an easy chair. "All those companies out there, like InUnison, sooner or later, have to start selling their products and they have to sell them out here where the business is. I'm positioned to do that."

Helen inhaled, started to make another point and gave up.

Wayne sighed. "I need to try again, Helen. We have the luxury to take risks."

"Financially, maybe," she said, wondering about the new dining room furniture she ordered without telling Wayne. "But mentally? You ought to consider that. I'm tired of 'conflicted Wayne'."

She turned and left the office.

***

Tyson's Corner, Virginia, was coming to life in the form of the usual morning gridlock on routes 123, 7, I-66, the Dulles Tollway, and the parking lot known as I-495, the Capital Beltway. InUnison's eastern headquarters, all four people worth, was located on Boone Boulevard, right behind the interchange of 123 and 7. The location afforded easy access to major routes around the Washington metro area, that is, once free of the perpetual Tyson's gridlock. The exponential growth of technology firms during the 90's spawned a building boom which taxed the infrastructure for automobiles.

The regional sales and systems engineering managers, federal sales rep, and federal systems engineer had individual offices in one of the football-shaped, red granite buildings. The plain, cream-painted offices along a curving hallway were shared by numerous other small high tech companies.

"Damn that Reaper!" Ken Presby lamented. "He's going to cost me my overachievement bonus!" Presby had just finished the weekly conference call with his sales troops. It was the first Monday of December and the pressure in software sales was at its maximum in the last month of the last quarter of the year. Joining InUnison early in the year from a "beltway bandit" consulting firm, he had worked to be the superstar Regional Director by cracking the whip. Or so he thought. His reps considered him utterly irrelevant to their lives. What did a services guy with a thin comb-over know about software?

Presby continued to review the forecast spreadsheet in front of him.

There isn't much gravy here, he thought. *Wait! Gatto! That New York prima donna! He has a bunch of stuff he could close if he could tear himself away from moussing his hair.* He quickly added up $250,000 in licenses, most of it from a bunch of no-name dot-coms.

Founded in early 1995 by Bill Engler and a few core engineers after a long career building cutting-edge software for the likes of IBM and Sun

Microsystems, InUnison's products acted like middlemen, enabling all the various systems in a corporation to share information, or be "integrated", in industry parlance. Normally, corporate information technology departments – or, more likely, expensive consultants – had to write lots of computer code to move data between systems. InUnison's out-of-the-box approach promised large development cost savings and productivity increases. Of course, still being in startup mode, their product was in some ways still working on that "promise".

It didn't help that there was no explicit marketing bucket for InUnison to be placed in. "Messaging" was too sterile and arcane but that was what InUnison's product did. After much lobbying with analysts, InUnison and their fierce rival, VibraWeb, were identified as the emerging leaders – at least in marketing awareness – in the so-called "Enterprise Application Integration" market ("EAI" for short). The new software segment was invented by some equally emerging analyst at Gartner Group, Giga or other market analysis firm.

The larger the company, the more computer systems there are to manage. New systems seldom replaced old software. The new programs simply added to the portfolio of indecipherable "spaghetti code", upon which the operations of the business depended. Enabling corporations to tie all of these software applications together cheaply and make some sense of the mess was touted as the "holy grail" of computing. Hype or not, being positioned in a hot new market segment was instant visibility for InUnison. The trick, now, was how to sell its products before the analyst grew bored with his market creation and chased some other new technology.

Presby's boat anchor of the region was Gary "Grim" Reaper, the Atlanta sales rep whose next dollar in revenue would be his first in two quarters. Reaper could always be counted on for excuses as to why he couldn't close deals, the latest of which was the delay in a new "connector" – software which could handle communication between the InUnison core information manager and some application. The latest connector would allow InUnison to talk to the big IBM mainframe computers found in almost every sizable corporation in America. It was true that revenue would be lost because of the release delay and Reaper clung to the excuse like a Titanic survivor to a floating board.

Giving up on Reaper, he returned to ponder his strategy to motivate his New York sales rep.

***

Tom Gatto stood in front of his bathroom mirror working his short black hair into spikes full of Paul Mitchell hair gel. Satisfied, he removed the towel that protected his triple-starched, white shirt collar and rechecked his tie. He had sales calls lined up and wanted his Brioni uniform in as perfect condition as was his slim and firmly toned five foot eight inch body.

He glanced at his Tourneau watch. Eight thirty. *Ooops. I missed another of my Regional Director's lame sales conference calls. Pity.* He eyed that watch frequently these days, wishing he could replace it with the Rolex he would get as number one sales rep.

Gatto looked out the front of his self-described "Central Park West condo" to check the weather. That characterization was a bit of a stretch. The apartment was really in the middle of West Sixty-Fourth Street, and, yes, he could see Central Park if he pressed his face to the window and strained to see the trees. Anyway, the gorgeous, yet vacuous women he tried to impress with his address didn't know the difference.

Gatto had eclipsed his Number for the year by July and was closing in on 230 percent of that Number, possibly ending the year as the number one sales rep at InUnison. It might be a small pond compared with an earlier haunt, Sun Microsystems, but the compensation was a hell of a lot better. With margins over 90% in the software business, there was plenty of incentive cash for management to ladle out to the sales force.

He put on his jacket, intending to run out for a cappuccino, when the phone rang. He turned, looked at the phone on his desk across the room, took a step out the door but just couldn't let it go. He sprinted back to answer it in case it was a sales lead.

"InUnison Software, Tom Gatto speaking," he said, with phony cheeriness. "How can I help you?"

"So, what sickness prevents you from calling into my conference calls?"

Great. Why do I let the telephone run my life? Gatto thought, lamenting the fact he would now be kissing Presby's ass instead of hitting on the cute new barista at his local Starbucks.

"I know you didn't get away with this disrespect at Sun. Or NeXT. Now there was a quality sales organization."

"Hey don't knock it. They helped pay for my Carnegie-Mellon education."

His mother had tried to push him toward pre-med at Harvard but the siren call of technology – computers specifically – drove him to Pittsburgh. He couldn't get enough of software and making a computer do his bidding through programming it. Control of the machine was seductive to Gatto. He also discovered the intoxication of enticing humans to do his bidding via sales. His first sales successes involved selling ice balls during the summers in Hoboken, selectively seducing lonely mothers along his route. But computers! They changed peoples' lives! It was the ultimate in control!

Gatto cut his computer sales teeth as a "campus consultant", as NeXT called them. At the time, NeXT was focused on the academic market. They had an impressive software development environment and word and document processing software. Unfortunately, customers had to buy very strange hardware in order to run Steve Jobs' "insanely great" applications. But no matter; Tom Gatto knew how to engage the imagination of his market and sold thousands of dollars of NeXT hardware to professors and students so that they could produce technical documents better than their peers.

Based on his outstanding sales performance at CMU, Gatto was rewarded with a choice sales district in New York. He attacked the market with zeal, expecting the Manhattan business market to be as wowed over the sleek black NeXT Cubes as the gullible academics he sold to. He was going to change the way Wall Street did business.

Nothing could have been farther from the truth. Except for very early adopters who wanted the productive development environment, corporate IT laughed the proprietary hardware – and those trying to sell it – out of their offices.

It finally dawned on the company that customers only tolerated its proprietary hardware to have access to the productive software. Deciding to convert the NeXTSTEP system to run on standard personal computers, NeXT abruptly halted the production of computer hardware, and fired half of the company's employees, including an incredulous Tom Gatto. He was stunned, hurt, jilted even, as if spurned by a lover. How could the ultimate and perfect system be dismissed? He blamed Steve Jobs, he blamed NeXT marketing, he blamed his mother, anything and anybody but himself.

Starting with Sun Microsystems – after a short mourning period – Gatto began a string of sales positions representing several companies' products to mostly Wall Street customers. However, Gatto never recovered his idealism from the trauma of his abrupt dismissal from NeXT. He compensated by developing an obsession with being the number one sales rep for whoever he happened to be selling for, and no tactic was spared in his quest for his Number.

"Look, I'm sorry I missed your call. I was on the phone to some prospects…"

"You're so full of shit, Gatto," Presby responded. "Are there really that many people ready to deal with you at 7:30 a.m.?"

"You'd be surprised. These startups I'm courting work wacky hours." He wasn't lying for once.

"It's those dot-com startups I want to talk to you about. First of all, the ones you closed last quarter haven't paid us. Second, for the good of the region and the company, we need you to close everything on your forecast for us to make the Number and it's a little heavy on the dot-coms. Can't you close a couple of the name accounts on your forecast? You've got Merrill Lynch on here."

"Ya know, Ken, I'm busting my ass to close anything possible when you know I'm already maxed out on the comp plan. I'm doing it for the good of the company."

"Gee, I'm sooo sorry Tom. I know 12 percent money isn't much motivation and the $30k you'd make from your $250k in closeable business is nothing but pocket change to you. We're grateful that you're still motivated to outsell The Swede and strap that shiny new Rolex on your wrist."

"Ken, can we get on with the forecast review and spare me the sarcasm?"

"What about Merrill?"

"I could close them tomorrow if we had the mainframe connector…"

"I don't want excuses, Gatto…"

"So, you want me to lie to them about it being pushed out to February?"

"Of course not, but a little "finesse" …"

"It's pretty black and white, Ken. They need it in January for development and we aren't going to have it. It's the same at Potential Investing and a bunch of other prospects. You want me to 'finesse' them all?"

"Well, it's your job to find a way to hurdle the barrier and bring in the business. Can't they start using a pre-release or something?"

Presby is starting to sound pretty desperate, Tom thought. *He must be worried about making his bonus. Serves him right for coddling losers like Reaper.*

"Look, these guys want to go *production* by February," Gatto said. "They aren't going to trust pre-release or beta quality software. If they don't trust it, they aren't going to use it. It's go/no go time for them. They need to *see* something from us *now*."

Presby wiped beads of perspiration from his upper lip. He had to get Gatto to come through for him and he thrashed his brain for some way to motivate Gatto. Unfortunately, Gatto was right. He *was* max'd out on his compensation and he was still a long shot to beat The Swede. Added to that, and unbeknownst to Presby, Gatto was getting "loose in the socket", and was considering several opportunities pitched by recruiters. His self-perceived star status did not allow for the kind of ham-handed treatment by a lesser light like Presby.

"Tom, do whatever it takes. Can't we throw an SE or Professional Services at the accounts? You know, be *creative*."

"What do you mean by 'creative'?" Gatto asked, hurt that he wasn't being given credit for his usual "creativity". "Look, you know my SE quit last month and that stiff, Murphy, is a pain in the ass to get down here from Boston, and damn near worthless when he does. You also know PS wants to get paid for engagements – it's end-of-year for them too – and most prospects aren't stupid enough to pay us to sell to them. It's a little late to be trying to schedule a PS engineer in there. Besides, what's in it for me? I'm better off letting deals slip into next year."

"Well, if you would call into the weekly conference call, you would have heard today that O'Rourke is going to establish a "New Account Bonus" for December. Five thousand dollars per new account, and double the revenue amount applied to the rep rankings."

Gatto was caught speechless for a few seconds. "You're not serious." *Our VP of Sales must be desperate, too.*

Presby knew that would catch Gatto's interest. "Yes, we are. So, let's do some quick math here. You have seven new account possibilities on your forecast, that's a quick $35k…" Presby said, using the "k" computer-ese moniker for thousands. "…plus the $30k for the total $250k revenue with rankings credit of half a million. Listen, we *are* going to blow the Number out one way or another. We're going to do another round of venture financing next year so revenue performance has to be met. So what if we pay out a little more as incentive? The VCs don't care about the margins, only that revenue goals are met."

Gatto reviewed his numbers again. *Hmmm, I really* could *still catch The Swede and strap on that Rolex! Maybe a down payment on a condo on the other side of Central Park…*

"Okay, I'll close these deals somehow. I'll be dancing around the mainframe thing, though."

"Great! Dance away! I knew you'd jump at the chance to be Number One!"

I'd like to tap dance on your ass, lard butt, Gatto thought.

"Oh, by the way, the kickoff meeting will be January fifth through the eighth."

"And what cool location have we booked this time?" Gatto asked.

"Need you ask? The absolutely *faaabulous,* Hotel Sofitel, Redwood Shores, California."

"Argh, not again! All that fake French crap all over the place, complete with authentically shitty French attitude. Ya know, I hear there are some great places in Napa…"

"Hey this isn't a Steve Jobs operation where they pack up the whole company and ship it to Silverado or somewhere. There's no way Engler would spring for that. He has this crazy notion that we ought to go public one of these days, maybe even be profitable."

"Why should we care about profits? No one else in the industry seems to care. The VCs keep shoveling money in. Even tightwad Engler should welcome that."

"Look, that's out of our control. I really don't care about IPO," Presby lied. He watched his stock option vesting calendar as regularly as anyone.

"Right, Ken. Anything you say."

"So, if that's all, let's go sell! Beat VibraWeb!"

Gatto hung up the phone. "Blow it out your ass, you loser."

***

The managements of InUnison and VibraWeb knew each other well, and loathed each other all the same. Khaybar Singh, VibraWeb's CEO, would sneer about Bill Engler's alleged moral superiority and Engler would rail about Singh's lack of business ethics. Worse, in Engler's hierarchy of sin, was Singh's loose technical discipline. Their attitudes trickled down through the sales ranks who liked nothing better than to use the rivalry to get more resources for their sales battles. A mention that VibraWeb was in an account would result in visibility all the way up the chain of command at InUnison and vice versa.

VibraWeb had a reputation in Silicon Valley for employing a "slash and burn" sales style: get in and get the money as soon as possible, if for no other reason than to keep it out of the competition's hands. This style had the effect of acquiring market share for the company but at the expense of profits. While revenue growth was significantly aggressive, there was a persistent view of VibraWeb as an arrogant company to do business with, that VibraWeb would eat their young. Most of their customers and partners were wary of their tactics.

Singh was a software engineer for Hewlett-Packard in the late 80's and into the 90's, moving up to managing workstation operating system projects. Frustrated by the "HP Way" and seeing colleagues making fortunes in Silicon Valley startups, he joined a series of startups that went nowhere. He fostered a reputation, though, as a demanding technical manager who, legend had it, never missed a release date, albeit usually at the expense of quality. Testing was a luxury at times.

He joined with longtime friend and partner Chin Tsai to start VibraWeb, whose first product was to be an "object-oriented messaging bus". Objects, or chunks of reusable code, were all the rage in the early 90's and his design for having these chunks talk across the Internet was viewed as revolutionary. His reputation – and the vast amounts of venture capital available – had VC firms lining up to fund his new company. Chin Tsai became Chief Technology Officer.

The pair assembled an engineering team and began work on the product. After 18 months, release 1.0 was ready and it was time to start selling. Unfortunately, no one had a clue what the messaging system was good for and Singh's initial sales efforts were weak. Like many engineering-driven startups, VibraWeb was a solution in search of a problem.

Hoping to ignite his revenue stream, Singh recruited an ex-Oracle sales manager, Simon Hager, to be his Vice President of Sales. Hager, like most Oracle sales managers of the era, believed he had a divine right to every dollar of every customer. Despite his fierce reputation, reps clamored to work for him as they knew he'd make money for them. Most figured that they needed to survive under him for a few years, make some big money and then move on or just plain burn out trying. Either way, they would be in demand by other companies looking for aggressive sales reps trained in the Hager Method – which boiled down to driving revenue, driving revenue, driving revenue. Empty a prospect's wallet for more licenses than they needed and move on to the next. Even he was surprised by how often he could get away with it.

Hager and Singh started to see the rise of the integration market and swung the company to position their products for the EAI space. They thought that all they needed was the right marketing message to make it work. It was tough going since their rather arcane products were hard to use, unlike InUnison's which were designed from the ground up to do integration. No matter. Simon Hager was on the case and assured them he could "sell the fucking shit".

Hager was deep into his high octane sales day, thoughtfully sharing his intensity with every person on his sales staff. From VibraWeb's Santa Clara headquarters, he was turning up the heat on the East Coast sales team.

His phone rang just as he was fired up to call his next victim.

"HAGER!" he said into his cell phone, spitting out his name with his customary, undisguised annoyance. It was Bill Thomas, his very successful rep in New York.

"Simon, I'm leaving the company. I'm tired of you and your bullshit! I just got off the phone with a very angry CTO at First New York who says you lied to him about the contract. You lied to me too, you bastard!"

Thomas had managed to insulate most of his customers from the arrogance of the Hagers of the company. In fact, several of his customers told him they didn't want that "bastard Hager" anywhere near them.

Hager had people resigning on a regular basis, both good and bad reps, so he was unfazed.

"You know what you are, Thomas? A pussy. 'Oh, my customers are complaining'. Big fucking deal. Let 'em. We got their money and that's all that matters. If that's not enough gratification for you, get the fuck out of here. We'll be fucking fine without someone who fucking coddles his fucking customers." He punched the END button on his cell phone. "Fucking pussy."

He immediately called George Means, his Eastern Regional Sales Manager and nominally Thomas' boss. He caught him in the kitchen of his New York office suite stirring cream into his coffee.

"George, that fucking wimp Thomas fucking resigned. Hope you have another fucking rep ready to make up for three fucking million in fucking revenue," he spat out.

Means was startled at the suddenness of the news and a bit offended that Thomas hadn't come to him first. While they weren't personal friends, he felt that he and Thomas had mutual respect. Still, Means wasn't surprised; he knew Thomas cared too much about his customers' success. *Naïve bastard should have just sold software,* he thought. *It's enough to give a rep an ulcer, worrying about his customers' success.* Means shuddered at the thought.

"Obviously, Simon, I'll jump on this."

"You better. You should have seen this coming, the way he protected his fucking customers." Hager hung up abruptly as usual.

Great way to end the year, Means thought. *All I have to do is hire someone ASAP in the most competitive market in the country.*

He wasted no time calling his best headhunters.

***

The late fall of 1997 was unusually warm in the New York area. The temperature never flirted with the freezing point and the skiers on the Port Authority – the "PATH" – trains into lower Manhattan moaned about the lack of any snow over the Thanksgiving weekend.

All was quiet, however, on the 30th floor of the sleek black steel building known as One Liberty Plaza. Only a few Security National Bank programmers had arrived by 7:30 and Porter Mitchell, the leader of the so-called "Integration Squad" was one of the early birds. Today, he regretted being so timely. He hadn't even visited the coffee machine before his manager appeared at his cubicle. The meeting was only ten minutes long, but changed his life.

"Porter? What's wrong?" Brewster McNaughton asked his cubical neighbor and project partner.

Porter lifted his head from his desk, ran his right hand through his rumpled, auburn hair, to reveal his ashen face, paler than normal. As a software engineer, he didn't see a whole lot of sunlight. The only feature to interrupt his ivory face was the stray pimple. He was twenty-seven going on sixteen.

"The apocalypse is upon us."

"Huh?"

"I'm not supposed to spread the news around, but fuck it. We're being outsourced. Norm Johnson gave me the word a few minutes ago."

"Outsourced? Who?"

"The entire Security National Bank Information Technology Department."

"To who?"

"EDS, Electronic Data Systems."

"What about our project?"

"Stillborn."

Porter, Brewster and two other computer programmers had been using the InUnison integration system to tie the bank's disparate systems together. The project team, under the direction of veteran project manager Norm Johnson, had successfully built several pilot systems and was expecting to get funding to go production in 1998. The entire team was thrilled to be doing something more interesting than maintaining installment loan systems, but Porter went further. He was now an InUnison fanatic and wanted to "change the world" using their cool technology. But now his lollipop was being taken away just when he had figured out how to unwrap it.

"What happens to us?" Brewster asked.

"We go back to loans until EDS figures out what to do with us."

"You mean we'll be working *for* EDS?"

Porter nodded and slouched in his chair.

"Oh, shit! What about Norm?"

Porter drew his hand across his throat.

"Have you called your wife?"

"No. I've been gearing up to do that. Brenda's going to freak."

Brewster and Porter stared at each other, speechless.

Porter spoke first. "I'd better get this over with."

"Me too," Brewster said, turning to leave.

It took several attempts by Porter. He kept picking up the phone, dialing his wife and then hanging up. He was trying to keep himself composed to tell her that he was now a proud employee of EDS and was failing miserably at it.

Again, he picked up the phone, dialed, and didn't hang up this time.

"Hello?"

"Hi, Baby."

"Oh, hi! What's the occasion? Good news?" Brenda said, curling her honey highlighted brown hair behind her ear and out of the way of the phone receiver.

Porter struggled to maintain emotional control. "Not exactly." Only two words, but his hushed tone told Brenda that something was very wrong.

"Porter, what's happened?"

"My project was cancelled. We're being outsourced to EDS, everyone, well, not some managers but …" He had to stop and fight the emotions all over again.

"Porter, I'm so sorry!" She paused to gather her thoughts. She didn't want to say the wrong thing. "You worked so hard on that integration thing and I thought it was going so well that –"

"It was," Porter interrupted. "But it doesn't matter anymore. Damn it, Brenda, they're letting Norm Johnson go!"

"Won't EDS still have to deal with the same challenges you were trying to meet?"

"Sure, but it'll be months before they get around to this again. They have their own ways of doing it. They won't use our work."

Brenda was as disappointed as Porter. He had been so bored with work before the integration project that he rarely talked about the office. For the past year, though, she'd had to tell him to shut up about work or they wouldn't have time to talk about anything else going on in the world.

"Brenda, I can't go back to … to … *loans!"*

"Baby, I know you must be disappointed but it's not a *death* sentence," she said, now pacing with their newborn, Stephanie, in her arms. "You could have lost your job entirely."

"It *is* a death sentence, professionally. There's all this great technology out there; Java, the Internet, eCommerce… This integration stuff is going to be huge! But it's going to pass me by, like, I can only wave as the train leaves the station. Stupid bank! Why was I so gullible? They recruited me from high honors at Rutgers into a freaking sweat shop. I busted my ass on that MBA for them, too. For what?"

She'd never heard Porter so down about his career. The reality, though, was that companies were dumping staff every day. It was to be expected, particularly in a large bank like Security National.

"I don't know what to say," Brenda said. She then had a thought, but debated whether to suggest it. Porter's mind was obviously not in a rational state. She decided it might snap him out of the depression. "What about InUnison?"

"What about them?"

"Well, you know a lot about their products, right?"

"Yeah, so?"

"And, you really get jazzed working with their software…"

She paused, hoping Porter would connect the dots. He didn't, so she tried again.

"And you always said the one bad thing about the company was the lack of dependable local technical talent."

"Yeah, so?"

"Hey, helloooo, anybody home?" she said, rapping the phone with her knuckles. "Maybe *you* could be their dependable local technical talent."

Porter sat straight up at that thought. He did know the stuff inside and out after using it for a year. What did that InUnison Systems Engineer, Sean Murphy, call it? "Developing scar tissue?" Murphy had come in from Boston a few times to help Porter and they had struck up a good relationship.

"Yeah, I can call Sean in Boston," Porter said.

"Right, call Sean in Boston," Brenda said, not knowing or caring who Sean was. She wanted to get Porter moving in the right direction. "You should be off the ledge by the time you get home to play with Stephanie."

"Thanks, Babe. I love you."

"I love you, too. See you this evening. Now, call Sean!"

Porter's attitude returned to the positive range, at least barely. He started to dial Sean, but hung up. *Not this again. I don't know what to say.* He decided to put off the phone call until after lunch so he could compose his pitch.

***

Sam Racker rubbed his graying temples hard between his right thumb and middle finger as he looked at his budget projections for the coming year. This was his first budget cycle as Controller and he was profoundly disappointed with what he had inherited. Why was it that Azalea Financial, with over $100 billion in assets, revenue in the billions and net of over $300 million, didn't have an efficient financial system so he could sort through all the lines of business and crunch the numbers? He and his analysts had to collect numbers from various reports and then enter them into spreadsheets so complicated that he was leery of trusting what he was seeing. Wall Street was starting to notice as well. Just that morning, Manley Brothers, one of the largest brokerage and investment banks in the world, downgraded Azalea's stock. In the words of the analyst, Jim Grabin, Azalea's financials were "opaque and indecipherable". He downgraded the stock to "underweight, underperform, sell" which was two positions from the bottom of Manley's ten point scale.

"What's 'opaque and indecipherable' is your stupid rating system," Racker murmured at the time, but knew the criticism was justified. Standard and Poors agreed and put Azalea's debt rating under review with "negative implications". The stock market reacted to the downgrades, knocking twelve percent off of Azalea's stock price.

Twenty-six floors below his One Seaport Plaza office, he could see the South Street Seaport restaurants coming to life with New York's Financial District personnel streaming in for lunch. He wouldn't be one of them except vicariously by ordering in from Pizzeria UNO.

"Connie, go ahead and order pizza for me, please."

Connie – short for Consuelo – Sanchez had been his administrative assistant for fifteen years, rising with him through the ranks at Citibank and now Azalea. She was the kind of admin partner senior executives craved and protected with their lives. She was his gatekeeper, organizer and sometime gift shopper. He made damn certain she was happy, especially if he was to replace Ralph Gibson, the current CFO, at retirement.

"Sammy, you know you need to balance your diet a little," she chided, pointing to his waistline where a belt held his paunch more up than in. She knew his idea of exercise was raising a cigar in one hand and a scotch in the other. "How about I find a good seafood salad somewhere?"

"Yes, ma'am. Also, can you see if our elusive Chief Information Officer, Stewart Miller, is available sometime tomorrow?" he asked Connie. "This reporting stuff is out of control. I need some technical help ASAP."

She reported back in less than five minutes.

"He says he has no openings for two weeks."

"What is he? Some kind of doctor? This is totally unacceptable. You'd think he'd be smart enough to not piss off his future boss."

"I don't think intelligence has anything to do with it," Connie said. "According to Gloria in Human Resources, he's convinced that he is indispensable to the company."

"Sure. Just like a warden is indispensable to a prisoner; he's the only one who can grant privileges. Well, we're going to start a jail break here at Azalea."

Chapter 2 Recruiting the Fat Bear

Sean Murphy pounded his fists on the desk in frustration. He was in his home office in Newton, Massachusetts, trying to install a new version of InUnison on his laptop and having little success. He was InUnison's Boston systems engineer and desperately needed some of the new features for a demo later that week. InUnison's phone support people weren't calling him back so he was particularly grumpy. *No wonder what little hair I have left is going gray,* he thought, as he restarted his system for the fourth time in the past hour. At age thirty-two, he looked progressively closer to forty as his bald spot expanded toward his forehead. Rogaine had failed to arrest the hair loss just like all the other treatments.

Expecting that Support was finally calling him back, he reached for his phone before the first ring faded.

"Sean Murphy."

"Hi, Sean. Porter Mitchell with Security National in New York."

"Good morning! How's our one-man quality assurance department?" he asked. Sean spent several days with Porter over the past year, helping him use InUnison's products. "I hope you're not calling for help on the beta. I'm ready to hurl my laptop into the Charles because it won't install."

"No, I haven't tried it yet and won't get a chance either," Porter said, with obvious disgust. He breathed deeply and plunged in. "Sean, are you guys hiring by chance?"

"Well, you should know better than anyone that we need someone in New York." Sean knew, though, that the reason for the opening was because the last SE couldn't stand working with Tom Gatto. "Why do you ask? Are you on the market?"

Porter described the outsourcing deal and then went into sales mode, giving Sean his prepared spiel. "….I really think that I could do a good job for you guys. I know the software and believe in it totally. It could really change how information is managed in business."

"Hey, you don't have to convince me. I've seen your work. Listen, while I check on this, get a resume together. That's the first thing they'll ask for. Look, it would be a no-brainer to bring you on board. You'd hit the ground running."

"Well, I am a little concerned about the presentation side of things. I have very little experience in public speaking."

"Not to worry. It's easier to teach a few presentation skills to someone who knows the technology than vice versa. Our products rarely sell themselves by demo or presentation. The customer usually wants to do a hands-on evaluation using their own systems. That's where your experience with real projects is invaluable. Anyway, I saw you demo your pilot to some of those department heads. You did great."

"Thanks, but I know you're simply being kind." Sean had indeed been present at that demo and half the audience had their eyes rolling up into their heads. It wasn't really Porter's fault, though.

Sean laughed. "Okay, they weren't getting it, but you did as well as we're doing right now. I'd have better impact if my audience were cardboard cutouts. At least they couldn't ask the usual stupid ass questions.

"Think about it; it's a bitch trying to describe something that is inherently invisible," Sean continued. "You can show the effects but what's going on inside is a mystery to most people. Go put that resume together and I'll get back to you."

"Thanks, Sean. I appreciate it." Porter hung up with relief. Maybe this job change wouldn't be so difficult.

Murphy kept his hand on the receiver as he checked the time. *Young should still be in his office in Tyson's Corner,* he thought. Sean punched the speed dial for his manager.

"InUnison, David Young speaking."

"Youngster! How the hell are you?"

"Well, the morning was fine but if I have to start off the afternoon talking to you…"

"Now, at least wait until you find out why I'm calling before starting with the trash talk. I have an opportunity to significantly enhance our presence in New York…"

"You're going to strangle Gatto! Great!"

"Well, maybe not that great, but pretty close. I have a great SE candidate. You remember Security National, Porter Mitchell?"

"I know the name. They're an Early Adopter, right? Aren't they about to go to deployment? It wouldn't be too smart to raid a customer, Sean. I hope you haven't –"

"Relax. He came to me. The project is dead. All the IT staff is being outsourced to EDS and he wants out. There's no opportunity for us there now."

"Oh, too bad. Would have been a nice reference for us." Young didn't mourn for long, though. "Do you have a resume?"

"He's drafting one as we speak. Dave, he knows our stuff cold, this should be a slam dunk."

"Sean, you have a special knack for oversimplification." Young knew that reality was seldom reflected in a resume or a recommendation motivated mostly by the $2,500 referral bonus.

"So, how do we handle this?"

"Get me his resume, ASAP. Presby and I will be in New Jersey to do some interviewing, both SEs and reps, next, um…" Young had to glance at his schedule, "…next Thursday, the 11th."

"Where again?"

"Newark Airport Marriott."

"I'll pass that along. Now, what do I tell Porter about Gatto?"

"That's a tough one. The good thing is that Presby is interviewing for a rep for New Jersey, Upstate New York and Connecticut so we can spin it that the SE would be covering that territory as well."

"Some spin. Having to work with two reps on a wide territory."

"Better than sentencing him to life exclusively with Gatto."

"True. I'll get him there."

***

Tom Gatto popped out of the N train station at 49th and Seventh Avenue conveniently located in the southeast corner of his destination, the boxy black building called 750 Seventh Avenue. Early for his nine o'clock meeting with George Melani, the Director of Strategic Systems at Potential Investing, he ducked into Timothy's for a coffee and a chance to rehearse his speech.

Potential was investing heavily in new Internet-based systems to broaden its trading and financial modeling product offerings. A strategic new addition to the service product line was an offering to automate foreign exchange futures swaps for importers. Using a web browser, importers could automatically lock in protection from currency fluctuations at the same time as a product transaction. The idea was that no software was necessary to put on the customer's machine – the so-called "thin client". Potential was using InUnison's products to coordinate the transaction with their existing systems at Potential and some of these were on IBM mainframes.

Gatto, almost never fazed by a sales challenge, was uncharacteristically nervous about this meeting. Melani had, in no uncertain terms, stood firm about the absolute need for the mainframe connector. Gatto was thrilled to see the connector still listed on the new price list. *Thank you, marketing morons!* It would be exhibit A with Melani. He might just have to sell some consulting services to hack something together.

He finished his coffee and went up to Melani's floor where the receptionist led him into a conference room.

"George will be in shortly. Help yourself to the coffee," she said as she left the room to return to her ringing phone. Gatto compulsively filled a foam cup from the pump style thermos – it was his fifth or sixth cup that morning – and stirred in some powdered creamer.

"Hi, Tom. I'm pressed for time so what's the news? Do we get the mainframe connector on time?"

"Check this out, George. The latest price list." He turned to the appropriate page and circled the entry, "Mainframe Connector".

"So? Does this mean that it's shipping?"

"By the end of the month."

"You're sure?" Melani said, raising his right eyebrow.

"Hey, the price list is like the Ten Commandments; it's set in stone! If it's on the list, I can sell it. They wouldn't want me to sell something that doesn't exist."

Melani grunted something unintelligible. "Can I get a beta? I'd really like to get my guys working on it."

"Absolutely! I'll find out where it is on the ftp site." Gatto hoped that little white lie would placate Melani and he would not have to deliver on it. "So, here we are, December 3rd. Can we get the PO processed by the end of the month?"

Melani gazed out the window, looking up Seventh Avenue. He was nervous about signing anything when he hadn't physically touched the product. But he needed to get this through before the new budget year. "Yes, if you fax the agreement to Purchasing, they'll send it to me for approval. I already got preliminary approval on my side so it will go through in a week."

"Actually, George, I have a new copy of the paperwork right here. We have some new boilerplate in the license language so I have an updated contract for you," he said, as he pulled the document from his briefcase. "I hope it doesn't mean we have to start the approval process all over again."

"Show me the changes."

Gatto pointed out some innocuous language about liability for use of the software. "If it's acceptable, simply sign this new copy and I'll take it to purchasing right now."

Melani gave it a cursory review. Noting that the bottom line, $255,000 in software and services hadn't changed, he signed. "You know where to go for purchasing?"

"Yes, I've been there before."

Melani stood up, all 272 pounds worth, and leaned across the table toward Gatto, his pony tail flopping onto his right shoulder. "You had better deliver that connector by Jan 2, or you won't have to worry about having children. You dig?"

While Gatto had never been on the receiving end of a Melani temper tantrum, word was he had a tendency to threaten people's genitalia. He was adept at controlling his customers and laughed to himself at Melani's attempt at intimidation.

"George, it's a done deal!" He stuffed the price list back into his briefcase and stood. Melani blocked the door briefly, giving Gatto one more evil look, and then left without further word.

Gatto, relieved, stopped by Purchasing and the deed was done. He was retracing his steps back to the subway when his cell phone rang.

"Gatto."

"You missed my call again," Ken Presby said. "I hope you can give me some good news to make up for it."

Gatto started to pace outside the subway entrance on Seventh Avenue.

"I'm closing deals, Ken! I dropped off the PO at Potential and Merrill should come in next week," *assuming I can work the same magic there.* "I just need some cooperation from Professional Services to fake some code."

"What do you mean, 'fake'?"

"Look, they can code up something that acts just like the Rule Agent. That's good enough for that Fabozzi guy down there to demonstrate the functionality. He's on board with that."

"Okay, I'm counting on it. It will be great to have Merrill as a reference."

"Sure, Ken." *Keep dreaming. They aren't going to allow that until we really bend over for them.*

"So, assuming we chalk up Merrill, that leaves you about $125,000 short. Where's that coming from?"

"Short of what? Don't you mean *you're* short, Ken?"

"Short of The Swede," he said, knowing that would get a rise from Gatto.

Damn, I hate being manipulated. I'm supposed to do *the manipulating.* "Yeah, sure, Ken. I still have those dot-coms to close. They're going to be down to the wire though. Look, I really have to get going."

"Oh, before you go, do you remember a Wayne Angelis?" Presby asked.

Gatto froze in his tracks.

"Yes, why?"

"We might hire him."

"NOT HERE! You can't cut my territory, damn it! I'm going to be number one! It just isn't –"

"Calm down! He'll cover Jersey and Connecticut. So what do you know about him? You worked with him at Realtime Analytics, right?"

Jersey, my ass. He'll be poaching in Manhattan as soon as he can, just like before. He wanted to shoot this down and had to think quickly.

"Yeah. He wasn't that hot there, though. I had to carry him," Gatto said.

Sure you did, Presby thought. *That's not what the VP there said.*

"Really? He's got a pretty stellar resume. Kicked ass at Wang."

"Hey, you asked my opinion. I think we could do better."

"Well, I'm interviewing him this week. None of the other resumes comes close. Get used to the idea."

"Don't expect me to share territory."

"Close strong and you won't have anything to worry about."

F' you! "Count on it, Ken."

"I know you can do it. Let's go sell! Beat VibraWeb!"

If I hear that one more time… Gatto thought, as he hurried down the steps to the subway platform.

***

Porter stood in his closet, staring at his clothes as if he had never seen them before. He was unbearably nervous about his interview coming up the next day and it was driving Brenda crazy. Normally the calm, unemotional, rational member of the family, he was now wound tight. Even his daughter was reluctant to be around him, clutching Brenda whenever he reached for her.

Brenda made sure she was there for this fashion session knowing that she would have to dress him properly. After five years of marriage, she knew he couldn't be trusted to dress himself for an important occasion. He wasn't color blind, but his idea of color coordination was that all blues went together, or that polka dot ties went with striped shirts. She wondered where his mother had been when he was growing up.

He took Wednesday through Friday off, supposedly to use up vacation before the end of the year. His soon-to-be-ex manager Norm knew better.

"Sure, Porter, take whatever time you need," he had said. "And by the way, if you get an offer, ask if they have any positions for a washed up IT manager." Porter felt guilty about Norm's plight, but the guilt irritated him. *I'm not responsible* he tried to tell himself, and he wasn't, but there was a lingering feeling that maybe if they, the Integration Squad, had done more, things would be different. Porter decided he had to focus on himself for a change.

"Brenda, are you *sure* I should wear this blue suit? It makes me look like a banker."

"This is an *interview*. You have to look presentable, business-like."

"Sure, but this is a Silicon Valley startup company. Maybe I should look hip or something."

Brenda bit her tongue. *Porter, I love you, but you couldn't look hip to save your life.* "Yes, but these are *East Coast* business types, and you'll be dealing with people, well, people like at Security National, who happen to be, duh, *bankers*!"

"Oh, hell, what do you know about this anyway?"

He immediately regretted that question. Brenda had, after all, served as administrative assistant to a Director of Human Resources for a Manhattan systems consultant firm and knew damn well what was expected for interview attire in New York. She narrowed her eyes and stepped to within an inch of Porter's face.

"Fine!" She stormed into Porter's closet and started to rifle through his shirts. "Here's what you ought to wear: your 'Byte This' t-shirt, and, oh, lovely, your jeans with the holes in the knees. Here." She draped the shirt over Porter's head and threw the jeans at his feet. "Oh, and don't forget the Converse high-tops." She stomped off to get a load of laundry, flinging a "You're hopeless" over her shoulder. Brenda was right. He hadn't interviewed since his senior year at Rutgers and was afraid he'd blow it by doing or saying something stupid.

Porter desperately wanted to talk to Sean Murphy. After several attempts, he finally caught up with him.

"InUnison, Sean speaking."

"Sean! Porter Mitchell. I hope that I'm not interrupting anything important…"

"Actually yes, but that's a good thing. I'm struggling with PowerPoint. What can I do for you?"

"I've got this interview tomorrow and want to have a better feel for the personalities. I'm meeting with Dave Young and Ken Presby. I'm not sure what they'll be looking for."

"Young, he'll be very friendly. He already knows you're solid with the technology. He will be more interested in how you present yourself, making sure that you don't have a hump back and three eyes or something. You should act like a banker."

Okay, definitely the bank uniform. Be sure to apologize to Brenda. "What about Presby?"

"He's a good guy," Sean replied, adding with disdain, "for a sales manager. He'll be more concerned about your business demeanor, so spout as much b-school BS as you can. Make sure you talk about providing business solutions, not only technology. He'll eat that up."

"So it sounds like he's not going to be impressed with my technical prowess."

"Oh, he'll appreciate that but he's down on SEs who are only technical. Like I said, that MBA will be valuable to him. Keep talking about how you want to show customers that using InUnison will enhance their bottom line."

"Anything else?"

"Don't be a geek, will ya?"

***

"I love the smell of revenue in the morning!" Gatto called out, feeling especially cocky this morning.

Over the past week, he had successfully uncovered a dozen high probability, albeit small, deals by canvassing Silicon Alley. The average deal size was in the $25 – 35,000 range for the software license, plus services. Once those PS consultants were in place in an account, though, they typically became a permanent fixture at the customer and yielded a steady revenue stream which counted as much towards Gatto's Number as licenses. Over a year the services revenue could easily double the value of the software license. Very important to him – crucial in the last month of the year – these dot-coms were in a big hurry.

He had three Silicon Alley sales calls scheduled and was packing his briefcase to head out.

"Mark? Ready to hit the street?" Gatto called out to his visiting SE, Mark Moskowitz from Virginia. "Our first meeting is in forty-five minutes down on 22nd Street."

"Are we walking or taking the train? You walk too damn fast and almost get me killed crossing the streets."

"Walking, of course! We're only eight short blocks away after all. It's a great, crisp morning to be out making money."

I truly hate your guts, Gatto. His USAirways Shuttle flight home couldn't come soon enough.

Gatto's desk phoned warbled again.

"Good morning, Tom. This is Frank Henderson of Henderson Recruiting. Do you have a moment?"

"A short one."

"I'll be brief. I'm recruiting for a Silicon Valley startup. They need to fill their New York sales manager position. Would you happen to know anyone available?" he asked, using classic headhunter code to ask if Gatto was available.

"Actually, I might."

"They have some of the most aggressive compensation I've seen."

"Yeah, that's what they all say."

"Okay, how does this sound; On-target earnings of $200,000 with accelerators at 125%, 150% and 200% with no cap."

"What are the Number and the accelerator rates?"

"Five to seven hundred thousand first quarter, 6% on-target, 8%, 10% and 15% for the steps on the accelerator ladder."

That got Gatto's attention. He did the math in this head. Since his ego wouldn't let him accept anything less than achieving 200% of quota, the take would be $180,000 for the quarter. *Hmmm, could be interesting.*

Henderson continued. "Options on 50,000 shares, four year vesting, 25% per year."

That didn't impress Gatto. He couldn't imagine staying anywhere for four years. That was one reason he liked most of his compensation up front.

"So, who is this charity?" he asked.

"VibraWeb. Do you know anything about them?"

Dumb headhunter. Doesn't even know we are direct competitors. "Only that I butt heads with them every day."

"Oh, really? You compete with them? Too bad. I guess you can't jump then," Henderson said, dropping the pretense.

"Non-compete agreement? Actually, I don't have one."

"You're kidding? Well, what do you think?"

Gatto thought about it. The money was terrific – better than at InUnison – and then there was Wayne Angelis. *I know he'll cause trouble.*

"Yeah, I'll talk to them. But there's no way I can start until February. I'm getting a big payday in January. I'd have to stick until then."

"I'm sure that would work for them. I'll get you in touch with the hiring manager, George Means."

***

Arriving at the Newark Airport Marriott almost forty-five minutes early for his InUnison interview, Porter settled into an arm chair in the lobby. He tried to read the *Wall Street Journal* but could hardly focus on it. His stomach felt like a towel being wrung out. *I can't blow this chance. I'll never get another one,* he kept telling himself.

He could not help eyeing up anyone who came into the lobby. *They could be competition. They could be Young or Presby! I have to look nonchalant. Don't be stupid, they don't even know what I look like. You ARE a moron. No, you can't get down on yourself…* On and on it went.

Finally, his digital watch clicked to 10:30 and beeped the alarm. He got up and walked to the house phone.

"David Young, please."

"Just a moment… I'll connect you."

"Thanks." The phone rang three times.

"Dave Young."

"Hi, it's Porter Mitchell. I'm in the lobby."

"Great! Come up to room 515."

Porter hung up and looked around. The elevators were behind the lobby in the middle of the floor. Now that the moment had finally arrived, he suddenly felt relaxed as he entered the elevator.

Exiting the elevator on the fifth floor, he found an obscure plaque directing him to the right for rooms 501 - 525. Finding the room, Porter took a deep breath and, noticing that the door was propped open with the security deadbolt, stuck his head in.

"Hello, Dave?"

"C'mon in!" Young got up from the sofa, clicking off CNBC as he did so. "Pleased to meet you face-to-face, Porter!"

"Likewise." *What a stupid thing for me to say,* Porter thought immediately.

"Any trouble getting here? I know traffic on I-78 can be tough."

"Sailed right through," Porter answered.

Young directed Porter to the sofa as he chose the armchair. "Coffee? I had a carafe brought up."

"No, thank you. I've had plenty today," Porter said. *Can we get started? I'm going to explode!*

"I don't know if you are aware, but your boss Norm Johnson called me the other day…"

Norm called? How did he even know? It wasn't too hard for Norm to figure out what company Porter would approach first. He had more InUnison logos around his cubicle than Security National's.

"…and I don't think I've ever heard a more glowing recommendation. The key thing he kept saying over and over was 'team player'. Your technical abilities are obvious, you can demo and you were essentially a player/coach for your integration team. That's huge for me." Young shifted forward, sitting on the edge of his chair.

"I have a boilerplate speech I give to candidates so that they know exactly what I expect from my SEs and what they can expect from the InUnison environment, so bear with me for a few minutes."

"Sure."

"First and foremost, I expect my SEs to own the process of securing the technical win at a prospect. That entails giving presentations; showing canned demos or creating custom demos; writing responses to Requests for Information – you know, 'RFIs'; and managing a detailed onsite evaluation or proof-of-concept. So the skills I look for are strong communication talents, project management expertise and, of course, technical depth. Patience and poise is critical as well."

"Poise?"

Young chuckled. "Because every meeting has at least one smartass who gets off on knowing every bit and byte of a subject and has to show it. I've been tempted to pack a gun in my laptop bag to deal with those freaks.

"Now, the other thing about InUnison is that we are still in startup mode. Those of us in the field have to fend for ourselves. There aren't any administrative assistants out here and help from HQ is problematic so we end up rolling our own resources in a lot of ways. You'll be expected, at least initially, to work from a home office. As we grow, we'll get shared office space somewhere in New York. In the interim, though, you must, *must* be a self-starter and use a lot of self-initiative. I can't baby-sit SEs from Tyson's Corner, so I have to be convinced that I can trust you. You have to get up in the morning, plan your day with one guideline: is what I'm doing on the path to revenue? If you have any doubt, you should question what you are doing. Your rep partners are going to expect that you can operate independently or else I'm going to get flamed."

"Stay on the path to revenue. Got it," Porter responded.

"The good news is that you won't need to travel overnight much. We'll have a few sales meetings – such as our January kickoff – usually in California. We will send you out there for any training you may need. Of course, you'll get a laptop. So, any red flags there for you?"

Porter felt like he had just experienced a fire hose blast to the face. He did appreciate that Young was being totally upfront about the environment.

Young continued before Porter could respond. "Hey, I know I threw a lot at you but it's better to get this out right up front and not waste anyone's time."

"Oh, I totally agree." Porter considered the environment Young described. The home office requirement gave him both pause and excitement. He was so used to the infrastructure at SecNat that he took it for granted. But at the same time it was like a prison. Space wouldn't be an issue. He and Brenda were lucky to have a large house in Bernardsville, New Jersey, thanks to financial help from Brenda's parents, a bribe to keep their daughter nearby. Mentally, he balanced the potential distractions against more time with Stephanie.

He realized that he was keeping Young waiting. "Sorry for the dead air. I was considering the home office thing. It would be a totally new experience but I have the room."

"The key question is: Do you have the discipline to block the world out?"

"Absolutely! If I can block out the crap that goes on around the cubicle forest at the bank, I can certainly do that at home." *Damn, that sounds too negative.*

"Okay, now let's move on a little. Because of your experience with our products, you would be one of the most knowledgeable SEs in the company about the software. My concern is that you lack presentation and sales experience. Now, normally we can teach those skills more easily than we can take a good talker and make him a propeller head. You say you've done presentations, tell me about them."

"Well, first I had to sell myself to some new management that I had the requisite skills to attack all these new fields of technology, like Java, HTTP, that kind of thing. These new managers were pretty skeptical that there was any in-house talent who could handle the job but my school background and, uh, extra-curricular activities overcame that. I strongly believe in investing in myself so I completed my MBA and made sure I was hands-on with all kinds of systems at Rutgers."

Very good! Young thought. *I like the "self-investment" thing.*

Porter realized his voice was moving into a louder range so he paused to throttle down a little.

"At the bank, we started to collect pilot project ideas. Believe me, it wasn't hard. People have been after this kind of thing for years. We had to decide which ones had the highest chance for success while still showing enough complexity to be interesting and, most importantly, quantifiable in a budget sense. The team chose four projects and punched them all out over the past year. At the close of each pilot, we designed as cool a demo as we could and presented it to the appropriate IT and business management. We ROCKED!" He stopped to calm down again. "Sorry."

Young stifled a chuckle. "Not to worry, that spirit is critical to success in sales. So it sounds like everything was hunky-dory. What happened to this emerging Shangri La?"

"The bean counters did some funky calculation which said they could save a bunch of money if they sold us all into slavery. I'd be put back into tweaking loan systems." *Why did he have to bring this up? I was on a roll.*

"So, what's wrong with that?"

"Nothing except that I don't want to be doing the same thing for the rest of my career."

"Well, lots of people are very happy with consistency. There's a lot to be said about the security of a big bank IT department, room to advance..." *C'mon, man, give me the answer I'm looking for!*

Porter was aghast. *You don't really believe that?* Porter thought. *Maybe I'm talking to the wrong guy.*

"Look, I don't know where you're going with this, but the simple fact is that if I go home at night and can't point to something new I learned during the day, I'm very cranky. The integration project was cool because it *demanded* that we constantly learn – learn about technology, learn about business processes, what really made the bank tick. I was never happier in my life than coming to work and finding a new challenge. I *crave* variety..."

OK! This is the GUY! Young raised his hands to wave Porter off from continuing but Porter's enthusiasm was unstoppable.

"You give me a problem; I'll figure the damn thing out..."

"Porter, please..."

"... and I'll take it down to the mat, hands around its throat...

"Porter ..."

"... until it cries for..."

"Porter! Stop! I'm sold! You'll still have to sell yourself to Presby but he'll end up deferring to me. You should expect to make a decision over the next couple of days."

Wow, this is moving fast. "I'm sure I will have some questions. It's fine to bounce some of that off of Sean Murphy, right?"

"Don't believe what he says about me."

"But he's already said a lot." *Shit, I hope he has a sense of humor.*

"Like I said, don't believe the bad stuff."

"Well, I'm not sure what to say, Dave. I'm flattered. I'm thrilled to be considered and will work my tail off for you guys. I know that Sean and I can work well together. Don't think I'm pandering here, but I certainly like your style. I was expecting to have to do a presentation or demo or something. A friend of mine had to do all that plus a dozen interviews for a software company he joined."

"Yes, I've been part of that kind of thing too, but I really consider it a waste of time. Some managers get their rocks off by putting candidates through a grinder. But, it's a seller's market right now and quality candidates are few and far between. I don't have the luxury of drawing the hiring process out because the candidate will simply find another hot job more quickly. Anyway, I strongly believe that, unlike mutual funds, past performance and behavior does indeed predict future performance and behavior. You've successfully shown the behaviors we are looking for. Enough about that. What other info do you need from me to make your decision?"

Porter had a laundry list of questions about the market, how sales compensation worked, the usual benefits questions and how expenses get reimbursed. Young patiently went into all the necessary details, amused that the guy still hadn't posed the important questions: base, bonus and stock options.

***

In another hotel room down the hall, Ken Presby closed his notebook, satisfied that he had all the information he needed from Wayne Angelis.

"Wayne, I'm very impressed with your experience. Is there any reason you aren't holding out for a management position?"

"To be honest, I'm a little jaded about managing right now. I'd like to take some time and get re-energized as an individual contributor. I know that there will always be management opportunities with a growing company. I'm in no hurry about that."

Thank goodness, Ken Presby thought. *With this resume you should have my job.*

"That's great, Wayne. You'll have plenty of chances to excel. Anything else you'd like to know?"

"I know that we've talked about the Number and territory but I can make a good case for some named accounts in Manhattan. For instance, I have a longstanding relationship with some people at Manley Brothers. Any chance I can carry them and others with me?"

Talk about touching the third rail, Presby thought.

"That would be tough to do. Our Manhattan rep will end the year first or second in the company. I don't think he will be amenable to giving up anything."

Wayne decided to press a little harder.

"Is he active at Manley? At Bank of New York?"

"To be honest, no."

"And you must realize that Manhattan needs multiple sales teams, right?"

"That's an obvious move as we grow. I don't want to piss the guy off. I think you know him, Tom Gatto."

Hearing the name was like being run through with a hot poker. Memories of hand-to-hand combat with Gatto over territory blinded him for a moment.

"Yes, we worked briefly together at Realtime Analytics. He's, uh, aggressive."

Presby detected Wayne's less than positive tone.

"So, you must know what his reaction would be if I tried to cut his territory."

"Yes," Wayne replied, pausing to tactfully craft his next comment. "Don't take this the wrong way but I'm surprised he's so successful at InUnison. He's a bit out of character for InUnison."

Presby knew what he meant – and agreed – but knew to hide the sentiment.

"Well, I can only judge on the results and he's tops," Presby said. He wanted to get off the subject. "Anything else we need to cover?"

Wayne thought for a few seconds. The Gatto revelation had thrown him.

He was sold on InUnison by their reputation for integrity and team environment but what was a character like Tom Gatto doing there? It was an oxymoron for "Gatto" and "InUnison" to be used in the same breath. He decided he had better dig a little deeper.

"I want assurances on the integrity of assigned territories. If I can't get a few named accounts in Manhattan, I don't want Gatto or anyone else coming up with lame excuses for New Jersey accounts."

"Of course, Wayne. I wouldn't have it any other way." Presby wondered why he needed to reiterate that point.

"One last thing," Wayne said. "I've been with a couple of startups and they turned out to be under funded and under managed. I'd like a higher comfort level with the financial health of InUnison."

"Are you saying that you don't trust me?"

"Nothing personal. I've been burned before."

"How would a phone call with Bill Engler do?"

"The CEO? You're kidding!"

"Look, we want A-players on our team and you're definitely an A-player. If it takes a few minutes of Engler's time, I'll make it happen. You'll find him very forthcoming."

"Yes, I have heard that about him."

"Perfect. I'll set it up for tomorrow or Monday morning. He starts early out there, one of the few in that God-forsaken valley. You can always tell who isn't a California native; they get to the office by seven."

Wayne laughed. He was always in his office by seven if not earlier.

"I appreciate it, Ken. If all goes well, I'd like to hit the ground running in January."

"Super!" Presby checked his watch. "It's time to do a swap. I'd like you to meet David Young, the SE manager for my region. He's awesome. He should be wrapping up with an SE candidate I need to talk to."

Presby and Angelis walked down the hallway to Young's room and knocked.

Young opened the door as he was finishing a question for Porter. "…so you need to be prepared to be in California on Sunday, January 4. I'll jot down the contact information for our travel agency before we leave today."

Presby raised an eyebrow at Young, whispering, "A bit premature, aren't we?" Young scowled back at him as if to say "don't blow this for me".

Presby introduced Angelis. "Wayne, this is our SE manager, Dave Young."

"Pleased to meet you," Dave said, then stepped back to allow Porter into the greeting. "And this is Porter Mitchell, our candidate for SE in the New York metro district."

"So, shall we switch candidates for about thirty minutes?" Presby said. "Then, if your schedules permit, can we get lunch downstairs together?"

"Sure," both Porter and Wayne replied simultaneously.

"Great! Porter, please follow me."

***

"Thanks so much for lunch. I didn't expect such hospitality," Porter said, trying to remember his manners.

"Yes, I appreciate the time we spent, and look forward to hearing from you," Angelis agreed, shaking Presby's and then Young's hand.

Porter and Wayne paused in the lobby as they put on their overcoats. Then Wayne spoke up.

"Well, it looks like we may be working together. You made a great impression at lunch."

"Oh, right, like when I dumped half my club sandwich into my lap."

"Sure! Your recovery was impressive. I don't think Presby even noticed. And that Young; he was too busy managing his own feed bag to notice."

"Man after my own heart," Porter said, as they strolled to the front door.

"Hey, do you have anywhere to go right away?" he asked Porter.

"I want to beat traffic if I can."

"Oh, right. I'd like to pick your brain about InUnison and get to know you better. You live in Bernardsville, right?"

"Yes."

"How about dinner at the Bernards Inn? Saturday? I know the owner, he'll set us up. My treat."

"Sure, we'd love to. My mother-in-law's been begging to watch Stephanie."

***

Brenda was ecstatic about a dinner out, especially at a restaurant other than Chili's or some other chain. An uncomplicated dresser, she chose a slim navy pencil skirt and a classic white silk blouse. For the second time in a few days, she played stylist for Porter, selecting tan khakis, white shirt, blue and tan striped tie and blue blazer. He hated the brass buttons but deferred to his higher authority.

The Angelis' were waiting for them. Seeing Helen, Brenda felt underdressed. Wayne's wife wore a sequined, spaghetti-strapped, black dress and spike high heels, contrasted with teardrop diamonds – large ones – sparkling from her ears. Her face and figure were stunning, as it should be from hours at the health spa and a few Botox injections. Brenda, still working off the extra pregnancy pounds, suppressed a wave of jealousy, rationalizing that Helen's attire was more Broadway cocktail party than conservative dinner, certainly not in keeping with the wood-beamed warmth and country charm of the Bernards Inn. She thought Wayne's gray wool slacks and burgundy Lands' End turtle neck sweater were more appropriate to the occasion.

The couples were ushered to a quiet corner table and ordered drinks. The Angelis' enjoyed their signature gin martinis while the Mitchells sipped Bud Light.

"So, I hear you are new parents!" Helen said, breaking the ice.

"Yes," Brenda said, proudly. "A gorgeous girl, Stephanie."

"Well, just wait. She'll be a teenager before you know it. I have two teenage sons and they –"

"Sooo, what do you recommend here, Porter?" Wayne interrupted, not wanting Helen to go there. Helen always vented about the trials and tribulations of playing chauffeur for two three-sport high school athletes, plus an eight-year-old daughter now going to ballet lessons twice a week. She beat Wayne over the head for not being around enough to help.

"I've never had a bad meal here," Porter replied. "They have something for everyone and it's all great. I love the tenderloin here."

Helen gave a snort as she reviewed the menu. Not the sort of French-inspired or trendy fusion food she was into.

Their waiter took their orders and the conversation returned to family topics.

"How long have you been in Scarsdale?" Brenda asked.

"Fifteen years. Right after Wayne left Wang," Helen replied.

"I prefer to remember it being just before Danny was born," Wayne said. Danny was the younger of his two sons, the other being Blake, born only fifteen months apart. They had intended to stop there, but Eileen was an "oops" conception. Helen insisted on a vasectomy shortly afterward, not willing to trust her contraceptive method any longer.

Wayne steered the focus away from his family to the Mitchell's.

"I understand you grew up around here, Brenda. You must be very fond of the area."

"Yes, my family has lived here for three generations," Brenda replied. "My parents live in my grandfather's house just over the hill from here. It's a great area to raise kids."

"But where can you go to work out?" Helen asked.

"I go to the Somerset Hills YMCA. It's not far."

"Do they have personal trainers?" Helen pressed.

"I don't know. I've never looked into it."

"Well –"

Wayne was grateful that the salads arrived to interrupt Helen's ongoing interrogation. He could see Brenda's eyes narrowing.

"Where did you grow up, Porter?" Wayne asked.

"Trenton. My father is an attorney there. Mostly corporate type work."

The small talk continued through the meal, with Helen thrusting, Brenda and Porter parrying, and Wayne playing referee.

"Shall we retire to the lounge for some aperitifs, Wayne?" Helen asked, as her husband signed the credit card slip. She knew that Wayne wanted to talk shop with Porter and she would take Brenda aside, assuming that Brenda would want the benefit of her life experience.

Once in the lounge, Porter ordered a Gran Marnier and coffee, Brenda another glass of merlot, Wayne a Drambuie and Helen, her fourth gin martini of the night. The wives drifted over to a pair of chairs by the fireplace while Wayne and Porter leaned against the bar.

"So, Porter, what's making you leave the comforts of corporate life for the insanity of a software startup?"

"I guess two reasons: my project got cancelled which means that I'd be back doing boring stuff, and I love the InUnison products. I was really accomplishing some great things at the bank with it. I think that it will be fun to be an evangelist and get paid for it."

How refreshingly naïve, Wayne thought. "That's a great attitude, Porter. Can't say that I've had a technical partner with that for a while."

"Wayne, I hope you appreciate what InUnison has to offer. This stuff is so awesome. You should come by the bank next week. I can show you what we did. It was going to really save the bank money…"

"That's great, Porter," Wayne said, stifling a chuckle. He could tell that Porter was only getting warmed up. He let him run for several more minutes.

"…and think if we got into some manufacturing applications! It would be way cool…"

Wayne couldn't hold back and threw his head back in laughter.

"Goodness, Porter, you really *are* a zealot."

"Sorry."

"Don't be. I love it!" Wayne said, candidly. Porter's energy and enthusiasm was infectious.

So, what's your story?" Porter asked.

"I'm in it for the money," Wayne said, rubbing his hands together for effect.

"Oh," Porter said, taking Wayne seriously and looking deflated.

"Just kidding, Porter," Wayne assured him, realizing that he had one gullible nerd in front of him.

"Sure, I do like the Number chase and compensation but I could do that anywhere, hell, selling vinyl siding even. But I really want to win with a startup where I can be part of building something up from almost scratch. I should have started with these guys a year or two ago, though. More stock options."

"Of course," Porter said, hoping to hide his incomprehension of the importance of stock options.

"I was frustrated that my two previous startups ended up selling out. The first one sold out because they were running out of cash and the other because management lost their nerve and decided to grab what they could for themselves, leaving crumbs for the rest of us." His lips tightened as he recalled the experience.

"Everyone talks about the 'pain' of a startup. What's so painful?" Porter asked.

I should get a napkin so this guy can dry himself behind the ears, Wayne thought. "It's the pace of change and the challenges all this new technology presents. I've been selling technology since the early 80's. We were revolutionaries! We sold Wang word processing to bank secretaries! They were practically throwing their panties at us in gratitude for freeing them from their IBM Selectrics. We all thought that change was blistering *then.* Looking back now, it's laughable, even with Apple, Compaq, Oracle, 3COM leading the way. Remember Compaq? 'Fastest billion dollar company'. They were simply the first stage of an industrial rocket of change.

"Also, back then I knew exactly who I'd be selling to: some lifer in the Information Technology Department – oh, excuse me, it was called Management Information Systems back then. There were only mainframe products to sell and MIS departments to sell to. No one outside of MIS knew anything about computer systems. As long as they got their reports on green bar paper, they were happy. Now, everyone seems to know everything about PCs, client-server… just think of all the new categories of software that sprang up over the last ten years; relational database, HTML, CRM, EAI, local area networks. And they all have companies with products represented by sales forces selling to all parts of corporate America, not only IT. It demands a different kind of sales force, a smarter, more nimble sales team…"

"I see…" Porter said.

"The challenge of selling this new stuff into a new environment is like a drug; with each new deal, the next one has to be bigger, more historic. It's intoxicating!"

"I can tell. But you're not in it for the money?"

"Not *just* for the money. But your record against the Number – and receiving the subsequent greenbacks, of course – is the scorecard. One thing you will soon learn is that nearly everyone at a startup wants to grab the gold at the end of the rainbow in the form of publicly traded stock. It's risk versus reward. Even with all the hype about IPOs, it's still long odds. Those who succeed do so through hard work and dedication, teamwork. Why go through that startup pain if you aren't rewarded for the dedication?"

"SEs too?" Porter asked, hoping that they weren't "just in it for the money".

"Especially the SEs," Wayne said, immediately regretting that he didn't soften the blow for Porter. "Hey, sorry, but once you get into a sales environment, that's what happens."

Well, it isn't going to happen to me, Porter thought, assuring himself that he would always put the technology first.

"So, you've already decided to join InUnison, Wayne?"

"Pretty much. I asked Presby if he could set up a conversation with Bill Engler, the CEO. I'd rather look him in the eye but it'll have to do. I want to be sure about the corporate culture. I've been burned in the past," Wayne said, the image of Gatto flashing through his mind.

As they finished their drinks, Brenda approached, pointing at her watch.

"It's past eleven. We need to pick Stephanie up."

Porter looked at Brenda, confused. "I thought we had until –"

"No, Mom wanted to go home by eleven-thirty."

Porter didn't argue, and helped her put on her coat as Wayne did the same for Helen.

At the front door, they said good night, wishing each other Merry Christmas.

Once in the car, Brenda opened up.

"I'm sorry, Porter. I just couldn't take that bitch any longer. She is so self-centered and egotistical…"

"I'm sorry you had a bad time, babe."

"Oh, Wayne is great. I can see why he's a good sales rep and I think you'll work very well with him. But I don't see how they ever became a couple. She actually tried to convince me we *had* to have a nanny to bring Stephanie up correctly. She scoffed, *scoffed*, when I said that I was confident raising her as a stay-at-home mom, especially with my mother so close. *Argggh!* Oh! And did you know we should already have her on a pre-school waiting list? She said she'd put a good word in for us at, at, oh, I don't remember the place, I'm so aggravated!"

Porter knew there was no stopping her. It was a very long fifteen minute drive.

Wayne had an even longer ride back to Scarsdale.

"Oh, what a cute little couple they were. So naïve…"

"Helen, I recall being pretty naïve when we got married."

"You think that you can succeed with that greenhorn, Porter? Trenton? What's Trenton? Might as well be from East Jesus."

Wayne almost pulled off the road but maintained control.

"Listen! Porter is inexperienced but knows what he wants and hasn't been jaded. I'm energized after talking to him."

"It's only a matter of time," Helen said. "You were the same silly way and look at what you've become."

Wayne regretted that he had to agree.

***

The next Monday morning, Wayne's phone rang exactly at ten. *Punctual. That's a good sign.*

"Good morning, Wayne. Bill Engler, InUnison Software." Engler's voice was so quiet and soft that Wayne wondered if he was under the weather.

At a bit under five feet nine inches with a runner's slimness, Engler was a non-imposing, bearded 50-something. He made up for that with laser beam blue eyes that burned into the listener. When speaking, he spoke softly, so quietly that his audience concentrated all the more on what he had to say.

His seemingly calm and unassuming demeanor gave the impression that Bill lacked "fire in the belly". Nothing could be farther from the truth. Bill had a huge chip on his shoulder due to naysayer colleagues who doubted he could succeed with his own operation. His fire could be witnessed on the basketball court. He was deceptively quick to the basket, possessed an annoyingly high percentage three-point shot and his bony elbows became lethal weapons under the basket. There was seldom a company or sales meeting which did not include time for lengthy and full-contact pick-up games.

"I appreciate you taking some time to talk, especially when it's seven your time."

"I'm usually here by seven-thirty to beat the traffic."

"I have a tough decision to make and, well, I guess I wanted to hear some things directly from the top."

"Certainly. I try to be open to everyone. What are some of your concerns?"

"Financial, mostly. You see, I was with two other startups, thought that they were well funded but they burned through the money and ended up selling out. We got very little out of the deals. So, what is the status at InUnison?"

"Wayne, you know that I am taking a big risk in talking about these matters."

"Yes, of course. It's just that I need to know."

"I know that it can be a leap of faith to join a young company such as ours. Let me put our position this way: given our current burn rate, we are funded into third quarter 1998. We will be embarking on a third round of VC funding in the second quarter. Now, we will be aggressive on the revenue side, and are gearing up the sales force for that. If we fail to meet projections, obviously the liquidity horizon shortens."

"And release schedules? Any hiccups happening there?"

"We have a dot release, 2.7, for January which includes mostly new connectors and bug fixes. We have a major release, 3.0, in March with an all new user interface for the tools plus a Rules Agent. We are on track for both except for a delay in a couple of connectors, such as the mainframe connector."

"With respect to the VC money, will existing investors participate?"

"Yes and a major new one from Wall Street. I'll keep that name to myself for now."

"I totally understand. Now, I've spoken to some reference customers that Ken Presby pointed me to. I was struck by how they consistently raved about how easy it was to do business with InUnison; how you backed up your customers. Now, I'm not so naïve to believe that one hundred percent are happy –"

"That *is* what I want; one hundred percent referenceability – if there is such a word. Look, I'm trying to build a big, enduring company here. Yes, I'm hoping for the financial reward, but not on the cheap and especially not at the expense of our customers' success. Going public too early risks being frozen in place, worrying too much about the stock price instead of product."

"I'm with you on that, Bill. That's the kind of company I want to work for."

"Based on what I've heard from Ken and Niles, we'd definitely like to have you on the team."

"A few other things, Bill…"

The two talked for over an hour, touching on all aspects of the company. Wayne came away totally impressed with Engler and the culture he was striving for the company to embrace.

"Bill, again, I really appreciate you taking this much time to chat. I'm looking forward to joining the team."

"Glad to hear it! Nothing is more important to me than having the right people in this company."

The Gatto issue still nagged Wayne, but he decided to chalk him up as the exception that proved the rule.

"Merry Christmas, Bill. I hope to see you at the kickoff."

"Merry Christmas to you as well, Wayne. Oh, hey, do you play hoops? I need a power forward at the kickoff."

***

"Here's the deal," VibraWeb's Eastern Sales Manager, George Means, explained to Gatto. "We go for the money. We find a prospect and ask for money. If there's money on the table you take it. If money isn't there for the taking, move on. We avoid prolonged sales cycles like the plague. Market share rules and we can't get it by getting into pointless proof-of-concept projects or long evaluations. I know this is different from the way those navel gazers at InUnison work, so if you can't deal with our way of working, tell me now."

Well, that certainly laid it out, Gatto thought. As he sat across the desk from Means in his Five Penn Plaza office, he mulled how to twist the obviously desperate sales manager. Gatto found out how Means was left high and dry in the final quarter of the year by Bill Thomas. Means might be talking tough about "navel gazers" but his New York office was sucking wind. This slovenly, off-the-rack Brooks Brothers, IT reject from the 70's didn't impress the suave Tom Gatto. He knew how to play him.

"George, that's exactly how I like to work, and why things aren't working out at InUnison. When I saw money, I took it," Gatto said, clenching his fist. "Frankly, I'm kind of hampered at InUnison. It's almost like they say to a customer, 'Sorry, we can't take the money until we earn it. How about an onsite eval?'"

Means liked that anecdote.

"No way does that happen at VibraWeb. We want everyone to be a fat bear."

"Fat bear?" *Sounds corny,* Gatto thought, but he figured he'd better seem interested.

"Ah, think of big grizzlies fishing for salmon. Some try to catch the one, perfect salmon and nearly starve until that one big fish comes by. But a Fat Bear, ah! He focuses on the easy prey, regardless of size, grabs it quickly, rips the head off with his teeth and tosses the carcass to the shore so he can get the next one. By the end of the fishing, he's got a pile of fish to enjoy. The other guy? He might have one or two. Our prospects are those easy salmon."

Means was very proud of being a fat bear. He also used it as a verb, "to fat bear a deal". He even bestowed a Fat Bear Award every quarter. He took credit for the analogy, though no one believed that Means was creative enough to come up with it on his own.

Hmmm, that's the way I like to work, Gatto thought, as his brain conjured up visions of headless customers.

"George, I guarantee you; I will be a very fat bear."

"That's the attitude, Tom! I think we can do business. VibraWeb is *the* hot ride!"

Means' impatience returned. "So what's it going to be? I don't have all day." He whipped out a boilerplate offer letter. "Look, here's our standard offer letter for a senior level sales rep. I can have HR fill in the blanks and fax this over in an hour."

Gatto sensed a transparent attempt by Means to railroad him. Now was the time to twist him a little.

"Look, I'm closing out my quarter, big time. I'm very impressed with your offer and the fact that you can turn it around quickly, but I need a few days to think about it. And you know I can't start until February."

"Sure," Means said, hoping the sweat on his upper lip wasn't showing. "But I need a commitment very soon."

"You don't care that I'd still technically be at InUnison in January?"

"I don't give a rat's ass. Just be sure to gather as much G2 as possible while you're there. Can you sneak away to our kickoff meeting?"

"When is it?"

"January sixth through the eighth in Santa Clara."

"That overlaps the InUnison meeting in Redwood City. I might be able to sneak away," he said. He usually blew off most of these sales meetings anyway.

"Okay, call me when you get out there."

Means got up and shook Gatto's hand. "Great! Pleasure doing business, you Fat Bear!"

"Thank *you,* George. I'll find my way out."

***

Alone, back in his apartment, Gatto pondered his future. He poured himself some coffee and gazed at his surroundings. Two days until Christmas and he felt as if Santa Claus stopped by his condo early. He'd have plenty to brag about at his mother's house in Hoboken. He thought he could finally put to rest the ridicule his older, supposedly more successful, siblings always laid on him. All six – all males – were doctors, lawyers or had an MBA and worked in investment banking. Sales – unless it involved securities – was not deemed worthy. This year he'd have quite a bank account to show off.

Yes, this could be the last few months in these sorry digs. He figured that if he could sell the lame InUnison software, how tough could VibraWeb be?

A killer quarter, a new job; this calls for celebration, he thought, as he pulled out his Palm Pilot, tapping on the phone list category labeled "Babes". Pressing the advance button a few times, he found an entry to his liking.

"Ah, Sondra!" he said, with a wide grin. "I wonder if she still wears that dental floss for underwear…" he said, dialing her number. She quickly accepted Gatto's invitation.

His social calendar set, he skipped into the bathroom and reached for his hair gel.

Chapter 3 Kickoff

It was only January 5th but the holidays might well have been months ago as the InUnison sales force assembled in Salon 2 of the Hotel Sofitel in Redwood Shores. The slate was wiped clean and the sales reps and SEs anxiously awaited any news befitting their high expectations.

The audience stood, applauding their beloved CEO, Bill Engler. For a very few, the cheering was sincere and heartfelt in appreciation for his success in building a growing concern but for most, the applause was because of his support for a generous sales compensation plan.

"Everyone in this room is to be commended," Engler said. "Because of you, we exceeded our plan, much to the pleasant surprise of the board. I, of course, had no doubts about your ability to blow out your Numbers.

"While I'm very satisfied with your financial performance, I'm equally pleased with *how* you've achieved them. You've upheld InUnison's standards for dealing with customers: honesty, integrity and partnership for success."

"Why does he have to say that every freaking time?" Murphy asked rhetorically.

"He really means it, that's why," someone near him replied.

"Idealist child," someone else commented.

He paused to allow the group to applaud themselves.

"And now, it is my great pleasure to introduce our VP of Sales, Niles O'Rourke, who turned our motley sales band into an industry juggernaut, I dare say, the best in the business..."

"This is such bullshit," Gatto said, clapping only enough to seem enthused. He didn't want to reveal his short-timer attitude yet. "We always come to this same lame hotel, with their worn-out wall coverings and crummy chairs so that we can listen to managers tell us what we already know."

"That being?" Joe Phillipson, Denver sales rep, asked.

"That, gee, our Numbers are going up while our compensation stays the same at best. Oh, and that our Business Development and Marketing departments have sales as their top priority. Total bullshit."

"Yeah, but I won't mind as long as O'Rourke leaves my territory alone. I've got a target rich environment for our integration engine and ..."

Yo, Joe, I really couldn't care less about your "environment", Gatto thought.

Niles O'Rourke ascended the stage to continued applause from the team. He has been InUnison Software's VP of Sales since the last kickoff meeting, blew out his Number for the year and was the company hero, putting them on the revenue track for a public stock offering later in the year, or so they all expected.

Across the room and in front, the new sales team of Wayne Angelis and Porter Mitchell were taking in this scene, each having very different reactions. Wayne smirked a bit at the rah-rah environment. *All sales kickoffs are the same*, he thought. Wayne had been in the business long enough, and become enough of a cynic, to know that this display was meant to fire up the new hires and impress them with the team's "go-go culture".

Porter, being new to the sales game, was simply bewildered. It was already quite a shock to move from the static world of Hayworth and Steelcase cubicles to the pressures and dynamics of sales in a fast growth software startup. When Porter entered his hotel room, he found his roommate, Sean Murphy, behind the television working with pliers in order to hack into the Sofitel's TV system so he could get free movies. Sean then helped himself to the in-room liquor, carefully prying off the vodka and gin bottle caps and emptying the contents into glasses so that he could refill the bottles with water and return them to their rightful places in the cabinet. He hadn't detected Sean's criminal mind while working on the SecNat project and he hoped he wasn't expected to adopt these kinds of skills himself.

Wayne sensed his new partner's nervousness.

"Hey, Porter, don't get too overwhelmed. All sales meetings are like this. The idea is that we get all energized and leave ready to take on the world."

"Does it work?"

"Nope. Reality will set in as soon as we get our Numbers."

"So, why do it?"

"Beats me. Some motivational consultant is counting his millions on a beach somewhere, laughing about how he sold this so-called motivational drivel to sales managers all over the world."

They turned back to the stage as O'Rourke raised his hands to settle the troops.

"Thank you all for the enthusiastic greeting, but it's all of you who deserve the credit for our tremendous year! Give yourselves another round of applause!"

Salon 2 erupted in cheers and the sales team rose to their feet again, giving each other high-fives. They all shared in the past year of success, with all but one district team – Grim Reaper in Atlanta, of course – qualifying for the first 100% Club trip at InUnison, the reward trip for sales overachievers. They would find out later where the trip would be, but rumor placed it at a Caribbean beach or resort, in short, a perfect place for the over-eating, over-drinking, over-carousing, and playing politics with the sales management on the golf course.

"Great, *another* helping of bullshit please," Gatto murmured. "Just give me my Number and shut the hell up."

"Why can't you bask in the collective adulation?" Joe teased, while trying to outdo the next guy in enthusiasm.

"I don't need no stinking adulation," Gatto said, in his best outlaw voice. "Except from O'Rourke's administrative assistant. I'm counting on a close encounter with Suzy tonight after the tequila shots. She does this thing when she's drunk…"

"I don't want to know, Tom."

O'Rourke continued to review the past year's glories, highlighting key deals, embarrassing the reps who were responsible and sometimes acknowledging the technical talent needed to win the deal.

He motioned for quiet and moved closer to the audience as the room calmed down.

"InUnison cannot sit on its laurels. Let's move to the coming year and our plan to continue our explosive growth."

The room was now silent as they knew what was coming, The Mother of All Numbers: the revenue goal for the company. The Number from which all of their Numbers would be derived. It was expected to be some magnitude larger than the previous year so as to impress the IPO market.

O'Rourke, wearing a wireless microphone so that he could pace across the full area of the stage, milked the pause for full suspenseful effect before advancing to his 1998 Plan slide on his presentation. He scanned the room as he drifted across the stage. *Yes, I have them now. It's time to lower the boom…*

A cell phone rang. Not a typical warble, no, it was a loud rendition of the William Tell Overture. About a dozen people in the back of the room reached for their phones, praying it wasn't theirs. It was, of course, Gary Reaper's phone and he frantically tried to turn it off amid the snickers around him.

"Gary!" O'Rourke shouted. "I guess you missed the message banning cell phones and pagers from the room? That'll be fifty bucks, pal." *I should take that phone and shove it up your ass.*

He walked the stage some more, hoping to rebuild the suspense. Once he saw everyone's eyes on him, he advanced his slide.

"Our revenue goal for 1998 is $70 million dollars…"

The audience gasped. The Number was worse than they could have fathomed: four times that of the previous year. Porter looked around at all the stunned faces.

"The Number is much higher than expected," Wayne whispered. "That means, one; the territories will shrink as the company attempts to hire an army of new sales teams, or two; territories don't shrink but individual Numbers go up even more than the revenue increase."

O'Rourke continued.

"In order to achieve this aggressive – but certainly attainable – goal, we will be equally aggressive on the recruiting front..."

There were hushed, but clearly audible "oh shits" from several in the crowd. This revelation would mean tough battles in the breakout sessions to retain choice territories.

"...and we have a few new faces already. For instance I'd like to introduce Wayne Angelis, a software sales star from New York. Let's give him a warm InUnison welcome! Stand up Wayne!"

While polite applause rippled through the room, Gatto smirked to himself. *Angelis. I'll be getting out while the getting is good.*

"So, a bit of competition, eh, Tommy?" Phillipson asked, assuming Gatto cared.

"No, knucklehead, it means he works for me," Gatto bluffed. "Besides, who are you to talk? See that tall blonde hard body by the door? She's going to cover the cable and media companies in Denver. Didn't you know?"

Gatto was pulling his chain – she was one of the hotel staff he'd been trying to hit on – but Phillipson was so gullible that Gatto couldn't resist.

As he could have predicted, Phillipson's eyes grew huge and he was blubbering about how unfair it was.

"I'm scratching out an existence in Denver and they're going to bring in this tart…"

Gatto salted the wound a bit more.

"So much for the target-rich environment, eh pal?"

Across the room, Wayne shook his head.

"Well, Porter, I hope you have some good shoes, because we're going to have to pound the pavement long and hard. Our Number is going to be aggressive."

"Oh, before I forget," Porter whispered to Wayne, "I got a call from my old manager at the bank. He's starting, today as a matter of fact, with Azalea Financial. According to the message, he's going to be doing almost the exact same thing as our old project. He wants to talk to us as soon as possible."

Wayne thought for a minute. "They're located down by South Street Seaport. Manhattan. That's not my territory. We need to talk to Gatto about it."

"You mean we can't work it?"

"It means *I* can't work it. You can. Remember, Young said you'd have to support me and Gatto." *Great, first day on the job and I'm already going to have to share Porter with the enemy.*

***

"Norm, are you all set up in your office?"

"Yes, Sam. Connie was extremely helpful with that. You've got a great admin. I'm going to get spoiled."

"Don't get too used to it. I don't share her very much. Usually only when Gibson's assistant is off or something. Anyway, I guess I need to do the honorable thing and introduce you to Stewart Miller in IT."

Racker dialed Miller's number and got the usual voice mail greeting.

"There are two certainties about our CIO: he'll never be at his phone and will never return the messages. That was my fourth attempt since yesterday and I'm out of patience. Follow me.

"Connie, I'm going down to the tenth floor to seek out Stewart Miller. I want to introduce Norm around down there. Hopefully this won't take long."

"Sure thing. Happy hunting."

He and Norm got off the car on the tenth floor and Sam was startled to see windows the entire length of the elevator lobby, through which he could see banks of equipment. They could feel a low, mechanical rumble as they watched numerous operators huddling over consoles and others yanking stacks of paper off of printers.

"Jesus, it really *is* a glass house," Racker said. "I thought that was an urban legend. Figures Miller would set things up this way; show off his manhood."

There were doors at either end of the lobby, both with security card readers. Racker took his company access card out and swiped it through one of the readers. The red light flashed, signaling that his access was denied. He tried a couple more times without success. He then walked to the other end of the lobby and tried that door. No luck.

There was a phone on the wall by the first door so Sam went back to that end of the lobby. There were no instructions about any extension to call so he simply picked up the receiver. It immediately rang someone.

"Raised floor. How can I help you?" said the receptionist, Becky Sharpe.

"Sam Racker to see Stewart Miller."

"Are you authorized for this floor?"

"I should be. I'm the Controller."

"I'm sorry, what company was that?"

"*This* company, Azalea, I'm the CON-TROLL-HER."

"Ken Treller?"

Stay calm; this is some low level receptionist. "Sam Racker. I sign your paycheck," Racker said, hoping she would get the joke.

"Very funny. The computer signs my paycheck."

"Today is payday. Do you have your check yet?"

"Yes."

"Whose name is in the signature?"

"Can't read it. Bad handwriting."

"LISTEN! You get out here and let me in, NOW!"

Sharpe didn't appreciate being yelled at and punched her mute button. "Hey, Herb," she called out to her Shift Supervisor. "There's someone out front who thinks he's some big shot and can wander in here like he owns the place. Should I call Security?"

"Who is he?

"Sam Racker. He claims to sign my paycheck but I don't see where–"

"YOU IDIOT! That *is* our Controller and future CFO! He sure as hell *does* sign our paychecks!" Herb Putnam sprinted for the door, ignoring Sharpe's question, "What's a 'controller'?"

"Mister Racker, Herb Putnam, Shift Supervisor. Sorry for the misunderstanding. Becky, well, she takes the security thing pretty seriously."

"I understand. We're here to see Stewart Miller. Can you show me to his office?"

"Sure it's right outside my cubicle. It's quicker if we cut through the datacenter."

"Herb, this is Norm Johnson," he said, introducing Norm as they walked. "He is our new Director of Financial Information. He's going to help sort out the confusion with our financials. I'm counting on some help from you folks, of course."

"Oh you know we're here to help, Mr. Racker." *Does Miller know about this new guy?* Putnum wondered. He led Racker and Johnson through the maze of machinery, pointing out a few things along the way, such as the dozens of StorageTek disk drives and automated tape vaults. Herb was especially proud of the ultra-high speed printers, claiming to run enough paper per day to stretch from New York to Los Angeles. Herb was disappointed that neither Sam nor Norm was impressed.

Racker hadn't noticed the noise of the machine room until he was startled by the silence of the office area. There were rows and rows of cubicles with offices and the odd conference room lining the outside of the floor. They came upon cubicle "10R9" which stood for tenth floor, aisle R, cubicle 9. This was Herb's home for the few minutes a day when he was away from the supervisor's console. It was close to the corner of the floor, where, of course, Stewart Miller's office was located. Miller was out of the office.

"He's around," Herb said. "He was there right before you came down. Heard his phone ringing."

No kidding. He saw that it was me calling and scrammed.

"You want me to page him?"

"Please. I'll wait in his office," Racker said.

Herb left them to return to his cubicle and wait for Miller to answer the page.

Racker and Johnson stepped into Miller's office, which was on the Water Street side of the building and looked out towards the heart of the financial district. All of the office's walls were covered by custom-built shelves populated with coffee mugs, all from computer software, hardware and services vendors. *I guess everyone needs a hobby,* Racker thought. He chuckled at what a waste it was that the mug collection obscured a decent view.

Behind the desk, hanging on a hook driven into the shelving, was a samurai sword. On the credenza below were the usual family pictures but also a large picture of Miller, wearing some tourist version of a samurai outfit and holding the sword with both hands above his head.

"So, this is the office of our problem child. Supposedly, he uses that samurai sword on uncooperative vendors."

One section of wall displayed numerous plaques and other mementos. As he examined them from top to bottom, he realized it was a professional chronology: Marine Corps, late 60's Vietnam – Connie had described his jar head crew cut as so perfect that you could practice putting on it – Piscataway Tech, IBM COBOL Training. Sam quickly scanned some of the other frames.

"Look at this, Norm; no bachelor's degree, classic internal career path. I'll bet he started out mounting tapes for a living."

Racker and Johnson sat down at the conference table in the corner to wait for Miller. *ComputerWorld* and *CIO* magazines were strewn on the table.

"He certainly has the IBM world nailed here, doesn't he?" Norm noted. There weren't any of the newer trade rags like *Wired, Industry Standard* or journals covering the emerging use of the Java computer language exploding on Internet applications. Sam leafed through a few of them before his impatience returned.

"Herb," Racker called out, "Any sign of your boss?"

"No, sorry, Mr. Racker."

"Can you come in here, please?"

Putnam walked just inside the door, nervously awaiting some directive. He wasn't comfortable being in Miller's office without being invited by Miller himself.

"Come on over and sit down. I'm still new here and I haven't met too many people. So, tell me about yourself. How long have you been with Azalea?"

Herb settled into the chair opposite Sam Racker. "Almost six years. I started out as a programmer analyst and moved into Computer Operations after a couple of years."

"Why the change?"

"I was a systems operator in the Navy and decided I liked that better than programming."

"After several years in Operations you must know a lot about what goes on here. Perhaps you can help educate me. I'm trying to make some sense out of our financial systems. For instance, this Oracle Financials implementation seems to be a little out of whack. What's your take on it?"

Herb recoiled at the question. *Talk about a live grenade! This might be a career defining situation here.* He decided to play dumb. "I'm not sure what you're asking. It's certainly late, no question about that, but if you're asking me why, I really can't say. I'm not involved in the project yet. I deal with code *after* it goes production." *Development is not my job, thank God!*

Sam leaned back, strumming his right fingers on his chin. *Herb deflected that question quickly.* "I see. But certainly you're aware of something as radical as bringing Oracle and PeopleSoft in. Must be quite a challenge for the folks in IT."

"That it is," Herb said. *It's definitely a challenge to stay the hell away from those subversive projects.*

Racker tried to ferret out a little more information. "Well, what I mean is, it must be quite a culture shock to see radical new equipment, like Sun servers, and packaged software come into this datacenter. How do you think people are handling it?"

Like ants handle Raid. "Uh, pretty well. There's a bunch of training going on for the new teams."

Racker gave him several more chances to go on, but it became clear that Herb wasn't going to volunteer much. The interrogation ended when Herb's pager went off. He looked at the number and recognized it as the main control desk. *Thank God.* "This is the Control Desk. I think I better return it."

Racker nodded his approval and leaned back in his chair pondering the slivers of information while Putnam called the control desk from Miller's phone.

"Control Desk."

"This is Herb. Did you page me?" He heard the console operator say "It's Herb" and then a shuffling of the receiver.

"Is he still there?"

"Who? I'm in Miller's office with Sam Racker."

"Shhhhhh. Just answer yes or no."

"Who is this? I don't have time for…"

"Shut up! This is Stewart. DON'T say my name. Answer yes or no. Is Racker still in my office?"

"Yes."

"Tell him you have to go."

"But –"

"NO BUTs! Tell him you have a production problem and you're sorry and all that. Then he'll leave."

"But –"

"I SAID…"

"I got it!" *I hate you Stewart.* Herb hung up and turned to Sam. "Mr. Racker, uh, I'm terribly sorry but there's a production problem that needs my attention. I need to get back to the datacenter."

"I understand. Thanks for your time. I'll find my way out. Oh, one other thing. Can you give me Miller's pager number?"

Putnam froze. *What do I do?* Miller had fired the last guy who gave the pager number out without asking, but he realized that Racker would soon be his boss' boss. It mattered.

Racker saw the panic on Putnam's face. He got up, crossed the room and put his hand on the shoulder of a nearly paralyzed Herb Putnam and said, "Herb, I won't tell him where I got it." Mildly relieved, Herb wrote it out for Racker.

"It was a pleasure meeting you," Herb said and fled the office.

Sam looked around for some note paper, finding it on Miller's desk. He wrote a quick note to Miller, asking him to stop by his office to meet Norm Johnson.

He and Norm returned to his floor. "Connie, this is the pager for Stewart Miller. Please keep paging him every ten or fifteen minutes until he calls back. Try using different numbers if he doesn't reply. You still have your cell phone, right?"

"Sure, Sammy. What do I do when, well, if, he calls back?"

"Tell him I want to introduce our new Director of Financial Information so we can get going on some reporting work." He started to go into his office but spun around, tossing his ID badge onto Connie's desk. "Oh, and figure out how I can get that badge enabled to enter the datacenter."

***

The InUnison meeting broke up just in time for a reception with open bar and hors d'oeuvres. This was a time to mingle, collect inside information, and get warmed up for the evening of serious drinking at the hotel bar.

Even within the frugal InUnison budget, the hotel provided a sizable spread of food spanning three or four tables. Being in California, though, the dishes were usually inscrutable to the out-of-towners. It would start with a couple of salad choices, move to a fish or chicken dish – all dusted with unrecognizable spices or simply soaking up a witches brew of marinade – and finishing with a bowl of soup from a large cauldron. It was a juggling act to keep it all together.

"What is this?" Porter asked his roommate Sean, gazing at a greenish, guacamole-type dip. "I didn't recognize anything but the salad at lunch either."

"Same crap every time." Sean replied, as he gingerly spooned through some fishy smelling salad. "You'd think they could at least put out some marinated shrimp or something."

"People really survive on this stuff?" Porter was looking down the line to see the West Coast folks eagerly loading up on some sort of soybean concoction.

Sean sighed. "They think we should all be vegans or something. We have to put up with it for a few days but it's become a tradition on the last night of these meetings for us serious eaters to head up to Gulliver's in Burlingame for the Full Bone Cut of prime rib. Biggest slab of bloody cow I've ever seen. But it would be frowned upon for us to disappear on the first day."

"Well, given your criminal habits, can't you rustle up something from the kitchen?"

Sean laughed. "You know, I might have to work out a way to scam room service, maybe try to have it sent to a different room and then intercept it or something..."

Around eight o'clock, the crowd started to assemble in the sizable lounge at the Sofitel. It didn't take long for the industry-standard shots of tequila to show up. Reps who had been with other software companies would relate stories of the quantities of agave consumed at their meetings, always casting InUnison as not up to snuff.

Reaper could be counted on to regale anyone who would listen about his glory days at Sybase. They were about the only glory days in Gary's life.

"Yeah, when I was at Sybase, that dude with the Greek last name – what the hell was his name? – he wouldn't let up on us. Tray after tray after tray of shot glasses... We got kicked out of so many bars ..."

"Oh, and *how* many shots was that, Gary?" Phillipson, while no superstar drinker himself, had heard this story at every meeting since joining the company. It was definitely old. The number had grown from 10 to 100 in one year.

"A SHITLOAD! I'm telling ya!" Reaper slurred.

Egging him on a little further was Gatto.

"So, Grim, how'd you end up at InUnison? You were doing pretty well there at Sybase weren't you? Why leave a good thing?" Gatto already knew the answer and he considered it sport to bait Reaper at almost every meeting. He also knew Gary hated the nickname "Grim Reaper". But Reaper was too involved in his story and tipsy to notice, disappointing his tormenter.

"Hey, we had a huge, I mean HUGE deal brewing at AT&T. Business Development fucked it up. I left because I got tired of them screwing up my deals. BD and those incompetent marketing people."

"But you're always going on about 'At Sybase we did this' and 'At Sybase we did that'," Gatto said, continuing to draw Reaper to the ledge. "You always make it sound like they were the standard for how to run a software business."

Reaper started to look sadly at his empty tequila shot glass. "They were when I started there. Then things went to hell." Gary was almost ready to start sobbing now. He was sure that he'd never see that kind of success ever again.

Gustavson, always the champion of the little guy, knew Gatto had blood in the water and interceded. He'd seen Gatto reduce people to tears with his merciless rundowns before. The Swede could talk trash with the best of them but never with malice.

"Hey, Gatto, you're always bragging about Sun. Why can't Gary brag about Sybase?"

"That's because Sun really was and *is* a good organization. We could do no wrong at Sun. Of course you wouldn't know a good organization if it fell on you."

"Yeah, and your shit doesn't smell, does it?" Gustavson said.

"Great comeback, moron." Gatto was already feeling the alcohol. Pretty soon he'd believe he could take on the whole bar.

"Who's calling who a moron, you Jersey Dago?" There was certainly no love lost between Gustavson and Gatto. But Gustavson had about five inches and fifty pounds on Gatto. "If I had New York, I'd have tripled your production."

Gatto pushed his chest out to meet Gustavson's, though his chest met at The Swede's lower rib cage. "Well, for your information, I happened to *live* in Jersey for a while, I'm not *from* Jersey."

Knowing he had nothing to lose by making up a legend, he went further. "Anyway, now I'll finally get the resources to do the job in New York properly. That's why they're bringing in Angelis and Mitchell to work under me."

Gustavson sprayed his tequila in Gatto's face.

"You can't be serious! You can't manage yourself let alone a team! Right, they bring in a serious player with a background in startups, some of which he practically started himself, and he's going to work for you. You'd best lay off of the sauce, my friend. Let's see, I seem to recall you losing UBS to me because they had no confidence that you could deal with a long, very technically involved sales cycle."

That ripped an old wound wide open since UBS Warburg had in fact pretty much chewed Gatto up and spit him out as not worthy of dealing with them. He tried to close them on a multi-million dollar deal at the second meeting and they literally laughed him out of the conference room. Financial services companies such as UBS Warburg were always at the forefront of technology and often had to build leading edge software internally before it was available commercially. Since they knew the technology cold, their evaluation criteria was some of the most brutal in the industry. But if you passed the test, it was usually worth millions.

Gatto couldn't back down now. He'd crossed the point of no return in the story, so why not go all the way?

Keeping a straight face, he continued.

"Yes, Number *Two*," he said, waving two fingers in the Swede's face. "I got the word from Presby himself. He's going to let Angelis in on it at the breakouts. Oh, and you can get used to being number *TWO* for a while," Gatto said, waving the two fingers in The Swede's face again. "As for UBS, you can have those elitist bastards and their fifty page RFIs. I closed six deals in the time it took them to decide which stall to take a dump in."

Even Gustavson had to laugh at this bit of hysterical hyperbole, as no one was buying it.

"Hey, back off, pal!" The Swede said, shoving Gatto out of his personal space. "Your hair is dripping grease on me. Even you know that one UBS Warburg is worth a dozen of the no-name accounts you conned into buying software from us."

Wayne was at the other end of the bar chatting with Ken Presby when he noticed that Gatto and Gustavson were glancing down at him. He saw how animated the conversation had become and figured that they were simply conspiring about territories.

It was a schmoozing kind of chat that Wayne was having with Presby, though he had hoped he'd get some confirmation about his territory. He wanted to lobby, again, for at least a few named accounts in Manhattan – like Azalea – but really didn't want to get into any kind of pissing match with Gatto. Presby, like most savvy sales managers, wasn't going to get sucked into any kind of serious discussion in public. It might have seemed as if no one was paying attention to them, but all eyes and ears from the East team were alert to any clue to come from Presby.

"… Anyway, Wayne, we're damn glad to have you. You are going to fit in fine here." Presby put on his best fatherly face.

"Well, I appreciate the vote of confidence, Ken. I'm particularly happy to be working with Porter. He certainly knows the technology."

Presby wasn't showing any recognition about Porter.

"He's that pale, slim guy with the unruly brown hair at the far table. You remember; SE from Security National Bank. He's been working with our products for over a year. You interviewed him the same day you met with me."

"Oh, right. I'm not thinking clearly. His company used our stuff? Security National? Hmmm, must not have been a big deal. Don't recall the name. Who sold it?"

"I suppose Gatto did."

"No, wait. Security National, they were an early adopter. I'm told that we pretty much gave them everything for free. No wonder I didn't remember. It was done before I joined the company and was never on a forecast. Either way, Gatto wouldn't have dealt with them. His deals always are obscure. He doesn't have a clue about strategic relationship selling. Always takes the short cut…" Presby caught himself as he was about to start really dissing Gatto. His eyes scanned the groups nearby to see if anyone had been listening in.

Wayne certainly took note. He wondered about what the relationship was between those two; Gatto may have sold to nondescript accounts, but he was still number one in the company.

Just then, Gary Reaper rudely stepped in front of Wayne to talk to Presby. Wayne took the opportunity to wander down to the end of the bar where Gatto and Gustavson were still jousting. He figured he'd better get the reintroduction over with.

"Tom Gatto, how have you been?" Wayne said, extending his hand in greeting.

Gatto shifted his newly refilled beer glass to his left hand to accept the handshake, spilling some on Wayne's shoes.

"Oh, sorry 'bout that. Fine, Wayne. Get anyone fired lately?" Gatto said.

Already playing head games, are we? Wayne sighed to himself.

"Actually, no."

"Still poaching accounts?" Gatto asked.

"I believe I should be asking you that question, Tom."

"Well, it'll be nice to be on the same 'team' again. I could use some help in Manhattan. You *do* know that you're working for me?" Gatto said, winking at The Swede and swaying into the bar.

"I see you haven't lost your sense of humor."

"I wasn't joking."

Gustavson had heard enough and came to Wayne's defense.

"I'm Bill Gustavson, Wayne. Welcome! And don't listen to this drunk. His Attention Deficit Disorder precludes him ever really getting a big account."

Gatto didn't appreciate his intervention.

"F' you. Isn't it time for your beauty sleep?"

"Actually, it is. I need my rest so I can continue to kick your ass tomorrow. See you guys in the morning. The first session is BD, right? It'll be content-free as usual." Gustavson downed the rest of his Anchor Steam and left the glass on the bar.

Wayne decided to cut his losses. He wasn't going to get anywhere with Gatto in his current state of inebriation and bad attitude, the latter of which had been aggravated by Gustavson.

"I'm going to turn in as well. It was nice to get, uh, reacquainted, Tom." Wayne said, extending his hand. "I'm sure we'll be able to work together well, just like old times."

"Sure thing." Spurning Wayne's hand, Gatto waved his glass at him instead and turned away.

***

Out at the edge of the lounge, the SEs congregated among the sofas and armchairs, filling the coffee table with empty beer bottles and drink glasses. The conversation was becoming more animated as the number of glasses increased. The standard religious arguments about Microsoft versus the true egalitarian nature of the software business were hashed out for the umpteenth time.

"Listen, someone ought to sue the Redmond boys and break them up. They are sucking in all the oxygen, strangling the industry."

"Please. What are you, some kind of retro-Commie? Maybe you missed it but the Berlin Wall came down a few years back. Gates has simply built an aggressive company. Government doesn't have a right to blow up companies because someone thinks that they are too successful. Sure, they seem to use tactics which should be reigned in, but blow up the company? I suppose you support the death penalty for jaywalking."

Sean Murphy spoke up. "Oh, guys, I just realized that I haven't properly introduced my roommate! This is Porter Mitchell from New York. He's been using our stuff for quite a while now so you won't be able to snow him with any technical or marketing BS."

Each of the eight SEs took his or her turn shaking Porter's hand and welcoming him.

"So, you must know Tom Gatto. How much money did he shake you guys down for?" asked Mark Maskowitz, the SE for Washington, DC.

"Never met him until this meeting. We were an early adopter before he even came on board. I started working with InUnison on version 0.8. Since we were plugged in directly to support and got the software for free, I guess he didn't see the point in spending time with us."

"Of course he wouldn't. Unless it lined his pockets, he wouldn't give you the time of day," Mark said. "We lost two good SEs in New York because they couldn't stand to work with the prick. I ended up shuttling back and forth from DC."

"I was part of the Gatto Shuttle as well," Sean said, referring to the fact that he was also a shuttle flight away in Boston. "He wants you to demo the same thing over and over, never really wants us to engage with the prospect; always says 'no' to a proof-of-concept or managed evaluation. Takes all the fun out of the job."

"Of course, he doesn't have a problem engaging if the prospect is female. Hi, I'm Julia Berkowski, Atlanta SE."

Julia, one of the most respected SEs at InUnison, had a software product engineering background, was an excellent communicator and had a wicked competitive streak which served her well in the sales environment.

She dreaded these sales events, though. A tall, slim yet buxom strawberry blonde, she had to fend off the sex fiends of the company but took full advantage of her sex appeal with the white males who still dominated IT management. At some point during every sales meeting, some tequila-buzzed rep would wander by and "chat" with her. The attempt to pick her up might not be blatant or overt but she knew the rep wasn't really interested in her latest demo techniques.

That sex appeal had not translated into any lasting relationships, though. Julia hadn't had a serious relationship for over three years, during which her suitors were all computer nerds who thought she was one of them and the last thing she wanted was a one-dimensional partner. Others, intimidated by Julia's strong conservative opinions and intelligence on a wide range of subjects, moved on.

As long as she was with the other SEs, though, she had a protective buffer around her. She was one of the guys with them, though they tended to think they were all her older brothers.

"So it sounds like you have more experience with the product than the rest of us put together. Beware; you'll be getting calls for help."

"I'd be happy to help out however I can. But you guys are going to have to give me some Sales 101 in return."

"Julia, don't you think your sales partner could give Porter some tips?" Sean knew this would get a rise from Julia.

"Oh, sure. Grim Reaper's Rule Number One: drop trou at the first meeting and beg for the business. Rule Number Two: when rule one fails as usual, offer your SE for long engagements in pointless projects that the prospect doesn't want or need."

Julia seethed at having to deal with the arrogant yet clueless Gary Reaper on a daily basis. She longed for the opportunity to really have an impact on a big deal. She was simply unlucky to live in the same geography as Reaper, forced to chase after prospects that had no use for integration software.

"I'm always the one to have the rejection conversation with the customer, along the lines of, 'I really don't know why Gary keeps bothering us. We keep telling him we aren't interested. You're very capable though, would you like a job here?'"

Everyone laughed, knowing it was true. It was especially funny to have a woman talking about a rep dropping his trousers to get the business.

Ron Defazio, SE in Los Angeles, introduced himself and offered some alternative advice.

"*My* Rule One: make sure your rep feeds you and picks up the check."

Sean interrupted, "Of course, Ron, being a California surfer dude is a pretty cheap date for a rep. 'Oh, could I have some fruit pizza please with a side of tofu?' Yuk!"

"Well, my body is my temple," Ron said while caressing his ripped abs. "I take care of it instead of hooking up to an IV of cholesterol like you heathens."

"I know Wiley worships your body, Ron."

Wiley Nelson, SE in Chicago, piled on using his best lisp. "Ooooo, big boy, be my roommate sometime so I can worship that body toooo?" This broke the whole team up as Wiley was about 6 feet 5, 260 pounds, practically a twin of his sales partner Gustavson.

"This is where I get off the bus." Julia loved these guys, but when the conversation degenerated to this level, it was time to call it a night. "Don't stay up too late. Don't want anyone sleeping through my presentation tomorrow."

"Don't forget to say goodnight to Gatto, Julia."

"I'll be sure to give him your room number, Sean."

"Hey, where's the Youngster?" Wiley asked. "Shouldn't he be buying these drinks?"

***

"So, what good news do you have for me?" Young asked O'Rourke, after being summoned to the bar.

"I wanted you to know that we have to hire about five SEs in the next two quarters."

"And where are these SEs going to be located?"

"Oh, not sure, maybe another in DC, Chicago; open offices in Dallas, St. Louis… We already have some reps ready to sign."

"Isn't that going to reignite territory battles?"

"No, I'm working hard to be sure everyone has set territories for the year. These are mostly new locations that weren't being worked."

This was a very depressing aspect of Young's job. O'Rourke always treated the technical side of the team as an afterthought even though the reps craved access to quality technical talent – dedicated to them, of course. When his hiring lagged the sales rep hiring, he felt tremendous pain.

"Shit, Niles, when was this decided? You know it takes twice as long to find SEs as reps, and then it takes a quarter for them to be proficient. In the meantime, my guys, and me of course, get run ragged." He'd made the argument for as long as he'd been an SE manager, and as usual, his VP didn't care. "Speaking of getting run ragged; you realize that we are going to have to add another SE manager to the mix. It's not so bad right now as we are one to one, SE to rep, but you add five or six more and I'm going to be doing nothing but playing traffic cop and wet nurse. My first choice would be Chicago to cover the Central Area."

O'Rourke gave Young that humoring kind of smile for which he was famous. It made the recipient feel like O'Rourke cared, but the effect wore off quickly.

"I'll take it under advisement. Youngster, I know you can meet the challenge. Where's your drink?"

Young decided that he needed something stiffer than a chardonnay.

"What single malts do you have?" he asked the bartender.

"Hey, where's this Kenneth Presby guy from room 847?" the Bartender called out, ignoring Young. It was closing time and he needed someone to pay up or sign out.

Shit. They did it to me again, Presby thought. He tried to hide his room number but at every sales meeting and company event, someone found out and started the tab on his room bill. *What would it be this time, four figures?*

"I'm Presby. Give me the damn bill." He made a show of snatching the bill and looking disgusted but it would be bad form to bitch too much.

Chapter 4 Switch Play

"We can't talk to your mainframe."

"Excuse me? Say that again??"

"Our mainframe connector isn't ready yet."

George Melani could feel his blood pressure spike. He was used to it after two years at Potential Investing. It was a very aggressive and demanding environment dependent on a lot of technology for its business. He was now in charge of the foreign exchange project which needed to pull together information from all over the organization and deliver it in real-time to customers.

But now he was realizing that what he was hearing was career threatening. He began to back Sanjay Chandra, a senior Professional Services Engineer from InUnison, into the conference room corner.

"*Your* company promised me you could integrate with my mainframe with *this* version," he said, as he waved the software CD an inch from Sanjay's nose. "*You* have been here for two months and only now figured out that we can't get to my mainframe?"

Chandra backed away from Melani but was running out of conference room to melt into. The usually very comfortable, wood-paneled conference room had turned into one of those interrogation rooms from an old spy movie and a hot lamp named George Melani was focused right on his face. As the lead engineer assigned to Potential, Sanjay was in the unenviable position of giving Melani the bad news that InUnison wasn't going to achieve the promised results. George was legendary at Potential for his temper, a weapon he used to get his way. This time Sanjay was the unfortunate target.

Stammering, Sanjay tried to explain.

"Well, uh, I don't know who misled you but the current version of our software was never meant to –"

Melani erupted.

"BULLSHIT! Your scumbag rep *promised* that the features were in THIS version!" he said, again furiously waving the CD. "We PAID for it!"

"Well, uh, well –"

"SHUT UP! So when do I get the real product I paid for?" He kept moving toward Sanjay who stumbled over a chair as he peddled backward.

"Well, uh, according to Engineering –"

"SHUT UP! You'll tell me anything at this point." He shoved the offending chair into the conference table and closed the distance.

Sanjay was now trapped in the front corner of the room. "But, George, it'll only be another…"

"SHUT UP and GET OUT!" he yelled, flinging the CD at the door. "Tell that bastard Gatto that if I ever see his ugly face in here again, he'll leave without it!"

Sanjay didn't need to be asked twice. He bolted out the door of the conference room and into the elevator. Catching his breath once he stepped out onto street level, he spotted the Crowne Plaza Hotel across Broadway and decided their lobby would be a safe place to get some coffee, settle down and call Tom Gatto about this. It had been another in a series of Gatto accounts where PS was supposed to implement the fantasy he sold. The engineers were practically in a mutiny and some refused to work on an account owned by Gatto. Sanjay himself had been flown in from headquarters to fix things.

Sanjay hit the speed dial for Gatto. It would be about 6:30 a.m. in California but he didn't care about waking him up. He didn't appreciate being set up for failure at Potential and wasn't in a mood to be courteous.

Gatto was still recovering from his morning workout – a highly aerobic romp with O'Rourke's admin, Suzy Kestral – when his phone rang.

"Good morning! This is Tom Gatto. How can I help you?" He answered pleasantly; after all, it might have been a prospect.

"Tom, Sanjay Chandra here. We have a problem."

"Who?" Gatto tended to forget PS people. They came *after* the sale and what did he care about that?

"Sanjay from PS who's trying to keep Potential Investing as a happy customer."

"Oh, sorry Sanjay. I didn't hear you right," Gatto lied. He had no idea who

Sanjay was. "So, what's going on?"

Sanjay got right to the point. "We finally had to tell Melani that we don't have our mainframe product ready and his project is in the toilet. He almost decapitated me fifteen minutes ago. Why is it you guys can't tell the truth?"

"Spare me. I had to get the deal and took a chance we'd have the product ready by the time Potential would need it." Gatto then applied a little textbook blame shifting. "Anyway, your boss committed to the project so I suggest that you talk to him."

"I'll do that. But don't you need to talk to Melani? He's saying he'll pull the software."

Suzy was alive again, and began stroking and kissing Gatto's inner thighs.

"Let him – Suzy please! – we already got paid. Besides, there's no commitment in the contract for the mainframe piece." *Thanks to my deft deletion of that clause from the contract,* he thought, patting himself on the back. He was aided in his editing of contracts by the fact that both InUnison and Potential used outside legal counsel who were overworked and disinterested, and usually waved drafts through. He also chuckled at how easy it was to evade responsibility when he had nothing to lose.

Sanjay had dealt with reps for a quite a number of years and was used to having to clean up messes but was taken aback by this level of arrogance. Even the most cynical reps would at least have some regard for their reputation.

"Dude, I can't walk away from this! Don't you care at all about reputations?"

"Well, *duuuude,* I don't have time for people like Melani who won't take responsibility for their decisions – oh, yes! Do that butterfly thing, Suzy! – He took the chance that we'd have the stuff ready for him. We don't. He fucked up."

Gatto had to lean back a bit to get out of the way of Suzy's bobbing head.

"This is a waste of my time," Sanjay said, realizing that he didn't have Gatto's undivided attention.

"*That* I agree with, Sanjay. Don't worry, I won't be around here much longer…I mean, I won't be around here in California, much longer and – oh, that's *great,* Suzy – I'll deal with Melani when I get back." He decided to lay it on a little thicker. "Hey! I have lots of new business in the pipeline that will keep your team busy!"

"That's what I'm afraid of." Sanjay hung up and stared out the bar window onto Broadway, wondering why he stuck with this business. He punched the speed dial for Jim Silvester, Vice-President of Professional Services. Jim never passed up a chance to bash sales reps who put his engineers in bad situations and this certainly qualified.

Gatto flopped onto his back, fully giving in to Suzy's talents.

***

Sean and Porter left their Sofitel room together, lugging their meeting binders and their laptops, ready for day two. It was inconceivable that any SE would sit through a business meeting without hacking some code to relieve the tedium.

"Hey, did you hear that?" Murphy asked Porter as they walked past the second door down the hall.

"Hear what?"

Sean led Porter back to the door and leaned in to listen.

"You're the best! You're great! You can do it all, Buster! You *know* you can!"

"What the hell is that?" Porter asked. "Some TV show?"

Murphy was snickering. "I didn't believe it, but it's true! It's Grim Reaper!

"Are you ready? *Are you READY!?* Then go get 'em, Tiger!" Reaper was audible all the way down the hall.

Porter and Sean heard him rustling in the closet barely inside the door and scrambled back to their room's door just as Reaper came out and charged down the hallway without noticing the two SEs behind him.

"What the hell was that, Sean?"

"Like I said, I had heard about it before but didn't believe it. Supposedly he stands in front of the mirror and gets himself all revved up. Pathetic."

The usual trays of breakfast breads awaited Sean and Porter inside the conference room. Porter already knew two things the Sofitel was good for: quality coffee and French pastries. The two SEs entered the ballroom together to see Wayne making some tea.

"Good morning, Wayne. Where are you sitting?"

"Second row on the aisle," he said, waving a croissant in the general direction. "Want to join me?"

Sean chuckled. "Suit yourself, roomie, but that's way too close to the front. They'd see me nodding off if I sat up there. Besides you can't crack jokes about the speakers if you're too close."

"Maybe if you hadn't been up half of the night watching porn you could stay awake."

"Hey, the dialogue was riveting; 'Oh, yes! Oh, YES! Give it to me! Oh….' How could you want to turn that off?"

Porter dropped his notebook next to Wayne's and returned to get some coffee.

"So, Wayne, the first session is Business Development. Just what is that?"

Always quick with commentary, Sean answered first.

"It's sales without quotas, hence no accountability. Not to jade you newcomers but Fred Lakota, our VP of BD is a total sleazebag. We call him 'Lucky Lakota'. He always seems to screw things up but never has to deal with the consequences. The smart reps keep him the hell away from their districts. It's particularly galling because we see press releases from VibraWeb on a weekly basis about some new partnership they made. Only last week, they had a major commitment from Perot Systems. Lakota's next partnership will be his first."

"Well, Porter," Wayne said, "in theory, BD is supposed to build partnerships with other companies in the industry to do things like resell our products or imbed our technology in their products or services. They also try to get the big consulting firms like CSC and Ernst & Young to adopt our products in their practices."

David Young entered the room.

"Now, there's one guy who doesn't take any BD crap," Sean said, loudly enough for Young to hear.

"Sean Murphy. Why is it that your voice is always the first one I hear?"

"I want to always be in your thoughts."

"Yeah, like a bad dream. Your references warned me about that. I should have wondered why they wouldn't hire you."

"We were discussing the valuable and productive role BD plays in our sales efforts."

"Shit. Counterproductive, you mean. I can't even talk to Lucky any more. The last serious conversation I had with him ended with me screaming into the phone about how my guys were always taking it up the ass for him. It's a good thing I'm not based in HQ. I'd have strangled the bastard by now."

Reaper returned to the coffee stand for a refill.

"This is always the most productive part of these meetings," he said. "BD has always helped me out. Way more than those losers in Marketing."

Porter watched as Young, Murphy and even Wayne's jaws dropped.

"You can't be serious," Young asked. "He's a total asshole."

"Be careful, Dave. He might be your boss one of these days."

"In your wet dreams, Grim."

Reaper gave Young a look of disgust and returned to his seat.

"Oh, excuse me a second." Murphy crept up behind Reaper. "So, Gary; are you *READY*, tiger?"

Reaper whipped around. "You have a problem, Murphy?"

"Nope. Making sure you're psyched for BD ... *TIGUURRR!*"

***

Arriving for the BD presentation, Niles O'Rourke was intercepted by Bill Engler. He asked O'Rourke to step outside to the parking area of the Sofitel. "Niles, what the hell is going on in New York?"

"I'm not sure what you mean, Bill. We've done pretty well there, as I think you are aware." O'Rourke wasn't used to having Engler in his face so he knew something must be really bugging him.

"Well, in the last day I've received at least five emails from accounts in New York who are really pissed off. I got one a few minutes ago from someone named Melani at Potential Investing threatening my first born and my gonads. He claims we lied to him about the mainframe connector. He further accused us of tampering with the contract during closing. He said that the commitment for the connector was in the contract at one point and then, poof, it wasn't in the final version. Do I have to eat my words from yesterday? Remember? The ones about how proud I am of our integrity, our customers' happiness?" Engler bit off the syllables through his gritted teeth.

"Let's get Presby out here. He would have the detailed information. But I have to point out to you, again, that we have to get someone internal to do contracts. The outside law firm doesn't exercise controls like being sure that line items are actually shipping product and stuff like that."

Engler winced. O'Rourke was right. He'd been warned multiple times by O'Rourke and his CFO, Jay Antoniazzi, that his controls were lax.

"Okay, find Presby and let's get this sorted out."

Niles ducked into the conference room and scanned for his Eastern Region sales director. He spotted him in the second row just as Presby happened to look back at the door. He gave him a quick index finger pointing to the lobby.

Presby let the door close slowly to avoid the clanging of the panic bar. He turned to see a very grim CEO.

"Good morning, Bill. You need me for something?" he said, not wanting to hear the answer.

"I want to know what the hell is going on in New York. One of our customers threatened my first born if we didn't get him his mainframe connector. Who was the wise guy who promised it in the first place? I thought we made it clear that it wouldn't be ready until Q2."

"What's the account?"

"Potential Investing, but I've got flame mail from several others as well, all from New York. So what's the deal?"

"Potential is definitely a Gatto account. He plays it pretty loose out there but it would be a stretch for him to blatantly commit to something like –"

"Commit, my ass! You mean he made it up, right?" Engler interrupted. "There's no gray area here. If he sold them this thing, then he was lying. It couldn't have been clearer about the status of that product. It wasn't on the price list after all."

"Ah, Bill, actually the connector *was* on the price list," Presby reminded Engler. "Marketing put it on, inadvertently, for a while in Q4 before the decision to delay release."

Engler gritted his teeth and seethed. "That's not enough of a fig leaf, guys. Look, find out what is going on with these New York accounts and get back to me. You know I place a high priority on having 100 percent of our customers as references. It looks to me like we have a lot of repair work to do in New York. Niles, I've grown to regret letting your predecessor hire Gatto. I didn't think his style was going to fly here. If he's become a loose cannon, then tie him down or throw him overboard. I won't have that here. I'm used to customers telling me how comfortable they are doing business with us. It is totally unacceptable for any erosion in that reputation. Is that understood?"

Engler alternated his laser-like gaze from Presby to O'Rourke. They both knew he was laying the responsibility on their shoulders. The last time they had heard him call something "totally unacceptable" and the situation wasn't rectified, the VP of Marketing disappeared.

"I'll get to the bottom of it today," Presby assured both Engler and O'Rourke.

Engler went into the BD presentation while Presby and O'Rourke hung back.

"Ken, I don't appreciate being Pearl Harbored like that. It indicates a lack of control on your part."

"Look, that's bullshit, Niles, and you know it. I inherited the bastard when I came in last year. Your predecessor hired him and I guess there was a different hiring profile that year. Besides that, our internal controls on contracts stink. Am I supposed to analyze every contract to be sure the rep is on the up and up? I'm trying to crack the whip here."

"You weren't cracking the whip a little too hard, were you? Or was the prospect of additional bonus so attractive that you and Gatto bent the rules?"

"I'm offended, Niles, that you would think such a thing of me! I simply wanted to motivate everyone to close out the year strong."

"Well, based on what seems to be transpiring, I'm not going to give Gatto credit for anything he closed in December, let alone double credit. It's tainted money. If he really did alter contracts, that's grounds for dismissal."

Presby wanted to ask if that meant he wouldn't get credit either, but quickly swallowed the question.

"I'm having breakouts this afternoon and I'll get to the bottom of it," Presby said, appearing to be in charge. "I already have a guy, Wayne Angelis, ready to go in New York if necessary. I'll figure out a way to shift things around."

"Do whatever it takes," O'Rourke said, jamming his finger into Presby's chest. "We won't be able to paper over this with Engler. He is taking it very personally, and frankly so do I. I'm holding you responsible for fixing this fiasco."

"Will do."

Presby slipped back into the BD presentation but couldn't focus on Lakota. He looked around for Gatto but couldn't find him. *Blowing off the meetings as usual,* he reminded himself. His eyes fell on Wayne, who had his hand raised to ask Lakota a question. He pondered how he could spin this in his breakout with Wayne. It would be a challenge to sugarcoat this mess for his brand new rep.

Lakota acknowledged Wayne's raised hand.

"Hi, Fred. I'm Wayne Angelis, covering New Jersey and Connecticut."

"Welcome, Wayne! Good to see a new face!"

"Thanks. I understand that you have responsibility for recruiting third parties to build connectors for us. Who on your staff handles that process? I have several good candidates in my district."

"Oh, boy, did he step into a pile of dog shit," Gustavson whispered loud enough for the back row to hear, setting off a new round of chuckles.

"I wonder what excuse he'll use this time," Sean Murphy said a little louder.

Wayne turned to see what the buzz behind him was all about. All he saw were shaking heads.

"Well, Wayne," Lakota started. "Right now, I'm dealing with that on a case-by-case basis. Since you're new here, perhaps we should take that offline."

"Oh, Fred?" Gustavson asked, standing and towering over the back row. "I think we'd all like to hear this. You didn't have any info for us at the last sales meeting."

"Bill! Good to see you! Yes, well, as you know we have requests for new connectors all the time so we are looking at farming out some of the work."

"You've been 'looking' at it since at least July," The Swede said. "What's the hold up? We are losing business because we don't connect to everything yet. Every deal now needs one more connector than we offer. Take that customer service application, Clarify. You promised someone to do that one in October. What's the status?"

"Engineering decided to do that one inhouse."

"How can they?" Young asked. "No one in Engineering has any expertise in Clarify. We have dozens of potential partners who know Clarify."

"Boy, did I hit a sore topic, huh Porter?" Wayne whispered.

"No kidding. Sounds like Murphy and Young were right about Lakota."

"I'm sure, but none of them have InUnison experience," Lakota replied. "That's a much harder proposition."

"That's bullshit and you know it, Lakota," Dave Young countered. "We can't expect our engineers to know all these systems we have to connect with. But we're losing a lot of opportunity because we don't have these connectors. We have to get going with third parties. Now!"

There were loud "harrumphs" and "fuckin' A, bro's" in agreement.

"I have plenty of beltway bandits who could write these things," Federal Government rep, Al Fisher, said. "It'd be no praaablem." Everything was "no praablem" to the hoarse-voiced Fisher.

"Gentlemen, gentlemen! Patience! You know these things take time," Lakota responded with a grin.

"You haven't signed one third-party yet. That's unacceptable," The Swede said, pointing at Lakota. More "fuckin' A's". "Who are you talking to right now?"

Lakota was still smiling. "Guys, I need to do a lot of prep work first; I don't have a contract ready, for instance. Heh, heh, you know how lawyers are."

"Can we at least see the draft?" Wayne asked.

"What good would that do?"

"We could start greasing the skids with our third party contacts. Also, I'm sure we could come up with sample agreements. We have a lot of experienced people in this room. I would think that we could fix whatever is wrong –"

That took the smile away from Lakota.

"There's nothing *wrong* with it! I have the responsibility to manage these things. I don't need twenty or thirty opinions on the matter."

"So, again, when can we get it?" The Swede asked.

"Soon."

"How soon?" Wayne pressed.

"Maybe by the end of the month."

"Maybe? Is that a commitment?"

"I'll give it my best effort, what did you say your name was?"

"Wayne Angelis."

"Ah, yes. Wayne. Well, you're new here. I'm sure it will take you a while to get acclimated. Now, moving on to our next topic, strategic partners…"

What the hell did that mean? Wayne wondered. He turned to Gustavson, who was still standing, shaking his head. The Swede could only respond to Wayne with a frown and a shrug.

"…and to cover that, I'd like to introduce our new Director of Strategic Partnerships, Wa Chu."

"Gesundheit!" Sean Murphy said, cracking up half of the room.

"*Another* director in Business Development?" Dave Young said, getting up and heading for the door. "This is fucked. I'm outta here."

***

Day three of the sales kickoff found several hobbling about the Sofitel or displaying black and blue fingers or patched wounds. Those badges of courage identified the wearer as a participant in Engler's basketball tournament. Back at headquarters, the CEO had his middle finger splinted to his fourth finger, having dislocated it on The Swede's face and Tony Tibbetts, the mainframe connector engineer, had his foot in a bucket of ice courtesy of being stepped on by Wayne Angelis, driving to the basket. The injuries were fewer than normal.

Once away from the reality distortion of the mass sales meeting, the past year was forgotten and the new year was laid out. At InUnison, the regional sales managers summoned each sales rep to his room for a "one-on-one". They would to discuss any new geographical alignments and of course, the new individual Numbers.

Reaper was the first to be ushered into Presby's room. He showed up fifteen minutes late and soaking wet.

"Gary! What the hell happened to you?"

"Well, Ken, I had to run out on an errand and, well, you know it's raining like hell. You know how Januarys are out here and it's been worse than usual this year…"

"Couldn't you have at least changed? I feel like I'm looking at a stray dog or something."

"Oooo, that's a good one, Ken!" Reaper said, laughing. Only it wasn't a joke to Presby who didn't appreciate falling behind schedule. He simply offered Reaper a chair and a towel.

"Listen, Ken, I have no business in my patch. You may think Atlanta is a major metro area with lots of growth companies, but believe me; I can't possibly make my Number this year without more territory. Every deal needs a lot of systems engineering resources and my SE partner is close to cracking. Marketing sucks and I don't get any professional services help. When I was at Sybase we…"

Presby had heard this before and would have none of it, particularly any more references to Sybase. While he welcomed a healthy back and forth with his reps, he was tough as nails when it came to whining reps who tried to put one over on him.

"Well, that's interesting, Gary. Let's see, you're partnered with Julia Berkowski, one of the best SEs in the company; BD has introduced you to lots of valuable partners and after all, you *almost* made your Number," he said, drawing out "almost" as if slowly pulling a sword out of Grim's midsection. "So, I'm confident that you can grow your business at least 100%. Have a nice day and let's go sell! Beat VibraWeb!"

After a few other Eastern Region reps had their opportunities to grovel, Tom Gatto's turn came up. Given his performance as Number One, he entered Presby's room with a swagger. He had been practicing his demands for days, including some trial arguments in between trysts with Suzy.

After the initial pleasantries with Presby, Gatto swung for the fences. He figured that he didn't have anything to lose; if Presby caved, he could still stiff VibraWeb.

"Okay, Ken, enough chit chat. This year, I'm not going to take any of your usual crap. I came through in December, I'm Number One. I want a district to manage with an admin and three reps reporting to me. Given my track record of two years blowing out my numbers and …."

Presby wasn't in the mood for this power play given his conversation with Engler and O'Rourke. He went on the offensive.

"Oooooo, mister BIG TIME!" Presby interrupted, laying on the sarcasm. "Well, I'd looove to hear how you're going to manage a cumulative number of $9 million, since that's what you'd get if I gave you a district to manage. And, of course, it's going to take you two quarters to staff your district, so what are you going to do to generate revenue in the meantime?"

"But, but, I've *earned* this!" Gatto said, shocked that his challenge was being met.

"Earned? How? Just by making your numbers? All the potential reps you'd inherit think that you're an arrogant bastard. How hard do you think they are going to work for you? What are you going to do to make sure that they fulfill their commitments? SEs hate your guts. Youngster would like to see you drawn and quartered in Times Square since we can't hold on to any technical talent in New York. And now I'm hearing that you like to play fast and loose with product commitments. You've managed to make your messes visible all the way up to Engler. What were you thinking promising people the mainframe connector?"

Shit, Gatto thought to himself. *How'd he know about Potential already? Must be that rep-basher head of Professional Services.*

"Look, that Melani guy is insane; he could be saying anything to save his ass."

"Gee, did I name anyone in particular? And there are five or six others out there. Any other time bombs you want to tell me about?"

He'd never seen Presby this confrontational, in fact, didn't think he had it in him.

Gatto counterattacked. "I don't suppose you remember our conversation in early December, 'close them however you can'? You remember; 'finesse' them, be 'creative'? 'You'll get double credit'; 'You'll catch The Swede!' Well, that's what I did. And where's the reward? I look like a total sap busting my ass for your benefit."

"I challenged you to help the company achieve its goals, that's all."

Bastard! He's going to hang me out to dry!

Presby seized back the initiative. "So let's take inventory here. To be Number One you lied to customers, possibly altered contracts without review by our outside counsel – oh, that's felony fraud – and put the reputation of the InUnison family at risk. And you think you should be a manager? Some example you set. You can't browbeat reps – or PS engineers, by the way – into submission. You need to show leadership and frankly, you've done everything but. We treat each other with respect and as peers. You don't even bother to participate in team conference calls. I happen to agree with your peers, you *are* an arrogant bastard and I'll be damned if I'm going to depend on you for a big chunk of my Number when you have the morals of a cobra. Your territory is enough of a liability, what with pissed off customers who think you lied to them about what our products could do for them. It's not the InUnison way. Oh, by the way; until these accounts get straightened out, you're not getting paid on them, and that includes what counts toward the rep rankings. So much for the Rolex, buddy."

He gripped his wrist where the Rolex was to go. "You *BASTARD*! This is how you treat your number one rep? You sucker me into doing your dirty work to make your bonus and then deny the whole thing? You and O'Rourke talk a good game, but in the end you're as manipulative and abusive as anyone. You make it sound like InUnison is the fucking Waltons. I think Corleone is more appropriate. 'Yo, Gatto, make 'em an offer they can't refuse'. You're all a bunch of gangsters…"

"That's enough! We've treated everyone equally and with respect. Your problem is you think the world should spin to your cycle, and it doesn't, pal, I'm sorry. We play by the rules, and that starts right at the top."

"Oh, you mean, Bill Engler, the Godfather? Ooooo, sorry, wouldn't want to upset the family atmosphere but I don't kiss rings, or any other body part. This sales team is pathetic, it's worse than mediocre and THAT starts at the top."

"I SAID THAT'S ENOUGH!!!" Presby yelled, standing now, and close to hyperventilating.

"AND I SAY…" Gatto said, raising the middle finger of his right hand, "FUUUCCCCKKK YOUUUU! This is the way you treat your best rep? Well, keep your fucking family, I'm OUTTA HERE!"

Gatto stormed out of the room, almost running into Wayne who was arriving for his one-on-one. He pointed his finger at Wayne and screamed into his face, "It didn't take you long to find that knife to stick in my back again, did it?"

"I don't know what –"

Gatto started to back Wayne up into a doorway. "Don't give me that shit! Watch *your* back, Angelis!" he said.

Presby appeared in the doorway. "Get the fuck out of here, Gatto!"

Gatto stormed off down the hall, shouting, "Watch out for those land mines I planted, Angelis!"

"Please come in Wayne," Presby said, composing himself. "I have some breaking news to share with you."

***

While the reps were having their breakouts, the systems engineers were back in Salon 2 getting an immersion of technical details from the Product Marketing and Engineering departments. This was to be a grueling session, as the SEs were in a very ugly – and still hung over – mood, frustrated with the lack of information coming out of Marketing about the forthcoming release. The SEs wanted to start demoing the pre-release of InUnison's new Data Transformation tool and Rule Agent but Engineering wouldn't allow it. Product Marketing, nominally in charge of such decisions, was in the middle getting pushed by the SEs and pulled by Engineering.

"Look, guys, I want to get this into your hands as soon as possible but I can't overcome the engineers right now." Phil Lansing, Director of Product Marketing was pleading for some understanding.

"Phil, the reps are already *selling* it for Christ's sake!" Sean Murphy said, ever the first to speak up. "Look, everyone knows that it is Samantha "Dr. No" Brinks who is the hang up. I think she needs to get laid or something."

"Are you volunteering?"

"Noooooo waaaayyy."

That loosened the tension a bit as everyone chuckled – including Julia – but the seriousness soon returned.

"Oh, I'm supposed to control Engineering," Lansing said. "But you guys can't control the information the rep gives out? We don't have a whole team of Gattos out there do we?"

Sean parried, "Nice try, Phil. We announced this at that San Jose show last month. If the field can't show it, why did you start creating demand for it? Doing that is like giving the reps carte blanche to start talking about it. And God only knows the extent of the fantasy they'll be spreading. Please tell me that it will at least be on time."

"Um, well…"

"I thought so." Murphy sat down in disgust.

Phil knew Sean was right. It frustrated Phil that while he was, in theory, responsible for the product development lifecycle, he was missing some key authority to discharge those responsibilities, authority zealously protected by VP of Engineering, Samantha Brinks. "Sean, we'll get it to you ASAP. I can't commit to a date yet."

While they could be tough to deal with, Phil had a lot of respect for the SE team and genuinely wanted to give them the weapons and ammunition to adequately sell the products.

Dissatisfied, Sean slouched in his chair and Phil moved on to other topics.

***

"Gatto imploded and won't be with us any more. Frankly, he never really fit in around here and …"

Wayne tried to understand the ramifications of this. It certainly explained the comments from Presby at the bar. He didn't know whether to laugh or cry. *Sure, not having to share the territory would be great,* he thought, *but dancing on the corpse of another rep? Even Gatto's?* Wayne knew it was bad enough to manage any account transition but an involuntary, cold turkey situation like this?

"Now, one thing you need to know is that there will be some issues to address with some of our New York accounts so you need to jump on in and get acquainted quickly."

"Not a problem, Ken, but what kind of 'issues'?"

"Oh, a few outstanding commitments Gatto made which need some attention. We'll get those to you right away. We've had a couple of product schedule slippages and we have to smooth some ruffled feathers."

Uh oh. The hair went up on the back of Wayne's neck. *There's a lot more to this than a few "issues".* He realized that this was worse than cold turkey; it was going to be Wayne flambé'. Before he could try to get Presby to elaborate about Gatto's "land mines" curse, he was getting the bum's rush out the door.

"…and I think your potential with InUnison is unlimited! Sooo, let's go sell! Beat VibraWeb!" Presby clasped his right hand in Wayne's, smiled broadly and ushered him out the door.

***

News of the blow up between Presby and Gatto swept through the InUnison sales meeting. There weren't too many reps upset that prima donna Gatto was out, especially in the Northeast region as they were relieved that they wouldn't be reporting to the Evil One, a rumor making the rounds.

"Can't believe he just up and quit. Not good for the reputation," sniffed The Swede. "No class." *I better find O'Rourke right away and remind him that I can handle some of those accounts from Chicago.*

Reaper, who fancied himself a friend, called Gatto on his cell phone.

"Gatto, what the hell are you doing? You already have somewhere to go?"

"It won't take long. I always have headhunters calling me."

"Well, old buddy, remember your friend, Gary. I'd love to work with you again." Reaper immediately set off to find Presby and offer to take over AT&T and any other accounts that might have an Atlanta presence. A P.O. box anywhere in the Southeast would do for justification.

***

Gatto closed his cell phone, shaking his head.

Yeah, he'd love to work with me. In his dreams, the mediocre bastard.

He was still fighting the urge to race back to Presby's room and wring his neck. He had never been so shabbily treated, even when he was let go by NeXT and he wanted a pound of flesh for his humiliation. He realized that his best chance would be with his former enemy, VibraWeb.

Gatto knew the way to the Santa Clara Marriott where VibraWeb was holding its kickoff meeting and jumped into his car immediately. Mid-day traffic on Route 101 was cooperative and he made it in 20 minutes, hydroplaning through the January rains. Concerned that he'd be recognized as an enemy agent, he planned to call Means from the parking garage.

"Means," George barked into the cell phone.

"Hi, this is Tom Gatto. Looks like I'll be able to start right away," he said, going on to explain what happened at the Sofitel.

"Outstanding! Can you get down here?"

"I'm pulling into the garage now."

"Okay, look for me outside the Monterey Boardroom. It's in the garden section of the hotel, out in the back."

"I'll be there in five."

He marched into the lobby of the Marriott, checking the direction signs for the Monterey Boardroom. The room was way in the back of the low rise rooms and the hallway was practically deserted except for a couple of people outside the conference room. He stepped up to the impatient looking man first.

"Hi, I'm looking for George Means?"

"You Gatto?"

"Yes."

"Great! Let's go out to the lobby and go over things."

Gatto ran to keep up with the high strung Means.

They made their way back to the lobby, stopped for coffee and settled into armchairs off the lobby.

In a moment, Simon Hager came storming through the lobby and detoured when he saw Means.

"What the fuck are you doing out here? Marketing is presenting and as usual has things all fucked up. Get your ass back in the fucking meeting."

Means could have strangled Hager for putting on a tirade in front of Gatto, but had to take it.

"Simon, I'd like you to meet Tom Gatto, our new sales manager for New York. We stole him from InUnison!"

"InUnison, huh. What makes you so fucking special?"

Gatto didn't flinch. "Listen, I was kicking your company's ass all over Manhattan. *That's* kind of special."

Hager liked that. "Excellent! Someone who won't take any fucking shit. Anyway, like I said … HAGER!" He answered his cell phone in mid-sentence. "No fucking way – you better get into the Marketing presentation – I said NO FUCKING WAY, what isn't clear about that? Five hundred fucking thousand or zero." A mother with her five-year-old in tow fled the lobby, horrified.

Means pulled Gatto by the arm and led him back to the Monterey Boardroom. Once Hager got on the phone, there was no way to have a meaningful conversation.

Inside the conference room, Gatto found it difficult to find an open seat. The room was cramped and the air was already getting pretty ripe even though the outside doors were open. He slipped into the back of the room and stood while the VP of Marketing continued his presentation.

"If we are to achieve our goal of being thought-leader, revenue-leader and technology-leader in our target product category, we have to have quality referenceable, deployed customers who are willing to participate in advertising and aggressive outbound communication initiatives …"

Gatto didn't quite grasp what he was talking about but hoped that maybe it was because he missed the first several PowerPoint slides. A young attendee got up from the back row of seats and stood next to Gatto.

Whispering to Gatto he said, "Make any sense to you?"

"Typical marketing bullshit."

"Eric Miller, Bay Area rep. Are you just starting with us?"

"Looks like it. New York."

"Oh, right, Thomas finally snapped. It was only a matter of time. He took this stuff way too seriously. Anyway, as usual the Bomber has latched onto the latest marketing craze without doing his homework. He's about as original as concrete sidewalks."

"The Bomber?"

"Yeah, that's Eugene Kaczynski. Unfortunate coincidence in names which we, of course, have no shame in taking advantage of. Gene is so anal he's an easy mark."

"Well, he's bombing with me so far." Gatto recalled Steve Jobs saying once that there weren't any good marketing people left in Silicon Valley because all the good ones were now CEOs starting their own companies. Over the years, Gatto decided he must be right.

Eric continued his commentary. "You'll love our partners people. Really know how to sign up those consulting firms. In the four companies I've been with, this is the first time I've actually seen production, I mean real business, from a partners group. They rock."

"I know what you mean. I'm not used to that."

"Where you from, Tom?"

"Um, could we step outside and chat? Sounds like you could give me a lot of insight into this organization." They stepped out into the hall.

"I left InUnison today."

"NO WAY!"

Tom laughed and tried to set his new best friend at ease.

"No, I'm no spy. They screwed me, I left. Simple."

"Weren't you making your Numbers?"

"Number one in the company."

"Okay, you were throwing down with the VP's admin then?"

"None of your business on that," Gatto said with a wink. "So, what inside dirt can you give me?"

"The management is a bunch of assholes but they have their eye on the revenue and IPO balls. Have you met Hager yet?"

"Yes, out in the lobby. Hyper dude."

"To put it mildly. I don't think the guy ever sleeps. He'll call you any time of day or night to go over your deals. He's also the most abusive manager I've ever seen."

"What about George Means?"

"I don't know Means all that well, but I haven't heard anything from the guys in the East about any interference. The usual bitching about pipeline reviews. It's Hager you have to watch out for. He'll sort of parachute into your patch and want to go on calls."

Gatto shook his head. "I usually avoid involving too many people – particularly sales management – in my deals. How do you manage that?"

"You can't. I try to stay under Hager's radar and make my Number. Be careful who you let Hager talk to. Most prospects end up hating his guts. But like I said, these guys are driven, especially Hager, Tsai, and Singh. Singh definitely has a chip on his shoulder. He really has a thing about becoming a legend in the Valley, right up there with Jobs, Ellison, and Clark. I tell you, it *is* infectious."

"Can you put Tsai and Singh in front of customers?"

"If carefully scripted. They *can* be trained. Chin Tsai can be awesome with senior technical people. He can do the vision thing like nobody's business and he's great at handling technical objections. Unfortunately, he's also an arrogant SOB who will rip a stupid customer apart if he senses weakness or if some prospect calls his baby ugly. We have to be very careful to control his visits. That's one of the reasons we do a lot with video. When we bring prospects in, we keep it pretty controlled. Kaczynski owns all that stuff. "

Gatto pondered all this. He had dealt with assholes before and succeeded. If what Miller was telling him was true, this would be the ride he was looking for. He was starting to feel comfortable with the change.

"Oh, hey, I have a tip for you. My cousin is CIO at Azalea Financial. He's fighting a battle right now with some new guy over integration issues. He could really use our software. I was home for Christmas and talked to him about it. I had passed it on to Thomas but I don't think that he followed up. I'll introduce you to him, Stewart Miller. He's a tough bastard and he's got clout."

"That's excellent! Thanks! Azalea is a pretty big fish."

***

The final night of the InUnison Kickoff Sales Meeting included the annual awards banquet. After another two hours of open bar, the well-lubricated group sat down to dried out lemon herb chicken, soggy green beans and tossed salad. Gary Reaper reminded everyone – as he did every year – that Sybase's banquet included filet mignon. As usual, no one believed him.

While there were some seriously coveted awards like Gustavson's Rep of the Year – courtesy of Gatto's departure – and Wiley Nelson's SE of the Year, it was the culture of the company to be sure "everybody got a lollipop", some hunk of Lucite or slate with the company logo embedded and some cute motivational slogan like "The Best of the Best". There would be an endless series of made up – supposedly humorous – awards such as "Unsung Hero", usually given to the SE unfortunate enough to be paired with the least productive rep. That award went to Julia Berkowski who didn't react as if it was much of an honor.

Finally, at the end of the awards, came the roll call of 100% Club; those reps, SEs and other key "friends of sales" from other departments in the company would be called to the stage. Once all the members of "the Club" were present, the worst kept secret of the meeting would be announced: the site of the Club Trip. Everyone knew it to be St. Thomas in the Virgin Islands. Suzy Kestral was known to have made several trips to scout the hotels and facilities, breaking the hearts of several reps who had volunteered to chaperone her.

Niles O'Rourke stepped to the front microphone, flanked by the club winners. He gave the signal for the video to start as he unfolded a couple of sheets of paper.

"Oh please, not a corny poem," Gustavson whispered to Nelson. He had heard from his contacts at O'Rourke's previous company that he aspired to be a poet laureate. The result was usually strained abdominal muscles, as no one wanted to be the one to guffaw in the middle of a serious literary discourse.

> "There once was a sales rep short of his Number
>
> who awoke late in the quarter from his slumber…"

***

Gatto was able to get a room at the Marriott for the final night of the meeting and was the toast of that night's libations in Champion's Sports Bar. He was quite a celebrity with his new sales colleagues for having jumped to VibraWeb directly from a key competitor. He was a bit late for the closing session – due to the late night and lingering tequila buzz – and slipped into the back of the Monterrey Boardroom where Hager was spewing fire and brimstone.

"Now, listen. I need you to get out there, FIND THE MONEY, and get it off the fucking table and move on to the next table. We need MARKET SHARE, MARKET SHARE, … FUCKING MARKET SHARE! And of course when you do that YOU will make a lot of fucking money. Where's Susan

Sheffield?" Hager asked, waving his hand across the audience looking for his top rep for the year. She had brought in several big accounts and ended up achieving 300% of her Number.

"There she is! Stand up! Don't be shy! Folks, this is our number one rep." He waited for the applause and cheers to die down. "How much did you make last year?"

Sheffield stood up, giggled nervously and tucked her bleached blonde hair behind her right ear. Like the majority of the crowd, she was pretty hung over and wasn't sure she was steady enough to stand.

"Uh, quite a bit, Simon," she said, not taking him seriously.

"Come on, don't be humble. How much? 500, 600K?"

"Really, Simon, I don't think…."

"HOW FUCKING MUCH?"

"Seven hundred fifty-five thousand" she murmured into her shoes.

"Didn't quite catch that, Susan!"

Totally pissed now, she yelled "SEVEN HUNDRED FIFTY-FIVE, DAMN IT!"

"See, that's what YOU ALL should be shooting for this year," Hager said.

Susan sat back down, feeling totally humiliated. Her head was really pounding now under the mix of rage, embarrassment and leftover tequila. Only Simon Hager could take an achievement that she was very proud of and make it feel dirty.

The rest of the team gave her a standing ovation, not so much in tribute for the accomplishment but more in sympathy. *There but for the grace of God…*

What wimps, Gatto thought. He would have been proud to announce his earnings in a loud clear voice. Reps seldom talked openly about their actual compensation but, fact was, every rep knew exactly what all the other reps were making simply based on their quota achievements and knowing the accelerators. Why not shout your achievements to the world? That was what it was all about.

As he recognized Sheffield's title along with the rest of the VibraWeb sales team he smirked to himself.

I intend to be the one standing next year, using Angelis' corpse as a riser.

Chapter 5 Landmines

Wayne was anxious to get home from the kickoff, so he took the United red eye to Newark and landed at 6:15 AM. United Airlines had a wide body plane on the flight which at least formed the illusion that the coach seats weren't so cramped. But having been a very frequent flyer, Wayne was able to upgrade to First Class, greatly improving the odds of rest on the flight. He was counting on it as he had to hit the phones early and often upon arrival home.

Wayne retrieved his bag from baggage claim and waited for the long term parking shuttle. It was an unusually warm January morning, well above freezing, as he walked to his car in the parking lot. The aroma from the Budweiser plant seemed more pronounced this morning, inducing a longing for a tall coldy.

He soon left the parking lot and headed north on the New Jersey Turnpike. He was glad to be across the George Washington Bridge by 7:05, before it really backed up, and zipped up the Major Deegan Expressway. He was home by 7:45, just in time to see his third grader, Eileen, off to her elementary school bus.

"Hi, Daddy!" she said, as she flew by, running to her bus stop a block away. His two older boys were long gone to high school. Helen was tying her hair into a pony tail in preparation for her aerobics class.

"Oh, hi! Didn't think you were coming home so early. I'm off to the club and then to the Junior League lunch. See ya this afternoon." She gave Wayne a quick kiss and jumped into her new BMW 740i sedan.

Gee, sorry you all missed me. As much as he had traveled in the past, homecomings like this still rankled Wayne. It seemed like they enjoyed not having him home. Being away so much in his last job was one of the reasons he took the InUnison position. He hoped that it would narrow his territory to driving distances or, even better, trains to Manhattan.

At least I'll have the house to myself. He was now working out of a home office which was a new experience. While the distractions were few at home, he was already missing the camaraderie of his old offices in Manhattan or New Jersey – on those rare days when he wasn't traveling – and his access to administrative help. He kept telling himself that access to the refrigerator and his back deck balanced out all that. His wife might not appreciate his newfound availability, but seeing the family more was a plus for him.

He made some coffee and started to hit the phones. First on his "issues list" was one George Melani at Potential Investing. Wayne had never heard of the firm so he did some research before calling him. Their website was not particularly informative but revealed that they were working to capture market share in online trading, particularly corporate treasury department futures trades and foreign exchange business.

Wayne listened as Melani's phone rolled to voice mail. Rather than leave a message, he hit zero to see if Melani had an administrative assistant who handled his schedule. Sure enough an efficient sounding voice came on the line.

"George Melani's line, Angela speaking, how can I help you?"

"This is Wayne Angelis of InUnison Software. Is Mr. Melani in today?"

"Yes, but he's in a staff meeting right now. Would you like voice mail?"

"Do you handle his schedule by chance? I'd like to set up a meeting as soon as possible. I'm the new sales rep on his account and I understand that we have some repair work to do."

"Yes, I handle his schedule. Who are you with again?"

"InUnison Software."

"Oh, yes, he *very* much wants to meet with *you.*" Her voice had suddenly changed to quite a sarcastic tone. "He'd *love* to meet with you on Monday at 9:30. Do you know our location?"

"Yes, right off of Times Square, right? Big black building?"

"That's right. Please be prompt."

"Sure thing, Angela. Any chance George could call me back today to give me a little background?"

"No way," she said, cracking her gum. "He's got budget meetings all day."

"Ah, well I hope he's including us in the budget requests!" he said, trying to loosen her up a bit.

"I wouldn't count on it."

"Well, would you be able to give me some background on your experience with our software?"

"Other than the fact that George gets real red in the face when your consultant is here, I really don't know. Look, I really have to get back to the phones here."

"Right, well thanks for your time and for setting up the meeting."

"Sure," she said with a chuckle that suggested she hadn't done him a favor.

Who's next? Wayne looked at his list. Merrill Lynch, Perils.com, Sampson Logistics, Merit Solutions, Filberts.com, and PensAndClips.com. *Including Potential, that makes seven. And these dot-coms, who the hell knows anything about them?* he thought. He noted that all of these accounts bought Developer Starter packages and should be targets for deployment in the first quarter. Deployments were the gravy deals, usually good for lots of server licenses.

Wayne continued to ponder the list. It irked him that the only recognizable name was Merrill Lynch. He tried to call the contact there, Stanley Fabozzi, but had to leave a voice message.

He picked up the phone and started to dial Perils.com, but stopped and hung up. He realized he ought to check out their website. There wasn't much there and what was seemed to be "under construction". Under "Company Info" it listed someone named Gilbert Jankowitz as Founder, CEO and CTO. No one else listed. Under "Products" there was a rather cryptic reference to "safety services via the Internet". No further elaboration. "Doesn't sound like a going concern to me", Wayne scoffed. He decided to put them aside for the moment.

He went to the websites of the other dot-coms, Filberts and PensAndClips. He expected that PensAndClips was some sort of office supply site and sure enough his browser was filled with graphics of pens and colorful paper clips. They focused on the Manhattan market and promised one-hour delivery anywhere on the island. They emphasized their ability to quickly supply hard-to-find items. *At least they have a full allotment of management,* he noted. He dialed the number for Craig Mansfield, noted as "Founder; Director, IT" on his file and on the website.

"This is Craig, can I help you?"

"Good morning, Craig, my name is Wayne Angelis with InUnison Software…"

"Where's that fucking asshole Gatto?" Mansfield interrupted.

"He's left the company and I've taken over his territory, so I'm calling to introduce myself."

"Good. I hope you aren't the lying SOB he is. When can I get the mainframe connector?"

Mainframe connector? Wayne scrambled to recall the product information from the sales meeting. Luckily he had his notebook from the meeting handy.

"Oh, and is that moron Lakota ever, *ever* going to return my calls?"

Okay, I'm learning the language here; Gatto means asshole, Lakota means moron. "I apologize. Since I'm new here I'm not aware of what BD has to do with you. Can you fill me in?" Wayne asked, still fumbling to find the connector product sheet.

"Sure. I have to put my software on site at some of our large customers. These customers have purchasing systems already in place and want to be able to automatically link to us without some human using our website. These are IBM mainframe systems and I need to connect to them. I'm essentially embedding your technology into mine, so this is sort of a Value-added Reseller, ya know, VAR, deal and I got vectored to Lakota for that agreement. After a fancy lunch here in New York, though, I haven't been able to talk to him. And the discussion during lunch was pretty much off topic except for Lakota puffing himself up and being condescending with us. I mean, I know we're starting out fresh but we've got some great customers lined up, people like Manley, Morgan Stanley, AT&T."

Now, that's what I call LEVERAGE! I could walk behind these guys into some big accounts, Wayne thought. He finally had the connector information in front of him now.

"Okay, according to my data, the connector is due for release in April."

"APRIL, MY ASS! GATTO PROMISED IT IN DECEMBER! I HAVE CUSTOMERS WHO WANT TO GO ONLINE IN FEBRUARY!" Wayne held the phone away from his ear.

"Craig, I got back from our kickoff meeting with this schedule. I don't know where the disconnect came in."

"I know EXACTLY where. I took Gatto at his word. He had to close end-of-year business and I fell for it. He jammed a Developer Pack on me with the promise of the mainframe connector and dumped me on Lakota. So, are you going to stand behind the commitment or resort to the 'I'm the new guy and don't know anything' bullshit?"

"Listen, I will always be straight with you. Let me check out the situation and get back to you on Monday."

"Fine, but if you can't fix this, we are going to pull the plug and find something else. This has to go live next month."

"I promise I'll call on Monday." Mansfield grunted a "yeah, right" and hung up. Wayne's idea of leveraging the relationship was vaporizing as quickly as it had appeared.

Next, Wayne investigated Sampson Logistics, a large company, with over $2 billion in revenue the previous year in the business of shipping and inventory management for the apparel industry. They had recently changed their name from Sampson Shipping to the sexier moniker of Sampson Logistics.

Wayne started to speculate. Logistics meant tight integration of systems, and that meant mainframes. It didn't take too much thinking to sense a pattern here. He dithered about whether to call Sampson or try to figure out the story of the mainframe connector. His whole quarter could blow up if all these accounts went south.

Wayne tried to call a few of the other accounts, but could not get anyone else. He thought of Rob Bailey at Manley Brothers. He had sold quite a bit of product in the past to Rob. When Wayne told him of his move to InUnison,

Bailey suggested that Wayne call him when he got settled. He told Wayne he was following InUnison for the venture capital people at Manley.

He called Bailey and left a voice mail message.

"Hi, Rob, this is Wayne Angelis. You may recall that you suggested that we get together after I started at InUnison. I'm off and running and would love the opportunity to show you what we're all about. I've got a great systems engineer to work with and we're ready to suit up. I'm wide open next week so let me know your availability. My new office number is 914-555-8422 and you have my mobile. Looking forward to it. Later."

Wayne continued to work down his contact list. After about an hour of fruitless calls, his message tone beeped as he picked up to dial again. It was Rob Bailey.

"Hi, Wayne! Damn glad to hear from you. Yes, we definitely want to get together. There's a new initiative here which we hope will help do away with all this homegrown middleware crap. I've penciled you in for Wednesday at 1:30 across the river. I've got some new responsibilities and I'm going to be in meetings the rest of the day so confirm with my admin. Looking forward to it!"

Happy to finally make some progress, he immediately reconfirmed the meeting. "Across the river" meant the Manley offices in Jersey City where most of the IT staff worked. He also called Porter's number to be sure he had these meetings scheduled. He got Porter's voice mail. *Hmm, must be taking the daylight flight. I'll have to introduce him to the glories of the red eye.* He left a message about the schedule and asked him to confirm as soon as he landed.

Just as he took his hand off of the phone, it rang.

"Wayne Angelis, may I help you?"

"Hi there Wayne! This is Fred Lakota, VP of Business Development?"

Oh, boy. Be patient. Give him a chance, Wayne thought. "Yes, hello."

"Very sorry I didn't get the chance to meet you at the kickoff. So many new faces!" There was a mysterious pause and Wayne wasn't sure what Lakota was waiting for.

"Well, we did sort of meet. I asked you about the third party connector program at the kickoff. So, Fred, what can I do for you?"

"Well, I'm coming into New York on Thurs and Fri, the 22nd and 23rd. Would love to go on calls with you. What can you set up for me?"

Typical BD. Blow into my patch expecting to be chauffeured all over town.

"Well, Fred, seeing as how this is my first real day on the job, I'm only now getting my schedule together for next week, let alone the end of the month."

"Now, Wayne, you don't want to miss the golden opportunity for me to help close some business! If I do say myself, I've proven to be a real business magnet."

"There happens to be one account where I need your 'magnetism' to work its magic. I just got off the phone with Craig Mansfield at PensAndClips.com. He says that he's been waiting to hear from you."

"Mansfield? PensAndClips? Oh, yes, I had lunch with them right before the holidays. Went to Union Square Café; a great lunch as I recall. Don't recall that it was much of an opportunity…"

"On the contrary, Fred, they want to embed our software into theirs which would be placed onsite at their large customers. He listed some very impressive customers, like AT&T."

"Wayne," he paused as if trying to choose words, "we have to look at the big picture. In BD, I have to triage all the wonderful opportunities our software presents for partners. I can't chase them all. This PensAndClips, well, how shall I say this, they are pretty small potatoes."

Wayne waited, expecting Fred to enlighten him with examples of worthy partners. None came.

So he asked, "Maybe you could describe who you *are* targeting?"

"We are working very hard to secure prime visibility with Flanderson Consulting and the Big Six firms, firms with large integration practices. The embedded opportunities like PensAndClips pale in comparison to the largest consulting company in the world."

"So, do we have any agreements with these integrators yet?" Wayne knew the answer was negative. This was one of the major complaints about Business Development at the kickoff.

"We are very close, Wayne. I can't get into specifics; things are at a delicate stage. In fact, one reason I'm coming to New York is to close with the Flanderson Consulting Financial Services Group in Manhattan. But keep that to yourself."

"Fred, forgive me being blunt, but I need partners with leverage, like this PensAndClips. Once they place their stuff into, say, a Morgan Stanley, I can ride right in there and upgrade them to a full license with practically no sales cycle. I can't do that if I'm dependent on some integrator who's using InUnison on some twelve-month project. I have a Number to meet *this* quarter. Can't you send them a VAR agreement to sign?"

"Wayne, with your experience, I'm surprised at how simplistically you view this."

"We *do* have a VAR agreement, right?"

"Ah, well, it's in Legal right now…"

Great. "How long before we can get it into the field?" Wayne wasn't hopeful given Lakota's tap dance at the kick off.

"Wayne, I don't have control over the process. Heh, heh, you know lawyers!"

"How long?"

Lakota lowered his voice to a whisper. "Most likely next quarter."

"YOU CAN'T BE SERIOUS!" Wayne yelled, now on his feet, pacing around his desk. "I was told that paperwork was done *last* quarter!"

"I don't know who would've told you that…"

"Presby."

"Well, now, he's a sales guy isn't he? Always promising…"

"Very funny, Fred. I suppose you think it's funny also that my Number is already in jeopardy because Gatto left me with several big messes to clean up, including PensAndClips."

"Well, you can't blame me for that…"

"But you could *help* me by closing the partner agreement with them. They are ready to roll."

Lakota sighed impatiently. "Sure, Wayne, I'll see what I can do. At the end of the day, Wayne, I put Sales first."

"So, you're going to call Mansfield ASAP, right?"

"Absolutely! I'll call first thing Monday morning!"

"Why not call today?"

"I have to run out to get my Benz serviced."

"You have a cell phone, right? Can't you at least *try* to get a hold of him while you're waiting for your car?"

Lakota responded with a very annoyed sigh. "Sure, Wayne, sure. I'll let you know if I get him."

"You have my cell number, right? Call me. Don't worry about the time."

Wayne wasn't going to hold his breath.

***

Porter couldn't wait to get his stiff back out of seat 18B on the Continental flight from SFO to Newark. Travel was a new experience for Porter and he didn't have any miles accumulated for first class upgrades earned by experienced travelers such as Angelis or Murphy. Sean would joke that he was known by the entire American Airlines First Class flight attendant staff. "Welcome back, Mr. Murphy, the usual gin and tonic and slippers? I'll be happy to massage your tired feet …"

The middle seat on the Boeing 757 was not conducive to anything but pain and no one was around in coach to massage Porter's ego let alone some body part. He also felt like he was still processing the "Full Bone Cut" from Gulliver's the night before. The flight might have been a bit more palatable if he hadn't been seated next to a huge woman – she was 280 pounds if she weighed an ounce – who reeked of cigarette smoke, and downed two Bloody Marys every time the drink cart came by.

The five hour flight at least gave Porter some time to work on the presentation slides Marketing had distributed at the meeting. Wayne had already scheduled meetings with some prospects so he needed to be ready.

The plane landed a bit early at 4:15 PM but burned that advantage away with an excruciatingly long taxi to the gate. He knew the traffic would be horrid. That was something he would have to get used to. He had a pretty strict routine during his bank days: up by 6:00, catch the 6:45 PATH into Manhattan, read the *Wall Street Journal* on the way in, coffee and bagel from the street vendor at 7:30, at his desk in Liberty Plaza by 7:45. It was like clockwork for five years. Now, all of a sudden, every day was going to be different, scripted mostly by Wayne

Angelis.

Sure enough, he crawled west on I-78 and didn't get home until after six. Brenda was playing on the floor with Stephanie. She was their first child and it killed Porter to be away from her for nearly a week.

"Hi, handsome! Tough flight?" She tried to hug him but it was a bit awkward to do with 15 pounds of baby in her arms. Stephanie burped and spat milk on Porter's jacket. "See? She missed you too!"

"The flight sucked. I was trying to work and this fat pig next to me–"

"Now, don't start with the names," she teased as she mopped the mess off of his shoulder. "I'll make you a drink and you can tell me all about the week. You weren't too talkative on the phone from California."

"Sean was always in the room. No privacy. And I kept forgetting about the time difference."

"Nice excuse. By the way, I heard your office phone ringing this morning. Did you remember to check messages?"

"No, I was concentrating on not getting killed on I-78. It was probably Angelis. He was going to be scheduling some things."

While Brenda fixed that drink, he walked to the spare bedroom, now his office, and dialed the message system. Two messages from Wayne and one from the bank. Wayne had scheduled meetings on Monday in the city at 9:30 and the Manley presentation for Wednesday. He was more nervous about the Manley one as he hadn't done the presentation yet. The Monday meeting at Potential seemed to be only a get-acquainted meeting. He fished around for Wayne's number and called to let him know that he got the message.

"Hi, Wayne. Any difficulty getting home?"

"No, I don't usually get held up when I come in on the redeye. Bet you hit the weekend traffic, didn't you?"

"Big time. It's going to take a while to get used to driving around here. I've lived here for ten years but really never had to drive during rush hour. So, I got your message about the meetings. I'd really like the chance to run through the presentation with you before Wednesday."

"We'll have time after the Monday meeting. We'll find a spot in one of the hotel lobbies around Times Square and go over it. But don't sweat it. Manley will be a friendly meeting. It's the Potential meeting I'm concerned about. I'm kind of going in blind since Melani wasn't available and his admin was cryptic about what we might be facing there."

"Oh, is this on your 'issues' list?"

"Right at the top. Can you call out to HQ and find out who the consultant was on this project? Call him and debrief. If he's still in the area, see if he can meet us for breakfast on Monday, say 7:30 at the Marriott Marquis."

"I'll track him down."

"Leave me a message over the weekend. Later." He abruptly hung up.

Porter immediately got on the phone to HQ. The drink would have to wait.

***

Monday came too quickly. Porter worked intensely on the presentation and demo on Sunday and had it internalized. He knew, though, that was only half the battle. At the sales meeting, the other SEs all had horror stories about dealing with vocal people at presentations, usually some know-it-all who tried to take over the meeting. Sean had tried to allay his fears by saying that Porter simply had to get some of these events under his belt. Porter wasn't so sure.

Porter bought a *Wall Street Journal* at the Marriott gift shop and waited on one of the benches facing the registration desk. Unfortunately, he hadn't talked to the Professional Services Engineer, Sanjay Chandra, directly. He traded voicemails with him to set up the breakfast meeting and got a little information about the mainframe connector being the missing piece at Potential Investing. He was able to talk with Phil Lansing in Marketing about the availability of the connector. Phil was very cooperative but indicated that the VP of Engineering, Samantha Brinks, held the leash on product releases.

Wayne appeared at 7:20, followed almost immediately by a tense Sanjay.

"Hi, are you Porter Mitchell?" he asked Wayne.

"No, I'm Wayne Angelis. This is Porter."

"What role do you play?" Sanjay eyed Wayne suspiciously.

"I'm the new sales rep for New York and Northern New Jersey."

"Hmmph. Pleased to meet you both." Sanjay continued to eye them. Wayne broke the nerve-wracking silence.

"Let's get some breakfast and chat about Potential Investing."

They walked over to the restaurant entrance, Wayne showing three fingers to the hostess. It was a hectic scene as many business people milled around juggling plates from the breakfast buffet. The three were led to a corner table by the kitchen door.

Wayne tried to lighten the mood. "Guess they don't want us riffraff up front."

"Story of my life," chimed in Porter. Sanjay, saying nothing, sat down and started to look at the menu.

"I suggest we order off the menu so we have a bit more time to talk," Wayne suggested.

"Fine by me," Porter agreed.

Sanjay remained silent, examining the menu. Finally, he set the menu down and looked at both Wayne and Porter.

"So, what do you want to know?" Sanjay asked with evident anxiety.

"I guess start at the top. When did you get involved at Potential and what is the situation?" Wayne replied, putting on his most sincere face.

"I came in December. I was supposed to help with the architectural design and project plan. Another consultant, Bill Dailey, was assigned to help mentor and train the Potential team. Our expectations were that this was a pretty straightforward, three-point integration – database, custom client-server apps and web server. We didn't know until we showed up that the mainframe was the key element in the project."

He paused so that they could order and then continued.

"As you know, our mainframe connector isn't ready and won't be until March at the earliest. Potential is on a very aggressive schedule so any slip in product would be fatal to the project."

Porter, looking quizzical, asked, "How was that requirement missed? I mean, they would have had to specifically order the product, right?" Wayne knew the answer, of course, but Sanjay replied first.

"You're new to sales, aren't you? Tom Gatto simply lied to them about availability but had it as a line item on the invoice without the performance clause in the contract. A masterful stroke of fraud, if you ask me. Now before we go any further," he leaned into Wayne. "I want you to understand that I've had it with you guys forcing us in PS into this kind of bullshit situation. I have a reputation at stake. I don't give a flying fuck about your Number or commission or any of that crap…"

Porter pushed slightly away from the table, as Sanjay's rage seemed to be only starting.

Sanjay turned to Porter. "You call me out of the blue with some cheerful bullshit about wanting to 'fix' the account. Well, I can't fix the damn account because the product doesn't exist. That animal Melani almost strangled me last week when he found out. Are you, Mr. wet-behind-the-ears SE, going to wave your wand and instantly come up with a solution?"

"Who had the scrambled?" The waiter interrupted Sanjay's rant with their breakfasts. Wayne took advantage of the interruption.

"Sanjay, I know you don't know me yet, but I care about my reputation as well. I didn't know the depth of the issues here. I guarantee that I will not knowingly put you guys in a situation like this."

Sanjay eyed him with skepticism. "Yeah, right."

"I talked to Phil in Product Marketing on Friday," Porter offered, hoping to lighten Sanjay's mood. "He can get me an early version of the connector next week if Samantha Brinks approves its release."

"I have no idea of the quality of the connector. I don't know which is worse; no product or buggy product," Sanjay said. "And I'll bet Brinks will say 'no'. It's her favorite word."

"It may be the only shot we have to regain some credibility here," Wayne countered.

Sanjay turned his head to look out into the lounge, pondering that fact. He couldn't deny Wayne's point. He frowned and turned to Wayne.

"You're right. Dailey is still working with the team over there and he's mainframe savvy. Phil's a stand up guy, I'm sure he wouldn't have told you he'd make it available if he didn't believe it."

"I may be wet behind the ears as far as sales, Sanjay, but I've spent several years on mainframes. I'll do what I can as well."

"Sorry about that comment, Porter. I've heard about you and your experience with our software. Dailey can learn something from you."

No one spoke for several minutes as they took time out to eat. Finally, Porter posed a question.

"Is there anyone on the Potential team we can trust to work with us?" Porter asked.

"Oh, sure. Frank McDermott. Great guy. He hates Melani, but works really hard. Even has a sense of humor, though it tends toward gallows humor."

Sanjay relaxed in his seat, and even smiled a bit.

"So, we have our meeting with Melani in an hour. What else can you tell us about him?" Wayne asked.

"Does your 'we' include me? After last week, I don't want anything to do with Mr. George Melani," Sanjay said, holding up his hands as if to ward off evil.

Wayne thought quickly and decided he better let Sanjay off the hook.

"No, Sanjay, this is my and Porter's responsibility now. But come now, he can't be that much of a beast."

"Listen, his team is scared to death of him. He jacked a guy up against the wall just for being late a couple of times, even though he'd been putting in 36 hour days. He screamed at him about how he was going to cut off his balls."

"Sounds like an HR issue."

"He's protected by his management since, at least until now, he's delivered. He *does* know technology. It's his, uh, interpersonal skills that need some adjustment."

"How did he get along with Gatto?"

"He didn't need to. Gatto gave him the software to try out, some SE time, and negotiated with Melani's purchasing people. George validates the technology and tells his management he needs it. They go buy it."

"So that gave Gatto the opportunity to play the miscommunication game."

"Right. I don't know for sure, but Melani probably told purchasing what he needed. Since they used Gatto's paper, they weren't in control."

"You seem to know the game pretty well, Sanjay."

"I've been cleaning up sales messes for years."

"Sanjay, I promise, I won't create any more messes for you." Wayne stood and extended his hand to Sanjay. "I really appreciate you joining us this morning. I hope we can do it again under better circumstances."

"I'm sure." Sanjay said, giving Wayne a sincere handshake this time. "And sorry for the rant, but it was very ugly dealing with Gatto's accounts. Good luck with George." Sanjay picked up his backpack and left.

Wayne and Porter watched as Sanjay walked to the round elevator bank. They didn't admit it to each other, but both were left wondering what they had gotten themselves into. They had about half an hour to compose themselves.

***

The thirty minutes might as well have been thirty seconds. Wayne reviewed his notes again, as Porter paced the Marriot lounge. They buttoned up for the walk up Broadway to Potential's building – the low thirties temperature was a first for what had been a warm January – and an uncertain fate.

George Melani stormed into the stark conference room, Sanjay's torture chamber. He had kept Wayne and Porter waiting for twenty minutes.

"Big surprise that motherfucker Gatto flew away after shitting all over my project. I suppose you're going to be different?"

Melani was lucky to still have his job but was on probation until the mess was cleaned up. Summoning his most contrite posture, Wayne tried to gain a modicum of confidence with Melani.

"George, I understand your disappointment –"

"UNDERSTAND? How can you fucking UNDERSTAND? You bloodsuckers almost got me fired! You are L-I-A-R-S!" Melani wrote the letters in huge strokes on the whiteboard.

"We can't automate the updates to the mainframe in R-E-A-L-T-I-M-E," biting off each letter as he wrote. "REEEEAAALLL TIME, my friend, means IMMEDIATELY, not when some human has time to key the crap into a stupid terminal."

"Yes, I understand –" Wayne said, inciting another Melani torrent. Porter sat still, dumfounded at Melani's display of rage.

"You don't understand shit," Melani continued. "My CEO ripped me a new asshole about how amateur our system looks to partners. Do you understand the idea of T-R-U-S-T?" There was another violent mashing of marker on board. "Our customers' hedge business is predicated on TRUST," he ranted, pounding on the board for further emphasis.

Wayne was sure he wasn't going to leave the room alive. Miraculously, after a final marathon rant, George took a seat and was silent, apparently spent from his tirade.

Wayne recomposed himself.

"George, here's what I'm prepared to offer. My SE, Porter Mitchell is a veteran user of our products. I'd like to offer him to you on our dime to help sort this stuff out and work with engineering on accelerating the promised functionality. I'd also like to put you in touch with some of our other customers so that you will know that your relationship with the previous rep was not the norm within InUnison."

"I've talked a bit with Sanjay from our Professional Services group," Porter interjected. "I've identified some areas where we can implement some things right now that will provide some of the functionality in the next release and …" Porter outlined the plan for getting the project back on track, emphasizing his experience not only with InUnison but with the mainframe. He was still concerned, though, about not knowing if he could indeed get the connector.

Wayne was impressed with Porter. He had taken the cue and Wayne saw that Melani was impressed as well with Porter's mastery of mainframe issues. Nevertheless, Wayne was worried. If all the customers on his issues list were like this, his quarter Number was going to be on life support. He was counting on at least some pipeline from Gatto but it seemed to be flowing out, not in.

After leaving Melani with a game plan for addressing his needs, they stopped at TGIFridays near Times Square for lunch and a chance to decompress. Wayne pulled out his list of issue accounts.

"Well, Porter, you handled that one great. I think George genuinely appreciates the way you stepped up to take responsibility for moving things forward."

"Thanks, but I only wanted to get out alive."

Scanning the issue list, Wayne shook his head.

"We've got seven accounts on this list from Presby. Potential is only the first. I suspect that we're going to see a pattern of complaints centered on the mainframe connector. We are going to have to wade into this and try to knock them down. Some of these are suspect, but others like Sampson and PensAndClips could be big door openers for us. And we have to get rolling with your friend at Azalea."

"I wouldn't worry too much about that. He's got a couple guys from the team already on board so we only need to supply him with software. So, who gets the next shot at us?" Porter asked.

"Pick one."

Scanning the list, Porter said, "Might as well go for gusto: Merrill."

"Let's not waste time." Wayne reached for his cell phone and dialed the contact while Porter began to devour his Philly cheese steak. It took more than a phone call to get between Porter and food.

"Fabozzi, here."

"Hello, this is Wayne Angelis of InUnison Software. I wanted to introduce – "

"Where's that asshole Gatto?"

Wayne took a deep breath, and then exhaled.

"I've taken over his accounts and would like to schedule a meeting to introduce us as your new sales team."

"Unless you are going to get me the Rule Agent by tomorrow, there isn't anything to talk about except how much we are going to sue your company for."

"Yes, I understand that we have some repair work to do with you folks. I really think that my SE and I should stop by World Financial Three and try to sort this out."

"What's to sort out? You promised me software by such and such date and haven't delivered."

"Stanley, I promise –"

"Why would your promises be any more reliable than Gatto's? And it's Stan. I despise Stanley."

"Okay, Stan, I don't know what else I can do but ask for the opportunity to prove our mettle. You've dealt with InUnison for a while now. Outside of Gatto, hasn't the company been reliable and responsive to your needs?" Wayne had no idea if this was true, but he had to go for it.

Fabozzi paused. "Yes, I have to say that your support team has been top notch. The purchasing people here were very impressed with the turnaround on contract issues. All right, I'll give you an hour tomorrow afternoon at two, but you better show up with a firm commitment for a delivery date on the Rule Agent."

"Great, Stan. I'm sure we will get things straightened out…"

"Oh, and where's my mainframe connector?"

Get in line, pal. "We will have an answer for that as well," Wayne replied, shaking his head at Porter.

Porter tried to listen while dispatching his sandwich.

"So, let me guess, he needs the mainframe connector too, right?"

"Of course. We meet with him tomorrow at two. What do you know about the Rule Agent? He's bitching that Gatto made a commitment about that as well. Stop me if you've heard this before."

"Gee, was the guy a pathological liar?" Porter asked.

"Textbook. I never turned my back on the guy."

"Anyway, about the Rule Agent, I haven't touched it yet, but by all accounts it's a cool addition to our messaging infrastructure. You can apply logic to the message delivery and data transformation while the message is in flight –"

"Great, when is it available?" Wayne interrupted. He really didn't care about the technical details, only what could be done to make Stanley, er, Stan, happy.

"Don't know. I'll call Phil."

"Jump on it. I'll need to get to Presby. We've got a big set of issues here and we may have to get senior management involved, or my quarter is toast. Now, let's finish up here and head back over to the Marriott. We can work on Manley's presentation stuff over there in the lounge. Onward and upward!"

***

Wayne paid the tab and they walked the few blocks down Seventh Avenue and crossed Times Square to the Marriott Marquis. As Wayne had hoped, the lounge area was nearly deserted. They chose a table away from the registration area and set up their computers.

Wayne and Porter went through the presentation slides four or five times, dropping a large number of them. It was later than they realized, almost 3:30, and the lounge was starting to see some action as the steam tables came out for the hot finger food. They decided to wrap up the presentation work even though Porter was still nervous about the slides.

"Porter, no matter where I've worked, and no matter what the presentation, you have to be prepared to junk the whole thing and merely chalk talk the material," Wayne reassured him. "Often the audience would rather do that than sit through monotonous PowerPoint slides created by Marketing."

Porter breathed a sigh of relief. His slides bored him to tears. He knew that if *he* was bored, his audience would be comatose.

Wayne reached for his phone. "Porter, while I work on the management side of this mainframe situation, try to connect with someone who can give you the skinny on the status of the product technically."

"Sure." Porter dug out his company directory to figure out which engineer to call. He had met several during the Technical Roundtable meeting at the sales kickoff but couldn't remember who was responsible for the mainframe connector. He saw the name of Tony Tibbetts and seemed to recall he was the one. He dialed Tibbetts' office number.

Wayne was already on the phone with Presby and seemed to be on the attack.

"Ken, you really weren't straight with me about these 'legacy' Gatto accounts, were you? When I call them, the first words out of their mouths were something like 'Where's that lying asshole Gatto' or 'Where's that fucking asshole Gatto'. It would seem that he promised the mainframe connector to several of these accounts knowing full well that it wouldn't be available when they would need it."

"Now hold on, Wayne. I didn't know the extent of this myself. I knew about Potential but not the others."

Wayne didn't buy it. Presby was practicing a bit of plausible deniability, Wayne knew, but he'd have to move on.

"Look, it really doesn't matter what you knew or when you knew it. But my quarter is already in jeopardy here, not to mention the company's reputation…"

Presby heard the words "quarter" and "jeopardy" close together and became more attentive.

"… New York may be a big town but word about vendors gets around fast, particularly in Financial Services. I need to get the mainframe connector into peoples' hands NOW."

"Let me put you on hold. I'll try to loop O'Rourke in on this." Presby knew he better send this right to the top.

While Wayne waited, he looked over to see Porter writing furiously in his note book, muttering "Uh huh, right, sure, uh huh".

Presby came back on the line. "Wayne, you still there? I've got Niles O'Rourke on and have briefed him on the situation."

O'Rourke took over the conversation. "Wayne, I feel badly that we've put you in this situation. Here's what we need to do. Get me an email ASAP with the details of each account you have product commitment issues with, and copy Bill Engler. He's the ultimate guardian of these decisions so we –"

"*Emails?* Excuse me, but I don't have time for emails! I will lose two accounts by Wednesday if I don't have answers for them. I need a go/no go decision NOW!" Wayne demanded, not satisfied with his management's lack of urgency.

O'Rourke paused for a moment. "Let me see if Engler is available."

Again Wayne was put on hold. Porter was off the phone, grazing at the hors d'oeuvres table while waiting for an opening with Wayne.

"What do you have, Porter?"

"A few of these little sausage pizza things, cheese sticks; stuffed mushrooms look kinda greasy…"

"NO, damn it, what did you find out from the engineer?"

"Oh, right." he said, while finishing the cheese stick. "I talked to Tony, the engineer responsible for the connector. He says that he's had it finished for weeks but the holdup is in QA. Our guys don't know how to do quality assurance on a mainframe. In fact, Tony has been lobbying to put the connector into customer hands for testing since he doesn't have any confidence in our normal QA procedures."

"Whose decision is that?" Wayne asked.

"Apparently our VP Engineering, Samantha Brinks."

O'Rourke interrupted. Engler was now in O'Rourke's office.

"Hi, Wayne," Engler said. "I understand that you have a product issue that threatens revenue."

"Yes, Bill …" and he went through the story for the third time in the past half hour. "… and Porter has a moment ago finished a call with the engineer who says he needs to get the connector into customer hands to do proper testing. I think we have a possible solution here."

Engler frowned and hunched his shoulders. "Niles, see if Samantha can come in here." This would be a battle. Brinks had made a career of saying "no" to sales requests for pre-release software or accelerated engineering schedules. Her stonewalling collided with O'Rourke's "revenue rules and sales is revenue" mantra and his relentless drive to change the InUnison culture from an engineering one to a sales and marketing driven one. Brinks' influence had been consistently eroded over the past year as O'Rourke's team racked up successes and she resented it mightily.

Upon entering the office, Brinks eyed Engler and O'Rourke with alarm. These meetings always added more stress on her narrow shoulders and she was near her limit, what with the imminent release of several connectors and core product updates.

Looking haggard and in need of sunshine, she fingered her reading glasses which hung on a gold chain around her flamingo thin, long neck. She wore her usual drab, baggy slacks – O'Rourke called them "PJs on a scarecrow" – attempting to camouflage her six-two, bean pole-like figure.

"Samantha, we have Wayne Angelis, our New York rep and Ken Presby, the Eastern Sales Director on the line here. We have an urgent situation with some accounts in New York, well, Wayne, why don't you explain it?"

Great, for the fourth time. Wayne calmly explained the situation for Brinks.

"…and we can satisfy at least a couple of accounts if we can put the connector in their hands…"

"Absolutely NOT! We don't EVER put pre-release software out," Brinks said, leaning her face close to the phone for full effect.

"Now, Samantha, we wouldn't do this if it wasn't urgent," Engler said, trying to get her to be reasonable instead of her usual obstructionism. He may have been an engineering manager himself once but as CEO he was steadily embracing a sales culture and losing patience with Brinks.

"Who's going to support it? Nobody in Support knows the product yet. I can't have Tony providing support; he's trying to finish the product." O'Rourke rolled his eyes. Based on Porter's conversation, she was either bluffing or out-of-touch. Either way he was going to call her on it.

"Well, we understand that the product is finished in at least beta quality but needs live testing which we can't do in-house."

"WHO TOLD YOU THAT? NO ONE IS SUPPOSED TO KNOW THAT OUTSIDE OF ENGINEERING!" *Ah! Bluffing!* Wayne thought, shaking his head. Porter, who was listening in next to Wayne's ear, panicked and started to mime, "Don't let him mention me and Tony!" Wayne waved him to calm him down as he put his phone on mute.

"Porter, he won't burn his sources," he said, and rejoined the call.

Engler was disappointed that O'Rourke had beat him to calling her bluff.

"Is that true, Samantha? If it *is* ready, let's help solve a sales issue and QA constraint at the same time," he suggested.

Brinks wasn't ready to back down, though. "This is a slippery slope, Bill. We start with a connector, pretty soon it's the logic agents and the whole nine yards, out to customers, willy nilly, every time a rep panics. That's no way to control the process."

"Fuck the process!" O'Rourke yelled. He wasn't going to allow this bureaucrat to get in the way of making his Number. "I'm responsible for revenue, this connector is on the path to revenue and we should damn well get it!"

"I don't have to take this from you, Niles." Brinks started to rise out of her seat but Engler waved her back.

"Samantha, I'm making the call on this. While it was inappropriate for a former rep to make these commitments, I have to back Wayne on this for the sake of the company. You know my policy, 100% referenceability."

"BILL, this will wreck our release schedule for two quarters!"

"Then we'll deal with it. End of discussion."

Brinks was aghast. She had never been overruled this blatantly. "I guess this is what happens when we flush quality technology for the sake of sales."

That's right, bitch, O'Rourke wanted to say.

"Samantha, we will discuss this more later, especially about the ramifications to the overall product schedule," Engler said, trying to sound conciliatory. "Wayne, you may commit to getting the connector into your customer's hands with the caveat that we have to work out the support logistics."

"Don't forget that Porter has a wealth of mainframe expertise and can be the first line of support," Wayne offered.

"Very good. We'll stay on top of it. Sorry for all this, Wayne, but we'll make it work out. Wayne, would you like me to personally call any of these accounts?"

Wayne considered that briefly. "Well, definitely PensAndClips. I'll have to think about Merrill or Potential."

"Don't hesitate to use me. I think we're done, right?"

"Excuse me, before we leave…?" Wayne asked.

"Yes?" three voices responded in unison.

"One other issue with PensAndClips. They started talking to us about a VAR agreement. They want to embed our stuff in their product which would get installed at their customer sites. This guy, Mansfield, says he's being ignored by BizDev. He's talking about names like Lehman, AT&T…"

O'Rourke glared at Engler who returned a "don't start with me on this" stare.

"I'll look into in this personally, Wayne," Engler promised, giving O'Rourke another "don't start…" reprimand. Engler knew that assigning O'Rourke would mean World War III in his headquarters. O'Rourke shot Engler a skeptical look in return.

"Thanks, everybody," Wayne said. "I appreciate the backup on this. Later."

Wayne was pleased with Engler's handling of the situation. He now had some hopes for the quarter.

***

After Brinks trudged out in defeat, O'Rourke closed the door.

"Bill, this situation highlights several continuing conditions..." Engler tried to start talking but O'Rourke pressed ahead. "… and I know you don't want to hear about it but we have to do something about contracts and this totally ineffective – destructive, actually – business development situation. Look, Lakota is dropping the ball on all these VAR and OEM deals, sacrificing millions in ongoing revenue…"

Engler finally raised his voice. "Look, I'm tired of you always picking a fight with Fred. He's working hard…"

"On what? I don't see a damn thing actually getting finished in his organization. They fly all over the country, pardon me, the whole damn *world* actually, and what do we have to show for it? PensAndClips *wants* to work with us, hell they're practically begging to work with us and we are making it almost impossible."

"Let it go, Niles." Engler opened the door and left before O'Rourke could press ahead.

Chapter 6 Building the Pipeline

Tom Gatto arrived at his new Manhattan office after a long and party-heavy weekend in San Francisco. Capping off the weekend, a former colleague from Sun allowed Gatto use of his thirty-five foot sailboat, docked in Sausalito. Gatto didn't know the first thing about sailing but he never intended to leave the slip. Actual sailing would interfere with his "Suzy" activities.

The office was in a shared space in 5 Penn Plaza, directly across from Madison Square Garden and Penn Station. He liked the location; a quick subway ride from his condo near Columbus Circle. There were several other software startup companies on his floor which made it good for intelligence gathering and networking. He knew InUnison wouldn't be there; they were too cheap to spring for real office space when a home office worked just fine.

He introduced himself to the receptionist as the new rep for VibraWeb, disappointed that she wasn't anything special in the looks department. She showed him to his office and handed him the key.

The office was nothing more than a windowless inside room. Gatto was amazed to find a neat pile of files on the desk waiting for him. His predecessor, Bill Thomas, had taken the time to organize his prospect information for whoever was replacing him. Gatto was impressed with the wealth of detailed information.

He sat down and began to study each file in turn, making his own notes and beginning to prioritize the opportunities. He had scanned the first few account files when he heard a knock on his door.

"Yeah, come in," he called without raising his head.

"Hi, are you Tom Gatto?" A short, pudgy, balding guy stuck his head in the door.

"Yes, can I help you?"

The visitor quickly burst through the door and approached Tom with his hand extended.

"I'm Marcus Sweeney, VibraWeb SE. Didn't get a chance to say hi at the sales meeting, but welcome! Better late than never, right?"

"I guess." Gatto shook his hand then yanked it away as he sensed something sticky. He looked at his hand and saw some kind of donut remnant stuck to his palm.

"Oh, sorry about that," Sweeney said, as he produced a napkin, "Just taking advantage of the free donuts. Want one? I'll show you around!"

"Fine," Gatto replied, still wiping his hand.

"This is a great facility. We have individual offices – oh, there's Means' office – there are great conference rooms, a T1 network and it's all included in the lease."

"Well golly, Marcus!"

"Thought you'd be impressed," Marcus said with pride, missing Gatto's sarcasm.

They finished the tour with Marcus showing off his office. Gatto had never seen an office quite like Marcus'. It looked like a computer service workshop, with machines and parts scattered across every horizontal surface. The floor was covered with stacks of books and trade magazines, leaving only a narrow path from the door to Marcus' desk.

"Is it only you in here Marcus?"

"Yep. Of course, you can use anything here."

I don't think I ever want to set foot in here again, Gatto thought.

"Let's go back to my office. I've been looking over the files Thomas left behind. Perhaps you can shed some light on the accounts."

"Sure, let me grab another donut and coffee."

Gatto sat at his desk as Marcus rumbled in, kicking the door closed with his heel. "So, what do you want to know about these accounts?" he asked, spitting powdered sugar as he talked.

"Let's go through them one by one, Marcus. Thomas had a lot of big accounts he was targeting and I need to know exactly where we stand with them. Deutsche Bank: what can you tell me?"

"They are still evaluating the software for use in their Fixed Income operations. I'm going over there tomorrow as a matter of fact."

Gatto flipped through the pages in the file, noticing that they had started the evaluation in October. "They've had the software for almost three months. Pretty lengthy eval, wouldn't you say?"

"Pretty typical. They have this whole process for getting software approved."

"How much time have you spent there yourself?"

Marcus licked his fingers and looked at the ceiling, trying to recall his activities at Deutsche Bank.

"I'd say about 3 weeks time since late October."

"That's not typical for these accounts, I hope."

"Just about. Thomas liked to build relationships and put skin in the game, ya know, that kind of thing. We were really good at that," he said.

"I think it's a waste of time," Gatto said, bursting Sweeney's bubble. "Next one, Merrill Lynch," then he spotted the contact name. "Oh, never mind." *Better not go back there.*

"Right, InUnison is in there already, but I guess you knew that."

"First Securities, wait, did Thomas do anything besides call on Financial Services?"

"Hmm, can't think of any now that you mention it."

"No dot-coms? I was able to close a bunch of them in no time."

"Like I said, Thomas was into relationships. He didn't think a lot of those firms would still be in business in a year."

"Doesn't matter to me as long as there is a budget today, Marcus."

"You have to remember that our stuff is pretty complicated," Marcus said. "You get into the technical weeds real fast which puts demands on my time. I think Thomas figured that if evals were going to get complicated, he'd rather do a half-million deal as opposed to ten $50,000 deals with no possibility of covering the professional services needs. There's only one of me. Juggling too many accounts at once doesn't work."

You have no difficulty juggling those donuts though, eh Tubby?

"We'll see. Keep these evals going for now but keep me informed about their progress. I'll start scheduling visits for next week."

They continued to review accounts and the same pattern kept emerging, large accounts, enterprise deals, long evaluations. It all added up to excruciatingly long sales cycles. Not Gatto's cup of tea, but they were on the forecast for the quarter. The reality of the situation depressed him. If he was going to make his Number, he'd better crank up the dot-com prospecting machine.

***

"This is a helluva sandwich!" Porter exclaimed, holding his beef and swiss up for Wayne to see.

"For a cafeteria, it isn't bad," Wayne agreed. They were in the Manley Brothers cafeteria, bulking up before their meeting. "So, do you have anything wild and crazy planned for the weekend, Porter?"

"I'll be chasing Stephanie around. That's our world right now."

"Yes, I still remember the days. You don't seem to mind it though."

"Not at all! She is such a cool kid."

Wayne smiled, recalling the early days with his kids and how he volunteered to take them off Helen's hands on the weekends. Like Porter, he couldn't get enough of his boys either. It was less than a month since he first met Porter, but he was feeling younger just being around him and listening to his family life antics. It was such a contrast from his current life.

"My advice: don't rush it."

"No way, Wayne!"

They finished lunch and entered the Manley meeting complex about thirty minutes early to set up their laptops and projector. The receptionist led them to a huge conference room with tables set up in a ring configuration.

"Wayne, this isn't going to be filled is it? I thought we were talking to a couple of project leads." He nervously set up his laptop, mishandling the video cable and losing it under the podium stand, forcing him to go onto hands and knees to fish it out.

"Well, when I talked to the business manager, Rob Bailey, he said it would be him and his two top IT guys, some guy named Chang. Maybe this room was the only one available." Wayne was becoming nervous as well. He didn't want Porter to be thrown to the dogs in his first meeting.

The receptionist returned.

"Rob called. He wanted to let you know that he cannot attend. The rest of the middleware team will still be here of course."

"The whole team?" Wayne asked.

"Oh yes, about 12-15 people. Can I get you guys something to drink?"

Yes, how about a double martini, Porter thought. "Just some water, thanks."

"Porter, I'm really sorry," Wayne said. "Rob wasn't up front about what was going on here. I've dealt with these guys before. The middleware team is a bunch of MIT, Carnegie-Mellon and Cal Tech Ph.D.s from all over the world. It will be like the United Nations in here. Don't even think about putting anything technical over on this group. They wrote their own messaging layer for Manley."

"Well, wouldn't they rather buy than build?"

"When they needed messaging, there wasn't anything on the market to buy so they built it themselves. Now their jobs are dependent on that software and we will be viewed as competition."

Soon, a parade of engineers started arriving, some with full plates from the cafeteria, filling the room with a blend of aromas. This was indeed a multi-cultural group. As they settled into their chairs, Wayne passed out business cards and marketing literature.

"Hi, I'm Charlie Chang, Vice President of Corporate System Interfacing," he said, shaking Wayne's hand.

"Pleased to meet you. I'm Wayne Angelis, District Representative and this is Systems Engineer Porter Mitchell."

Chang went around the room and introduced his team. The titles were all something like "Messaging Engineer", "Network Protocol Designer" or

"Queuing Analyst" and all had "Ph. D." next to their names.

Chang continued. "Rob told us all about your product and since we've read the InUnison white papers, you can dispense with most of the marketing stuff and go right into the technical presentation. We have to vacate the room by two-thirty."

Porter turned to Wayne with a "help me" look. They had practiced the pitch – which consisted of the corporate presentation, technical architecture overview and demo – and the shortest they had been able to get through the presentations and demo was 90 minutes, and that was without questions. Chang was giving them only an hour. Wayne rolled his eyes and grimaced at Porter in agreement. He turned, smiling again, to Chang.

"That's fine, Charlie, but I would like to do a few slides to update you on things which are not on the website yet. Porter will then do a few slides on our architecture." Porter had finally tamed the cable and Wayne began.

"InUnison was founded in 1995 by William Engler who is a pioneer in the packaged integration market. He's been well known in Silicon Valley for over fifteen years at places like IBM and Sun Microsystems where he spearheaded their object-oriented work, including the submission of their work to the CORBA specification…" He moved forward through slides on their management team, highlighting their experience either with the technology of messaging systems or their experience with startups.

"Now I'm going to turn things over to the smart guy on the team, Porter."

Porter took a deep breath and a swig of water before stepping up to the podium. He pressed the 'enter' key to advance to his first architectural slide. He hoped to get through these quickly so he could get to the fun part, the demo. He had worked hard on some new demo tricks and was anxious to try them out.

He would never get the chance.

"Here we have a high level block diagram showing the layers of InUnison as a seven layer pyramid. You can see that we have abstracted out the network and other low level layers…'

One of the engineers interrupted.

"I don't see how you can make that work."

"Uh, well, perhaps it will be clearer in a few slides. Now, see how we have also abstracted out the important integration services from the low level –"

"So, what you are saying is that you have applied your own proprietary API to the messaging layer, right?" another asked, still chewing on his lunch.

"Sure, it *is* our API but it's totally open –"

"Do you supply the source code?" asked an engineer on the opposite side of the room.

"Of course not. That's our intellectual property after all. The whole point is to give you the tools to tie applications together without dealing with the underlying complexity of the –"

"So, if we were to use your products, we'd be dependent on you? You must realize that we couldn't do such a thing with such a strategic part of our infrastructure," sniffed the original interrogator, waving his hand as if to ward off a gnat.

Porter tried to continue. "I think that if you let me continue, you will see that we bring quite a bit of value which would compensate for any perceived –"

"Vat whalue ees it to vis da meeessing mass vit cruz?"

Okay, this Russian may be a genius but he's been playing hooky from his English as Second Language classes, Porter thought.

"Are you using centralized queuing?" another engineer asked, while Porter was still trying to decipher the previous question.

Wayne finally broke in.

"Given the short time we have, I really think that we should hold questions until the end."

Chang tried to be the courteous host and regain control. "Yes, let's let him finish, folks."

"As I was saying, we have these abstraction layers which comprise all the necessary services. So, at the middle of the pyramid, we have all the low level network protocol services like TCP/IP, security, naming and such encapsulated for you. If you are using our messaging –"

"But if you have centralized queuing, how can you scale to the enormous volumes we deal with?" the smart-ass queuing analyst asked, clearly intent on showing off, regardless of Chang's request to defer questions.

Now I'm getting pissed. Porter raised his voice and kept going. As several of the engineers got up and unceremoniously left, two of the others were clearly nodding off by the top of the seven layer pyramid.

"So, you can see that for most of your integration needs, we already have the services in place which relieve you of most of the coding involved in the integration process. Any questions?"

"So, we can't get the source code?

Now, Porter was *really* getting pissed.

"Well, why would you want to? Is it really Manley's business to write and have to maintain infrastructure software?"

Wayne winced. No matter how annoying the prospect might be, he didn't want his SE to start challenging him, particularly these guys who owed their livelihoods to writing and maintaining this kind of code.

A heavyset Indian leaned forward. "You haven't addressed performance. You must know that we have the most demanding environment in Financial Services, perhaps in the whole world."

Porter knew something about high volume applications in Financial Services and didn't think that Manley had any need greater than what he'd dealt with at his old bank job. He also knew that he didn't want to get sucked into anything at the first meeting.

"We will be releasing benchmark information in the near future. Otherwise, we would be happy to get performance requirements and perhaps replicate them in our lab." Wayne signaled his approval of the answer with a subtle thumbs up.

"You couldn't possibly replicate our volumes," the cocky queuing engineer said with another dismissive wave of his hand. He got up and left, making a show of leaving the InUnison literature behind by slapping the brochures onto the table.

It was now two-thirty and there was an impatient group outside the door waiting for the room.

"I'm sorry, but we will have to close the meeting," Chang said. "Thank you for coming. We are drafting a Request for Information document and should be releasing it next week."

"I guess Rob will be involved from your side in setting requirements?" He wasn't pleased with Chang's answer.

"No. It is not necessary," Chang said. "We fully well know the requirements Rob's department needs. Actually, he's leaving that department anyway."

That meant that the decision process was going to be almost exclusively in the hands of the techies and therefore a decision to do nothing was the most likely outcome. Wayne would be talking to Bailey about that.

"How many vendors are you releasing the RFI to?"

"We've narrowed the list down to thirty or forty."

Narrowed *it to thirty or forty!* Wayne gave up at this point.

"Thanks, Charlie, and thank you for organizing the meeting."

"Sure. We learned a lot." Wayne knew he was only being polite.

Porter was finishing with the packing up of his laptop and notes. He started to apologize to Wayne about the meeting but Wayne whispered to hold his comments until they had left.

They exited the building and crossed the street to the retail plaza, on the other side of the PATH stop. Porter was sure Wayne was going to rip him for allowing the Manley people get under his skin and worse, letting it show.

They found the coffee stand halfway down the concourse and sat on the edge of a planter in the atrium.

"Wayne, I'm really sorry. I was totally unprepared for that barrage of questions."

"Don't worry. They took me by surprise too. There's really nothing you can do about people like that but you have to go through the dance with them. If there is anything positive about this, it means that they are under some serious pressure to get something done."

"And what's up with all the foreigners? Is this some diversity exercise?"

"Porter, be grateful they are here. There wouldn't be much of a software industry without them, given the sorry state of education in this country. Schools can't seem to punch enough quality engineers out of the public school system."

Porter hadn't thought about that.

Wayne refocused the conversation to the issue at hand. "The RFI will be a bitch, though. It's not like we don't have other important things to do."

"God, yes. We used to have to create those at the bank. What a waste of time. There were some seriously sadistic people in IT who figured that it was a chance to abuse vendors. These are the same people who as kids would tear the legs off spiders to watch the thing twitch. At least now that I'm on the other side, we can hand it off to Marketing to answer, just like the vendors I used to deal with did, right?"

Wayne shook his head. "Well, in case you didn't notice, we are a little shorthanded in Marketing. Phil Lansing is the only guy who seems to have any bandwidth to work on this stuff. Like I said, you need to be his best friend."

"Great."

"Hey, it's the perfect learning device, right? Answer all the questions about our products we don't know the answers to yet!"

"Nice spin, Mr. Sales Rep. But I'm concerned about all this coming on top of fixing these accounts. We're talking about trying to manage four or five projects, and do this Manley response. I'm not sure I can handle all this myself."

Wayne decided to change tactics and give Porter some tough love. January was shaping up to be a real bitch and he couldn't afford to have his technical partner cave in this early in the month. "Welcome to sales, Mitchell. You didn't think this would be all fun and games did you, like sitting around hacking code all the time? This is real serious business and you need to step up to the challenge, starting with the mainframe connector at Potential tomorrow."

Porter hung his head while pondering how he would ever get used to sales.

***

Early the next day, Thursday, Gatto looked around the Bear Stearns building entrance on Park Avenue for his SE, Marcus Sweeney. He hoped that Marcus wasn't one of those chronically late people. After ten minutes, he dialed Marcus on his cell phone.

"Marcus Sweeney here."

"This is Gatto. Where are you?"

"Oh, hi Tom. How are you? I'm here waiting for you."

"Where? I don't see you in the lobby."

"Oh, that's funny. I was waiting for you out here on the plaza." He saw Tom through the window and started to jump up and down, waving his hands.

"Yeah, that's great Marcus. Can we go up now?" *Dumb moron doesn't even think of looking for me in the lobby.*

They rode the elevator up to the meeting floor and the receptionist escorted them to the assigned conference room. The projector for their laptops was already set up so both Gatto and Sweeney pulled out their computers and booted them up.

"Now, Marcus, remember what we went over. I'm going to ask all the questions about their business needs, project plans, and, of course, their budget for integration software. I have to find out where their pain is and rub salt into the wound. Then I'm going to do a few slides on VibraWeb's product direction. If they are still interested, I'll turn it over to you for the demo. We won't raise any technical detail unless they ask. Follow my cue."

"Right. Gotcha. Boy, you sure take command. That takes a *lot* of pressure off of me."

Just then Phillippe Marshon, Director of Trading Technology, came in. Gatto and Sweeney introduced themselves, exchanging business cards and pleasantries.

"So, Phillippe, who all will be with us today?" Gatto asked.

"Myself and Susan Fitzgerald, my top software architect. She'll be along soon."

Right on cue Fitzgerald entered the room and the business card dance started all over again. She was a waif-like woman with unruly raven hair. *Bad hair day?* Gatto wanted to ask. He preferred silky blondes. He didn't like "archs" since they were always tough questioners. They were the ones with "big picture" thoughts and were supposed to be the visionaries. He girded himself for her tough technical questions and hoped that Sweeney could rise to the challenge as well.

"Pleased to meet you. Shall we begin? I have a few background questions to ask, a few high level slides on our company and then Marcus has a demo. Then we can see where to go from there, hopefully to a purchase order, right?"

Marshon rolled his eyes toward Fitzgerald who was now in "show me" mode, folding her arms across her chest.

"First, I could use some background on your organization. Phillippe..."

"Phil is fine."

"Great. Thanks Phil. Who do you report to and can you describe your sphere of influence?"

"I guess the best way to do that is to draw an org chart for you."

Marshon got up to the dry erase board and drew out a reasonably detailed organization chart, starting with the Executive Vice-President of Equity Trading. To Gatto's dismay, Phil wasn't particularly high in the hierarchy. He was about six levels of management below the EVP and even three levels down from the top of the trading information systems team. It turned out that there were five Directors of Technology, and Phillipe only did evaluations; "playing in the sandbox" as sales reps liked to say.

"Okay, thanks Phil. That helps me out a lot." *It tells me that I don't want to deal with you.* "Can you address the budget for integration?"

"Well, not in any concrete terms. This guy," he pointed to a Vice-President three levels above him. "...is the guy with the budget. Of course he defers technical decisions to us..."

"Certainly," Gatto said. "And his IT budget is, what, ten million a year?" He knew that it was several orders of magnitude larger.

"Oh, my, it's about ten times that, especially if you include all the market systems. That's what we have to integrate, of course."

Bingo! That's *who I want.* "So, what are your goals for integration this year?"

At this point Fitzgerald came to life. "We have to take all these market feeds and merge that real-time data with our back office systems, ya know, mark-to-market kinds of things. We understood that VibraWeb was already tying things like Reuters feeds and Fedwire together." She looked from Gatto to Sweeney and Gatto gave Sweeney his cue to jump in.

Sweeney's eyes fluttered between Gatto and Fitzgerald. There was a distinct lack of comprehension in his eyes.

"So, Marcus, can you give them a summary of our Financial Services customers and what they are doing with VibraWeb?" Gatto asked, deciding that Sweeney needed some prodding.

"Uh, sure." Sweeney screwed up his mouth and wrinkled his nose as he racked his brain. "Oh, we worked with, let's see, Goldman on a trading floor project, well, actually, our partner, Trading Systems used us as a messaging bus. Yeah, I'm sure they had to do a Reuters feed for foreign exchange. 'Course they coded that…"

"So that feed isn't part of your product?" Fitzgerald asked.

"Oh, no, of course not. That's why we have the programming interface," Sweeney said, assuming that was a good thing. "We couldn't possibly productize something like that."

Gatto eyes grew wide and his face turned burgundy. *I can't believe this slug said 'no' to a prospect!*

"Perhaps if you document the systems and feeds which you have to interface with, we can respond with more detailed answers…" Gatto said as evenly as he could. He fought to smile as he said it.

"Oh, we can do better than that," Philippe said. "We're about to release a Request for Information with all that sort of detail. I assume you'll want to respond."

Sure, I'll respond. Right up your fucking rectum. "Oh, I'd be thrilled. When can I get that?"

"We'll send it out in early March."

"When will you be making a decision?"

"Well, if we release it on March 1, oh I mean March 2 – that's a Monday –" Marshon said, checking his DayTimer. "We'd like responses in a week. Then a couple of months to digest…"

Gatto's mind immediately switched off. *Right. I'm going to waste my time on an RFI in the last month of the quarter with no decision in sight.*

"…and we can decide how and whether to proceed."

"Okay, let's touch base in March then, shall we?" Gatto started to get up and gather his equipment."

"Sure."

"Tom?"

"Yes, Marcus?"

Marcus leaned close to Tom and whispered, "We haven't done the demo."

Gatto tried to wave Marcus off. "Thank you both for coming. I'll await your document. In the meantime, please feel free to call me with questions."

Sweeney persisted, only louder. "Tom, you said I'd demo."

"I'd like to see the demo," Fitzgerald said, winking at Gatto.

I don't have time for this, you vixen. "Sure, Marcus, take it away."

Sweeney then embarked on his thirty minute demo in which he expertly built an application which moved data between two Internet browser-based applets.

"That was *very* impressive, Marcus," Fitzgerald offered. Sweeney beamed. He had been working on that demo for weeks. "Now, if you could incorporate some data feeds into that, I'd be really excited." She licked her lips at Gatto, picked up her notepad and left the room.

Sweeney couldn't have been prouder.

Gatto gave Fitzgerald a weak smile and then turned to Sweeney. "Let's go Marcus. Two more meetings to get to."

After a silent elevator ride to the lobby, Gatto finally spoke.

"Marcus, don't ever, *ever* do that to me in front of a prospect again!"

Sweeney stepped back and looked at Gatto, clueless about what he had done wrong. "What do you mean? I hardly said anything."

"You humiliated me in there. You actually said 'no' to them. Never ever say 'no', especially if it's true. Didn't Thomas teach you anything?"

"But, we don't do those things and Bill wouldn't have wanted to mislead –" Marcus tried to say.

"There's a difference between saying 'no' and not saying 'yes'. We have to hook them. They can find out about the truth *after* we get their check. And another thing: the meeting was obviously over and you insisted on doing a demo. Those people were a waste of our time. Wasn't it obvious? That wench knew it and wanted to piss me off. It's called vendor abuse. From now on only speak when spoken to…by me."

Marcus looked at his feet. "She seemed pretty nice to me. Kinda sexy too, didn't you think?"

"I don't care if she was Pamela Anderson naked. I have a Number and low level sandbox players aren't going to get me there. Is this the kind of prospect Thomas always sold to?"

"I…I guess so."

"Great."

Marcus picked up his pace, trying to keep up with the power walking Gatto as they headed toward Grand Central Station and the shuttle to Times Square.

***

Light on his feet with high expectations for success, Porter breezed up Broadway through light snow flurries on his way to Potential's building. Melani's man, Frank McDermott was summoned by the receptionist.

"Hello, I'm Frank. I assume you're Porter?"

"Yes. Pleased to meet you."

"You have the 'goods'?"

"The connector? Sure." Porter patted his briefcase.

"Great! Dailey is here as well. We can jump right on it."

McDermott escorted Porter back to a windowless lab area filled with PCs, Sun workstations and mainframe terminals.

"Now, if I understand things, the connector can talk through a 3270 gateway, like Microsoft SNA, right?" McDermott asked.

"Yes," Porter confirmed. "But we can also use TN3270 directly if it's available."

"Cool! That makes things sweet. We can do either."

"Porter? I'm Bill Dailey." Dailey had been sitting in front of a laptop and rose to shake Porter's hand.

"Oh, you guys haven't met before?"

"No," Porter replied. "I started with the company this month."

McDermott gave him an icy look.

"Don't worry. I've been using InUnison for over a year," Porter said. "I know the products and I know mainframes."

"Nothing personal," McDermott said. "We're a little nervous about you guys after the Gatto thing."

"I understand. But I have all the confidence in the world we can overcome that."

"Remember, you don't have immunity from the wrath of Melani while you're here. If we don't succeed it's *shwing!*" He drew his extended fingers across his throat."

"Oh, no, it's *shwing!*" Porter drew *his* fingers across his groin. "Poor man's vasectomy."

All three laughed nervously. "Now, Mr. Melani isn't going to be in here, is he?"

"Anything is possible with George. He can be like a ghost, sort of appearing and disappearing. Maybe we ought to call him Casper or something. The last sighting I had of him was in the control room supervising some performance testing."

"Let's get at it then," Porter said, reaching for the software CD from his briefcase. Phil Lansing had sent it overnight for delivery to Porter the day before, and he spent the previous evening on the phone with the mainframe software engineer, Tony Tibbetts. He was able to install and connect into the test machine in HQ successfully. This exercise gave him a high level of confidence that he would be able to get things rolling at Potential. Tibbetts had even offered to make himself available while Porter was onsite at Potential. That was not something to be taken lightly as it meant that he would have to be in the office by five in the morning, Pacific Time. The California engineers usually rolled in around ten or ten-thirty and worked past midnight.

McDermott showed Porter to the PC server which had been configured for the main InUnison software. As he had done on his laptop, Porter installed the connector and was able to exchange data with the main InUnison message broker. McDermott was impressed.

"Well, don't get too excited yet. The hard part is actually connecting to the mainframe," Porter cautioned.

"So, what do we need?"

"I have to enter the address for the TN3270 service on your mainframe."

McDermott had anticipated that and had it ready. Porter added that information to the connector configuration. The connection test succeeded and the connector was able to talk to the mainframe.

"Now, what type of transaction can we access? We have to introspect the data structure and map that to a message structure."

"Got it right here." McDermott shuffled through some notes and found some transaction numbers to use.

In a few minutes, Porter was done with his configuration.

"Okay, now, here's the real test." Porter launched the InUnison QuickTest program which would send the request message and display any results. "I need a customer number to enter for the request."

McDermott dug around in his notes again. "Here, customer 339A4."

Porter entered that into the input field, paused, said a silent prayer, and hit ENTER.

Nothing came back. Three heads sagged in disappointment.

Porter launched MessageCommander which would trace the messages as they flowed through the system. "I should have done that in the first place."

He entered the customer number again. This time the trace told them the request made it to the mainframe and the connector was waiting in vain for a reply. In fact, the connection was live, then dead, and then live, dead, live, dead. Neither Porter nor McDermott recalled seeing a mainframe behave this way.

"Frank, this is really strange, don't you think?"

"Yes, it's almost like someone is switching it on and off."

Then Melani entered the lab. "I see you are back to salvage your sorry ass. So, is it real or is it bullshit?"

Dailey and McDermott both turned to Porter, moving aside to give Melani a clear path to him.

Porter composed himself. "George, we have the connector up, it's connected to the broker and the mainframe. Our request didn't trigger the transaction, though. We're only now trying to figure that out. It keeps losing the connection."

"I knew it. You really don't know what the fuck you're doing, do you? If you did, your precious connector would know to forward requests only when the partition is up."

"George, we literally ran this test moments ago. We were about to –"

"Don't back-talk me, boy. You're no better than Gatto, are you? This is all some charade, isn't it? ISN'T IT?"

Porter couldn't take this seriously. *No one could be this irrational after one failed test,* he thought. Still, he had this bear of a man towering over him with a face full of rage.

Melani clenched his fists, took one step toward Porter but stopped short. McDermott and Dailey averted their eyes. Porter was frozen; his flight or fight response not making any decision on the matter.

Then Melani broke into a smile, a rare and shocking sight for McDermott. Melani reached for the telephone and dialed the extension for the central console. "Joe, it's George. You can leave it up now."

Melani started laughing the most evil laugh any of the three had ever heard.

"GOT YA!" Melani could barely talk through his guffaws. "I saw you guys connecting… in… when I was on the con…sole …and took your connection up and down just…just to screw with you." He was so out of control he had to support himself on the equipment rack next to Porter.

Porter turned to the screen and tried the request again. Instantly, the return data flashed on the screen. *You are the biggest asshole…*

Melani leaned over and slapped Porter's back so hard, his nose left a print on the monitor. "Great! Keep up the good work!" He left, his hysterical cackles echoing down the hall.

Porter turned to look at his comrades. McDermott looked like he was going to collapse and Dailey's eyes gazed up to the heavens as if to thank Providence for his deliverance.

"I don't know about you guys, but I need to change my shorts," McDermott said.

Porter smiled and stroked his hair back while shaking his head. "Let's see what else we can do here before the evil trickster strikes again."

***

Back at his office – and still lamenting Marcus' performances on sales calls – Gatto checked his list of phone calls to make. The first one was to Stewart Miller at Azalea.

This should be interesting, he thought as he dialed.

"Stewart Miller."

"Good afternoon. This is Tom Gatto with VibraWeb Software. How are you today?"

"Fine. Get on with it."

"I was encouraged, by your cousin, Eric, to give you a call. He told me that you could definitely use our integration system in your projects."

"Doubt it."

"Now, I'm sure you must have a need for applications to communicate with each other. It really is a universal problem in corporate America."

"Not here. I don't appreciate Eric giving you my direct number. If you want to send me some literature or something, fine. I'll contact you if I'm interested. Thanks for calling."

Gatto heard a click and then dead air.

***

Back at Potential Investing, McDermott learned how to configure his own transactions and began to build a family of messages to move data back and forth. By the end of the afternoon, he had built the minimum set of interactions he needed to satisfy Melani.

"So, shall we show our proud baby to George?" McDermott asked.

"Frank, I think you should have that honor," Porter replied.

"Absolutely!" Dailey added, as he quickly packed up his laptop. "In fact, we're going to leave you to accept the glory all by yourself. After all, we are merely vendors."

"Bastards," McDermott muttered.

Porter and Dailey darted for the elevator, lest Melani capture them for more torture treatments. Feeling safe, they paused in the lobby.

"Hey, Bill, you want to grab a cold one? I think this deserves at least some celebration. I want to check in with Wayne as well. I think he could use some good news."

"Sure, Porter. I'd love to. Who's Wayne?"

"He's my rep partner. We started together at the kickoff meeting. I like him a lot so far. He includes me in his strategy sessions, buys lunch…"

"He has to be better than Gatto."

"Hmmm, there's only about a million places to go to here…"

"I know one of the bartenders at the All-Star Café. He'll give us some free stuff."

"Food?" Porter asked with wide eyes.

"You bet."

They made their way down the few blocks to the other end of Times Square where the All-Star Café was located. It was very busy as it was now happy hour but they were able to secure bar stools in the section Dailey's friend worked.

"Order me a draft of something. Doesn't matter. I need to step out to call Wayne. It's too noisy here."

Porter ended up going all the way back down to Broadway since his cell phone reception was poor inside the building. He hugged the outside wall of the restaurant merchandise shop and called Wayne.

"Wayne! Porter here!"

"Please tell me you have good news," Wayne said with a hopeful sigh.

"Hey, Mr. Grumpy, we hit a home run at Potential. We got the connector up and running, defined a bunch of transactions and things just worked. Well, they did after Melani quit toying with us." Porter went on to describe Melani's idea of a practical joke.

Wayne was relieved. *Finally, something going my way.* "Can you replicate that at the other accounts?

"That's what I wanted to talk to you about. I now know what information we need to define the instance of the connector. If we get those other accounts to get that ready for us, we should be able to knock them down. Now, the idea I had was to get Sean or some other SE in here to help and we could get them done in a week…"

"Whoa, boy! Be careful what you commit to. We can't summon resources by snapping our fingers. And I'm skeptical that all the accounts can be as easy as Potential, and Melani's trickery aside, it was almost too easy."

Porter was a bit deflated by Wayne's lack of enthusiasm. "Hey, where's your 'can do' attitude? After all, didn't management commit full support to fix these issue accounts? C'mon, man! Let's go for it!"

I don't want to burst your bubble, Wayne thought about saying*, but it isn't done. I've never gotten that kind of support and don't expect it here. No, stop being negative.* "Porter, here's what we should do. You call up your boss, Young, and tell him what you think you can do. I'll run a parallel track through Presby and see what we can do."

"I already have some spin ready for Young. This is a great opportunity to get SEs trained up on this new product. We also have Bill Dailey from PS on board."

"Okay, Porter, go for it. Let's touch base later."

They hung up and Porter immediately dialed Young.

"Hey, Dave, this is Porter Mitchell."

"Porter! I've been meaning to check in with you! How are things going?"

"It was great today! We got Potential Investing up and running on the mainframe connector! They are actually happy!"

"Fantastic! Tell me about it." Porter launched into a detailed rundown of his day at Potential.

Young was impressed. "Porter, that's exceptional leadership and cool that you exhibited. Great job! So, where do we go from here?"

"That's the main reason I'm calling," Porter replied. He took a breath before making his request. "You know that we inherited all these pissed off accounts from Gatto, right? Well, if I had some help, I could train them up on the connector and then divide and conquer. Could we get Sean and/or someone else up here next week?

"Kinda short notice; it's already Thursday. I know that Mackenzie is busy with some things in Philly…"

Porter couldn't hide his impatience. "Dave, look, Engler himself committed to doing 'whatever it takes' to clean up Gatto's messes. We can clean them up in a week if I get –"

"Porter, don't lecture me. The visibility of your situation was driven home to me at the kickoff. I have to try to balance things and do it efficiently. I'll get you your help."

Porter acquiesced. "Sorry, Dave. I guess I assumed –"

"…that I'd be a prick about this, right? Well I'm not a prick to my SE team, only reps who abuse the resource. Let me check on availabilities and get back to you. It would be great to get Julia up there. She needs the connector as well."

"Okay, thanks, and sorry for being impertinent."

"Hey, if you keep up this quality of work, you can be as impertinent as you want to be. We'll get you some help by Monday."

Chapter 7 Divide and Conquer

Wayne and Porter met at the Exchange Place coffee shop prior to the Monday conference call in order to go over their plans for the potentially pivotal week. Porter was coordinating the efforts of Sean Murphy and Julia Berkowski at the mainframe accounts and Wayne hoped to push the ball forward at Azalea and other new prospects.

"Looks like a plan, Porter. I'll bet you'll have everything straightened out in no time."

Porter wasn't so sure. He felt like he was sailing into uncharted territory, in effect, managing vastly more experienced SEs. Sean and Julia seemed anxious to help out, though.

They each dialed into the conference call on their mobile phones. Ken Presby was just connecting in himself but wasted no time with pleasantries.

"Wayne, what's your status?" Ken Presby asked, bracing himself for negative news.

"Actually, I have some good news," Wayne said, shooting a smile at Porter. "I tried to get you Friday but missed you. Porter was successful at Potential Investing with the mainframe connector. We seem to have gone a long way to bringing that account back from the brink."

"How'd you get that connector?" an incredulous Gary Reaper asked. "It isn't even in beta yet."

"Well, we would – and still could – lose a lot of business up here if we delay things further. We think that with some help we could solve –"

"I'm sure *my* productivity would go up if *I* had access to everyone else's resources like their SE. This is really going to hose me. If –"

"Gary," Presby interrupted, "Engler made the commitment to support Wayne and we are following through on it. You'd want the same treatment if you were in the situation that Wayne's been stuck with."

"Also, Gary, this gives Julia a great chance to get trained on the connector," Young added. "Then you can go after your own opportunities with it. Sean Murphy will be in New York as well."

"I don't know. At Sybase the SEs would never, ever –"

"Gary, the decision is made." *Damn you, Grim, can't you even spell 'team'?* "Go ahead, Wayne."

"I appreciate the help, Ken. The other new opportunity this week is at Azalea Financial. Porter's ex-boss is now forming a financial reporting group under the controller. They will need to gather information from a lot of –"

"Hey, Azalea is based here in Atlanta!" Reaper said.

"Ah, no, they are based here, down on Water Street. Anyway, as I was saying, this guy Norm used to –"

"Ken, I've been calling on Azalea Insurance for months –"

"Funny, it hasn't shown up on your forecast. Continue, Wayne."

"To clarify; Azalea Financial is the parent of Azalea Insurance."

"Right, but Insurance is an autonomous –"

"Please, Gary, let it go," Presby said. "Wayne."

"Right. Anyway, we think we have a high-level way in. That's about it since we're just starting –"

"Hey, if you need any help, call."

"Sure, Gary." *You can help by staying out of the way.*

"Thanks, Wayne," Presby said. "Oh, before I forget, we need your help next week at a show at Javits, something called IntegrateNow! It's being driven out of Marketing but we should have a sales presence there. Get with Maureen Madsen, Marketing Communications, for details. She'll be there as well. She generally has things all set up and you simply have to show up."

"Sure, Ken, I'll take care of it." He chalked up the need to work a trashy trade show as another drawback to being at a startup. He never *had* to do a show before. Sometimes he'd go hold meetings with key customers, but hang out by the booth? Forget it.

Turning to Porter he put his phone on mute and said, "Well, next week's a waste. Have you ever gone to a trade show?"

"We went to local ones. The bank was too cheap to send us to any out of town."

"Did you meet Maureen Madsen at the meeting?"

"Didn't meet her. Oh, wait, Sean said something about her. Must be attractive, he said she was 'some spinner'. I asked him what a 'spinner' was and he only laughed. He said I'd know when I met her."

"You got me. I'll get the scoop but we need to block out Monday through Wednesday."

"Oooh, lucky guys," Sean said, as if on cue. "Maureen's a babe."

"Watch your mouth, you pig," shouted Sims-Acheson, the Philadelphia sales rep, known as the team's "femi-nazi". "I could file a complaint for sexual insensitivity."

"My apologies," Sean replied. *Bitch.* "Oh, by the way, Ms. Political Correctness, did you see the *Drudge Report*? Your hero, Boy Clinton, has been throwing down with an intern."

"Sean, don't start…" Presby said, trying to head off a cat fight.

"I wouldn't put any stock in what Matt Drudge puts out," Sandy countered. "He's offensive. Anyway, it's nobody's business what the President does with his private life."

"Right, I forgot, lying doesn't matter anymore."

"Let's wrap up," Presby said firmly. "I know I talked to each of you individually last week, but thanks again, everyone, for a great kickoff. We've got a great regional pipeline and we could start off the year with a great Q1. Don't leave any stone unturned! Thanks for calling in. Let's go sell! Beat VibraWeb!"

"Ah, Ken? Can you hang on for a second? I have a couple things to go over which…"

"Gary, I'll call you later. Bye, everyone!"

"Porter? We'll be seeing you in about an hour, right?" Sean asked.

"Right. I'm across the river. I'll be over as soon as we wrap."

"Can't wait," Julia chimed in.

Porter and Wayne clicked off their phones and started to pack their things. Porter was due to meet Sean and Julia at the Marriott World Trade Center while Wayne was headed to Dow Jones, there in Exchange Place, and then to his first meeting with Norm Johnson at Azalea Finance.

"So, is Reaper going to be a problem?" Porter asked.

"Nah. Just the usual sales rep posturing. I'm willing to bet he hasn't done more than put a phone call in to them. I'll do the honorable thing if and when we get a deal and let him get a cut if something gets deployed down there in Atlanta. The insurance subsidiary *is* one of the largest parts of Azalea. Anyway, it's way too early to talk splits."

"I'll be sure to get the scoop from Julia."

"Good idea. People tell me that Gary spends more time trying to horn in on other reps' business than concentrating on his own."

They stood up to go their separate ways. "Oh, Wayne, good luck with Norm this afternoon. I'm sure that you will hit it off with him."

"I hope so. That organization could make my year. Later."

***

Gatto stepped off the subway at Penn Center, walking as if he was going to attend his own funeral. He had been with VibraWeb only two weeks but he had already developed a wariness of his sales management. He had been treated to many stories about the constant anal exams performed by the sales management. On this Monday, his immediate manager, George Means, wanted a pipeline review.

He walked into his office to see Means already using his desk and phone. Means hung up upon seeing Gatto.

"So, what do you have for me today? You didn't email me any visit details or an updated forecast."

Hey, good morning to you too. Gatto opened his briefcase and extracted his forecast. "Sorry, I thought that I had emailed it. Anyway, here's a hard copy." He had, in fact, emailed it the previous Friday but Means, as usual, didn't bother to read it.

"I don't see any changes on here. Are you saying that there hasn't been anything to add since last Monday?"

"Nothing that changes the status. I met with several accounts last week but nothing transpired which would raise the completion percentages. I have some calls this week which should add a couple of accounts to the forecast."

"Like who?"

"Chase, Bank of New York, Tables.com –"

"Not another dot-com, please!"

Gatto decided that trying to explain, again, that dot-coms have money like everybody else would only prolong the agony. "George, I'm getting some good traction and have the rap down so you'll see some pipeline growth over the next few weeks…"

"But you still don't have me scheduled to meet with anyone, do you?"

"I'd prefer to bring you in later in the sales cycle. All of my meetings this week are initial sales calls."

"How convenient. I'll let you off the hook this time but I want to go on some closing calls very soon."

Means grilled him on about every account on the forecast for close to an hour and a half.

"Oh, I almost forgot, we need you at IntegrateNow! next week."

"Argh, not a show! Can't Marketing handle it? You really don't want me to be wasting time talking to a bunch of mullet-topped techno freaks with no budget, do you? I already have sales calls scheduled," he pleaded.

"Sorry. Be there. With an SE. Call Cindy, our event coordinator in HQ, for details."

He unceremoniously closed the door in Gatto's face as he reached for his ringing phone. "MEANS!"

***

Reaper was still steaming from the sales conference call. He stood up and paced around his bare bones office. He stopped to gaze out his window which faced the huge Perimeter Center retail complex just down the hill.

I'll show that poacher in New York what's what. He began sorting through his stack of business cards to find the one Julia had given him for the Azalea Insurance CIO. "Spencer Carlton," Reaper said and reached for the phone.

"This is Spencer."

"Good morning, this is Gary Reaper with InUnison Software. How are you this morning?"

"Busy, of course. I really don't have time to talk right now," Carlton said, employing his anti-vendor defense shield.

"That's fine, Spencer. I'd like to get on your schedule sometime this week to update you on our products. I know that Julia Berkowski has met with you in the past and…"

Carlton tried to remember, *Julia Berkowski, oh yes, that tall blonde…smart…built like a…yeah, I can make time for her again…* "Yes, I met with her not too long ago. Smart lady. You have interesting software. I didn't have the right project, though. I do have integration challenges but your earlier stuff looked somewhat unbaked. And there wasn't any mainframe connectivity. Has any of that changed?"

"Absoooluuutely, Spencer! You won't believe your eyes. We have some new releases which I'm sure will interest you. When do you have a couple of hours free?"

Carlton checked his online schedule. "Thursday afternoon, say one o'clock?"

"That's great. I'll see you then."

Take THAT, Wayne Angelis.

***

Porter climbed out of the familiar bowels of the PATH station at World Trade Center, wove through the throngs shuffling past the shops of the huge underground mall, and crossed into the lobby of World Trade One. Porter squinted as he made his way toward the Marriott lobby. Morning sunshine, reflected from the glass of buildings across the West Side Highway, streamed through the tall, skinny windows into the elevator lobby.

In the Marriott, he scanned the lobby past the registration area, but did not see either Julia or Sean. Glancing at his watch, he realized he was a bit early so he settled down into an armchair to wait.

The three of them were going across the highway to Merrill Lynch's World Financial Center office to install the mainframe connector. Porter planned to use Merrill as his training exercise for Sean and Julia. If all went well, Sean would go to PensAndClips, Julia to Lehman in Jersey City and Porter would stick at Merrill to train a couple of Stan Fabozzi's people.

"Porter, good to see you again!" It was Julia striding up to where Porter was sitting. He had been gazing out the window watching traffic navigate around the construction on West Street and jumped up a bit startled.

"Julia! Hi!" Porter reflexively stood up and straightened his hair as if he were meeting her for a date. "Thanks so much for coming up to New York. I hope you didn't have to rearrange your schedule too much." Porter was taken by surprise by her attire. At the kickoff, she was all jeans and loose sweaters. Here was a thoroughly professional Julia in a figure flattering – and boy did it – blue pinstripe suit, and white faux wrap blouse. Her previously free-flowing, reddish-blonde hair was under control in a French twist.

"Are you kidding?" she said as she dropped her coat and briefcase next to a sofa opposite Porter's armchair. They both sat down. "Grim hardly ever has anything scheduled."

"Well, he put up a fuss on the conference call today."

"Oh, that's all show. I'm excited to get out of Atlanta for a while and actually do some productive customer work. It looks like you have things jumping up here."

"They're jumping all right. Down right hopping mad you might say."

"Gatto left some messes behind, eh?"

"Wayne calls them "landmines". But if things go as easily as they did at Potential last week, we can turn things around. I do want to find out from you about the Azalea Insurance work."

"Oh, that's all bullshit too. Gary has a friend over there that he golfs with. He's got granite where he should have brain cells. It never occurred to him to actually try to sell in there. Now, *I've* got a couple of good technical contacts, including the subsidiary CIO, so if you ever need something, let me know. We'll get you down to Alpharetta."

Porter became very comfortable with Julia as they chatted about the mainframe connector and some other technical matters.

"Hey guys!" Sean Murphy appeared. "Sorry for being a couple minutes late. Kyle had me on a quickie conference call with Fidelity."

"I figured you were trying to hack into the TV system."

"Wouldn't you know this place has OnCommand; it's hack proof. But the liquor…yeah!"

"Well, let's get on it. We only have to walk across the bridge from Tower One to get to World Financial."

The trio gathered their gear and made their way to Merrill Lynch. Stan Fabozzi met them at reception and showed them to their test lab where his lieutenants, William Best and Sergio Cruz, were waiting. Stan made introductions and left them to work. It was obvious from their expressions that Best and Cruz were skeptical. Porter, flush with confidence from his experience at Potential, went right to work.

"So, if you point me to the server with our broker on it we can install the connector. Did Stan pass on the email about IP addresses and transaction ID's?"

Sergio turned, pulled a sheet from the manila folder on the desk behind him and handed it to Porter without comment.

"And which machine is the server?"

"Here," Best said curtly, pointing to the machine behind him. He stood to get out of Porter's way, and leaned against the door frame.

"You might want to gather around to see how this installation works," Porter suggested. Neither of his new Merrill friends budged.

I guess I can't expect a whole lot of help from these guys, Porter thought. He started to feel some dampness under his armpits.

Julia and Sean gathered around Porter as he installed the software, asking a few questions along the way. Best and Cruz paid attention but maintained their silence.

The moment of truth approached as Porter defined the communication method and address for the mainframe partition. As it had worked at Potential, the connector immediately recognized the mainframe and vice versa. Porter looked at the transaction information on the sheet from Best and launched the message definition utility.

Turning to Best and Cruz, Porter waved them over. "You will definitely want to see this. This is how we map fields from the transaction to message fields."

Best sort of shrugged. "I'm sure we can figure it out. Continue."

Porter looked at Sean for help in engaging the Merrill guys but the best he could do was a subtle "I don't have a clue" expression. Porter decided to press ahead.

Porter entered the transaction ID and then defined a message to be sent through the InUnison system which would contain the information. It all seemed to be working.

"Now I'm going to use our testing program to publish a request for this information and then wait for the reply message with the result."

Best and Cruz gave each other a knowing look and Sergio gave him a backhand wave saying "Sure, whatever you say."

Porter clicked on the send button in the test interface, and was quickly greeted with bond information for a ten year US Treasury issue in Merrill's inventory.

Porter slid his chair back so Best and Cruz could see his achievement. "See, it just works!"

"Try another transaction," Sergio challenged, pointing to the paper. He and William moved directly behind Porter, displacing Sean and Julia, and squinted at the screen while Porter defined a new message. He then went back to the test program, entered the new request and hit send. Again, the correct information was displayed, this time client information.

Sergio looked at William and then back to Porter.

"It can't be this easy. Let's do some more," he said.

"Here, you drive and see for yourself," Porter offered.

Sergio sat down and mimicked the steps that Porter had followed. He fumbled a bit when defining what fields went where in the message but had his own transaction running in less than ten minutes.

"Wow. That mainframe stuff has been nothing but a big pain in the ass. And this is a beta version? Not bad. Bill, you want to drive?

Best sat down and replicated the work Cruz had done.

"Boy, I have to be honest," Best said, "we figured you'd bring some canned thing, make it look good and then split. We had next to zero confidence in this."

"Gee, we hadn't noticed," Sean said. "You greeted us so warmly."

"Yeah, sorry. But you have to admit our track record with you guys isn't so hot.

"New sheriff in town, dude," Sean said, dramatically hiking up his pants and pointing to Porter.

"Yes this looks so easy that even Sean could do it," Julia said.

"You can go back to Hicksville, Georgia Peach."

Porter retook control. "So, Bill, Sergio, I have to get these guys set up elsewhere but I'd like to stay and make sure you are off and running."

Bill and Sergio were already at work on other transactions. "Whatever."

Porter, Sean and Julia stepped out to the reception area.

"I'm so psyched!" Porter said. "This stuff is going to work out great. So you two know where you're going, right? Divide and conquer! Wayne's going to go nuts when we tell him that we've cleaned up all these accounts."

"Yes, I'm doing PensAndClips up on 21st Street," Sean said.

"And I'm going to Lehman across the river," Julia confirmed.

"You have my cell number, right? Great! I need to get back to these skeptics."

"Ah, Porter? Aren't you forgetting something?" Sean asked.

Porter thought for a few seconds, and then raised his palms. "I dunno. What?"

"Ah, the software? Our CDs?" Julia said, catching on.

"Oh, right. It's still in the machine. I'll get it."

"You *do* have more than one, right?" asked Sean.

Porter had turned around to go get the CD but the realization stopped him cold. "Oh, shit."

"Yea, 'oh shit'. So, newbie, how do we 'divide and conquer' with one copy of the software?" Sean was enjoying bringing Porter back to earth. Julia joined in the game with a raised eyebrow and an annoyed hand on her hip.

Porter could not have been more embarrassed. *Way to go, Slick. That's quality planning.* "Let's sit down and sort this out."

The three InUnison SEs gathered around a coffee table in the reception area. Porter wrung his hands. "Here's a thought. Both of you could go over to Lehman in Jersey City, install it, then you, Sean, can take the disk and head up to PensAndClips."

They thought about that scenario and Julia raised an objection.

"Porter, I'd be all for that but aren't we walking into unfriendly territory?

Shouldn't you at least make introductions? They might think that you're abandoning them again."

"I see your point. But these guys here are critical. I can't piss them off, either."

"As usual, I have the answer," Sean said. Julia rolled her eyes. "I think these guys are good to go here. I'll stay here, just in case. You go with Julia, come back here and I'll take the hand off."

"I'm reluctant to admit that Sean actually has a good idea," Julia said. "It works for me."

"It makes sense. Sean, let's go get the disk, I'll make apologies to Bill and Sergio."

***

Wayne approached the Azalea offices hoping that this meeting would be more productive than his Dow Jones meeting. His contact there represented himself as a Dow Jones executive when he was in fact a consultant hoping to ride Wayne's coattails into the firm. Wasting time was guaranteed to put Wayne in a surly mood.

He was wandering around Norm's floor looking for someone who might direct him to Norm's office. He stopped at Connie Sanchez's desk to ask directions.

"Hello, my name is Wayne Angelis with InUnison Software. I'm looking for Norm Johnson."

"You've come to the right place. I'll show you to his office."

Wayne glanced behind Connie's desk and spotted "Sam Racker, Controller" on the name plate next to the office door. His research of Azalea turned up the fact that Sam Racker was heir apparent to the CFO, and was pleased to see that Norm wasn't exaggerating his proximity to power.

Norm's office was three doors down from Racker's. Connie paused to see if Norm was on the phone then gave a quick knock on the doorframe.

"Norm? I have a Wayne Angelis here to see you."

Norm got up from his desk to greet Wayne.

"Pleased to meet you. Have a seat. Coffee?"

"No thanks. Had plenty at lunch."

"Thanks, Connie."

"So, Porter tells me you've quite the gig here," Wayne said. "What's your mandate?"

"My job is to rationalize all the information in the corporation that relates to financial reporting."

"That sounds pretty comprehensive. Why isn't that in IT?"

Norm chuckled. "Well, *officially,* it's because we need to be a cross-functional section, dealing with all departments and subsidiaries and more importantly, the function needs to be performed by financial experts, not systems people."

"And the unofficial reason?" Wayne suspected what was coming.

"IT sucks here."

"Is Stewart Miller still the CIO here?"

"Sure is. You know him?"

"I never met him but I sold some stuff here in a prior life. He had a reputation as a vendor abuser."

"I don't know how he treats vendors but he certainly has a lot of people around here intimidated. He won't even meet with me yet. He keeps canceling meetings."

Wayne quickly made some mental notes. *Reports to Controller, getting held up by IT.*

"What kind of budget do you have?"

"Not wasting any time are you?"

"Well, what you've described sounds like a quagmire. I know you have the backing of the Controller but…"

"Not only backing, this team is his baby, he's the heir apparent for CFO, and he has board support."

"I know, but this will be an expensive effort, right?"

"I have a budget in eight figures over two years. But we have to show something very, very quickly." Norm began to steal control of the meeting from Wayne. "That's where you come in. I know what InUnison can do and I've hired two guys who worked with Porter at the bank. I'd like the software and some of Porter's time to get something up and running quickly."

"Whoa! I still don't really know what the opportunity is here. You're asking for a lot." *And he thinks* I'm *being aggressive…* Wayne thought.

"Wayne, I don't have time to screw around. You strike me as a smart rep. You know this is exactly the problem InUnison was designed to solve. I've got the backing of the Controller who is still in his honeymoon period here and who has secured serious funding for this project. I've got a team experienced with your product. If we are successful, your products will be standard across the corporation. What more opportunity do you want?" Norm raised his hands as if to say "Isn't this obvious?"

"It certainly does look like a great opportunity," Wayne said, hoping to humor Norm. "I'd feel better if IT had some involvement in this effort. Don't take this the wrong way, but you're new here and IT isn't going to like being pushed around, Racker's honeymoon notwithstanding. I've seen so many of these kinds of projects get torpedoed because it was viewed as a rogue operation. Isn't there some other alliance you can make, some subsidiary?"

"Insurance in Atlanta is an obvious one. But with the kind of backing I have, I can be in the driver's seat."

Just a little cocky, aren't you? Wayne thought.

"So do you have a plan for dealing with Miller?"

"We can't go frontal on him. His shields will go up and deny us everything. We plan on flanking him. We think that we can co-opt the Oracle Financials team."

"'Frontal', 'flanking'? You used to be in sales, weren't you?"

"No, why?"

"Those are classic sales strategy terms."

"I'm a war buff and those are classic battle tactics. Miller thinks that way as well; has something to do with being in the Marines."

"Sales, war…" Wayne's hands were doing an imitation of a scale.

Norm laughed. "I may be a technologist, but I have to sell what I do. Otherwise I don't get funded. One has to think strategically."

Norm and Wayne drilled down into more of the details of the pilot project. At the end of an hour, Wayne felt that he had gathered as much as he could. He liked Norm but did not sense enough political instinct needed to pull off this coup.

"I'll arrange things with Porter about software and be sure he can commit some time here. Don't try to hire him."

"I won't guarantee that. It's up to you folks to treat him right otherwise I'll snag him faster than you can say 'quota'."

***

Across the country in Redwood City, the InUnison leadership was reviewing the state of the company. The mood in Silicon Valley continued to be hyper-bullish, with valuations pushing more and more startups toward public stock offerings. The InUnison board of directors was as infected as anyone. Engler was not in any hurry to go public and tried to dampen their expectations. He was only partially successful.

"Niles, the forecast looks pretty healthy. How confident are you in these numbers? Any bogus deals in here?" InUnison CFO Jay Antoniazzi asked.

"Jay, I scrub these things pretty hard. The last thing I want is to be held accountable for phantom deals."

CEO Engler broke in. "Neither do I. The board is totally focused on revenue run rate. This next funding round should be our last before IPO so reliable, predictable, revenue is king."

"So, what is our cash position and burn rate right now?"

Engler nodded to Antoniazzi to brief O'Rourke.

"We have six million in the bank, but we're burning one and a half every month at current revenue projections. Our hiring plan will increase that burn rate to over two million very quickly." He paused to let O'Rourke take that in.

"That's quite a bit higher than expected, isn't it? I thought we were confident that we would have at least nine months cash."

"Well, to be honest, the board was assuming over-achievement on the sales side," Engler said. Almost inaudibly, he added, "…and more leverage from partnerships."

"I *told* you not to count on BD for hard revenue…" O'Rourke said. He knew where this was going. "And who represented new direct sales numbers to the board? It wasn't me. If you recall, I last did a detailed presentation on sales expectations at the board meeting in October. You know I take my commit seriously and I presented realistic numbers to them based on our approved headcount and pipeline. Betting on over-achievement is dangerous."

"Niles, enough about BD and don't get defensive. It doesn't change the facts. We are accelerating the next round of funding, but the new investors will have to see us hit the targets for this quarter. And…" Engler glanced at Antoniazzi and back to O'Rourke. "…we have to raise the target a bit."

"You can't be serious! I went through hell setting everyone's Numbers! You can't ask me to do it again!"

"If you hit your hiring targets, the rolled up quota for those new hires would account for the increase, say, a million dollar quota per hire," Antoniazzi said.

"Spoken like a true bean counter. 'Go hire a bunch of reps with a million dollar quota each' he says. I've finally settled the team into the new year with new territories; I have chaos in New York and now you want me to defocus everyone by tearing up their territories…" He sank into his chair, shaking his head.

Engler tried to be conciliatory. "Niles, I don't like this either but what else can we do? While we aren't in danger yet, we have to act now."

"I'll tell you what you do; you fire that fucker Lakota and his Monty Python Flying Circus and get a guy who knows how to wring revenue from partnerships. *That's* leverage."

Antoniazzi gave a look of agreement to Engler who had been counting on support instead.

"Look, for the last time, I'm not firing anyone yet."

O'Rourke blew up. "Why the hell not? What has he committed to and come through on? This is total BULLSHIT! My team has fucking *delivered* and you reward me by making a scapegoat of sales instead of taking that bastard out onto Route 101 and letting him play in traffic!"

"Niles, you need to –"

O'Rourke couldn't control himself.

"What does Lakota have on you, Bill? Pictures with little boys or something?"

Antoniazzi's eyebrows shot into his forehead as the CEO's eyes bore into O'Rourke. O'Rourke was sure he'd be fired but he didn't care.

"Niles, for the last, and I *mean*, the last time, lay off of Lakota." O'Rourke's head was spinning.

O'Rourke thought that was the end of the subject for now as Engler rose to leave. Instead, Engler turned to O'Rourke. "What if I cut you and your guys loose to pursue partnerships and VAR agreements? Will that help?"

"It certainly will, as long as we don't create some kind of channel conflict. There are effects on the comp plan as well."

"At this point I don't care what we pay out as long as the revenue comes in. As far as conflicts, well, let's run with this and I'll play referee."

"I'm all over it," O'Rourke said, feeling like a dog let off his leash.

"One last thing. The cash situation is to be kept within this circle. Lakota isn't aware of it. We felt that we had to discuss this with you because of the effect on your organization."

"Bill, sales reps aren't stupid. When the plan changes they know it's for a reason. That will generate rumors for sure."

Engler opened the door for Niles.

"I know. Let's at least practice some plausible deniability. We can't allow the perception here or in the market that we may be facing a cash crunch," Engler said, lowering his voice as an engineer walked by.

***

Engler collapsed into his desk chair, stroked his beard and stared at the ceiling. He hated these constant confrontations between his senior management leaders. His admin, Sharon, entered the office with some mail.

"Okay, Bill, what's today's crisis?"

He continued to stare at the ceiling for a moment before responding. His only acknowledgement of the question was a low moan of pain. Finally, though, he sat up.

"Please close the door."

Sharon took a seat in one of the chairs facing Engler's desk, knowing what was coming. She had been Bill's assistant for several years and knew when he needed to vent.

"You know, Sharon, I started this company because I knew we had some great ideas. I had no doubts, though, that it took a lot more than ideas to build a successful company. I also didn't think I needed to be CEO."

"Yes," Sharon interjected. "That's why you brought in Chris Morrow, right?"

"Right. He was supposed to be the smart, experienced business guy. And look what happened? We didn't even have a product out the door, and I had to fire him, take over the CEO title and let go most of the people he hired into senior management. Only Lakota remains." *And he might be next,* he thought to himself.

"You didn't have much choice, Bill. Morrow spent more time drinking vodka martinis than running the business."

Engler shook his head. "But all the VC people recommended him! Where were they when he was screwing up? On *my* doorstep asking about when we'd start to see revenue. My worst fears are coming true. I can't focus solely on product anymore. I have to be referee between all these managers, not to mention the board. I wish people like O'Rourke and Brinks understood that."

"They all think their group is the most important. That's to be expected, isn't it?"

"I guess," he said, as he stood and gazed out his window toward the marina. "I really thought that I went into this with my eyes open, that we'd be one happy, hard working family."

"Bill, families squabble too, you know. It doesn't mean that they don't come together when necessary."

"I haven't seen much of that lately." He turned from the window to face Sharon. "I guess I have to deal with it. Thanks for listening, as usual."

***

It took Porter over an hour to get back to Merrill Lynch and Sean was getting a little nervous. Best and Cruz were entering uncharted territory and Sean was getting concerned about what they were attempting. They were clearly in a heated frenzy to test out all their scenarios. They were also extremely friendly now that they were being productive with InUnison.

"Sean! Check this out! We're getting automatic notifications of inventory changes! Do you have any idea how long we've wanted to do that on PCs? The analysts are going to be sporting some serious wood!" Sergio said, while grabbing Sean by the shoulders and shaking him for emphasis. "They've been screaming to tie things into their God-awful spreadsheets for years! You guys are fuckin' *geniuses!"*

"That's, ah, great, Serg," Sean said while trying to back away from Cruz's grasp. "Now, about the spreadsheet thing…I'm not clear how…"

It was too late. They were off and running again as Porter came into the lab.

"Sean, sorry it took so long. Lehman wasn't ready for us…" Porter was out of breath again.

"I was trying you on your cell phone. Did you turn it off?"

"No, we were in some bunker kind of thing and the cell phone didn't work. We got the connector installed, but we can't get the damn thing to work. They don't know their addressing schemes or anything. Julia decided that I better get this back to you…" he said, holding up the CD, "…so you can get going."

"Shit, Porter. It's already after two o'clock. We were supposed to be there right after noon."

"Yes, I know; they've been leaving me nasty messages. I called them back to say you are on the way. I think I have to get back to help Julia. How are things here?"

"Scary. These guys are doing things I don't think we knew could be done with our software. The good news is that they can be left alone."

"Porter, my MAN!" Sergio seized Porter by the arm and dragged him over to show what they had accomplished. Sean scampered out the door, heading for the elevator and then the cab stand on Vesey Street. Porter really wanted to get back to Julia but felt that he had to indulge these guys.

"Guys, this is really great stuff you've done. Would you mind if I went away? Julia needs some help and…"

William responded by waving his hand, saying, "We have your phone numbers. We'll check in later. JESUS! Look at that!"

Porter was out the door and onto the PATH for the fourth time that day.

***

Once back at Lehman's lobby, he paced like a child in need of a bathroom. *Please, I hope Julia has something working…why is this elevator so slow?* The car finally arrived and took him to the tenth floor. He stepped out and stopped to compose himself.

Why am I so flipped out about this?

Luckily someone was leaving the office so he was able to slip through the card access door without having to announce himself to the receptionist. He thought that he had turned into the right corridor but after passing the same administrative assistant three times, she stopped him.

"Hey, pal. I don't know you so can I help you or do I need to call security?"

"I'm sorry," Porter said, "I was looking for the computer lab. I was here earlier and thought I knew where I was going."

"Follow me, Hansel. I'll show you the way to the Wicked Witch's house."

She led him through the cubicle wasteland.

"Here you go. Hope you left some crumbs to find your way back out," the admin chuckled as she left.

"Julia, sorry it took me so long."

"Didn't miss you. We got things going here after they finally figured out the right names and addresses."

A wave of frustration flowed through him. *If you didn't need me to come back…"* It must have been obvious to Julia.

"Now, Porter, don't give me any shit. I still need you here. I don't know anything about mainframes and when they get out of their staff meeting, they are going to want to do real transactions. If you could help out on the first one, I can carry on."

He collapsed into a chair, still trying to slow down his pulse.

"Porter, you look a bit stressed."

"Stressed? Why would I be stressed? I'm only trying to fix three accounts at once and running all over town. I'm going to have to run back up to 21st Street to calm down PensAndClips. I feel like I'm screwing up right now."

"What are you bitching about? You have help. I know Sean and I need some training but imagine if we *weren't* here?"

"I know and I really appreciate it. I'm not used to juggling several things at once."

"At risk of being insensitive, get…used…to…it. Be glad you have the activity. I'm normally twiddling my thumbs."

Porter tried to snap out of his panic mode. "So, how are these guys treating you? Are they smart?"

"Yeah, pretty smart. Not like those Merrill guys though. Now, there's one creepy guy, Curt Weldin… if he keeps leaning on me and trying to look down my blouse I'm going to kick his balls into his cranium."

Porter winced and reflexively closed his legs a little tighter.

"I'll see if I can distract him."

Just then the three engineers returned to the lab. Weldin didn't waste time trying to return to his position behind Julia. Julia was ready for him though. When he got within one step of the back of her chair, she jumped up, pushing the wheeled desk chair straight back into his legs with a strong force that caught him directly in the knees.

"Oh! I'm so sorry, Curt," Julia said, as Curt gasped in pain. "Didn't see you there."

Porter had to suppress a chuckle and the knowing looks on Weldin's colleagues' faces revealed that they were in on the joke as well.

Memo: don't get on Julia's bad side, Porter thought, as he reached for his ringing cell phone.

"Porter, I need you up here," Sean said. "We can't get this thing installed. By the way, did you know they want to run this on Linux?"

"What the hell is Linux? I thought they were running Windows NT."

"It's open source UNIX. These guys are planning to use Linux on their production servers. We don't support it yet, and I don't think there's the newest Java for it yet either."

"Let me guess…did Gatto promise them that too?" Porter shivered at the thought.

"Thank goodness no. This is a recent decision by PensAndClips. They want to try our UNIX version out on it."

"Sean, I don't know what to do about this. What's your instinct?"

"Punt."

"We can't punt."

"Well, it won't work."

Shit. What do I do? I'm flying blind here. Hey… "Why don't you call Tony in engineering? Maybe he can figure something out." *This is going to be a nightmare.*

"I can't leave yet. We are at a crucial stage here. These guys aren't as quick as the Merrill guys."

"I'll call Tony and get back to you. We may have to defer until tomorrow anyway. The team here has some other things to finish tonight. That might buy us some time."

"I'll await your call."

Porter turned back to the group huddled around Julia in time to see her lean back from the screen.

"Pretty cool, huh?" Julia folded her arms in triumph and surveyed the Lehman team members, hoping that they were appropriately impressed. Wang Ling spoke first.

"That is very exciting to see this process. May I?"

"Absolutely. Have at it." Julia stood up and relinquished her seat.

She and Porter stepped just outside the room.

"Porter, I think they are off and running finally. They're a little thick but that last example pushed them over the hump."

"Speaking of humping, you made your point with Curt. He's been giving you some space."

"Occupational hazard. So, we've fixed Merrill and these guys are fixed. How's Sean doing?"

"Not well." He explained Sean's situation to Julia who didn't have any better ideas.

"He's going to check in with us after he talks to Tony."

"I have a suggestion," Julia said. "Let's get out of here before they find something else for us to do, go back to the Marriott and wait for Sean there. I need to pick your brain about some things."

"Great idea! That will give me a chance to update Wayne as well."

***

Phil Lansing picked up his InUnison logo coffee mug, took a sip of lukewarm coffee and grimaced in disappointment. He got up to walk down to the kitchen to get a refill of Peet's hazelnut brew.

Inside the "café", as they called it internally, he walked past some engineers perusing the Silicon Valley trade newspapers on the kitchen island counter.

The normally chatty engineers were whispering to themselves as Lansing made a beeline to the coffee makers on the long black granite counter.

"So, how are you guys doing?" he asked.

"Oh, peachy, dude," Alex Belky, an engineer working on the InUnison tools crankily replied.

"What did Brinks do today? You get some new requirements or something?"

"No. Wondering when we will see some revenue for our hard work."

"Can't help you there much. I know sales are under the gun."

"Big fuckin' deal," Belky said. "This software should sell itself. We shouldn't be in this situation."

Paul Linsky, the other engineer in the kitchen, gave Belky a panicky shake of the head.

"What do you mean by 'this situation'?" Lansing asked.

"Well, Linsky here overheard Engler talk about a 'cash crunch'. Revenue isn't happening, dude."

"Oh, c'mon. We have plenty of cash."

"Look, man, I know what I heard," Linsky said. "It's only a matter of time before layoffs happen."

Lansing didn't want to believe this. "Look, guys, the first quarter is always a down quarter and most orders close late in the quarter anyway. No doubt they figured that into the equation."

"Well, I'm not going to sit still with a loser," Belky said. "I can do better elsewhere where my stock options will be worth something."

Lansing started to panic on his own. He couldn't afford to start losing engineers for his products on unfounded rumors. *But what if,* he thought.

"Look, let me check into this."

"Yeah, dude. Quickly."

***

"Wayne? Porter. Where are you right now?"

"I'm hanging out in Timothy's on Water Street. How about you?"

"I'm here with Julia in the Marriott lobby waiting to hear from Sean."

"Are you guys wrapping up for the day?"

"Depends on Sean. He was having some difficulties at PensAndClips."

"Damn. That's one I really need…"

"Don't panic. We left Merrill and Lehman in good shape." His call waiting beeped. "Oh, that might be Sean. Hold on Wayne." He hit the "send" button. "Hello, this is Porter."

"Sean here. They kicked me out for the day and I didn't get a hold of Tony yet. I left messages all over HQ for him. Surprisingly they aren't pissed at us here. We did get things installed on a Windows NT machine."

"How far did you get with it?"

"Really only installed it and made a connection. Then they had to split and asked me to come back tomorrow."

"That works for you, right Sean?"

"Not really, but I'll do it anyway. Where are you and Julia?"

"We're back in the Marriott lobby. Come on down here. We'll debrief and plan for tomorrow."

"I hope debriefing includes cold adult beverages."

"You bet, Sean!" They hung up. Porter started to put his cell phone into his pocket when it rang.

"This is Porter."

"Did you forget about me?" an annoyed Wayne said.

"Oh, shit, sorry. That was Sean. He's coming down here as soon as he can jump on the subway."

"Great. I'll be there after making a few more phone calls. I'll buy dinner. Later." He hung up before Porter could say "thank you".

He sat down next to Julia, leaned back and rubbed his eyes. "Sean and Wayne are both on their way. Julia, please tell me this kind of day is abnormal."

"Like I said before, I'd love to have more of 'this kind of day'.

"I feel like I don't have control…"

"You don't. Don't expect to."

"But, how does anything get done?"

"What do you mean 'get done'? The only concrete event in software sales is taking down the order. But that simply guarantees that we, the SEs, get more work with a customer. It never ends, Porter."

They decided to drop their briefcases in their rooms, make some phone calls and await Sean.

***

Porter, first to return to the Marriott lobby, spotted Sean Murphy running through the Marriott lobby.

"Porter! Great news! Tony let me know that we have already tested our UNIX versions on Linux, and with a few tweaks, it just works! He called me about it when I got out of the subway."

"That's a relief. I don't suppose we can get that version early, can we? Brinks will freak out won't she?"

"She freaks easily. I was amazed that you got the mainframe connector without going out there and burning your own CD."

"You can do that?"

"As long as you grease some palms in Engineering. Although, Brinks caught me once. Boy, did she make a stink with Young…"

"I should have guessed that you would have done a black bag job. How did you pull it off?"

"I was out in HQ for a customer visit when Kyle calls up all panicked about Berkshire Holdings hitting bugs and needing an updated version. So I'm there late at night, sort of hanging out, and, gee, the server room just happens to be open and there just happens to be a CD burner in there, and gee, I just happen to find a blank CD which miraculously finds it's way into the CD burner and somehow the new version of the broker got written onto the CD. Showed up at Berkshire the next day via the miracle of FedEx. Unfortunately, Brinks found out from an engineer and bitched to the Youngster."

"What did Young do?"

"Oh, he read me the riot act about how we can't be ripping off Engineering or giving pre-release stuff to customers, blah blah blah."

"How can you be so blasé about pissing off your manager?" Porter was still in awe of Sean.

"Because right after he chewed me out, he shook my hand and said 'keep up the good work.' After all, we closed a quarter-million dollar deal because of it." Murphy broke into a very lecherous grin. "Kyle bought me a case of Jack Daniels on that one. So, where's Julia?"

"We both went up to our rooms and dropped our bags."

"You're staying here?"

"I thought we might be wrapping up late and didn't want to get home late only to stagger back into town tomorrow."

Sean grinned at Porter. "Separate rooms, I hope. Or do you have that 'adjoining room' thing going?"

Sean collapsed in laughter as he saw Porter's face turn beet red. The rooms were in fact adjoining but opening the intervening door hadn't occurred to Porter. Sean twisted the knife further.

"Watch out, Porter. She's a black widow. She'll eat you after sex."

"Sean, that's one of our esteemed colleagues you're denigrating." *After that balls and cranium thing at Lehman, though, I believe it.* "But I'll take it under advisement."

"Now, she didn't say she 'respected' you, did she? I was in Atlanta helping her on a project last year. One night, we went out with a couple of her college buds, gorgeous like Julia. I was alone with one of the friends and asked if Julia was seeing anyone. She laughed. 'No, Julia hasn't found any one to respect yet'. I asked what she meant by that. Apparently, Julia has a fetish about men she can respect. Really turns her on."

"Well, I guess we all have something that's a turn on," Porter said, uncomfortable to be talking about Julia's "fetishes".

Julia walked up, her timing uncanny as usual. "Hi, guys. Still no Wayne? Porter, what's wrong with your face? It's all blotchy."

That comment didn't help his "blotches".

"Wayne's on his way. Why don't we go into Tall Ships and get a beverage. He'll find us in there."

The three of them walked through the etched glass doorway into the bar at the corner of the hotel. They found a table next to the outer door and ordered a round of drinks.

"There's Wayne now," Porter said, waving to Wayne who was outside talking on his cell phone. He put up a finger to acknowledge the wave and indicate that he'd be a minute.

"Helen, please. I have to take care of these people. They are really getting me out of a jam. If I'm going to make my Number this quarter…"

"I don't give a damn about your precious Number, Wayne. You sold me on this job over something stable like Oracle because you'd be home more. And it's not only dinner tonight; you said you'd have to stay in town for that show next week. I'm tired of being a single mom."

"Oh, right; I always equate Oracle with home life stability. Anyway, you *should* care about my Number; it's what's going to keep you in beemers and the kids educated in those swell private schools you adore."

"Are we still going skiing this weekend or are you going to be obsessing?"

Damn! He had forgotten about the Catskills trip.

"What's the point? There's no snow. It hasn't even been cold enough to make snow up there."

"Wayne, it isn't really about skiing. It's to check out the McCarthy's condo to see if we want to buy it."

"Listen, we aren't buying a condo. Forget it."

"All our friends have one."

Wayne refused to continue the debate. "I have to go."

Helen wasn't going to let him.

"I don't suppose you would consider a *real* job…"

"Don't start this again!"

"… at a *real* company. Maybe then you'd feel comfortable owning a ski cottage."

"I'm hanging up, Helen."

"Go ahead, be a masochist. I'm tired of playing therapist with you."

"Gee, thanks for your support." *Therapist, my ass.*

Wayne pocketed his phone and gazed up Liberty Street toward Broadway before turning to enter Tall Ships. *I'm used to having* some *revenue always coming in. I can't confidently see a single dollar yet this quarter.* He tried to pull himself together as he entered the bar. He never wanted to be negative in front of Porter who was rapidly becoming his fountain of youth.

Watching his partner's phone conversation through the window, Porter could tell it was not a pleasant one. He hoped the news of their progress would cheer him up.

"Hey, Wayne. You know these guys, right?"

"I certainly remember Sean," he said, reaching over the table to shake his hand. He turned to Julia. "I don't think we met though. Julia, right?"

"Yes Wayne, pleased to meet you. You've got quite an exciting patch up here."

"I could do with a little less of this kind of 'excitement'. So, what's the good news?"

"We've nailed down Merrill and Lehman for sure. PensAndClips pulled a bit of a fast one on us," Porter said. Sean explained the Linux situation to Wayne.

"…so you may have to fight with Brinks on this."

"Well," Wayne said, enjoying a sip of his draft beer. "…I think I still have the support of O'Rourke." He thought for a second. "You know, this could work to our advantage. We could possibly push PensAndClips into the win column by creating a special deal for Linux…" He trailed off into thought.

"That's so cool," Sean said. "I love a rep who thinks strategically."

"So do I," Julia said. "I never get the chance to see it at home."

"You mean Gary?" Wayne asked, re-engaging in the conversation. "I don't want you to violate any confidences but…"

"Oh, not to worry," Julia said, interrupting. "The guy is totally clueless. I don't know how he ever got this far in sales. He sits by the phone most of the time thinking that leads will simply drop on him like manna from heaven," she said while raising and lowering her hands, wiggling her fingers. "When, miraculously, a lead does come in, he seizes it without adequately qualifying the opportunity. Then he throws the account to me to figure out how to make it work technically so he can go back into phone stakeout mode."

"What do you know about Azalea in Atlanta? Porter mentioned to me that you knew someone there. To be honest, I don't want to share, but if we get something up here we'll logically like to spread it out to the subsidiaries."

"I don't know him real well but I met the CIO for the insurance business at a seminar – what was it, Gartner or some analyst organization like that, doesn't matter – name was Spencer Carls…bad…ton…something like that." She silently cursed herself for not remembering. He was one of the most attractive men she had met recently, sort of a Pierce Brosnan look-alike, with a swagger to match.

"Anyway," Julia continued. We talked for a long time. Smart guy, seemed to get what we do. I passed his card on to Grim and of course he didn't follow up."

The waiter arrived. "You folks want to look over the menu?"

"Yes, we need a couple minutes," Wayne replied. "By the way, I'll pick this up tonight. You guys have done a great job bailing me out."

"That's another good sign of a quality rep; takes care of the talent," Sean said, raising his glass in appreciation.

The server left menus as Wayne refocused the conversation.

"Now, Julia, I shouldn't do this but…"

"You want me to call the Azalea guy, and not tell Gary, right?"

"You sort of read my mind, but no; I only want the guy's phone number. I'd like to prod Porter's friend Norm to engage with him. We'll clue Gary in when we need to. But it would be totally improper for me to talk to this Spencer guy without letting Gary in on it. Johnson made it clear that he wants to drive the bus on this. Frankly, I have real misgivings about putting all my eggs in his basket." He saw Porter put down his beer, a hurt look crossing his face. "Porter, he's a good guy but I don't think he knows who and what he's up against."

Julia reached into her handbag and rummaged around for her Palm Pilot. Finding it, she looked up the Azalea contact.

"Here he is; Spencer Carlton. You have something to write this down on?

"Here, zap it," Wayne said, pulling out his Palm Pilot. They exchanged the entry electronically.

"Don't you love that? It's like electronic sex," Sean offered.

"Sean, can't you ever keep comments to yourself?" Julia asked.

"I'd hate for the world to miss my pearls of wisdom…"

She turned back to Wayne. "This guy is sharp and he's carved out his own organization at Azalea. He doesn't seem to get much interference from IT."

"And now for something completely different," Sean said with a big grin. "Wayne, did Porter describe how we managed to work in three separate locations with one copy of software?"

"C'mon Sean, can't we let it go?" Porter's face deflated into shame.

"Well, the Keystone Kops would be proud of your boy here…" Sean launched into a detailed account of the day, never missing an opportunity to skewer Porter. He tried to defend himself but was no match for Sean Murphy, the seasoned roaster. Porter was especially anguished when Julia offered some jabs as well.

"To a great team of SEs," Wayne said, raising his glass.

"And especially to Porter," Julia added. "Welcome to sales!"

***

The next day, Porter, Julia and Sean went their separate ways, continuing to "divide and conquer" the remaining issue accounts. Sergio at Merrill Lynch had been kind enough to let them burn extra copies of the software so that there would be no more running around with a single CD.

After a very odd solo performance with Sampson Logistics in a Jersey City apartment, Porter returned to the Marriott where he would check in with Julia and Sean from the comfort of the second floor lobby. The first call he placed was to Wayne, thinking he could use some good news. Porter reached him in his home office.

"Wayne, I figured you'd want an update on our progress."

"I'm all ears," Wayne said as he leaned back in his chair and put his feet up on the desk.

Porter went through each account: Potential Investing, Merrill Lynch, Lehman Brothers, PensAndClips.com and Merit Solutions.

"Porter, I'm truly amazed. You three really got us out of a hole."

"I'd love to take all the credit, Wayne, but without Sean's and Julia's experience, I would have screwed it up."

"C'mon, Porter. Allow yourself some ego-boosting credit. You got all the activity organized, after all, and had to essentially train Sean and Julia on the new software…"

"All one copy of it."

"Hey, if it had been that big a deal, they wouldn't have teased you about it."

"Wayne, I really *am* psyched about getting these accounts straight. We're on a roll, aren't we?"

"Yes, I'm psyched!" Wayne lied. He shook his head, knowing that all of Porter's Herculean efforts only brought them back to square one.

"Potential and Merrill are likely to upgrade and the PensAndClips deal is still moving, right?"

"That's topic numero uno with Fred Lakota Thursday."

Wayne sat back up as he reviewed some of his notes. "Hey, you haven't told me about Sampson Logistics. What went on there?"

"Oh, my," Porter said. "I wanted to have a good long talk with you about them. I went over to their systems office…"

"Fort Lee, right?"

"No, Jersey City, in an apartment building. I get there, thinking that I've got to be in the wrong place. Sure enough they have converted a three bedroom apartment into a computer center. Now, get this, the whole team is comprised of Russians. The lead guy, Boris Morosov, treated me like I was some spy. He wouldn't even let me *see* what he was doing. He installed the software and started hacking stuff. All the other engineers got excited for a while but then went back to work. As soon as he was satisfied with the connector, Boris rushed me out the door."

Wayne started to laugh. "Those Russkies are all over Wall Street. What I'm told is that there are a lot of smart Russian computer people over there with time on their hands. They are supposed to be amazing. See, back before the Soviet Union blew up, they pirated software from all over the world, particularly the US. Since they seldom had documentation, they'd reverse engineer the stuff.

They also are supposed to be math geniuses."

"Is it legal?"

"Porter, sometimes you don't want to know. All I know is that it's a trend, legal or otherwise."

"Well, I'm not comfortable parachuting our software in and then leaving people to their own devices."

"Actually, you should wish for more people like these. Makes your job a hell of a lot easier. There's a finite number of smart customers, ya know."

"But how are we going to get more orders out of them when they are so secretive?"

Wayne fished for the Sampson account folder. "Let's see… right. I thought there was another contact at Sampson and he doesn't sound Russian. Mike Giuliano, Operations Director, based at HQ in Fort Lee." Wayne glanced at his watch; five-thirty. "Let's try him."

He put Porter on hold and dialed Giuliano. As luck would have it, he answered.

"Hello, this is Wayne Angelis of InUnison Software. I wanted to introduce myself as your new representative."

"Oh, yes. Just got a glowing review from our software guys. They can be a rough bunch but were thrilled to get the new software."

Porter shook his head.

"Yes," Wayne said, "my Systems Engineer, Porter Mitchell, was with them today." He introduced Porter over the phone. "I have to say that it was a, um, different type of visit for him."

Giuliano laughed. "Let me guess. Boris wouldn't let him in the office?"

"Oh, I got into the office; I couldn't see anything," Porter said.

"Well, you got farther than most. Look, don't take it personally. I have to beat the shit out of those Russky jaggoffs sometimes to find out what they are doing. Once I had to withhold their pay."

"I'll get right to it. Now that we've finally fulfilled our initial commitment, I'd like to schedule a visit and see what future opportunity there may be at Sampson for InUnison."

"Sky's the limit. We need to talk about an enterprise agreement ASAP."

Wayne swooned, steadying himself with the arms of his chair. He managed to rally himself and calmly continued.

"We'd like to see that as well, Mike. When can we meet?"

"Friday, one o'clock."

Wayne swooned again. "In Fort Lee?"

"Yes, our office is on Fletcher Avenue, near CNBC."

"I know it well. See you at one o'clock, Friday."

Giuliano said goodbye and the beep indicated he had dropped off of the conference call.

"Wayne? What just happened?"

"He wants to do an enterprise deal. The whole smash."

"Just like that?"

"Just like that." *And pigs will fly,* he thought. *I'm going to walk in there Friday and he's going to tell me he was kidding.*

Wayne ran through the developments in his head. *Hey! Things* are *looking up and maybe we* are *over the hump. Sign PandC to a VAR agreement; upgrade Potential and Merrill; close this major agreement with Sampson; should at least get some developer licenses from Azalea…yes, the quarter is finally coming into focus.*

"Wayne, you still there?"

"Sorry, Porter, I was thinking…yes…the quarter might not be a lost cause."

"Great! Oh, one more thing. I've been asked to stop by Azalea on Thursday. Apparently they have made some progress but IT isn't giving them access to the mainframes. I could head there right after our breakfast meeting."

"That would be great. Glad to hear they are off and running." *Yes, developer seats, at least.* "Well, you get going and tell Sean and Julia thanks again. I'll figure out a way to show my gratitude."

Wayne went over the opportunities one more time to be sure he wasn't imagining anything. Satisfied, he shut down his office for the day. His wife was astonished to see him emerging from his home office before six o'clock.

"So, do I interpret this surprise as good news or are you giving up?" Helen asked.

"I'm declaring that we are over the hump, and the Number is in my sights."

"Well, that's quite a change in demeanor from last week. But no doubt something will intrude before long."

"Thanks, burst my bubble. What's for dinner?"

"Dunno," Helen said. "Blake, Danny and Eileen just finished mac and cheese."

"Homemade?"

"Get real."

Wayne was the only real cook in the family and never passed up the opportunity to remind her.

"Fine. I'll fire up the grill," Wayne said. "I know we have some strip steaks somewhere. Think you can handle some salad, at least?"

***

"Stewart? This is Mordecai. Norm Johnson called, again, about the mainframe access. I guess that McNaughton guy gave up or is kicking it up the line. We don't want to piss them off any longer, do we? Next step is Racker, right? I don't feel comfortable pushing them off."

"Keep your skull cap on, Mordi," Miller told his Data Security Manager, Mordecai Rozensweig. "Drag it out a little longer. Wait until lunchtime to call them back. Then tell them to come down and get the forms."

"They say they need access by Thursday, something about a vendor or a consultant coming in."

Hmm. Who could that be? It would be nice to know who they are dealing with. "Get them set up with the absolute minimum. Then offer your services to them for Thursday. I want to find out who the vendor or consultant is. What can they really accomplish anyway? There's no way they can pull off what they are trying to do." *It will be simply another failed attempt to circumvent my authority.*

Chapter 8 Friendly Fire

Porter arrived at the Waldorf-Astoria by seven a.m. and Wayne was not far behind, appearing in the ornate lobby before Porter could find a chair.

"Porter, I love your attention to time. I never feel like I have to remind you a million times where to be and when. Some of my other SEs couldn't get from point A to point B without their mother's help."

"Thanks, but getting here from the PATH isn't rocket science. Oh, before I forget, Young wants me to do some SE interviews over the next few weeks."

"Fine with me," Wayne said. He was lost in thought and then... *Oh, no!*

"Where are these SEs going to be based?" he asked Porter.

"I think New York or New Jersey."

"Did he say anything about more reps coming on board? I can't imagine that we'd be hiring SEs without reps. Much as I'd love to have some more technical talent around, it would be unprecedented to have more SEs than reps."

"Now, don't panic about territory yet. Let me try to find out some things first. Maybe they are only going to add someone in New Jersey."

"Well, that's still my turf. If it wasn't for the blasted Gatto accounts, we'd have been doing some prospecting over there. Christ, AT&T alone has stuff all over the place, Johnson&Johnson, ADP …" he said while closing his eyes and slouching back in his armchair. *Why wasn't I at least making some phone calls? Damn, damn, damn!*

"Guess I shouldn't have told you about the interviews, but you really may be overreacting."

"Porter, my naïve Porter," Wayne said, patting Porter's knee. "In a growing startup like this, there will be a constant influx of new reps and splitting of territories. It pays to be paranoid about these things; I can't afford to ignore it. Plan on doing a New Jersey blitz after the show next week." *I'm not going to make it easy for Presby to take it away.* "You *do* still remember how to demo?"

Porter suddenly realized that in his almost three weeks with the company, he still had presented precisely once, at Manley Brothers, and that hadn't gone all that well. A wave of anxiety washed through him.

"Well, I guess I can get some practice at the show…" *More likely I'll be working late again on demos and PowerPoint…*

Wayne noticed a gentleman wearing a shiny, black silk, double-breasted suit, complete with white handkerchief in the breast pocket. His jet-black hair was slicked back. *Ah yes, I remember the style.* "Porter, our breakfast host has arrived, direct from Gentlemen's Quarterly."

Porter looked up and recognized Fred Lakota as well. Wayne stood up and gave Lakota a wave of his hand. Lakota returned the gesture with a quick tilt of his head and advanced briskly across the lobby.

"Good morning, Fred. Wayne Angelis and this is Porter Mitchell."

"Pleased to put a face with the name, Wayne," Lakota said, forgetting, again, that he had indeed seen Wayne's face at the kickoff. "Shall we go to Peacock Alley? I find their breakfast exquisite."

"Kinda pricey, though, Fred. I think we could find something a little more reasonable."

"Not to worry, Wayne. I find the atmosphere of this restaurant so conducive to business that it is well worth the cost," Lakota said, as he turned to head toward the restaurant. Wayne and Porter raised their eyebrows at each other and followed.

They were led to a table in the middle of the floor. Lakota protested the location.

"Sir, this is not acceptable. We are having an important meeting. Could we have something a bit more discrete?"

The maître d' scanned the room and offered a corner table.

"Yes, that will be fine. Thank you so much."

"So, Wayne," Lakota said, without looking up from his menu. "How's business?"

Wayne closed his menu and turned to Lakota. "To be honest, it's been a struggle. I think that you are aware that Porter and I have had to clean up some messes left over from the Gatto tenure."

"Certainly, Wayne. You should know that, at the end of the day, you have nothing but 110% support from Business Development," Lakota said, karate chopping the table for emphasis. "What can I do to help you sell, Wayne?"

"Fred, I really need two things from you: a Value-Added Reseller agreement for PensAndClips and some major partnerships signed up."

"I'll get to the VAR contract, but…" he looked from side to side very dramatically, and continued in a very subdued tone, "…I think we will be able to announce a major partnership with Flanderson Consulting soon. I'm meeting with them today, as a matter of fact."

"When is that meeting? It doesn't conflict with PensAndClips this morning, right?"

"Of course not, Wayne. I saved lunch for Flanderson," he said with a wink. "I'm taking them to Tribeca Grill. Bobby might be there."

"Whose Bobby?" Porter asked.

"Please! Bobby DeNiro! He owns the place. I thought everyone knew that."

"Impressive," Wayne said, sarcastically. "But back to the terms with Flanderson…"

"May I take your order?" interrupted the waiter.

Lakota ordered first. "I'd like the eggs benedict. Please check that the hollandaise is hot this time, will you? Last time, it was abysmal. Thank you, my good man. Oh, and a mimosa."

The waiter made a note and turned without expression to Wayne. "I'll have the fresh fruit plate."

"Three egg cheddar omelet, sausage," Porter ordered.

"Fred, about Flanderson –"

"Would you like breakfast potatoes?"

"Yes, please."

"So, Fred, about Flanderson …"

"Toast, sir?"

"Yes, wheat," Porter answered, hoping there weren't any more questions.

Wayne tried again. "What is going to be our arrangement with Flanderson? It's my understanding that they usually want equity and several projects which they can use prepaid licenses for."

"Wayne," Lakota said with a condescending smile, "have you ever negotiated a major partnership like this?"

"Personally? No. But I've participated –"

"Well, then, Wayne, you should know that these things are very complex, very touchy. We have to build a strong personal relationship among our peer managers before even talking about money. We are very close to talking monetary details; that's how successful I've been with them." He took a triumphant sip of coffee, pinky finger out.

Wayne breathed deeply. "So what's the target date?"

"Please, Wayne, I can't be held to a certain 'date'," Lakota said, hooking his fingers in the air. "We look to do partnerships when the relationships are ready for them."

"How do you know when it's 'ready', Fred? It's really just another form of sales."

"I'm surprised at you, Wayne. I would have thought that with your experience, you would have more appreciation for the 'dance'," Lakota said, with dancing fingers in the air.

Dance? "I'm trying to get a handle on where we are with any partnership agreements and what your strategy is for going after them." Wayne continued for fifteen minutes trying to open up Lakota to no avail. He paused when the waiter arrived with their breakfasts.

Lakota tested his sauce.

"Is the hollandaise acceptable, sir?"

"Marginally. Please inform the kitchen that their quality is clearly on the decline."

"Certainly, sir. And your breakfasts, gentlemen?" he said, looking at Wayne and Porter.

"Fine, thank you," Wayne replied. Porter, already with a mouthful of toast, nodded in agreement.

As the waiter turned to leave, Wayne noticed a raised eyebrow directed toward Lakota.

"Look, Fred, we have no partnerships. None. Now, I can go sign up a bunch of local boutique firms but I need a standard agreement. Even so, they aren't going to drive demand. I need a big player like Flanderson to give me some pull in my market."

"Wayne, at the end of the day, we, all of us in BD, have that goal as priority number one," he said, hand chopping the table again. "And we will achieve that, not only with Flanderson but with CSC, Ernst and Young, EDS, Perot, you name them, we are going to go after them."

"So, discussions are underway with all of those?" *Riiiight.*

"As soon as we wrap up FC we will work on the others."

"So, there aren't any other discussions…"

"Wayne, these things take time…"

"Certainly you have some goal in mind."

"Now, heh heh, Wayne, I know how you sales reps work; I give you a date and you'll run with it, telling everyone. Pretty soon I'll actually have a *deadline*."

Heaven forbid. "Well, it would be helpful to have some idea –"

"To do what? If I told you Q2, what would you do about it?"

"I'd start marketing to them immediately, do some seminars, stuff like that."

"That would be up to us, Wayne. That's our responsibility."

"So, you *don't* want Sales to sell with Flanderson?"

"Of course I do. That's part of the relationship-building."

"But you haven't used Sales yet to start building this relationship. When can we get involved?"

"Soon, Wayne. Soon."

"Weeks, months?"

"Soon."

Wayne clenched his teeth. "So, maybe you could expand on what your vision is for how we are going to work with them on the ground."

"It's a work in progress."

"You have discussed that with them, right? You have to set specific rules about account control. Otherwise we'll end up selling in conflict with them."

"Wayne, trust me, we will own the sales cycle."

"So, how will that work? Frankly, I'm skeptical."

"Wayne, why is this so important?"

"I'm trying to get control of my territory, so if you're going to close with Flanderson soon, I need to include that in my planning."

"I see. Well, at the end of the day, it's still a work in progress. Very touchy right now."

Porter devoured his breakfast while watching this tennis match between Lakota and Wayne. Wayne's bulging neck veins told Porter that his partner was ready to snap.

"Give me a straight *fucking* answer!" Wayne shouted, reaching the end of his patience.

Porter choked on his bite of sausage. A couple of neighboring tables halted their conversations, and glanced over at them. Lakota sat up straight and delicately dabbed his mouth with his napkin.

"Wayne, I don't appreciate your choice of words. Perhaps an apology is in order."

"I'll apologize when you explain where we are with these partnership efforts."

"They are ongoing, Wayne."

Wayne gave up. "We need to finish up here and get over to PensAndClips. Do you happen to have the VAR agreement with you for me to review?"

"Of course not, Wayne. I haven't received it back from Legal."

"Fred, you *promised* me that you'd have it for this meeting!" he said, fighting back more obscenities. "We cannot go in there empty-handed. There would be no point to the meeting."

"Wayne, we need to do more qualification anyway."

"BULLSHIT!" Wayne couldn't help himself but quieted down quickly. "There is no point in you attending this meeting without the paperwork."

"Suit yourself, Wayne. But, at the end of the day, there won't be an agreement without my involvement. Check please!"

"Wayne, I have to get going," Porter said. "Norm Johnson is expecting me at Azalea. They seem to need a hand with the mainframe connector." Neither noticed that Lakota was making a note.

"Thanks for breakfast. I'll let you know how you can continue to 'help' me," Wayne said, adding emphasis with his own finger quote marks.

The sales team walked from the restaurant.

"The week started so well. We, sorry, you, fixed all those mainframe customers, your update yesterday was great, the opportunity at Sampson is awesome. I was really turning myself around and after one meeting with Lakota I'm back on the ledge. I'm going to get crucified at PensAndClips. Now I know what Dave Young meant by not being able to hold a productive conversation with that guy." He glanced at his watch. "I have an hour before PandC. I have to get Presby."

"I'm off to Azalea. Hang in there, Wayne."

"Hey, one last thing. Check that Norm made contact with his counterpart in Atlanta. I'd like to know what he thinks about any angle we can play there."

Porter disappeared onto Park Avenue to hunt down a subway downtown as Wayne dialed Presby.

"This is Ken."

"Ken, Angelis here."

"Good morning! How you doing? Got any good news?"

"Yes I do, but first the bad news." He recounted the breakfast with Lakota.

"The Waldorf, huh? Just like that swanky bastard."

"Ken, I really don't care about his taste in hotels or men's haberdashery. What am I supposed to do about PensAndClips? They are expecting the VAR agreement."

"So, why don't you give them one?"

Huh? Is he playing some game here? "Ken, Lakota won't give it to me, says it's still in Legal."

"That's a lie, and you know he doesn't control VARs anymore."

"Excuse me?"

"Oh, I'm sorry. I guess we haven't talked since Monday. Engler gave O'Rourke the freedom to close these VAR deals through the sales force. Didn't Lakota tell you that?"

"OF COURSE NOT! He said, quote, 'all VAR deals have to go through me'."

"Well, again, he's either misinformed or lying as usual. Anyway, do you have access to a fax machine? I can fax the draft agreement."

Wayne, briefly flummoxed, gathered himself and realized where he was. "Hold on Ken." He walked back to the Waldorf's registration desk. "What's your fax number?" A desk receptionist handed him a card with the hotel phone numbers. He ran his finger down it. "Ken, it's 212-555-3399." He turned back to the receptionist. "I'm not staying here. Can I get a fax sent here anyway?"

"It would be my pleasure. There will, of course, be a courtesy fee," he said with a friendly grin.

Naturally. "Okay, Ken, go ahead. I'll call you in a few minutes to confirm."

The receptionist delivered the fax in less than five minutes. Wayne turned to leave.

"Oh, sir?" the receptionist asked.

"Oh, right," Wayne said, reaching for his billfold. He peeled off a ten. "Is that sufficient? Please give me a receipt."

The receptionist returned with a handwritten receipt, but no change. "Have a nice day, sir."

"Thanks." Wayne scanned the agreement. *Looks straightforward. Upfront license structure, royalty fee schedule for deals with InUnison embedded into the VAR's product.* He stuffed the pages into his briefcase and dialed Presby as he left the hotel.

"Got it, Ken. Thanks."

"So, I know you're in a hurry but what was the good news?"

Wayne stopped on Park Avenue to figure out which direction to go, but also to compose what he would tell his boss.

"The SEs did great. We have the mainframe connector installed at most of the problem accounts. At least Potential and Merrill have indicated that they will be buying more. If the VAR thing works for PandC, we should see revenue there as well."

"That's it?" Presby didn't hide his disappointment.

"Shit, that's a lot! We fixed all that crap Gatto left, what more do you want?"

"Revenue, of course."

What an asshole. It never ends, Wayne thought. *There's no way I'm going to talk about Sampson yet. Remember, 'under promise, over deliver'. Besides, it's too good to be true.* He had returned to "glass half empty" mode.

"I ought to get *some* credit for getting us back to zero."

"I'll give you a hearty handshake next time I'm in the Big Apple. By the way, I'm taking a long weekend, so if you need me, leave me messages; I will be calling in for them but don't expect immediate turnaround. Until then, let's go sell! Beat –"

"Oh, Ken there's one other thing. I'm hearing that..." Wayne stopped himself. He was about to ask about the interviews but quickly decided that until he could stuff his pipeline, he shouldn't let Presby know that *he* knew. "Oh, never mind. That was for Porter."

"Like I said, let's go sell! Beat..."

Wayne clicked off before having to endure Presby's tagline.

***

Julia was not glad to be back in the office. It would mean having to deal with more of Gary Reaper's reality distortion. She normally worked out of her home office, like most of the InUnison field sales teams, but Reaper had insisted that he needed the "cachet" of a business address and Presby's predecessor had relented. She only used the stark, undecorated office when Gary asked her to come in, as he had in his voicemail of the prior day.

Julia left her Alpharetta, Georgia home at seven o'clock hoping to miss the horrendous morning traffic on Route 19 inbound to I-285, the beltway – or "perimeter" – around Atlanta. There was also the small consolation that she would have a couple of hours or so before Gary showed up. He always complained about the traffic but it apparently never occurred to him to change his routine to miss it or even think about working at home for a while.

She was wrapping up the emails and her overdue expense reports when Reaper joined her in their shared office. She tried to be civil.

"Good morning, Gary. You survive without me?"

"I guess so. Of course, I had to cancel some things since you were sent to New York."

What bullshit, she thought. She knew he had been either hanging out in the office or playing golf.

"So, what's up? You said you needed me in here today?"

"Yes, we have a sales call today and I'd like to adjust the pitch a little."

"Gary, we always end up doing the tried and true no matter how much we play around with it. So, who's the victim anyway?"

"Spencer Carlton at Azalea Insurance," he said, not making eye contact.

Uh, oh, she thought. "Oh, that's cool," she said, feigning enthusiasm. "Are we collaborating with the New York guys then? Porter and I worked really well together."

Gary turned his back on Julia, shuffling some papers. "Uh, I'm sure we'll be able to leverage each other's work."

"So, what did Wayne have to say?" she asked, hoping that he had indeed talked to Wayne Angelis.

"Uh, I, I..." Gary had to pause.

Go ahead Gary; be creative with your fiction, Julia thought.

"I left him a voicemail but haven't heard back from him…"

Julia figured that Reaper had done nothing of the sort. "When is this meeting?"

"In half an hour. We need to change the slides –"

"*Thirty minutes??* And you expect me to be prepared?" *How am I going to get word to Wayne?*

"They're practically next door. Just on the other side of Perimeter Center. Okay, we don't need to change the slides. You can do this stuff in your sleep. We should go now anyway, I guess," Reaper said, still not making eye contact with Julia.

As they packed up to leave, Julia hoped for one last, desperate chance to get word to Wayne or Porter.

"Gary, let's take separate cars. I have to run a couple errands afterward."

He finally looked at her, and with suspicion.

Once in her car for the ten minute drive, she dialed Wayne but only got voice mail. She didn't leave a message but tried Porter instead. She failed there as well.

"Damn you, Reaper!" she said. As she turned onto Peachtree Dunwoody Road, she saw Reaper was already in the office parking lot looking for her. She put her phone away, frustrated.

***

"Julia, thank you very much for that update. That Rule Agent demo is especially impressive," Spencer Carlton said. "With these improvements over what you showed me a few months ago, I'm much more interested in the product." *And in you,* he wished he could say.

"Thank you very much, Spencer. I look forward to –"

"Spencer, I'd like to offer Julia's time to get a project going…"

Damn you! Julia resented Reaper's interruption which caused Spencer to turn away from her.

"…provide knowledge transfer, mentorship. When can she start?"

"Whoa! Gary, slow down. I have to see what resource I can bring to bear and what would make a likely pilot project. I'll certainly take you up on your offer, but not until I figure out what they would work on." He reluctantly allowed his fiduciary duty to overcome his desire to see more of Julia around the office.

"Well, you should know, Spencer," Julia began, "that there is some talent in your New York headquarters."

"Oh, really? Who is that?"

Reaper shot a look of pure hatred at Julia. "Julia, we really shouldn't…"

She kept her gaze on Spencer. "A guy named Norm Johnson. He's head of an effort to pull together financial data from around the corporation. Sounds like they are well on their way to a completed pilot. You might want to tag along." She went on to describe what she got from Porter about the Controller's pilot.

Carlton thought about that. *Who is this guy and how is he getting away with this right in Miller's backyard?"*

"I'm surprised that you didn't bring this up earlier, Gary."

Reaper began to slouch, making eye contact with everything in the room except Spencer or Julia. "Uh, well, I, uh, didn't want to, uh, didn't, ah, yes, wasn't sure there would be any connection," Reaper said, wracking his brain for a response. "Oh, and it's not like I can really *reference* them, you know."

Keep slithering, Gary, Julia thought. She was embarrassed more than usual.

"Spencer, before we leave, I'd like to present you with some pricing information. I took the liberty of scoping out your needs…"

What are you doing? Berkowski wanted to ask, glowering at Reaper. *You can't possibly give him a price proposal…*

Gary, seeing the daggers flying out of Julia's eyes, avoided her steely gaze, quite an accomplishment as she was still sitting across the table next to Carlton. She had not moved since she finished the demo.

"…and have printed up some scenarios," he said. He slid the document across to Spencer.

"Gary, I appreciate your, uh, efficiency, but this is most premature. And with the team in New York leading the way…" *Only until I get going, of course.*

A pained smile spread across Reaper's face. "Spencer, while the team in New York is certainly a crucial part of this, I'm responsible for the Azalea account. In short, I'm your guy."

With that Julia slammed her laptop closed, which startled both Reaper and Carlton. "Gary, aren't we going to be late for our next meeting?"

This time Gary returned the daggers. "You are mistaken, Julia. We have all afternoon here."

"Maybe you do," Carlton said, noticing the rising tension between his two visitors. "But I do not. I have a meeting in ten minutes and I have to gather some notes for it." He collected the InUnison literature that Gary had pressed on him, including – much to Julia's chagrin – the pricing document. "Gary, I'll review this," Spencer said, holding the proposal up, "and forward it to this Norm Johnson in New York. He'll be interested, I'm sure. Thanks for coming, and thanks again for the great presentation, Julia." He shook hands and left.

Julia finished packing up her machine and notebook without looking at Gary. They left silently.

Out in the parking lot, Julia wheeled on Gary.

"*You* had absolutely no business giving any pricing to them. Are you actually trying to sabotage Angelis? Surely you don't believe that you can take this account?"

"And *you* had no business bringing up New York. I run the sales strategy here and I'll decide what and when to tell prospects things. As my partner, I would expect you to back me up."

"*Partner?* Partner to you means me, me, me! Wayne and Porter are breaking into Azalea and you ought to be kissing Wayne's ass to help out, not trying to subvert him. Oh, I suppose that's something you learned during your wonderful days at Sybase."

"Don't you want to be compensated for this deal?"

"Of course, and I will, even if I don't have anything to do with it. It's none of your business but my bonus isn't tied only to *your* performance," thank *God,* "It is half regional performance and half national."

"Well, I'm going to get my piece of this deal. I'm not going to let this newbie poach my territory…have to protect myself…"

"You're pathetic." She turned and walked briskly to her car, thankful that they had driven separately.

***

"Porter! Good to see you! How were your holidays?"

The question stumped Porter for a few seconds. Christmas was less than a month in the past but seemed like ancient history, given the pace of his new responsibilities.

"The holidays were great. It certainly helped to have a new job to look forward to." Porter took a moment to take in Norm's surroundings, especially his view down Water Street. "Nice digs, Norm. A step up from that windowless partition space you had at the bank."

"Not bad at all," Norm agreed.

"So, what's the deal here? Brewster said something about getting some friction from IT."

"Yes, IT is dragging their feet on some access issues. It's the usual BS from outfits like that; they are control freaks and their pride is bruised because my boss, Sam Racker, is going around them to get some things done. Anyway, to be honest, we are using you as an excuse to put some pressure on them."

"I don't mind. I need some friendly contact for a change. This week was a track meet." Porter gave Norm the *Cliff's Notes* version of his week.

"You seem to be adapting well! That's quite a bit different from sitting in your cubicle coding all day."

"Well, I'm a little worried though. My sales rep doesn't think that we are generating enough leads or doing enough selling because of being burdened with all this cleanup."

"I hope that I convinced him of the opportunity here. This is a big, expensive project that will revolutionize how things are done here."

"Oh, he definitely has Azalea as prospect Numero Uno. So, am I here as human scenery or is there something productive I can be doing?"

"We'll find something for you. Let me show you to Brewster's cubicle."

They walked down the hallway to Brewster McNaughton's desk, picking up Peter Chaplin along the way. Brewster jumped up upon seeing Porter and gave him a punch in the shoulder while shaking his hand.

"It's damn good to see ya again, Porter!"

Being together with the team was bittersweet for Porter. The good memories of working together at the bank came flooding back but also the cold dose of reality: the projects, politics and wasted careers.

"So, what are we waiting for?" Norm asked, seeing the team all sitting around.

"Our Director of Security is supposed to be up shortly to personally give us our access codes. Don't know why email isn't good enough," Brewster said.

They engaged in some more chit chat for another fifteen minutes when a new face appeared at Brewster's cubicle. He was looking at the nameplate on the partition and smiled at the fact that he had successfully navigated the halls to the correct location.

"Good morning, I'm Mordecai Rosenzweig, Director of Data Security."

He shook hands with all, took out a folder and handed it to Brewster.

"Here are the access codes for the Oracle instance and mainframe login ID's for you and Peter."

Brewster glanced at the forms with Peter and Norm looking over his shoulder. "Great, thank you. We are going to jump right in then. Porter, here, is with InUnison Software, the integration platform we are using in our pilot."

"Do you mind if I stick around?" Rosenzweig asked. "I'd love to see how you are doing this. It could really benefit all of us if it works."

Brewster looked to Norm for approval. Norm didn't think anything of it, shrugged and nodded approval. "I need to get back to my office, so I'll leave this in your hands, Brewster."

It became a bit crowded with Brewster, Peter, Porter, and Mordecai all in one cubicle but they were able to find chair positions and still see what was going on.

Brewster began. "We already have the message broker set up with connectors to our local test database and message definitions which simulate the information we've needed from Oracle and the mainframe. Porter, you have the mainframe connector, right?"

"Here ya go. Installs like all the others."

Brewster loaded the software and began to configure the addresses for the mainframe partitions. "This says the test machine is called, Saigon? What's up with that?"

Rosenzweig sighed. "It's Miller's naming scheme; Saigon, Danang, Mekong. He's never left Vietnam."

"Saigon it is." Brewster completed the configuration and ran the connection test. It came back immediately with a "green light" icon indicating success. "Hey, it just works."

Brewster then reconfigured some of their message definitions to be delivered to the mainframe, and others to retrieve data from Saigon's processes. Within about fifteen minutes, he was able to trigger a simple request on the IBM machine and the connector reformatted the mainframe data into a message for the requester, a Java application on his PC. He continued to add new messages to the mix, including an automatic "publish" of changes made to a Microsoft SQL Server database.

"Now, the *pièce de résistance*," Brewster said in Georgian-accented French. "I'm going to merge similar data from Saigon, the Oracle Financials tables and the SQL Server, and update this Excel spreadsheet report," he said, switching from window to window on his PC. This took somewhat longer than the previous tests as he needed to add some logic to properly do the merge of data. Brewster was thankful that Porter was there to get him through the rough spots. They succeeded in updating the spreadsheet within about half an hour.

"Way cool," was all Peter could think to say.

Mordecai was taking this all in with genuine fascination but increasing alarm. Here, from a single desktop, these guys were able to reach out and touch multiple systems. *Think of the security headaches I'm going to have now! This is going to totally freak Miller. What did Miller say? "There is no way they will succeed…" Yes, Stewart, way.*

"Oh, look at the time. I need to get back downstairs. Thanks so much, this was fascinating. Good luck!" He couldn't get down to the raised floor fast enough.

***

The PensAndClips office was stuffed into what looked like a hastily rehabbed tenement on West 21st Street, part of what had become hyped as New York's "Silicon Alley", an area roughly described by a few blocks straddling Fifth Avenue between the Flat Iron Building where Broadway intersects with Fifth in the north, and 14th Street in the south. Many of the clothing industry's former workshops – sweatshops to some – were now home to a new type of weaver: weavers of new products and services on the World Wide Web.

Craig Mansfield was such a weaver. PensAndClips was his third startup, and in the true spirit of "third time's a charm", he was hitting his stride. He had leased a huge abandoned warehouse on the Upper West Side, turning it into a squeaky clean, highly automated repository of about six Staples superstores-worth of office supplies deliverable in under an hour to satisfy the insatiable demands of Manhattan's offices.

Mansfield established the philosophy early on that PandC would buy rather than build software for inventory, shipping, accounting and dispatching systems, not to mention all the other internal systems such as payroll. Before the 90's, the paleo-IT managers of the 70's and 80's considered buying packaged software unmanly. They hadn't built up a cadre of loyal programmers for nothing. However, top management finally realized that it was not in their core business or budgetary interests to write and maintain custom software. Scores of programmers were cut loose or outsourced – as Porter had been – and replaced with off-the-shelf software. The challenge was to get all those shrink-wrap applications to cooperate with each other. That's where the InUnison system came into play.

While the integration of these systems was easily accomplished by the InUnison system, one piece of Mansfield's vision was to allow customers to automatically order directly from whatever internal purchasing system his customer already had in place. This was to be a key differentiator for PandC as all of his competitors forced a customer to adopt their proprietary system, or install a complex and expensive Electronic Data Interchange – EDI – interface. Many customers who previously passed on the opportunity to automate their purchasing were very interested in what Mansfield had to offer.

But to bring that vision to a reality, he needed his systems to talk to mainframes and if he was going to use InUnison, he needed that piece from them. Craig was approaching a go/no go decision point. If he couldn't get a deal from InUnison he would have to look elsewhere, even though it might set him back temporarily.

Wayne entered their building and walked down a hallway lit only with a single bulb ceiling fixture. A small, handwritten sign directed him to the rear of the building where a rickety-looking freight elevator stood with its grated door open.

He entered the car and squinted to read the buttons. He found "2" and pushed. As the elevator slowly ascended, he had a thought of Glenn Close ripping off Michael Douglas' pants in a similar freight elevator in *Fatal Attraction*. No such luck for Wayne.

"Hello, Wayne?" Mansfield asked his visitor as the elevator stopped at the second floor.

"Yes, Wayne Angelis," he said, extending his hand as he stepped into the office.

"Sorry for the elevator," Craig said. "We didn't view it as a priority to put money into. When we want to show off the company, we take the prospect to the distribution center. It's way cool. We'll be moving these temporary offices there soon."

"As long as it gets me up and down safely, that's all I care about."

Safety was not an idle concern for Wayne. Three steps out of the elevator he stumbled over network cables duct taped to the floor. He paused to look out for other hazards and, sure enough, there were numerous wires and oddly placed electrical conduit to avoid. He noticed that there was a path of sorts worn into the ancient floorboards and tried to stay within its limits.

OSHA would have a field day in this place, he thought.

Mansfield showed him to the front of the building where an open conference area had been assembled. Four long folding tables were pushed together with metal folding chairs set around facing a whiteboard on wheels.

"I thought you were bringing Lakota."

"He had a, uh, complication come up. He won't be joining us."

"Fine with me. I don't like dealing with empty suits, particularly empty silk suits. Now, I hope you have the agreement…"

"Absolutely!" Wayne was proud to confirm. He reached into his case and pulled the fax out, handing it to Mansfield for review.

Mansfield sat down around the corner of the table from Wayne, stooped over the paper, stroking his chin slowly. Towards the end of his review, he started to nod.

"Looks pretty straightforward. Is there any flexibility on the royalty terms?"

"Craig, we can negotiate about anything. To be more honest than I should be, we would really like a good value-added reseller reference to prove how easy our technology is to embed." Wayne leaned in closer for the next part. "Craig, there's one other benefit we would like out of this arrangement: referrals. We will waive the royalty fee altogether if you give us access to your customers. We're confident that when your customers see how powerful your use of InUnison is, they will want to use it internally, which is forbidden in the VAR agreement."

Craig pondered that for a moment. "I don't see a downside as long as I am not expected to be a sales arm for InUnison. I have enough of my own sales efforts to deal with."

"That's our job."

"Excuse me a minute." Mansfield took the agreement and disappeared toward the back of the office. While he was waiting, Wayne got up to look out the window. The office overlooked 21st Street. It was a crowded street, with many buildings like this one lining both sides. *What a mess this area must have been.* Wayne pondered the irony of the area being taken over by high tech companies.

Hearing footsteps on creaking floor boards, Wayne turned away from the view and towards the back of the room. Mansfield was returning, and not alone.

"Wayne, this is Steve Powell, my CFO. Steve, this is Wayne Angelis of

InUnison." Wayne and Steve shook hands and sat down on folding chairs.

"I wanted Steve to get involved since he is, after all, the money man."

"Wayne, I have to say, this is a most generous agreement. You will, of course, put the waiver of royalties that Craig described to me in writing as well as the commitment for productizing the Linux version."

"Of course. We have to protect ourselves as well."

Mansfield exchanged nods with Powell. "Let's clean up that royalty language and get this done. Now, forgive me for being paranoid, this doesn't depend on Lakota, does it? I really need this in place ASAP, particularly now that we are in development using your new connector. By the way, that Sean Murphy is a real piece of work."

"Yes, we love him…especially at arm's length. Anyway, the answer is no; our respective legal contacts can work directly and use me as liaison if things get confused. We've decided to channel VAR recruitment through the direct sales force since we are the ones on the ground with organizations like PensAndClips."

"Okay, get that new agreement to me and let's go from there," Mansfield said in closing.

Back outside on 21st, Wayne breathed in the cold air and let out a long, satisfied sigh. *Finally, something getting pushed forward.* He walked to Sixth Avenue then up to Penn Station where he could get a train home. Once there, he would get the VAR agreement nailed down, and start hitting the phones again. *Gotta fill that New Jersey pipeline…*

***

Mordecai Rosenzweig hunted for Stewart Miller in vain. He hiked from the hulking mainframes to printer room to storage units, leaving messages with Herb Putnam and Becky Sharpe. Giving up, he camped out in his cubicle, hoping that Miller would finally return his numerous pages.

"So, what's so urgent that you had to put a dragnet out for me?" Miller said, suddenly appearing in Rosenzweig's cubicle, causing him to almost topple over in his desk chair.

"Goodness, Stewart! Damn near went into cardiac arrest!"

"So? I'm still waiting."

"I spent most of the morning upstairs with that new Financial Information team and –"

"It's a big joke, as I expected, right?"

"Not exactly, Stewart. They have some pretty impressive things already working, stuff that's been on our "to do" list for awhile."

"Oh, please; they've only had a couple of weeks. It's kids playing in the sandbox."

"Stewart, it wasn't two weeks, it was a couple of hours *this morning*." He proceeded to describe in detail all he had seen in Brewster's cubicle. "This InUnison stuff is something."

"Mordi, it's some vendor trick…"

"Stewart, aren't you listening? I *saw* them start with almost nothing, and in no time they had major applications: mainframe, Oracle, a spreadsheet, all sharing data. We haven't been able to simply get Oracle synchronized with the mainframe apps, let alone a damn spreadsheet."

"I still think you're being snookered."

He left Rosenzweig's desk without saying anything else, heading back to his office to digest Mordecai's report. *Can't be as good as he says it is, but what if it is?*

Miller was still skeptical but turned around and went back. "Mordi, what's the name of the guy up there who did all this?" *Must be Jesus F. Christ.*

"Brewster McNaughton. And the vendor guy helped a little. Why, you going to see for yourself?"

"It sounds like I better." He dialed Brewster's extension from Rosenzweig's phone and put on his best demeanor.

"Brewster, here."

"Hi there, Brewster! Stewart Miller, here. How are you? You're new here right? Welcome to Azalea!"

Porter and Chaplin were still working with him and he gave them a look of terror as he covered the receiver. "It's, it's, Stewart Miller! What do I do?"

"Brewster? You there?"

"Yes, yes, sorry, someone just dropped something off here."

"Well, Mordecai gave me a glowing report on your progress. Mind if I come up to see? He says it's amazing stuff."

"Uh, I guess so. It's not much, though. We're going to finish some more work and then put together a presentation. Perhaps that would be more productive for you," Brewster said, pleased with his clever recovery. It was short lived.

"No, I'd love to see it *right now*. I'll be up in ten minutes."

"But…" The line went dead.

"Shit. He's coming in ten minutes. Where's Norm?" He got up and ran down the hall to Norm's office. He was relieved to see him in but apprehensive at the same time.

"Norm, Stewart Miller wants to see what we've done."

"Tell him no. He can wait for the presentation. I don't want to show our hand yet."

"Uh, sorry, but he's on his way up."

"What? Why didn't you –"

"Look, he's the head of freakin' IT! What was I supposed to do?"

"Say no, that's what. Listen, knucklehead, you don't work for IT anymore, you work in the Office of the Controller. Damn it!" He paced around his office to figure out what to do. "Is Porter still here?"

"Yep."

"Okay, let's get over to your desk and put something together, fast."

They sprinted back to his desk. "Porter," Norm said, "can you do a quick presentation on InUnison? It will buy us some time to figure out how and what to show Miller."

"It's on my laptop. But I haven't done it in a while and –"

"It'll have to do. Use my office."

Miller rounded the corner just then.

"Hello, Brewster?" he asked, looking at Norm.

"No, I'm Norm Johnson. Pleased to meet you finally," Norm said, trying not to be too sarcastic. "This is a little sudden; we aren't really organized to show –"

"Oh, it's no big deal. Mordi was really excited after spending the morning up here and I figured I'd pop up and take a gander."

"Well, Brewster has to set up a couple of things first, so I thought I'd let Porter here from InUnison give you a quick technical overview of their integration platform. Then we can show you our progress."

Miller started to object, but thought better of it. *I guess I better learn something about this stuff. "Know your enemy…"*

"That sounds great. Not too long, mind you."

"Oh, fifteen minutes, right Porter?"

Porter nearly fainted. *NORM! It's more like an hour! What are you doing to me?*

Norm's on-his-knees-begging face said "make this work, will ya?"

"Well, we can cover the basics in fifteen…"

"Great! Porter, you know the way to my office, right? I'll be right there."

Porter began his death march to Norm's office while Norm turned back to McNaughton and Chaplin. "Now, let's do this…"

Porter opened his laptop, started up PowerPoint and scanned the slides quickly to figure out what to show and what to skip.

"If you don't mind, Porter," Miller asked, "why don't you draw the pieces of your architecture on the white board. I don't have time for all the fancy marketing stuff."

Relieved, Porter closed his machine and selected a blue marker from the tray. He started to draw, but the marker was dry. "Heh, funny how that always happens," he said. He tried three more markers before finding a fresh green one.

He drew boxes to represent the system parts and then talked about the flow of messages between connectors and the message broker, emphasizing how the connector worked. He thought that Miller would be most interested in how nothing had to be installed on the host system in order for InUnison to work. Miller was not giving Porter any clues as to what he thought of all this but Porter noticed that he was taking a lot of notes.

"So, that's it in a nutshell. Pretty cool, huh?"

Cool? It's a goddamn virus! Miller thought. *There's no way I'm letting this in my shop. Every department will want to tap into everyone else's systems. No f'in way!*

"Yes, Porter. Thanks for the overview. It was very educational."

Porter led Miller back to McNaughton's cubicle, hoping that they were ready and relieved to see that they were in fact all set to demo.

Brewster started by describing the problem they were trying to solve, which was synchronizing duplicate data between several applications. He built some message definitions to show Miller how the tools worked and topped the discussion off by showing the three-way update on the spreadsheet which Rosenzweig had seen.

Norm, Brewster, Porter and Peter all stepped back and watched for some reaction from Miller, who was standing in the back of the cubicle, hand on chin and staring at the computer screen.

"Well, very impressive," he said, coming out of his trance. "Thanks for the demo. I'll be interested in your progress." He shook their hands and left.

The team looked at each other. "Norm," Porter said, "how did we do?"

"Perhaps too good. I really didn't want him to know what we were doing until we had the whole pilot done, at which time it would be a *fait accompli.* If he gets worried too early, he might try to rip the project out of our hands."

"Well, I don't know what we at InUnison can do to help you with your internal politics, but…oh, that reminds me; Wayne asked if you had called that guy down in Atlanta at the insurance company."

"As a matter of fact, no. As I told Wayne, I really don't want to get on anybody's radar yet. I don't know anything about that Atlanta guy; he might have his own agenda. I want to get our pilot done, another couple of weeks or so. Then we'll be operating from strength."

"Wayne's worried that IT will squash this in the cradle. We have a team in Atlanta who could –"

"Read my lips, Porter. You're selling to me and you'll follow my lead," Norm said, thrusting his finger at Porter. "I'll bring the Atlanta guy in when I need him. You tell your buddy Wayne that if he goes around me, he'll screw this up. Then where will he be?"

Ouch. Now I really *feel like a vendor.* "I hear you."

On his way out of the building, his phone rang. It was Julia.

"Oh, Porter, I'm glad I got you. I've been trying to get Wayne."

Porter looked as his watch. "He must still be at PensAndClips. What's up?"

"We met with Spencer Carlton at Azalea a few minutes ago. Did you guys know about it? Gary claims that he left Wayne a message."

"No, I don't think he knows anything about it. And I got an earful from Norm Johnson about how he doesn't want anyone else at Azalea to know what he's doing yet. Shit. This is going to really piss him off. He just got Pearl Harbored by IT so he's sensitive about secrecy right now."

"I'm sorry I couldn't wave off Reaper. He sprang the meeting on me when I got in today."

"Okay, I'll work on tracking down Wayne," Porter said.

He was now standing inside the Water Street door to Azalea's building, banging his head on the wall. *This is not good.* He dialed Wayne and got his voicemail. He gave him a review of the Miller visit and then gathered himself for the next item.

"Wayne, I also wanted to give you a heads up about a meeting Reaper and Berkowski had with Azalea in Atlanta this afternoon. I'm hoping you already know about it but, well, give me a call. Oh, and Norm and Spencer Carlton have not talked. He's trying to keep things close to the vest, he says. Call me."

***

"Mordi, come into my office." Miller put his phone down and sifted through his inbox, trying to find something. Rosenzweig appeared quickly.

"What's up?"

"I saw that stuff they're doing upstairs. It's a menace. Ah, here it is. I thought I remembered getting this." He threw a brochure across his desk toward Mordecai. "I want you to go to this IntegrateNow! show next week. If we are going to have to battle these guys, we better know what the hell the market has. Gather as much G2 as possible."

"I wouldn't mind getting out of the office." He started gazing at the brochure as he started to leave.

"Oh, Mordi? Get me some coffee mugs."

***

"I don't know why we are wasting our time with this Lakota. He can't seem to take a hint," Carl Hunt said. Hunt was just arriving at the Tribeca Grill with Larry Liu, the Flanderson Consulting Financial Services partner.

"What, you don't want to have a decent lunch on InUnison software?" Liu teased as they entered the tiled foyer. "Consider it a 'Last Supper'. Maybe he will finally get the hint Monday morning. Funny how these things work out; frustrating actually. In many ways we'd much rather be working with InUnison and Tom Gatto." *Funny, I haven't heard from him lately.* "But this Lakota guy…" he said, jotting a note to look up Gatto.

The maître d' returned to the podium. "May I help you gentlemen?"

"Yes, we are meeting Fred Lakota."

"Very good, gentlemen. Mr. Lakota is already here. Please follow me."

The two Flanderson colleagues dutifully followed the maître d'. They walked along a dark mahogany and brass rail partition leading to a back table where Lakota was reviewing the menu. He jumped up at the sight of Liu and extended his hand as the maître d' held their chairs for them.

"Very good to see you again, Larry," Lakota said.

"Fred, you remember Carl Hunt, my head project lead?"

"Yes, certainly. We will be filling up your timesheets with InUnison projects!"

"Uh, yes, I'm sure," Hunt said while shaking Lakota's hand and giving Liu a sideways glance.

The trio ordered lunch and Lakota started to regale Liu and Hunt with an update on news from InUnison.

"We have a major new release of the core platform coming in March, version

3.0. It will significantly flesh out our coverage of operating systems and the suite of connectors will expand…"

Liu and Hunt smiled and nodded, but had already pretty much tuned Lakota out.

"Now," Lakota said, still in lecture mode, "I hope we can finalize our partnership soon. I've become aware of some great potential opportunities, right here in New York…" Liu put his fork down and started to pay attention. "…such as Azalea Financial, Merrill Lynch and an interesting one at PensAndClips.com."

Liu couldn't believe his ears. *Think; did I sign a non-disclosure agreement? Hell, even if I did, the NDA might not stop me from chasing business, maybe not talking about their technology.* "Well, Fred, I'm impressed that you are so forthcoming, but without an agreement I really can't represent these opportunities…"

"Larry, of course. I'm so excited about what is going on at InUnison that I want you to know how we will be able to work together to our mutual benefit. We will be able to build a *framework* for our, uh, *relation*ship."

Liu now wished that he had indeed listened to Hunt. *I really don't want to know some of this. It's going to put me in conflict. This guy is such a fool!*

Whether he intended to or not, Carl Hunt came to his rescue.

"So, Fred, tell me more about the technical stuff of 3.0?"

Carl's question set Lakota off down a long and winding path which consumed the rest of lunch. They all exchanged pleasantries and Lakota departed from the restaurant hailing a cab, leaving Liu and Hunt at the door.

"Carl, I should have taken your advice and not come. I've now got to figure out whether I can act on his information or not. I know our new 'friends' will be interested in those opportunities. I don't know if I can tell them directly. I'll have to look at the language in the NDA."

Carl shook his head slowly, with a look of disbelief on his face. "That guy amazes me. I may be a simple technical geek, not savvy in the ways of sales, but what did he want to get out of this meeting? Assuming we were still interested in a partnership with InUnison, wouldn't he want to come away with some tangible evidence of progress? We've been doing these meals for months."

Liu smiled. "We made progress in the form of full stomachs."

He hailed a taxi for the return trip to their midtown office.

***

As he exited the train station in Scarsdale, Wayne noticed the voicemail reminder on his phone. Hmmm, why didn't I hear the ringer? Oh, damn, forgot to turn it back on after the meeting. He speed dialed his mailbox and listened.

Ah, good boy, Porter! Always updating me…demo for CIO...May not be a bad thing to involve IT...Reaper?...WHAT?...OH SHIT!

***

Fred Lakota was back in a taxi, heading up to the Waldorf-Astoria. Checking his notes from earlier in the day, he saw a reminder to himself to call Craig Mansfield at PensAndClips. He found the number in his Palm Pilot.

"This is Craig."

"Good afternoon, Craig. Fred Lakota here."

And the day was going so well… "What can I do for you?"

"I'm calling to apologize for missing our meeting this morning. I had a little bit of a fire drill to deal with. You know how it is."

Mansfield didn't respond, so Lakota continued.

"Was Wayne able to stand in for me?"

"'Stand in' for you? It was *his* meeting after all, and, yes, we got quite a bit done. We have a couple of fairly minor changes to make in the reseller agreement…"

"He showed you the agreement?" *How did he get it? O'Rourke!*

"Yes, and we need to nail down some language which Wayne is working on as we speak. We should be able to sign next week and get rolling."

"Craig, Craig. I believe that there has been a misunderstanding. That agreement hasn't been approved yet. We are still working on our internal changes. I don't want to undercut Angelis, but he's jumping the gun a bit. I have ultimate authority on the agreement."

Mansfield collapsed into his chair. *This can't be happening. Angelis couldn't have been more explicit, or… he couldn't be another Gatto, could he?*

"Fred, I'm very confused. Wayne was very clear about the terms…"

"Again, I apologize. He does not have the negotiation authority for VAR deals and I will take responsibility if he has misled you."

"But he very clearly said that his management *specifically…*"

"Again, I assure you that he is mistaken if he has said that." The taxi stopped at the front of the Waldorf. Lakota was juggling the phone and his wallet in order to pay the driver. "Craig, I will straighten this out."

"Please do. I don't have time to screw around anymore."

"Don't worry, Craig. At the end of the day, I'm your guy!"

Chapter 9 Control

Spencer Carlton had his feet up on his desk looking through the InUnison software documentation that Reaper had left with him.

Pretty cool stuff, if it works. He began to make some notes about possible proof-of-concept or pilot projects. After a few quick ideas, he put the documentation and his notes down. He started to think about other strategies.

When should I call this Johnson? If he's new, he's going to get chewed up by Miller. If I were him, I'd want to keep this covert for a while; that's why he didn't call me yet. But if he's going to do real reporting consolidation he has to come to us at some point. Very interesting. I'm going to have to monitor this. This is the kind of project to put that dinosaur finally out to extinction.

He picked up the business cards from Gary and Julia.

Ah, Julia. Very impressive, indeed.

***

Wayne was frantically dialing anyone he could get a hold of: Reaper, Mitchell, Berkowski, all to no avail. He had been working on the VAR agreement while also trying to find out what was going on at Azalea. In between call attempts, his phone rang with a 212 area code on the caller ID. It looked like a familiar number, one he had dialed recently, so he answered it.

"Wayne Angelis."

"Wayne, this is Craig Mansfield at PensAndClips."

"Oh, hi, Craig, I've just received a new version of the agreement from HQ. Can I fax it to you?"

"Is this some kind of sick joke?"

Wayne recognized Mansfield's tone from their first conversation. "Craig, I don't know –"

"Look, if you're another Gatto, I'm not going to put up with this bullshit. I'll simply find an alternative like VibraWeb. At least they –"

"CRAIG! What is the PROBLEM? I have an approved agreement right in front of me," Wayne pleaded.

"I got off the phone a few minutes ago with Fred Lakota…"

That asshole, Wayne thought, closing his eyes in pain.

"…and he says you have no authority to negotiate this deal. He said 'I'm your guy'. Now, I know I shouldn't believe a snake like him, but the best face I can put on it is that InUnison is the most fucked up company…"

Yeah, I'm beginning to agree.

"…or you're no better than Gatto."

Think quickly, "Now, we came through for you on the mainframe connector, right? I should think that the company bending over for you on that should mean something. When was the last time a software company gave you special pre-release software like that?"

Mansfield thought about that. *I really want to trust this guy; he* has *come through in a very short time period.* "You have a point. But you know the saying, 'fool me once…'".

"Yes, and I am not fooling you here. I'm faxing this over and I'll be here to go over any questions. Now, if you want, I can try to get the VP of Sales to confirm my instructions…"

"That would be great. I'm sorry, Wayne, but I need some reassurance here."

"I may not be able to set it up today, but will you be available tomorrow?"

"Yes. I'm sorry, Wayne. Let's keep things moving."

"You have nothing to apologize for, Craig. As you said, we look pretty screwed up. I'm the one who owes you an apology." *I should beat one out of Lakota.* "I'll fax the document shortly."

The call ended with Wayne's emotions cycling between relief, despair and rage. He tried to get control over himself as he faxed the reseller agreement to Mansfield. As the fax machine started with page two, he heard his email emit the ding-dong signaling arriving messages. A message from Mike Giuliano from Sampson Logistics appeared.

Damn. He's canceling our meeting for tomorrow. Hmm, I guess I shouldn't read too much into it; he wants to reschedule for next Wednesday.

Wayne replied to confirm the schedule change. The fax was starting on page four when his office phone rang again.

"Hi, Wayne, it's Julia Berkowski," she said, sheepishly. "I think we need to chat."

"Yes, Julia, we do. What is Gary trying to do to me?"

"First, Wayne, I'm very sorry I couldn't give you a warning. Gary kind of sprung it on me and I couldn't get a message out." She gave Wayne a blow-by-blow rundown on their meeting with Carlton, as well as her parking lot confrontation with Reaper.

Wayne was aghast. "Did you get a look at the pricing info?"

"Unfortunately, no. We were wrapping up, or so I thought, and he kind of whipped it out. He's always premature with that kind of thing but this was bad even by Grim's standards."

Wayne still had enough sense of humor to laugh again at the nickname.

"Oh, Julia. This is surreal. Talk about dropping trou! I can't let Norm get anywhere near that pricing document."

"Don't you think you have to simply disavow any knowledge of it?"

"I've never had to deal with this situation before. Sure, I've had fights with reps over accounts, but, goodness, I've never had a rival who went so far." *Well, except for one.* "I mean, a smart, hell, even a mediocre rep would never want to be locked into a proposal at this stage in the sales cycle."

Wayne's email signaled again. He quickly noted that Mansfield was acknowledging receipt of the fax and another from Giuliano at Sampson confirming Wednesday's appointment. *Just as well he cancelled. I won't be in the mood.*

"Julia, thanks for the call. I don't want you in the crossfire that's going to erupt."

"Crossfire? I'll be in your trench, Wayne, not out in the middle. Frankly, I hope they fire Reaper's ass over this."

"We shouldn't talk in those terms, Julia."

"You're being too civil, Wayne. What do you think you are going to do?"

"Unfortunately, Reaper isn't my only challenge. Frankly, I've come to a fork in the road."

"Please, Wayne. Get off the ledge. They'll work these things out." She attempted a little humor. "You know what Yogi Berra said about forks in the road?"

Wayne laughed. "Of course! 'When you come to a fork in the road, take it'. You're not a New Yorker if you haven't memorized all those Yogi-isms."

"I need to go but at least I'll leave you laughing. Call me if you need anything on this."

You're a good soul, Julia. "Thanks, again, Julia."

Now what do I do? I can't have Norm find this out from Carlton. He'll think I'm 100% slime.

He picked up the phone to call Norm Johnson and dialed the number.

No! He slammed the receiver down before it started to ring. *If I call him, he's going to think I can't control things. What's worse, being a slime ball or just stupid?*

Wayne got up from his chair and paced his office, squeezing his increasingly throbbing head with his palms. Think!

What if I call Carlton? What do I have to lose here? Maybe I can wave him off calling Norm or sending that damn proposal. He paced a bit more, and then started nodding his head faster and faster. Yes, what do I have to lose? Worst thing that can happen is I expand the project which is what Norm should be doing anyway.

He sat back down at his desk and pulled out his Palm Pilot to get Carlton's number. He started to dial, *414-…* Again, he slammed down the phone. *Aaaaaaah! Reaper! If Carlton takes over the project, Reaper'll get the deal!* Wayne got up and started to pace again.

I can't take the chance that Norm gets shoved aside. I'm in command as long as Norm is, at least nominally. But he's already losing it to Miller and I have no control there.

Wayne left his office to get a glass of orange juice from the refrigerator so he could take some Tylenol for his now ripper of a headache. He opened the bottle of juice and started to pour. His mind became more and more focused on his predicament, so much so that he didn't realize that the glass had filled and an orange juice lake was forming on his countertop. It wasn't until the edge of the lake started dripping onto his Nikes that he noticed.

Goddamn it! He capped the juice and reached for the paper towels.

After cleaning up, he took his medicine and returned to the office. Sitting down again at his desk, he tried again to think through the situation.

I need to control Norm to fend of Reaper, but I need Carlton to grow the deal and fend off Miller. But I need to fend off Carlton, else he grabs control from Norm. Round and round we go…

He took his hands from his head and looked blankly at his computer screen. *That's really what this is about: control. I can still have control over this so start controlling, Wayne. Stop reacting. Reaper screwed me; that's done. I have to keep Carlton out of his claws. I don't care what Presby might say later, I'm going to control Azalea. I know what to do.*

He checked the Palm Pilot again and dialed.

"This is Spencer."

"Hello, Spencer, this is Wayne Angelis calling from InUnison Software in New York. How are you?"

"Fine. I seem to have become very popular with you guys lately. What can I do for you?"

"I wanted to fill you in on what's going on at Azalea in New York…"

"Yes, Julia Berkowski brought it up at our meeting yesterday but didn't give me very many details. It didn't seem like Reaper wanted me to know about New York."

"Yes, that's one of the reasons I'm calling to clear up some of that confusion. You see, Gary really wasn't clued into what's going on up here at your headquarters…" Wayne said, emphasizing "headquarters", "…and I take responsibility for that. It was rather coincidental that he scheduled that meeting with you when we are only now heavily involved with Water Street. Julia was aware of some of it because she was up here helping my SE with some other accounts."

Coincidental my ass, Spencer thought. *I can tell when there's account conflict going on. Reaper is as transparent as window glass, and about as interesting. Now, who is poaching who?*

"So, fill me in."

"Your new Controller…"

"Racker, yes."

"Right. He's formed a team to provide consolidation of financial information…"

"Yes, that's what Julia told me. Look, Wayne, let's cut to the chase. It's obvious to me that you and Reaper have some sort of tug of war going on here so don't bullshit me about how 'coincidental' our meeting was. Reaper clearly can't fire more than a couple brain synapses at a time so prove to me that you're any better."

Damn.

"Fine, you're right. Let me start at the beginning." Wayne began with how Norm got the job, Porter's relationship, the fact that the Controller was trying to be the focal point without IT, that is, Miller's, involvement.

"Well, if Miller has already seen something, it's too late. I'll bet you one year's salary he's going to slam the door on Johnson."

"How can he do that? He'll be reporting to Racker soon. It would be stupid to piss him off."

"Never underestimate the power of the dark side. Miller is a survivor, first class one. He figures that if he defeats this project, Racker is out. Might even be true. It's happened before."

"So, how did you gain so much autonomy?"

"It doesn't hurt that we're seven hundred-some miles away. We're the biggest subsidiary and the most profitable. We already had a self-contained IT department when we were acquired and the CEOs told everyone to leave us alone. Miller still tried to gain control but we beat him back. He's had it in for me ever since, and frankly, the feeling is mutual."

"I've been trying to get Norm to make some alliances. I don't think he appreciates what he's up against," Wayne said.

"I agree. I'd like to see this succeed but the onus is on him to work with me. I can appreciate that he tried to be covert but that's blown now. He should bring us in."

Now for the delicate part, Wayne thought.

"I agree, but I think that it is best for the project to be under the Corporate HQ umbrella since the mandate is through the Office of CFO."

"Very nicely done, Wayne. Keep the control."

Can't put much over this guy.

"Okay, that's part of it, but you have to admit…"

"That's fine with me, Wayne, and you're right. It should have the veneer of

HQ control. But between you and me, we should accept who is best at driving the strategy here. I'm always willing to help our new folks deal with Miller."

"Very nicely *said*," Wayne said, echoing Spencer. "So we're in agreement?"

"Yes, one other thing. Keep Reaper out of here. Now, Julia can visit as often as she wants and I don't mean because she's good eye candy."

"Yes, understood. Oh, speaking of Reaper, I understand that he gave you some pricing…"

"Extremely nice pricing. I think it will make a good start for negotiations," Spencer said, laughing.

"How much to make it disappear?"

"Oh, dinner, a very nice dinner, when I'm in New York in a few weeks."

"Done! And before you destroy it, can you fax that to me? I'd like to know what Gary was up to." Wayne gave his fax number to Carlton.

"On the way. Hey, thanks for calling! I think we can do some business."

That went about as well as it could have, Wayne thought. *I'm going to have to stay close to Carlton. Now, how do I break this to Norm?*

Wayne sat back in his desk chair and gazed out at his frosty backyard. As he watched some snow flurries start to collect on his back deck, he tried to take stock of his overall situation. *Sampson is blowing me off, well maybe not; Lakota is trying to screw me – damn, he's poison; Reaper is like a terrorist, but maybe that's under control; oh, don't forget, your territory is going to shrink. This company may really be fucked up and I don't think I want to be at the scene of an accident.*

Deciding to bring this situation to a head, he dialed Ken Presby hoping that Presby's cell phone worked in the mountains. Unfortunately, he could only leave a message.

"Ken, this is Wayne Angelis. I'm sorry to bother you while you're off, but some grave issues came up today. Actually, they've been building since day one. I won't go into details, but I'm encountering some unacceptable meddling in my sales activities. I've never, *never* in my career encountered the level of internal interference in my sales activities. I simply can't function in such an unprofessional atmosphere. Call me."

Hope it was cryptic enough. He left all of his phone numbers so that Presby would not have any excuse for not reaching him. *This is all going to be resolved, NOW.*

***

Presby called after eight that evening. A couple of Bass Ales during the wait calmed Wayne down.

"Look, Wayne. Let's not panic here…"

"I'm not panicking. It's a simple analysis of the chances for my success here at InUnison. I can see the business. I don't see a whole lot of competition from VibraWeb or anybody else. What raises a red flag for me is the level of interference from within. Brinks doesn't want to let software out until it's perfect; Lakota is a loose cannon going off randomly; Reaper is actively sabotaging me…"

"How's that? You could have brought him into Azalea, you know."

"Oh, please! We have only stuck our toes into the account waters here in New York. I don't have a deal yet there, let alone something I'd expand until I had better account control. This Norm Johnson is paranoid – rightly so – about too many Azalea groups becoming a party to his project. I have my doubts about that, but he is my way in right now. Depending on circumstances, I'd go to Atlanta but not yet. Hey, IT'S MY CALL, DAMN IT, NOT GRIM REAPER'S!"

"Don't yell at me, mister. I don't like it either but –"

"*Ken!* He gave the Atlanta guy *pricing* at the first meeting, for chrissakes! You should see the mindless discounts he put in there." Wayne began to think that Presby was part of the problem, like most of his sales managers had been in his career.

From his getaway in the Maryland mountains, Presby was trying to be neutral in this conflict but knew that Wayne had the moral high ground. *I know that you're right,* he thought, *but I have to balance this somehow.* He was wracking his brain. *I can't lose my New York rep, especially after a month.*

"Wayne, I hear you. Look, I will communicate in no uncertain terms that you own Azalea and will drive strategy. In short, Reaper will work for you on Azalea matters. Is that acceptable?"

"Absolutely. Now, what about Lakota? I need someone, preferably O'Rourke, to call Mansfield *today* to confirm that he is dealing with us, not Fred Lakota."

We ought to have Engler call, Presby figured. *He's the one who didn't tell Lakota.* "I'll set it up." He looked at his watch, five-thirty West Coast time. "In fact, let's try him right now. Hold on."

He put Wayne on hold and got his VP, Niles O'Rourke, on the phone.

"Niles, I've got Wayne Angelis on hold. Here's the situation…" He went on to quickly brief O'Rourke on the PensAndClips fiasco with Lakota.

"THAT MOTHER FUCKER…"

"Now, Niles, is it possible that Engler never told him?"

"Maybe not. He's been focused on, well, he's been focused on other things and you know how Fred is never around the office. Let's bring Wayne in on this and I'll make the call."

Presby hit his send button to add Wayne.

"Wayne, Niles is on."

"Good evening, Wayne. Ken has briefed me on the VAR matter and I'll be more than happy to call your contact at PensAndClips to clear this up. I apologize, Wayne. It seems that Engler didn't clue in Lakota. Even Fred wouldn't have been so brazen if he had known what Engler told us to do. What's the guy's name and number?"

Wayne recited Craig Mansfield's number from heart. "Any chance we can do this as a conference call so that I can hear exactly what is said?"

"I'll loop you in from here and then we will call Mansfield."

"Sooner the better," Wayne said.

"Is that it?" O'Rourke asked.

"Yes, Niles, that's all."

"No, Ken, there's one more thing. I'm hearing that my territory is going to be broken up. Let me make this perfectly clear; I don't appreciate –"

"Wayne, where did you hear that?" Presby asked.

"Well, when Porter tells me that he's been asked to interview SE candidates for New Jersey, I know reps aren't far behind."

"Wayne, it shouldn't be a surprise that we are going to be growing aggressively…" Presby started to say.

"Hold it right there. First, you interview me for New Jersey because Gatto was still in New York, but held out the carrot for some named accounts. Then Gatto splits and you give me Manhattan, loaded with landmines, in addition to keeping New Jersey. So now after Porter and I have most of those accounts on the path to success, you screw me because I haven't had time to work New Jersey. Ken, that is a slap in the face."

"Wayne," O'Rourke said. "It isn't a cut in territory. You were switched to Manhattan. We have to backfill you in Jersey. Simple as that."

Wayne could accept the backfill argument but wouldn't let them off the mat. "Well, let me be perfectly clear. I don't deserve getting a cut in territory yet. In fact, after the job we've done in January, we, particularly Porter, ought to be rewarded. If you want more revenue out of New York and New Jersey, I suggest you hire a couple of young go'fers to work under my direction with another SE and you'll see some real production out of the district."

"With a higher Number?" O'Rourke asked.

"Goes without saying," Wayne replied. "But I know the business is there. Keep people like Lakota out of my way."

O'Rourke was stunned. He couldn't remember the last time a rep was wiling to accept a higher quota, let alone ask for it.

"We should consider that, Niles," Presby said.

"I agree," O'Rourke said. "We'll think it through. Wayne, please believe that we are indeed grateful for your work," O'Rourke said, hoping to push Wayne back into the 'happy' column.

"That goes double for me, Wayne," Presby said, not wanting to appear any less grateful than his boss.

"Thanks, but I need to see action. Gentlemen, I will need to make a decision on my future very soon."

O'Rourke was disappointed that his attempt at flattery failed.

"I promise you that we will make things work out."

They all dropped off the call. O'Rourke, in his office in Redwood City, could only shake his head. *I hope Engler is still in. I'm going to read him the riot act.*

Presby, wanting to be out on the Maryland slopes, saw his long, peaceful weekend severely damaged. W*hat* do *I say to Reaper? I should fire his ass.* He began to compose in his mind what to say, knowing that Grim Reaper would take it as yet another sign that Presby was out to get him.

Wayne gazed out the door to his back deck again, not confident he had accomplished anything with the phone call. *Well, the ball is in their court,* he told himself. *We'll have to see if they can do something with it.*

He decided to start packing for his own skiing weekend to take his mind off things but wanted to update Porter on his conversations with management. He shook his head as he dialed Porter's number. He found it ironic that he finally had a technical partner he believed in, but the relationship might not be long lived.

***

"Okay, Wayne. I understand," Porter said. "I guess the path was laid out for us, huh? I bet Norm was bullshit when you told him about Reaper's meeting in Atlanta."

"I haven't told him yet. I've got to think through the strategy."

"Can't we simply be honest with him?"

"Porter, I'm always honest but I'm not going to go in without thinking through the spin. Look, I need your help with that too. Let's talk at the show. I'm too burned out from all of today's crap to think clearly."

"I'll give it some thought over the weekend."

Brenda had watched him from just outside his office door.

"Why the long face, Porter?"

"That was Wayne Angelis. It would seem that he's running out of patience with some things."

"What's been happening? You've been pretty upbeat about how things are going. You were able to fix…" Just then a wail came from the nursery and Brenda and Porter left his office together to see what Stephanie was up to.

"She's hungry, as usual. Anyway keep talking." She reached into the crib for Stephanie, who immediately quieted down for Brenda. She sat down in the rocking chair she used for nursing, and Stephanie assumed the position.

She never quiets down that fast for me. Don't have the right equipment, I guess. "Anyway, yes, we fixed a lot of things and see some good opportunities but he's frustrated with some internal interference. I told you about that guy in Atlanta…"

"Sounds childish to me…no biting Steph…God help me when you have teeth…"

"Maybe, but something I've learned already is that these reps defend their turf to the death. More disturbing though is what it means for Norm. We failed to follow his lead."

"Is that all that Wayne is concerned about?"

"For good reason. Also, we are hiring more reps, meaning his territory would shrink."

"I don't know. Isn't New York big enough for more than one rep?" she asked.

Porter laughed. "Not in the mind of a rep. I think if they only had one rep for the whole country, he'd bitch when they hired a second one. Territorialism is part of their DNA. I think they mark their ground every morning like a wolf.

"This guy, Lakota, is particularly troublesome. He seems to be made of pure bullshit. But again, it comes down to turf. Wayne doesn't want to let any account control out of his hands, especially to someone outside sales."

They stopped talking while Porter stared out the nursery window, collecting his thoughts.

"So, you haven't told me how this affects you." Brenda said, breaking the silence and looking at him with a raised eyebrow, seeming to expect some bad news.

"I honestly don't know. If Wayne goes, they hire someone else and I'll be working with him or her. I could deal with that. I can't say the same about the threat to my relationship with Norm. I owe him a lot."

"Hey, Porter, your business cards say 'InUnison' now, not 'Security National'. It's obvious to me that you've bonded with Wayne already. He didn't have to call you today. You're a team in more than name, and that's pretty cool, I think. You need to do all you can to rescue that relationship. Aren't the other reps and SEs tight like that?"

"Hmmm, don't really know. Well, Reaper and Berkowski certainly aren't. Don't really know about Sean and Kyle…"

"They sound like a band…here, I have to go to the bathroom and get some diapers," Brenda said. She handed Stephanie over to Porter and draped a towel over his shoulder.

"And don't just stand there. Burp her." She fled down the hall to the bathroom.

"You've got me in your sights, don't you?" He thought he detected a mischievous grin on his six-month-old's face before putting her on his shoulder. It only took two taps on the back to produce a very wet sounding burp and the cascade of pabulum, most of which missed the poorly positioned cloth diaper.

Brenda returned to the nursery. "Got ya again, did she? Good girl!" She took Stephanie back from Porter to rock her for a while. "There must be something more to all this than a territory dispute. It can't be the first time he's encountered that."

"No. What I've decided about Wayne is that he is almost desperate to be part of a startup that hits it big. He talks about it a lot. He was pretty bitter about his last two companies selling out for what he considered peanuts. I think he's worried that InUnison will turn out to be another one."

"Well, she's not going back to sleep any time soon," Brenda said, putting a wriggling Stephanie on her play mat on the floor and handing her a rattle. "What do you think?"

"No, she doesn't look sleepy to me either."

"No, dummy, about InUnison's chances."

"Oh. I don't know. I'm too new at this. All I know is that we have cool technology that can streamline business. We have to get it in front of people who will recognize our value."

"So, you're happy so far, right?"

"Absolutely?"

"And Wayne has been a big part of that, right?"

"Yeah." *Oh, oh. She's doing that Socratic thing to me…*

"Then I think you should figure out a way to get Wayne off the ledge and back inside. Sounds to me like he's a winner." She gave him a quick peck on the check and left for the laundry room with an armful of towels.

He started to say something but instead watched her go down the hall, disappearing down the staircase.

I hate it when she does that. Damn psych major…

***

The next morning, Niles O'Rourke was at his desk in Redwood City when he saw his CEO walk past the door with his Vice-President of Marketing, Kirk Kincaid. Having missed him the prior evening, he was all the more anxious to confront Engler.

"Bill? Could I have five minutes of your time?"

Engler shuddered. He never seemed to have calm discussions with O'Rourke anymore. "Excuse me a second, Kirk. I'll be right there."

He turned around and entered O'Rourke's office. "What's up?"

"Did you explain to Fred Lakota that VAR deals like PensAndClips were going to be handled by field sales?"

"Yes, I phoned him right after our meeting on Monday. I told him that because the sales force was closest to those VAR-like organizations, and would be potentially co-selling with them, it made sense for them to be done by the direct sales force."

"What was his reaction?"

Engler stroked his beard, trying to remember. "There wasn't much of one. He asked if it was a final decision and I said that we would see how these deals evolved and review it at the end of the quarter. He did spend some time trying to talk me out of it but, frankly, I was surprised that his reaction was so muted."

"Well, he very nearly blew up our PensAndClips deal. I gave Angelis the draft agreement. He presented it to PandC and, after a few revisions, was ready to close the deal. Lakota called the guy there, and told him that he was still in charge of VAR deals. Naturally, that pissed him off since Angelis told him that *he* was responsible. I just got off the phone with Angelis and Craig Mansfield at PandC trying to smooth things over.

"Bill, this was a premeditated hit job on us. Fred went out –"

"Now, hold on! I simply can't believe that. Why would he want to blow up a deal? Talk about cutting off your nose …"

"When are you going to accept reality about him? He speak with forked tongue," O'Rourke said, wigging two fingers by his chin.

"Niles, I still want to hear his side. Let's get him on the phone."

O'Rourke shook his head, sighed and pulled out his phone list. Engler closed the door.

This should be good, thought O'Rourke, as he punched the numbers on his phone.

"Lakota, here."

Engler stepped closer to the speaker phone. "Fred, this is Bill and Niles."

"Good afternoon, guys. How are you Niles? We haven't talked for a while. How's the quarter going?"

O'Rourke closed his eyes and bit his tongue. "Fine, Fred. Thanks for asking."

"Fred, uh, we seem to have a misunderstanding about VAR deals," Engler said. "I thought I explicitly told you that Sales will run VAR deals. Is that your recollection?"

Lakota was silent for several seconds. "Well, you told me that the field sales reps were going to manage the relationship, but that I would still own the product. I think the misunderstanding was on the sales side. Luckily, I was able to wave off Wayne Angelis at PensAndClips…"

O'Rourke had heard enough. "No, you almost fucked it up…"

Engler put up his hand for O'Rourke to stop. "Fred, when I said that Sales would manage VARs, I thought that it was, uh, explicit that it meant that Business Development was out of the VAR business. I *did* say your focus should be on national and global strategic partnerships."

"Well, now Bill, in my mind, 'focus' doesn't mean 'to the exclusion of all else'. I clearly heard something different from your intent. It never occurred to me that I wasn't still in charge of the VAR agreement."

Bill, please see through this bullshit. He's playing you for an idiot, O'Rourke thought, practically begging Engler with his eyes to show some semblance of understanding.

Engler, however, exhibited only his usual poker face. "Okay, let's be very, very clear here, Fred. Going forward, neither you nor anyone in BD has anything to do with VAR deals."

"Now, Bill, what is a VAR and how does it differ from…"

"BILL! PLEASE!" O'Rourke mouthed.

"Niles, what's a VAR?" Engler rhetorically asked with his best withering stare.

"A VAR is a customer with a software product within which they want to use InUnison software. Their license restricts their use of our product to the application they sell and we get royalties from their resale of our product with theirs. Simple enough for you?"

"Now, what happens if they embed us in their product but it isn't visible to their client?" Lakota asked. "That's more like an Original Equipment Manufacturer and OEMs are different…"

"Bill, we can't do this over the phone. Look, Fred, you nearly blew up PandC for Angelis and I had to smooth things over. We can't tolerate –"

"Okay, you're right, Niles," Engler interrupted, sensing that he was going to lose control over the conversation. "Fred, we will talk about this next week when you get back. But until then, do not talk to any accounts where direct sales are working as VAR accounts."

"Yes, I look forward to clearing this up. You know I have extensive experience in these types of deals and should still be involved. Frankly, Niles, your boy Angelis is not up to the task on PandC. It's a very poorly qualified opportunity which will only come back to haunt us. If I were you…"

Engler hit mute as O'Rourke exploded. "Listen, you greasy, slicked-back bastard…" He stopped, accepting the futility of continuing.

"Niiii-uuullllls…" Engler said, waving a finger at his Sales VP. He took the phone off of mute. "Fred, we will discuss more next week. Goodbye and have a good weekend." He reached for the off button but Lakota wasn't finished.

"Oh, Bill? Just FYI. I had a great meeting with Flanderson yesterday. They were very anxious to move forward. I've definitely hooked them. They were very interested in our work with Azalea and PensAndClips, but of course I pooh-poohed that one…"

"You talked to them about *deals*?" O'Rourke asked. He gave up and started banging his head on his desk.

"That's great news, Fred! I'll look forward to hearing more when you get back." Engler finally hung up.

O'Rourke collapsed into his chair and covered his face with his hands. "Bill, please tell me you aren't buying any of that BS. He couldn't close a door let alone a major partnership deal."

Engler looked at his shoes. "Niles, I …" *I'm coming around to your point of view,* he couldn't say out loud. "Niles, I hear you. We'll resolve this next week. Sorry for the screw up. I take responsibility."

"Bill, that's a mistake. You should hold people like me, Fred, Kirk responsible. You didn't screw up PandC. Lakota did. You should hold *him* accountable."

Engler nodded silently and left O'Rourke's office.

Chapter 10 Showtime

The commuter train was not nearly as full as usual. *Probably because I'm so damn early,* Wayne thought. Anyway, he had his choice of seats so he took one in the back of the passenger car and settled in to review his newspapers. He turned to his usual survey of the *Wall Street Journal*, noting that VibraWeb was listed in the company index. He turned to page B9 to see the news.

"Shit!" The headline read, "Flanderson and VibraWeb Ink Strategic Partnership". Wayne's face got progressively more flushed as he read the article. He seized his cell phone and speed dialed Ken Presby.

"Ken, did you see this Flanderson deal with VibraWeb? They've got an equity deal and pre-paid licensing. Jesus, Lakota was recently talking to them. They actually met with him even though this deal was set. Unbelievable."

"Well, good morning to you too, Wayne."

"So, is Lakota a liar or purely stupid?"

"Both." Presby pulled up his email from O'Rourke reprising the conversation he had with Lakota and Engler. "Damn."

"What?"

"I was just reviewing the email I got from O'Rourke. You were copied, didn't you see it?"

"No, I was away this weekend and didn't check email."

Presby read the email to Wayne.

Wayne was incredulous. "He let them in on Azalea and PandC?"

"Why did you tell him anything?"

Oh, that's rich, blame the victim. "We talked about PandC of course since he was supposed to go there with me but we didn't talk at all about Azalea. He must have picked up the name from Porter talking about going there. Damn. We were trying to fly under the radar at Azalea…I bet they've called them already…no, Norm would have told me, but, well, maybe they called Miller in IT…shit, my quarter is toast…"

"Wayne, snap out of it! Look, let me see what HQ has to say about it and what they know. I'll be honest; since we depend on Lakota for this stuff we were probably in the dark."

"Okay, but let me know if there's any damage control on my end."

He pocketed his phone and tried to return to his paper. He couldn't concentrate on reading so he stared out the window. The weekend in the Catskills had done nothing to improve Wayne's mood or stress level, indeed the pressure from Helen only increased. She fell in love with the condo and talked the whole way home about how she would decorate it. It wouldn't have mattered if the house was a shack. It was the *idea* of owning a ski condo that closed it for Helen. Wayne sighed at the thought of yet another luxury item to maintain.

***

Both Porter and Wayne entered the Javits Convention Center by 10:00 a.m. as instructed by Maureen Madsen. The keynote speeches opening the show were from 9:00 to 11:00, so there wouldn't be any traffic in the exhibit area until after that. They found the booth but no Maureen.

The booth was a typical trade show display that unfolded from its cylindrical shipping container umbrella style to form a self-standing wall. Dozens of exhibitors had the exact same booth, as it was cheap and portable.

The background was covered with a tight-loop, black carpet-like fabric on which a back lit logo panel could be mounted. The green and red InUnison logo was silk screened onto this panel and illuminated.

"Did you see this, Porter?" Wayne showed him the article about the VibraWeb partnership.

"How can that be? I thought they were talking to us?"

"Well, they won't be talking any more."

A bundle of energy in the form of an aerobics-honed blonde female arrived at the booth. "HI guys! I'M Maureen! Happy to see you here! This is GOING to be a GREAT show, RIGHT?! Porter? *Wayne*?"

Porter was transfixed by the topography of her seemingly painted-on InUnison logo T-shirt. "InUnison" was rendered in vertically stretched, block letters, the "In" red, and "Unison" green. A white swoosh encircled the words, providing a handy target on Maureen's chest. "Huh? Oh, *definitely*." He was also still trying to figure out the spinner thing.

"Looks like you have things pretty well set up. I hope you had some help erecting the booth." Wayne struggled to keep his eyes above her shoulders as well.

"OH, SURE!" Maureen gushed. "The guys from Freeman Decorating always do the HEAVY stuff! I NEVER have a problem with them!"

I bet you have a really hard time getting help, Wayne wanted to say.

She went over the demo stations which had laptops set up to show InUnison's tools and a self-running presentation complete with video clip of CEO Bill Engler speaking. Nothing too difficult. The demo was usually a waste of time anyway, since few visitors would stand still long enough to watch the entire thing.

"Oh! And we have these really COOL Exer-Globes with our logo on it! You can really get that stress out by squeezing! Try one, Wayne! Yeah, *squeeeeeze* it."

An obedient Wayne complied, imagining the ball was something else…

"Cool. Mind if I check out who else is here? We still have about 30 minutes, right?" Wayne asked.

"OH! Sure, Wayne! You go right ahead!"

"Is it safe to leave you alone with her, Porter?" he whispered on the way out.

"I don't know, she might hurt me, *squeeze* me to death," Porter replied without averting his eyes from Maureen who scurried back to the front podium.

"So! Porter! Where are you from? How'd you join us? C'mon! Tell me about yourself! You married? Kids? *Come on!* …"

Wayne wandered down the aisle. The usual suspects were there, Oracle – we can do it all as long as it looks like a database, IBM – we can do it all as long as we put enough people on it, Iona – all the world is an object, Sun – the network is the integrator?…*hmm.* Netscape had a big booth touting its web server as an integration server. *A bit of a stretch,* Wayne thought. The majority of the booths, though, were occupied by small or unknown companies all saying they could integrate your business systems. He reminded himself that InUnison wasn't exactly a household word yet either.

He turned the corner and saw VibraWeb's booth down the next aisle. He stowed his floor pass in his pocket, so he could check them out incognito.

He needn't have bothered. The booth was unoccupied. He helped himself to their literature and kept wandering. After a complete circuit of the exhibition floor, he returned to the InUnison booth.

"Here's some light reading for you, Porter. I expect a complete analysis by the end of the day. If you can tear yourself away from Maureen, of course."

"Hey, she's actually pretty good. She stands out in the aisle and people stop by." *No mystery there*, Wayne thought. Porter shuffled through the VibraWeb literature. "This is interesting stuff. We don't seem to have a whole lot of competitive analysis on anyone."

"HEY! Here they come!" Maureen gushed at the opportunity to greet show attendees as they poured out of the keynote auditorium. Sure enough, she jumped out into the aisle, handing out squeeze balls and showcasing her own "hardware".

***

Two aisles away, a freshly coifed Gatto found the VibraWeb booth just in time for the onslaught of show attendees. He was more than a little miffed to be standing alone in the booth. *Where was that lame SE, Marcus Sweeney? And the marketing coordinator?* Just then, a group of four approached his booth.

"So, what is VibraWeb?" asked a particularly scruffy looking lad. Gatto couldn't make out the company name on the badge.

"We are a messaging-based platform for integrating systems."

"Oh. Does that have anything to do with user interfaces?"

"Not a thing." Gatto reached into his pocket and found a quarter. "Here's twenty-five cents. Go buy a clue."

He shook the bewildered consultant's hand and turned away.

***

The day loped forward as countless tech-heads and nerd-faced visitors meandered through the hall, stopping every so often to pick up a tchotchke or take in a product demo.

Porter was getting hoarse from talking so much. His voice was not used to this kind of abuse, made worse by having to talk over loud music coming from a nearby demo stage. Wayne noticed that his partner's energy level was on the wane as it was already past five o'clock and he hadn't had so much as a bathroom break since the exhibitor floor opened.

"Porter, you don't have to be a martyr. You *are* allowed to leave the booth once in a while. Why don't you wander off and get something to eat or drink. The traffic seems to be dropping off a bit."

"Didn't realize how late it was getting. I've been trying to keep up with Maureen. Does she ever stop bouncing around? Can I get you something?"

Yes, bouncing. Wayne nodded, "Yes, a bottle of water."

"Oh, I meant to ask you about Norm. You *are* going to call him about the Atlanta thing, right?"

"Yes, I traded voicemails with him today. He's at some offsite meeting today and tomorrow so I suggested breakfast on Wednesday. He lives in Jersey, right?"

"Yes, Teaneck actually."

"Perfect. We can meet him in Fort Lee before our Sampson Logistics meeting. Then it's a quick trip down to Salomon in East Rutherford. I'll leave him a final message to meet us at Chelsea Deli in Fort Lee, say seven thirty."

"Better to be in public. He might want to strangle us or something," Porter said and left for his break.

As Porter was exiting, a stylish Asian man with a speaker ribbon attached to his show badge approached the booth.

"InUnison, is Tom Gatto here by chance?"

"He's no longer with the company, can I help you?" Wayne asked. He took a step back thinking this might be another of Gatto's landmines.

"Oh, didn't know that. I'm Larry Liu with Flanderson Consulting," he said, extending his hand to Wayne. Wayne noticed that his title said "Financial Services Partner", a fairly significant title at Flanderson. *Was this the guy Lakota met with?* he wondered. "I know Tom from his days at NeXT and Sun Microsystems. We did quite a lot of business together, especially when he was at Sun. I was hoping to renew the acquaintance. He was a great guy to work with. No BS."

Wayne hoped that his face didn't reflect his incredulity. *"Great guy to work with? No BS?* Having spent most of January cleaning up after Gatto, Wayne figured Liu must be talking about another Tom Gatto.

"You wouldn't happen to know where he went?" Liu asked.

"Sorry, I don't know. It was kind of abrupt. Also, I started with the company in January."

"Your loss."

"Well since you're here, would you like to hear about our integration products? I bet we could help in your consulting practice."

"Sorry, we just announced a tight relationship with VibraWeb and since they are your competitor…" Liu said with a shrug.

"Now, there's always room for two isn't there?"

"Not when we have an equity investment involved. We actually liked your stuff better, from a technical standpoint. But your BD guys seemed to want to come into town from Silicon Valley only to do lunches and dinners. Also, we were interested in an investment play. My advice? Get someone other than that Lakota guy as a front man. When we dealt with VibraWeb it was all business."

"That's too bad. But I know Lakota met with someone from Flanderson last week. This deal with VibraWeb just happened, right?"

Liu grinned. "I know what you're thinking; why did we bother…"

"You were there?"

"Yes. And my project lead. Hey, it was a great lunch and content-free as usual."

"So, I'm sorry that you guys couldn't get something going, but I'd still be happy to engage your team on an opportunistic basis. Is that still possible?"

Liu frowned but didn't want to close the door entirely. "Well, I don't want to mislead you. I can't bring you into any deals but, sure, I'm always looking for business. You'll have to bring the deal to me."

Of course, you'd dump us as soon as you got inside, Wayne thought.

Liu suddenly stepped out into the aisle. "Well, speak of the devil! There's Gatto now!"

Wayne jumped out into the aisle as well. It *was* the greasy one wandering up the aisle. Just at that moment Gatto saw Liu, smiled and waved. Then he glanced to Liu's right, saw Wayne and the smile faded.

"Tom Gatto! How the hell are you?" Liu greeted him like a long lost friend. "I was telling Wayne here what a great guy you were and here you are!"

Gatto looked at Wayne with disdain but put out his hand in greeting.

"Angelis," Gatto said, with undisguised scorn. "How are things going at the old InUnison?"

"Fine, Tom." He glanced down at Gatto's exhibitor pass to see that he was with VibraWeb.

Liu, still incredibly pleased to see Tom, clapped him on the back.

"Tom, where are you now?" he asked, not thinking to look at the badge.

Gatto had a smirk as he said, "Oh, I didn't go far. I'm with VibraWeb."

"What? That fast?" Then looking at Wayne, Liu asked, "What? Aren't you guys smart enough to have non-compete clauses? If he's anything like he used to be, you're not going to get any business in New York!"

Gee, thanks for that gut punch.

"Oh, funny thing," Wayne countered, looking squarely in Gatto's eyes, "Haven't seen VibraWeb all month. Any idea why that was, Tom? Didn't want to go slumming in your old accounts? Potential Investing really misses you."

Gatto's eyes narrowed as the face of George Melani flashed in his mind.

"Some accounts aren't worth my time," he growled through his teeth. "I hope George didn't hurt you much."

Wayne closed the distance between them. "Nah, he's a pussy cat. We're great friends now that Porter mopped up the shit you left." He hoped his breath wasn't fresh.

Liu stepped in. He hadn't intended to instigate a brawl, and this was starting to look ugly.

"Well! Hey! Tom, where's your booth? I'd like to stop by. Now that I know you're with a partner of ours we can do some business again." He gave a warning scowl to Wayne.

Wayne broke his visual lock on Gatto and turned to Liu.

"I've got some other people to chat with here, so you'll have to excuse me. Pleasure meeting you." He went back into the booth to great some of Maureen's catch.

Liu and Gatto walked away from the InUnison booth. Out of earshot, Liu asked Gatto about that exchange.

"Well, they brought that snake in and he immediately tried to poach my territory. My former management indicated in very clear terms that I wasn't fitting into their long term plans."

"Were you making your Number?"

"Of course! You know me. I was number one."

Liu shook his head. "I have to wonder about the management over there. You know we have just announced a great partnership with VibraWeb. I was stopping by to offer condolences."

"Yes, were you responsible for that?"

"Mostly. Gotta be honest with you. We liked the InUnison stuff better, from a product standpoint. But the relationship couldn't get off the ground."

"Bet you had some great lunches with Lakota, though, right?"

Liu chuckled. "Last week, as a matter of fact. Anyway, it's great that we'll be able to work together. Why didn't you let me know you moved? I've got a lot of business to throw your way."

"Anything you can toss my way today? That big mouth Lakota must have told you what InUnison was up to."

"Well, I'm kind of in a bind on that, Tom. Yes, he mentioned a couple of things but I'm not sure what I can say about them. We were under a non-disclosure agreement."

NDA, shmen-DA. "C'mon, they'll screw them up anyway."

Liu looked around. "Okay, but I'll deny ever telling you. There's a deal at something called PensAndClips…"

Well, can't go back there… Gatto thought.

"...Merrill Lynch…"

Ditto. This isn't exciting me, Larry…

"…and Azalea Financial."

"Well, to be honest, I took InUnison into PandC and Merrill. Angelis is reaping the benefits. As far as Azalea, turns out the cousin of the CIO works for us on the West Coast. He gave me a heads up about something going on there. I tried to use his connection but that guy, Stewart Miller, gave me the brush-off. Supposedly he's one of those old-fashioned IT guys. Thinks he can do it all with Big Blue."

"Hey, that's not all I have. That's what Lakota brought up."

As they walked up to the VibraWeb booth, Sweeney was deep in technical talk with a bunch from Citibank, so Liu and Gatto chatted for quite a while about other possible joint sales opportunities.

***

Wayne decided to stay in Manhattan during the show rather than commute back and forth. The exhibit floor opened earlier than the first day and he didn't want to have to awake at 5:30 to make it into the Javits Center on time. Porter considered staying as well – Wayne tried to bribe him with a steak dinner at the Palm – but Porter really hated being away from his daughter for even a night. Wayne was amazed that there actually were limits to Porter's lust for food.

Waking up before his five thirty alarm and wakeup call, Wayne wasted no time dialing into email. While his messages started to download, he brushed his teeth and started the coffee maker. He returned to the desk and scanned the first message titled "Niles O'Rourke Promoted", a company news release which was going to go out that day. Wayne burst into laughter as he read.

FOR IMMEDIATE RELEASE

Niles O'Rourke promoted to Senior Vice-President, Sales and Business Development at InUnison Software.

InUnison Software is proud to announce the promotion of Niles O'Rourke, formerly Vice-President of Sales for InUnison, to the newly created position of Senior Vice-President – Sales and Business Development.

Says William Engler, Chairman and CEO, "Niles has proven to be a world class sales manager who has formed a team which has performed second to none in the software industry. As we continue to grow, we felt that the roles of sales and partnership management needed to be consolidated."

"I'm humbled and pleased that Mr. Engler has shown such confidence in my abilities," O'Rourke said. "More important, it recognizes the hard work of the entire sales team in 1997 and the fast start we are off to in 1998."

InUnison also announces that Fred Lakota, formerly Vice-President of Business Development for InUnison, has decided to pursue other interests.

"I want to express my appreciation for the trust that Bill Engler has given me over the last two years," Lakota said. "I've decided for personal reasons to slow down, spend more time with family and then pursue opportunities after an appropriate period of rest and relaxation."

About InUnison: InUnison is the leader in message-based Enterprise Application Integration. Its products are installed across the spectrum of enterprise applications and are used the world over. InUnison is funded by Superior Venture Partners – Fund IV, Broadscape InfoMillenium Wealth Managers, Founders VC International and other private investors.

Business press - direct questions to Joyce Welland, Director, InUnison Corporate Communications, 408-555-9890, jwelland@inunison.com **or visit www.inunison.com.**

Well! I've got to find out the scoop on this, he thought. He dialed Presby.

"Ken, Wayne. So give me the scoop on this O'Rourke thing."

"Oh, it was a piece of beauty. Engler saw that Flanderson announcement yesterday and totally flipped out. He called up Jones – you know the building manager out there – and had him bring up a bunch of boxes to Lakota's office. He ordered him to pack up all of Fred's stuff. Lakota…" Presby paused to control his chuckles, "…he shows up around eleven in the morning, sees all his stuff in boxes and…" Presby was losing control again, "…and… and…he still doesn't get it. He goes to Betty in HR and asks if they were moving to another building or something. Now, Betty *knows* what is going on since she had to get the exit paperwork together but she can't *tell* him. She sends him to Engler who has gone totally ballistic. O'Rourke was with Bill when he shows up. Engler tells that scum bag to sit down, still with O'Rourke there, and tells him that he's fired. Lakota asks why, and Engler says, 'Because you're a lying sack of shit' and throws a copy of the *Journal* article at him. He starts blubbering about how he was taken in by Flanderson and crap like that. Engler told him to get his stuff, sign the papers and get out, and if he says anything bad about him or the company he'd sue his ass."

"Isn't that out of character for Engler?"

"He puts up with almost anything, but not lying. He goes ballistic if he thinks he's been lied to, especially if it's someone in the inner circle."

"So, Fred's out, just like that?"

"Just like that."

"Amazing. How did they get that quote out of him?"

"Oh, please. Our corporate flack put that in. Can't simply say 'we fired his sorry ass', after all."

"I should have known."

"So, Lakota won't be around to screw up your deals any longer. Does that help get you off the ledge?"

"Well, not like I want to dance on someone's grave, but yes, it helps."

"Good. Wayne, I'll say again how impressed we are with your efforts in such a short amount of time. We need you. Oh, and O'Rourke approved hiring a New Jersey sales team reporting to you."

"Don't worry, Ken. I'll hang in there. Oh, before I forget, guess who surfaced at VibraWeb?"

"Haven't a clue, Wayne."

"Tom Gatto. And he's apparently a good friend of the Financial Services partner at Flanderson Consulting."

"Wayne, I really wouldn't worry about him. You've got a much better organization behind you." Presby tried to allay any fears Wayne might have about Gatto joining the competition.

"I suppose but I had to sign a non-compete. How can Gatto get away with this move?"

"Look, we only now started to do non-competes. It's kind of a legacy of Engler's 'we are family' style but O'Rourke is trying to inject some reality here. This ain't no encounter group, it's *sales*. Gatto and a couple others balked at signing one and were kind of grandfathered. I suggest that you forget about Gatto and Flanderson and continue to cultivate local partners."

"You're right, Ken. I need leverage. Porter can't handle all the technical issues and he certainly can't get sold into proof-of-concept slavery all the time."

"Right. Anything coming out of the show?"

"Not much. We've had good traffic but only a few quality leads to follow up."

"Well, thanks for doing it. I know it's a pain. Of course, Maureen's there right? Can't be too bad then," he chuckled.

"Hadn't noticed, who's Maureen?"

"Yeah, right."

"Oh, you mean Miss Hard Body with the bouncing logo balls?"

"That's her! Her chest generates more leads than half the sales force. Get back to work! Let's go sell! Beat VibraWeb!"

"Later," Wayne said.

Wayne hung up the phone and began to put his work away but stopped as he was about to shut down his computer. He fished through his pockets for a business card, found what he was looking for and went back into email.

He selected the email with the press release attachment announcing O'Rourke and Lakota's moves.

First, Craig Mansfield. This should solidify our relationship, he thought. He smiled as he typed the email title: "I'm your guy". In the body he wrote:

> **Craig, the attachment speaks for itself. I hope we can conclude our business very soon.**
>
> **Wayne Angelis, InUnison Software**

Hmmm, what about Larry Liu? Wayne debated. He knew that it would be fruitless – and a little petty – to forward the announcement to Liu but somehow he felt that there might still be an open door with Liu. He fished through more pockets for Liu's business card, finding it in his khakis from the first day of the show.

He typed a short message to Larry:

> **No Free Lunch**
>
> **Larry, I regret to inform you that there will be no more free lunches from InUnison – see attached news release.**
>
> **I was very pleased to meet you yesterday and hope that we can do business at least opportunistically. You'll see in the attached news release that we have significantly upgraded our Business Development personnel.**
>
> **Wayne Angelis, InUnison Software**

He triumphantly clicked on 'send' and jumped into the shower.

***

Porter flashed his vendor pass at the guard leading into the main exhibit hall. The forest of booths and displays were at peace – except for the whine of a vacuum cleaner in the distance – and the aisle carpets were pristine for the time being. He had come to the exhibit floor an hour early so he could rehearse his demos, anticipating that Wayne would be scheduling a bunch of presentations.

He connected his laptop into the booth's network hub so that his demo could use resources such as the Oracle database on Marketing's show computer. Following his first abortive demo at Manley Brothers, Porter struggled to properly show their products work on one screen but there wasn't enough real estate. So, he had been working on a presentation which would use both his laptop and Wayne's.

"Wayne!" Porter said, with a start. "How long have you been there? You startled me."

"I didn't want to disturb you. From what I could see, it's pretty cool stuff. Are we going to be able to do that two-machine thing ourselves?"

"That's my plan. I'll need to load some stuff on your machine."

"Hey, if it punches up our presentation, I'm all for it."

Porter shut down his laptop and stowed it in the cabinet in the rear of the booth.

"So, Wayne, how's the attitude?"

"Pretty good, actually. Significantly enhanced by the announcement this morning."

"What announcement?"

"Didn't you check email this morning?"

"No. I wanted to get back in here early."

Wayne gave him the news.

"Well, I can't say I'm disappointed," Porter said. "With O'Rourke running both areas, cooperation should be better, right?"

"Should be. It's a huge help for us to own VARs. I think we can make some quick hits on that theme using PensAndClips as a reference. I'm dying to talk to Mansfield. I forwarded the press release to him."

"Gee, that might be our first deal, huh?"

"Could be. I think we can close it real soon."

"It's good to see you smile like that, buddy. You were so grim last week."

"I know. I have to stay focused on the business and the Number. Oh, also, Tom Gatto is now with the competition."

"VibraWeb?"

"Yep."

"You've never told me what the deal was between you two."

Wayne wished he hadn't brought the subject up. He didn't want to go into the details. "It wasn't complicated. He thought the whole world was his territory. I had to make a stand and, luckily, management backed me up." He wanted to leave it at that with Porter.

The announcement came over that the exhibit floor was now open and attendees started to trickle in, making their way down the blue aisles.

"Where's Maureen? She *is* going to be here today, right? She's the only thing that makes this event tolerable. I hope she brings her 'friends'," Wayne said, squeezing the air with his hands about chest high.

"You hound. She didn't say anything to me. Oh, oh, this is trouble…" He nodded toward the rather lost looking soul staring at his floor map.

"You know him?"

"Yeah, he's the dude from Azalea IT, the Data Security Officer, Mordecai Rosenzweig. He's the one who tipped off Miller after seeing us work on the pilot. Seems like a nice guy, but all spies are like that."

Wayne scratched his chin. "We better get him in here. I'd like to pump him for some info." Before Porter could beat him to it, Wayne was out into the aisle, extending his hand.

"Hello, Mordecai. I'm Wayne Angelis of InUnison Software. How are you this morning? Enjoying the show?"

Mordecai shook Wayne's hand rather robotically, wondering how he knew his name.

"Uh, yes, pleased to meet you," Mordecai managed to say. "Do I know you? You weren't at the demo, were you?"

"No, you met..." he turned to point to Porter, "...Porter Mitchell who is here as well. Come on in. Wouldn't you like to see what else we have to offer? From what Porter's told me, you only saw a snippet of what we can do."

"Hello, Mordecai. Good to see you again," Porter said.

"Call me Mordi. Everyone else does." He had long since given up on fighting the abbreviation.

"Porter, can you show him that new stuff you were going over with me?" He wanted to hang back and observe how Rosenzweig reacted to the demo.

Porter embarked on a lengthy overview of all the existing and soon-to-be released products. Rosenzweig was very attentive, nodding frequently to acknowledge his comprehension of the key points that Porter was making.

"So, Mordi," Wayne asked, "what do you think?"

"Thank you very much, Porter," Mordi said, then turned to answer Wayne.

"I was very impressed at the first demo, and even more so now. You have a very comprehensive yet easy to use system here. You're able to shrinkwrap capabilities we, or some expensive consultant, would have to code directly."

"You're the Security Officer, right? So, you must know a lot about all the different systems at Azalea?"

"Sure do. I'm also on the steering committee." He was very proud of his place on an important committee. It gave him significant visibility.

"With all these new packaged applications coming along that must be a big challenge." *I'm sensing a problem crying out for a solution, an InUnison solution,* Wayne was thinking.

"You bet. I wish that there was some sort of standard all of these systems could adhere to for security. I know there are things like LDAP coming but it isn't baked yet. And then there is the customization to our home grown systems, ouch."

Porter decided to jump into the discussion. "Actually, Mordi, we have customers doing pilots with us that demonstrate single login capabilities," Porter said. "They use a front-end authorization which then interrogates a database for a particular user to find out what systems that user has access to. There's even one project where they are going to use digital certificates. We already handle those for using secure messages."

About time you weighed in, Porter, Wayne thought.

Mordecai was thinking about Porter's scenario. *Hmmm,* that *would be something I could really use. And the fact that they adapt to the system instead of vice versa...* "I have to say that you've allayed one of my biggest concerns about InUnison. I came away from Brewster's demo fearing that everyone in the world would be able to jump into every system willy-nilly. If we can use your infrastructure to manage access…" He trailed off for a moment. "…and you do digital certificates so Internet stuff would work…" His mouth scrunched up into one of those knowing, impressed frowns.

I don't have a clue what you're talking about, Mordi, but you do seem to know what you're doing, Wayne thought. "Mordi, you seem to be pretty up to date. What's your background?"

"I spent about ten years in government."

"What part of government?"

"Federal."

"Okay, department?"

"Defense."

Are you some kind of spook? A frustrated Wayne thought. *I'll keep trying.*

"Army?"

"No, just Defense Department. Ft. Meade, Maryland. I'm really not at liberty…"

"Oh, I understand," Wayne said, even though he had no idea what went on in Ft. Meade. "How did you end up at Azalea? I shouldn't say this, but you seem overqualified for Azalea."

You're right about that, Wayne. "Basically, I wanted to be home here in New York. My parents are older and I wanted to be near to them."

"We didn't get a whole lot of feedback from Stewart Miller after his demo. Can you shed some light there?"

"Well, I don't really know. He must have been intrigued enough because when he came down he just told me to come to this show and check out this new integration stuff. He wanted me to get a contact list together. To be honest, I don't see a whole lot of substance at this show. You guys, and maybe this VibraWeb thing…" He pulled out a VibraWeb marketing brochure. "But the guy over there was a jerk."

Wayne and Porter suppressed their chuckle.

An alarm bell went off in Wayne's head. *Contact list?*

"What does Miller want with a contact list? I heard that he hates dealing with vendors, at least directly."

"You got that right. Joke around the datacenter is that they don't get into his office unless they bring a logo coffee mug he doesn't already have. Then he does that stupid samurai routine…" Mordecai stopped himself from going any further over the "bash Miller" line. "Anyway, that's what he wants me to do."

"Well, I hope you don't think we're jerks, and sorry, we aren't handing out coffee mugs. Norm Johnson used our products at his last job and, as you saw, is off and running at Azalea. I think he can vouch for our character. Do you anticipate being involved with that project?"

"For better or worse, I'm involved in everything. I keep trying to get Miller to reorganize my section. He's stuck thinking that data security means having a login to the mainframe. It's a lot more complicated than that."

"How big is your section? I assume you manage it."

Geez, Wayne, what is this, twenty questions? Porter didn't think this was going anywhere and there were other visitors to the booth so he snuck away to meet them.

"There are four of us, and, yes, I'm the director. Got here six months ago." Mordi shivered a bit recalling the past six months under Miller.

Wayne felt that he was bonding with Rosenzweig and continued to schmooze. Mordi seemed to enjoy having this innocuous conversation. After another fifteen minutes during which family pictures were shared amidst talk of skiing in the Catskills, though, he decided to take his leave. He thanked both Wayne and Porter and moved on down the aisle.

Porter was finishing with some consultants and collared Wayne in between demos.

"Wayne, what was that line of questioning on Rosenzweig? He's the enemy!"

"I'm hurt! First of all, I don't think that he *is* the enemy and if he is, I think he can be turned. He knows where a lot of bones are buried in that datacenter. He's smarter than he lets on."

"I didn't notice. Seemed like an IT grunt to me."

"Listen to you. You were an IT grunt a month ago. Look, after selling for as long as I have, you get a sense about people. I'll bet we can turn Mordi. Norm should be nice to him and co-opt him into his pilot."

"Doubt that will happen."

"If he doesn't work with him, I will."

"You can't! We owe it to Norm, don't we? He's bringing us in."

"Forget for a second that he's your buddy. If I see an opportunity to raise the probability for a sale, I'll do whatever I have to do to secure the deal. Hell, if Miller suddenly sees the light, I'd jump on that bandwagon just like I'll jump on Carlton's in Atlanta."

"But what about Norm?"

"Who cares? He will still get his project, but we get a bigger deal."

I didn't notice the ice water in your veins before, Wayne, Porter thought. *I don't think I like it.*

Wayne saw Porter's dismay. "This is why I couldn't talk to you about this over the phone last week; I knew you'd get emotional. Porter, remember who you work for now."

Porter wasn't going to give him the satisfaction of knowing that Brenda agreed. "Don't we work for our customers?" he said instead.

"As long as they are on the path to revenue."

"God, 'path to revenue'. I'm starting to get tired of that phrase."

"Porter, revenue and the Number rule. It will make sense to you eventually. Usually by the last week of the quarter."

Porter reflexively wanted to protect his former mentor somehow but couldn't construct a retort that put InUnison's interests first. It finally dawned on him that his relationship with Norm had fundamentally changed now that he was on the selling end. But had he lost all credibility, simply by joining a software vender? So many of the booth visitors scoffed at what Porter told them – truthfully, in Porter's mind – about his products. Their skepticism hurt more than his sore throat.

Wayne gave Porter that kind of scolding, fatherly "you'll learn like I did" look that Porter used to hate from his own father.

"Can I count on your support tomorrow morning when we have to talk to Norm about the Atlanta fiasco? Or is this going to be a conflict for you?" Wayne asked.

"Wayne, don't question my loyalties. I know where my future lies and Azalea is only one account. But I won't stand for any dishonesty."

"Porter, don't confuse spin with dishonesty. Spin is putting the facts in the best light. That's all I'm doing here. I don't lie to anyone, Porter. Not even to customers," Wayne said with a wink and grin.

Chapter 11 Sandbags

Mordecai Rosenzweig struggled to his desk, weighted down by the two canvas bags of contraband from the IntegrateNow! trade show, most notably the dozen or so coffee mugs he'd snatched for Stewart Miller. He dumped everything out on his desk, sorting the literature into one pile, items he was interested in keeping for himself in another pile, and then put the mugs back into one of the bags for delivery to Miller. He dug into his briefcase for the contact list he compiled from the show and shoved that into the bag with the mugs.

He checked his watch: twelve thirty-two. He hoped Miller would still be at lunch so he could slip into his office, drop his bags and get out without the usual Miller abuse. He lifted the bag of mugs too aggressively, causing the mugs to clank loudly.

"Hey, Mordi, keep it down," his neighbor complained. "You doing dishes over there or something?"

He walked down the corridor to Miller's office, mugs clinking the whole way. He was disappointed to see Miller in his office polishing off a sandwich from the cafeteria deli.

"Mordi, how ya doin' today?"

"Good, Stewart. I was organizing the stuff from the show for you. It's all in the bag."

"Mugs! Good job!"

"There's also literature. I compiled a contact list of the companies I visited like you asked. What are you going to do with it?"

Mordi didn't think Miller had been paying attention as he was busy examining the mugs and deciding which would go where on his shelves.

"Stewart?"

"Huh? Oh, I'm going to look them over and decide which ones will do as sandbags."

"Sandbags?"

"Yeah. I'm going to slow that Johnson guy down. See, he's only looking at one vendor for his project." Miller put a white and red Oracle mug back on his desk. "Already have one of these. You want it?"

"No, thanks. So, I'm still not following you."

Miller found a place for two more mugs. "See, we have a policy here that before you bring any software in-house, it has to be evaluated against the market and, of course, internal capabilities. Oooh, that's a cool one!" He admired a bright orange and yellow striped mug, giving it a place of honor directly behind his desk. "So, it doesn't matter how well he demos anything. He can pilot and demo until hell freezes over but nothing's going production on my system until I'm satisfied it's the right stuff. Shoot, got that one too." He put another duplicate mug on his desk.

"Well, they are doing some impressive things and what I saw at the show reinforced that InUnison seems to be out in front on this EAI market."

Miller spun to face Mordi. "I don't give a rat's ass. It's *my* domain and I will, WILL control what software or hardware gets into Azalea Financial."

"So, I still don't see what the contact list…"

"RFI, Mordi. 'Request for Information'. I'm going to – actually *you* are going to – draft an RFI to send to this list of vendors, especially InUnison. It will take weeks for them to reply, during which I will figure out how to rip that financial project out of their hands."

"But won't that piss off Racker? He keeps saying he can't wait for that kind of process."

"That's what they always say." He found homes for the remaining mugs and sat down, pulling out the contact list. "I don't recognize any of these companies…okay, IBM, but who the hell is Iona? Oracle; they're like a plague." He scanned to the last page. "VibraWeb…VibraWeb…why is that familiar?" He stared at the name, racking his brain for the reason the name triggered something. He reached for his business card file, next to his phone.

Flipping quickly to the "V" tab, he pulled out several cards and flipped through them.

"Ah, that's why! My cousin works for them. He was bragging about them at Christmas. Very interesting." Miller looked up at the ceiling, flicking Eric Miller's business card with his middle finger. A smile crept across his face.

"Mordi, I think we can get some help for you on this RFI." He reached for his phone and dialed his cousin's phone number.

"VibraWeb, Miller speaking."

"Eric, this is cousin Stewart. How're you doin?"

"Fine, Stewart. This is an unexpected, uh, pleasure. How're things at the bank?"

"Great, couldn't be better, Eric. Say, we're going to do a study of this EAI market you guys are in, you know, do an RFI, maybe a pilot project, that kind of thing. Would you be able to pass me some good information to better formulate a questionnaire?"

Eric paused, a bit suspicious of Stewart's motive after the earlier brush-off. "Well, first of all, Stewart, you should meet with our rep out there, Tom Gatto. Remember the message I left with you about him?"

"Gatto, Gatto? Oh, right. He called a while ago. I'll call him right away. So what else can you do for me?"

Eric wanted to dump Stewart on Gatto but he knew that would irritate both. *Wait, we just got something from Flanderson…* "Stewart, just a second. I need to find an email." He scanned the last couple days of emails and found one from Marketing which had an Adobe Acrobat attachment.

"Stewart, I'm sending you a document from Flanderson Consulting. They, uh, independently analyzed the needs of corporate America with respect to EAI and came up with a set of criteria in the form of a questionnaire for people like yourself to use when evaluating products in our space."

"How did you get it?"

"Flanderson offers it to all their clients."

"Well, send it along then."

"Now, Stewart, I'm going to call Gatto and give him the heads up on this. Please don't embarrass me. Take his call."

"Sure thing. I'll look forward to it."

"Bye, Stewart. The email is on it's way."

Stewart hung up and smiled at Mordecai. "Like I said, I got you some help."

He turned to his PC and checked for email. Among ten new messages was the one from Eric. He opened the attachment and scanned it.

"Beautiful. Mordi, here's your RFI. Sanitize it of any reference to Flanderson and you're good to go. When you're done, give it to Sandy to distribute to everyone on the contact list. Oh, write up a cover letter like this." He reached into his file for his standard RFI cover letter. "Put a response date of, oh…" Miller glanced at the calendar, flipping to February. "…February 9th."

"That only gives them a week. Is that really enough time?"

"No way. But I'll bet that VibraWeb will submit it in time."

"Why is that important?"

"Competition and we control the process."

***

While Miller plotted his moves, Gatto fretted about his forecast. He looked over his spreadsheet in his Penn Center office, continuing to curse his predecessor for saddling him with long sales cycle deals. Means wouldn't listen to reason about the low probability of closing the accounts and refused to remove them from Gatto's forecast.

His phone interrupted his thoughts.

"Tom, this is Eric Miller in HQ."

"Hey, how are you? Sorry we haven't talked all month. Been heads down."

"Likewise. Hey, I just got off the phone with my cousin, Stewart, you know, the Azalea CIO. All of a sudden he's doing a study of EAI. I sent him that new so-called independent RFI document we got out of Flanderson. He's going to issue it to a bunch of vendors."

"Oh, shit. I don't have time for RFIs. What did you do that for?"

"Settle down. Part of what we got from the Flanderson deal was this questionnaire and of course the proper responses. It only asks questions that we already have the right answers for, product-wise."

"Now, that's the way to do RFIs! Sorry I bitched. Now, is he going to finally show some interest in us?"

"He'd better, or I'll get my aunt to bring hellfire on him. I'm suspicious why he's doing this all of a sudden."

"InUnison is in there with a group in the Controller's office and that triggered a red alert in IT."

"That makes perfect sense. He's going to sandbag them. But that may mean he isn't serious about us."

"Could be, Eric. But at least I won't have to invest a whole lot to find out. Maybe I can sniff around and see about an opportunity." *And maybe create some havoc for Angelis.*

"Let me know if I can help."

"Thanks for the tip."

***

It was now Friday, two days after the trade show wrapped up, and Wayne was in his home office, trying to catch up on his prospecting. He was interrupted by the familiar screeching noise of his fax machine coming to life. He rolled his desk chair over to see what was coming in. The name on the cover page made his heart leap.

"Pens and Clips dot com," he whispered. The message was a signed VAR agreement and purchase order for software and services. The bottom line read "$175,000".

"YES YES YES!" he screamed, pumping his fist.

Helen came running. "What's the commotion? You scared the dog!"

"Oh, nothing much, just my first order at InUnison. Fuckin' A!"

Helen wasn't impressed. "Grow up. You'd think you had never sold anything before."

"Hey, after the month I've had? I've been in serious withdrawal. I needed the fix."

"You're such a child," She stomped out of the office.

Party pooper. He turned back to the fax machine to see what was still coming out. "Oh my! This is AWESOME! Lehman, Citicorp, Ernst and Young, AT&T…outstanding!" Craig Mansfield from PandC included contact information for his customers in his fax.

"Porter," he said to himself, "strap on, we're going in."

***

"You *are* a Fat Bear! I love to see POs come in bunches."

"As I told you, George, I've struck a lode here with these startups," Gatto told his manager.

"Of course, they're small…"

Here it comes…

"…and Hager will complain about the risk of startups…"

"Okay, you want me to call these guys up and say never mind?"

"NO! I, uh, we, needed $175k this month. And don't forget the Early Bird bonus since this is the first month in the quarter."

"I should get a couple more tomorrow, so that would put me over $250k for the month."

"FAT BEAR 'EM! Get 'em in!" Means screamed before cackling uncontrollably.

"I'm glad to make you so happy, George."

Melani got himself under control. "So, when can we close Azalea?"

Azalea? Oh, shit. "George, how do you know anything about Azalea? I'm only now getting to the plate with them."

"Miller mentioned it to Hager out in HQ. Hager says you're in the 'fucking driver's seat', giving them our boilerplate RFI and such."

"George, I haven't even met the CIO yet, you know, Miller's cousin. I'm heading down there shortly. But I think that he's going to use us."

"For what?"

"He wants to blow up an outside group's project so he's going to slow them down with the RFI. I don't think he wants us any more than he wants InUnison."

"They're in there?"

"Yes, but not with IT."

"Then get in there. Hager says he wants 'a big fucking name account'."

Great. Just the kind of visibility I don't need.

"I really don't want to set expectations…"

"Well, then you shouldn't have it in your forecast."

"It's not in my forecast…"

Means started to giggle again like a schoolboy in on a prank. "Yes it is. Hager wanted it on your 'fucking forecast' so I entered it."

"Gee, thanks. You're so helpful." *You mother…*

Gatto hung up the phone only to glance at the time and realized that he was running late for his meeting with Stewart Miller. He snatched his Burberry coat and briefcase and raced to the elevator.

In about thirty minutes, Gatto was exiting the elevator on the tenth floor of Azalea's headquarters on Water Street. *Typical IT. A security card reader instead of a human…*

He walked over to the wall phone and, per the instructions, lifted the receiver.

"Hello, Datacenter," the ever present Rebecca Sharpe said.

"This is Tom Gatto with VibraWeb to see Stewart Miller. Can you buzz me in or whatever?"

"Please hold while I verify the appointment."

He started to pace as far at the phone cord would allow.

"He's expecting you," Sharpe said, surprised that was the case.

The door buzzed loudly as he hung up the phone. He entered and spotted a short portly woman in a tight flowery dress coming towards him. *Oooo, this one definitely bit the hose,* Gatto thought as he put on his best smile.

"Hi, I'm Tom Gatto."

"Becky Sharpe," she said. "Come this way." She led Gatto through the datacenter to Miller's office.

They found Stewart Miller with his feet up on his desk, leafing through *CIO Magazine.*

"Hi, I'm Tom Gatto." Miller gave him a painfully firm handshake.

"Stewart Miller. Have a seat," he said.

"What can I do for you, Stewart? Your cousin says that you want to do an evaluation of the EAI market."

"Yes, exactly. As CIO it's my job to stay on top of trends in the industry and such. I've started to see lots of references to EAI in the trade rags," Stewart said, pointing to *Computerworld.* "My cousin Eric is, of course, very high on your offerings in the field and encouraged me to check it out."

Yeah, and it's taken you weeks to bother. "Right. What do you know about us so far?"

"Between Eric and my new expert on EAI, Mordecai Rosenzweig – who you'll meet shortly – I've learned quite a lot. Has to do with messaging and adapters, right?"

"That's certainly the foundation of it but we take an object-oriented approach…"

"Riiiight, object-*oriented*…" Miller repeated, pursing his lips in recognition.

"Yes. We believe that you can encapsulate your business processes better that way, maximizing reuse. That also allows a layer of abstraction between the lower level technologies and your applications."

"Yes, abstraction. I saw that immediately from your literature."

Abstract, like your brain, Gatto thought. "How are you going to approach this effort?"

"Let's get Mordi in here. He's in charge of the project." He reached for his phone to summon Mordecai and he appeared almost instantly.

"Mordi, this is Tom Gatto from VibraWeb."

"Yes, we met at the show," Mordi said, recalling how Gatto wouldn't give him the time of day. Gatto said nothing, simply nodding acknowledgement.

"Tom, Mordi is the man on this," Miller said. "Mordi, tell Tom about your plan for the EAI evaluation."

Mordecai's eyes widened. "Uh, plan?"

"Ya know, the RFI…" Miller said, trying to lead him a bit.

"Yes, we're sending the RFI out today."

"The RFI is based on the Flanderson EAI document, right?" Gatto asked.

"Yes," replied Mordecai. "Then when the replies come back, we will choose three or four to do a proof-of-concept, present the results and then decide upon a course of action at that point." He looked at Miller for approval, hoping that he was saying the right things.

Miller nodded. "Very good, Mordi." He turned to Gatto. "Now, based on strong recommendations, I'd like to get something started with VibraWeb right away. Can we get some loaner software and some onsite technical talent to work on a quick demonstration project?"

Demonstration project? Who's going to manage that? Mordi wondered, suspicious that he was the lucky party.

"Yes, it so happens that we have a package that will equip one to three of your developers plus five days with a professional services engineer. The package lists for $15,000 –"

"Ah, I don't think you understand," Stewart said, reaching for his samurai sword. "We aren't going to pay to essentially borrow your software."

Gatto was keenly aware of the sword as Miller pulled it partially from its sheath and admired the etching.

"Oh, well you should know that the software portion of the cost will be applied when you deploy, as we know you will. We've found that to be a very fair –"

"Fair?" Miller said, raising his voice and removing the sword fully. "I don't see how it is fair to pay you to prove your worth."

Knowing what was coming, Mordecai was slowly moving away from the desk.

What is the bullshit with the sword? Gatto wondered. *He can't seriously…*

"Stewart, as I said the 15k is list, we can negotiate –"

Whump! Miller brought the sword straight down with two hands onto a tablet conveniently placed on this desk, slicing through the first few pages.

Gatto froze. *He's insane! I know this is theatrics but he could have split my skull with that thing!*

"Stew…Stewart, I'd appreciate it if you'd put that thing away. Now, about the price…"

Whump, whump, whump! Miller was turning the tablet into confetti.

Gatto jumped his chair back at least three feet, one for each whack.

"Okay, okay! What do you want?"

"I want Mordi here," he said, using the sword to point at Rosenzweig, "to get your latest software and a technical resource to work with him. It should only be for a week or two."

Gatto tried to hide his shaking hands in his lap. "Stewart, I can arrange that. My systems engineer can be available. He'll deliver the software personally tomorrow, if that's good for you, Mordi."

Mordecai slouched in his chair, his worst fears confirmed. "Yes, that's fine." *And Stewart, what do I do about my other responsibilities?*

"Great!" Miller said, returning the sword to its scabbard. "Mordi, work out the scheduling details. You know what we need to do, right?"

"Well, I…"

"Yes, you know, an example of what the CFO wants," he said, winking and pointing up.

"Oh. I see. Like what we saw those guys…"

"YES, yes, that's right," he said, making it obvious that he didn't want Rosenzweig to name them. "Now excuse me, I need to get upstairs to a meeting with the CFO. You guys go work this out."

***

Wayne forwarded the purchase orders and was about to sit back down for some more calls when the fax machine came back to life.

What could this be? He returned to the machine to see what this was.

"OUT-FUCKING-STANDING!" he yelled, outdoing his previous performance by prancing about the office in addition to the fist pumping.

"Act your age, will you please? The neighbors…" Helen scolded.

"IT'S ANOTHER HUNDRED TWENTY-FIVE FROM POTENTIAL!"

"I'm leaving! Call me when you recover."

"I wish I had a big fat cigar to light up," Wayne said, as he flopped into his chair, very satisfied.

***

"Okay, that's about it. Thanks for coming," Azalea Chief Financial Officer Ralph Gibson said, wrapping up his weekly staff meeting. "Stewart, Sam, please stick around. I need to cover a few more things with you guys."

The rest of the staff gathered their things and left the executive conference room, passing portraits of the founders and previous CEOs that hung on the oak paneled walls.

"I had an interesting conversation yesterday. A good friend of mine, Larry Liu of Flanderson Consulting was telling me about some new technology…"

Both Miller and Racker winced, dreading another attempt by Gibson to be "with it" and talk technology. In Gibson's case, given his position in the company, it usually meant more work, and heartburn, for his lieutenants.

"…Enterprise Application Integration. He seems to believe that it's going to revolutionize how we do business by *seamlessly* tying our systems together." He brought his hands together to emphasize the future togetherness of his business processes.

Miller relaxed. *For once, I'll be ahead of him.*

"Isn't this what you're trying to do, Sam?" Gibson asked.

Oh, shit, thought Racker. "Yeah, sort of."

"Larry Liu," Gibson continued, "runs the Financial Services practice here in New York and has created new teams for this emerging eeee-eye market."

"Excuse me, Ralph, it's E-A-I."

"Right you are, Stewart. You know about this?" he asked, embarrassed by the correction.

"Yes, we kicked off a market evaluation this week."

"Larry was high on this one company, uh," he searched around his desk for Liu's card on the back of which he had written some names down. "…yes, VibraWeb. He says that they are, in Flanderson's opinion, the company in the vanguard, yes; he used the word 'vanguard', of EAI. I hope that you are including them in your study."

Do I tell him they hold equity? No need. "Way ahead of you there, Ralph. Yes, I've already met with their representative and they've graciously..." *heh heh* "…offered to get us up and running with their software. They seem to be a real straight-up company."

Racker had heard enough. "Ralph, you recall that we have a team working on our financial reporting?"

"Yes, of course." *And I recall that I didn't see why we needed it when Stewart does such a good job.*

"Well, what they are doing, as you so correctly perceived, is essentially an integration effort to gather financial information from other systems and organizations within Azalea." *So that we can actually do the reporting which you haven't given a damn about for years.*

"I see," Gibson said. "And how are you going about it?"

"We are *successfully* using software from a company called InUnison. In fact, Stewart has already seen some of our progress." *Unfortunately.* "In fact, our pilot will be presented on Monday." *Take that, Miller.*

"Yes, it *was* interesting…as an academic exercise. But it's not something that's industrial strength," Miller sniffed, frowning.

"How would you know?" Racker asked. "You are only now getting started with a 'study'. We have tangible and…" turning to Ralph for emphasis, "…accurate reporting results. I'm talking about reporting we can take to analysts."

You bastard, Gibson thought. *Our reporting has been just fine; I don't care what the board says.* "Well, I'm glad to see you both are investigating this stuff. Keep up the good work."

Stewart broke in. "Ralph, uh, I think we are going to be duplicating our efforts. I think that it would be better for Sam's team to work with our EAI study team before getting too far along –"

"And how are you going to 'study' this market, Stewart?" Racker asked.

"We are issuing an RFI today, may have already gone out, actually. Then we will review the responses, do some proofs-of-concept, economic analysis…"

"RALPH! You know we can't wait for all that!" Sam was standing now. "Look, the board isn't going to wait six months for the IT bureaucracy to do some study. We have results…"

"Results?" Miller interrupted. "It's a sandcastle. They're playing with toys in the sandbox, Ralph."

"No, it's real," Racker said, shaking his finger at Miller. "Norm Johnson has been doing this stuff for a couple of years. *Your* team ought to be working with *us*. You might learn something. We already have the experience. Ralph –"

"Enough! Both of you! I didn't think I was going to set off World War III here." Gibson stood up and paced. "Okay, Stewart, continue with your evaluation –"

"Oh, Ralph!" Racker rose again.

"Wait, Sam. Because of your urgent needs, you should continue as well. Stewart, we don't have time to do the usual thorough market study. It would seem that we have two capable candidates in this VibraWeb and Uni, Uni, what's the name?"

"InUnison," Sam sighed.

"Right. I know! Let's do a bake-off! You can both build something and let the best man win!" Gibson was very proud of his balanced solution.

They winced again, more visibly this time, annoying Gibson. "Both of you should be able to work together on this. Make it happen."

"But, Ralph, there has to be some structure on this, else it becomes apples and oranges," Miller challenged.

"Stewart, take the project this Johnson guy has pursued and use that. Oh, I know what! Let's get that Atlanta guy, Spencer, oh what's his last name? His datacenter will need to be involved, right? He should be in on the independent analysis."

That's what I don't need; that prima donna involved, Miller thought. "I don't think that's a great idea. It will only complicate things."

"I think that's a great idea, Ralph!" Racker said, flanking Miller.

Miller started to argue another point but was frozen by Gibson's glare. "Okay. I guess I'll need your cooperation too, Sam." He got up and left.

Racker was livid. "Ralph, he doesn't have the organization to do this. He's woefully behind the times."

"It's bad form to bash a peer, Sam. I expect better of you."

"Look at how he operates. He runs that datacenter like it's his little fiefdom. Are you blind to that?"

"Stop right now, buster! Stewart Miller has been like the Rock of Gibraltar, keeping the data humming around here. He's bailed me out numerous times. No, you are off base," Gibson said, shaking his head and waving his left index finger.

"Ralph, I can't succeed with him."

"That's your problem. Look, I know you're here to replace me but I'm not gone yet. If I were you, I'd figure out a way to get along around here and not be the bull in the china shop."

You're hopeless. "Ralph," Racker said, rising to leave. "I think we'll see who the bull is around here."

***

The next day, Porter arrived early at Azalea to work with Brewster McNaughton on their pilot. He was hoping to avoid Norm after their rather unpleasant meeting two days earlier when he and Wayne told him about the Atlanta fiasco. He briefed Brewster on the breakfast meeting.

"Brewster, I've never seen him so rattled. Think about the last eighteen months. Have you ever seen him as anything but an iceman?"

"Never. But I have to tell you that he's really under the gun here. Even before the Miller demo he was feelin' the pressure to get somethin' done. And he's been pushing that pressure down to us."

Brewster paused to see who was calling his phone.

"Uh, oh. It's Norm." He gingerly picked up his phone. "Hey Norm," he answered.

"Hi, Brewster. How's the progress?"

"We're movin' along fine, in fact with a little help we should be able to do some extra credit."

"Got something to show me?"

"Pure sizzle. Come on over!" He hung up.

"What?" Porter asked. "He's coming over?"

"Yes. Is that a problem?"

"Weren't you listening to me? I'm 'Judas'. He's going to kick my ass out of here."

"Okay, Brewster let's see…" Norm came around the corner into Brewster's cubicle and stopped upon seeing Mitchell. "Oh, hi, Porter. Didn't know you were here."

There was a very uncomfortable pause as Norm shuffled around, avoiding eye contact with Porter.

"Ah…Brewster, give me a minute. Porter, can we step into my office?"

They went back to the office and Norm closed his door. Mitchell was more than a little apprehensive.

"Norm, before you start…"

"Wait, wait. Look, I'm sorry for the 'Judas' thing, but you guys betrayed my trust…"

"Norm, it isn't like that…"

"How else can I read it?"

"Like what Wayne told you; our Atlanta guy tried to screw *us*."

"Oh, that makes sense. Why would one of your own people try to screw up a deal?"

If you only knew what we've been through… "In his twisted way, he was trying to grab the deal for himself."

"I'm not buying it. I'm not turning my back on you guys, just so you know…"

There was a knock on the door and Norm stood up to open it.

"Sam, good morning. Come on in."

"Oh, sorry to interrupt," the controller said. "Stop by when you have a minute. Gibson just threw me a curve ball."

"Actually we were wrapping up. This is Porter Mitchell. He's the technical sales guy from InUnison who worked for me at the bank."

"Oh, very good," he said. "This involves you." He stepped into Norm's office and closed the door.

"Norm, my worst fears are coming to pass. You know I wasn't happy about that Miller demo, right?"

"Yes, I certainly do," Norm replied, remembering the obscenity-laden dressing down he endured from Racker. "But as promised, we are way ahead on the pilot and –"

"Not so fast. I got cut off at the knees by Gibson." He started to describe the meeting he just left with CFO Gibson and CIO Miller.

"Excuse me," Porter interrupted. Racker gave him a mildly annoyed look while Norm raised his eyebrows. "Could we get Wayne Angelis on the phone? I think that he has some thoughts on strategy here."

"Who is this 'Wayne'?" Racker asked.

"He's our sales rep from InUnison. I found out on Wednesday that he went around me to Spencer Carlton in Atlanta."

"Norm, that isn't how…" Porter protested.

"Carlton? He's the Director of IT down there, right?" Racker asked.

"Yes. These guys sent a team in to sell to him."

"Mr. Racker, that's not how it happened. Yes, we screwed up but, well, it's an internal thing. Look, can we get Wayne on the phone? He can help clear the Atlanta thing up and can help deal with the CFO."

Racker was skeptical. "First of all, Gibson isn't the problem, it's Miller in IT. He's a real inside player." He rubbed his chin, trying to figure out the situation. *Norm's lost control of this thing, the horse is already out of the barn.* He walked over to the window to think. *Won't hurt to listen. I don't think Norm can get us out of this jam.*

"Okay, let's get him on the phone."

"SAM! We don't need him," Norm pleaded.

"Why can't we hear him out? Norm, I can believe what this young man said. Sales reps fight like hell for deals and if one cuts across territories it gets ugly. I want to hear what he has to say. Perhaps we can use this to our advantage. He owes us, I figure."

I've lost, Norm thought, as he put his phone on speaker and dialed Wayne's number.

"Wayne here."

"Wayne, Norm Johnson here. I'm in my office with Sam Racker and Porter."

"Hello all."

Sam took over the conversation. "Wayne, this is Sam Racker. First of all, I appreciate all the help you have given us for our pilot. I've gotten rave reviews from Norm's team."

Hmmm, when was that, Sam? I've never really talked to you about that, Norm thought.

"You're welcome," Wayne replied. "We look forward to doing business with Azalea."

"Play golf?" Racker asked.

"You bet, ten handicap."

"Well, no golf, no business."

"That I can arrange, my friend. Where do you like to play?"

He's already your friend, Wayne? Porter thought.

"Oh, all around. Westchester, mostly."

"Likewise! You know that water hazard on the tenth…" Wayne continued on the golf thread, trading stories and dropping names.

"Oh, and how about that dogleg on fifteen?" Racker asked Wayne.

"Yes, I always overshoot it. Well, it looks like our games have a lot in common…"

Okay, can we get down to business? Porter was bored with the verbal stroking.

"So, what can I do for you?" Wayne finally asked.

"We have a situation here," Racker said. "Ralph Gibson, our CFO, had lunch with a friend of his from Flanderson Consulting who got him all lubed up about EAI and some company called VibraWeb…"

"Let me guess, the partner was Larry Liu," Wayne said.

"Yes, that's the one. You know him?"

"We just met." *That snake took Lakota's info and ran with it.* "You do know that Flanderson recently invested in VibraWeb."

"What? That's just great. Gibson thinks Flanderson can do no wrong. Anyway Gibson tells us this and Miller brags about how they are already on the case – no doubt because he saw what we were doing." He shot a disapproving look at Norm who avoided his gaze by studying his shoes. "He wanted Gibson to shut us down. Luckily, I was able to remind Ralph about the urgency of fixing our financial reporting and that we were well on the way to a solution. So he ended up cutting the baby in half. We're able to move ahead but Miller gets to do his so-called eval." He paused to let that sink in a bit.

"I think that we have a couple of options," Wayne started to say. "You may have a friend in Spencer Carlton in Atlanta. I recommend that we recruit him into a larger scope project."

"Gibson is way ahead of you. He wants Carlton to run the pilot because he thinks that he will be independent. So, how do you know about someone in Atlanta anyway?"

Uh, oh. "We had a little misunderstanding with our sales team in Atlanta who paid a sales call on them."

"How did you know to go call on them?" he asked, shooting another look of disgust at Norm.

"Our SE down there met Spencer Carlton a few months ago. The rep decided to call him up. I'll plead guilty to not controlling him. Anyway, I talked to Carlton and he's cool to the situation."

"That being…"

"That he would follow your lead. Unfortunately, I guess, that's by the boards now."

Wayne was momentarily distracted by arriving email. He glanced at one from Rosenzweig. *Oh, no.*

"Hey, folks, I got an RFI from Miller's group on email this morning. Did you know about this?"

"Yes, Miller brought it up at our meeting."

"How the hell did they whip this up in what, three days? Miller saw that demo last Monday, right?"

"You tell me how he did it." Racker said.

Wayne thought it through. "Well, they got help somewhere. You don't start on Monday knowing nothing about a new technology and then write an intelligent questionnaire simply from marketing glossies gathered at a trade show. This thing smells. Now, the good news is that the contact is Mordecai Rosenzweig who Porter and I met at the show. He seemed open to working with us. Norm, I know you don't…"

"Right. Sam, we can't engage IT on this. All along you've said 'no IT'."

Racker looked at Norm. *You're still not getting it.* "That's moot now. Gibson is forcing their involvement." He turned to face the speaker phone. "Any ideas, Wayne?"

"Can we engage Atlanta as an ally?"

"Not likely. That Carlton guy is supposed to be the arbitrator between the pilots."

Damn. There goes my potential champion, Wayne thought. *I'm left with nobody but this Racker dude and he just had his nuts cut off.*

"Sam, I'll come up with something. We'll take the initiative on this pilot."

"Is there any way Miller can duplicate what we've done?" Racker asked.

"No way," Porter said. "The VibraWeb stuff involves way too much programming. If we are aggressive with the delivery dates, it will give us the advantage."

"That may not be enough. We need something to put Miller – and VibraWeb – on the defensive."

Connie Sanchez knocked and stuck her head in. "Sammy, your ten o'clock is here."

"I'll be right there. So, we are all together on this, right?"

"Yes," Wayne said. Norm was stone faced.

"All right. Let's get on it. Thank you, Wayne. Don't forget about that golf when it warms up."

"Porter?"

"I'm here."

"I'm going to forward this RFI to you. The questions don't make sense to me. Can you review it over the weekend?"

"Okay."

"Then let's get together on Monday to start working on it before our sales calls. You want to come up here?"

"I'd love to see the Angelis estate."

"Have no fear, the fridge is well stocked."

"Great! I'll be there in time for the Monday conference call."

"Thanks. I'll touch base with you on Monday, Sam. Later."

"Fine. Bye." Racker hung up the phone and turned to Norm, who looked like his puppy died.

Feeling uncomfortable, Porter decided to make his exit. "I better get back to Brewster. Can't leave him to his own devices, you know." He waited for some acknowledgement of his humor but none came, so he left the office.

***

It was the tail end of Friday and Wayne had his feet up on the desk making notes about Azalea Financial. A strategy was forming in his mind and he was satisfied that while he didn't have 100% confidence that he could get total control of the situation, he did indeed have a chance.

Now it comes down to the chess game; move the pieces to the right places at the right times and checkmate. Why did there have to be a brainless RFI though?

He took his feet off the desk, tossed the bound journal notebook onto his briefcase and stood up, intending to wrap up for the week. Instead, the phone rang.

"This is Wayne."

"Wayne, this is Phil Lansing, Product Marketing in HQ. How are you doing? How's business?"

"It's looking up, Phil. Had a tough January but it's been a good week."

"So I hear. There were a couple of bell ringings in your honor this week."

"Bell ringings?"

"Yes, you know, O'Rourke rings a fire truck bell mounted outside his office when orders come in. We were getting a little nervous since it hadn't rung all month until PensAndClips came in."

"Okay, well, there will be a lot more from them. What's up?"

"Just wanted to give you a heads up that I'm sending you an RFI that came in."

"Never mind. Already got it."

"Huh? It looks like they only sent it to us out here."

"I got it direct from Azalea this morning."

"Oh, this isn't from Azalea. It's from Manley Brothers. O'Rourke said to send it to you right away. It will be in your email shortly."

I'm screwed. "Damn it, Phil, Manley is a loser. We went there first of the month and they beat the hell out of us."

"Hey, I'm only the messenger as usual. O'Rourke seemed to put a lot of urgency on it. I'll warn you it's big, over forty pages of questions."

"Gee, thanks Phil. Don't suppose you know when it's due?"

"Yes, hold on. It says…uh…February 13."

"God! Forty pages in two weeks! We have this Azalea one as well but at least that represents Q1 business. Manley doesn't represent squat. Phil, you gotta help us on this."

"Dude, I'd love to and maybe if it is as urgent as O'Rourke seemed to indicate, I can get my priorities reworked. Don't hold your breath, though."

"Don't we have a 'frequently asked questions' document on EAI or something?"

"That's on my 'to do' list at around item number one gazillion. Right now, getting out the beta of version 3.0 is my priority. I'm getting beat up daily by Brinks about how this is a zero-sum game and every feature that goes in means one goes out blah blah blah."

"I hear you. Please do what you can."

"I promise I will. But don't expect a whole lot."

Wayne hung up the phone and collapsed into his desk chair.

Helen, having seen Wayne in high spirits earlier in the day, was hoping to lure him away from his office with their traditional Friday martinis.

"Hey, Wayne, it's time for…" She saw him bent over his desk with his face in his hands. "I'll make it a double."

Chapter 12 Just Say Yes

In between play sessions with Stephanie, Porter spent the weekend analyzing the RFI from Azalea. He had concerns about answering the questions in a positive fashion and those worries kept running around his brain as he struggled to find Wayne's house in Scarsdale. He was repeatedly diverted from his intended path as he slowed to admire one massive, immaculately landscaped home after another. Even in winter, the grounds of these houses were lush.

"Ah, there it is," Porter said to himself as he finally found Wayne's street. He had made a couple of wrong turns which made him circle right around the correct street. Rather than admit that he was distracted or hadn't studied the map properly, he chalked it up to an unmarked one-way street in Scarsdale.

He cruised slowly down Wayne's block, finding his house on the left side of the street. Porter quickly counted windows on the front of the white, painted-brick colonial, estimating six bedrooms at least. A covered porch extended the full length of the front and he could see a three-car garage in the back. He parked in the turnaround behind the house.

Wayne spotted Porter through the kitchen window. *Seven fifteen. Damn if he isn't punctual.* Porter had promised to arrive in time for the seven-thirty Monday conference call. Wayne was prepared for Porter's insatiable appetite, having stocked up on cinnamon raisin bagels from Scarsdale Bagels.

"I can almost set my watch to you, Porter," Wayne said, opening the back door for him. "Come on in."

Porter entered, careful to wipe his feet on the doormat so not to trudge dirt into Wayne's elegantly appointed kitchen.

"Pretty exclusive neighborhood.

"Not exclusive enough for some of us," Wayne said. Helen was making noises about where they should move when the boys started college, alluding to The Hamptons. "So, are you hungry?" he asked, waving a bagel at him.

"Need you ask? You bet."

"Toasted? Cream cheese?"

"Yes and Yes."

"Help yourself to coffee," Wayne said, pointing a bread knife at the Krups machine before slicing the bagel.

"So I read that Azalea RFI over the weekend. It's fixated on object-orientation and CORBA standards. It's almost as if VibraWeb wrote it, since that's what they harp on in their literature. I know that's a stupid thing to think…"

Wayne laughed. "Porter, my boy, you've confirmed my suspicions. I'll bet they did write it. One of the first rules of sales is – well it should be – don't respond to an RFI unless you wrote it."

"We wrote ours at the bank. They were supposed to be objective."

"But you consulted vendors for the criteria, right?"

"Some, but we also used Gartner Group, Forrester…those independent analyst groups."

"And who do you think gives *them* the criteria?"

The toaster popped. Wayne reached for the hot bagel, juggling it over to a plate.

"Ah, vendors?"

"Ding!" Wayne said, retrieving cream cheese from his SubZero. "I suppose there are still a few saps out there who actually do the research themselves but RFIs are a big joke as far I'm concerned. Here, you do the honors." He handed Porter the plate, knife and cream cheese.

"Wayne, I'm taking Eileen…oh, I didn't know you had a visitor," Helen said.

"You remember Porter, right? The smart guy on the team?"

"Frankly, wouldn't take much to be the smarter guy on Wayne's team," Helen said, giving Wayne an exaggerated smile.

"Thanks a lot," Wayne replied, offended that she would rip into him, even playfully, in front of his sales partner. "You were just leaving, weren't you?"

"Yes, Eileen has to get her science project to school in one piece so I'm driving her. You here all day?"

"No, only until ten or ten-thirty. Then we have some sales calls."

She blew a kiss to Wayne and was gone.

Wayne glanced at his watch. "Let's go to the office and dial into the conference call." He led Porter to his home office in the opposite end of the house.

"Oh, some bad news. We have another RFI to do. It's the Manley Brothers one, remember them?"

"How could I not? You never forget your first time."

"Well, it's forty pages of crap but according to Phil Lansing, O'Rourke says we have to do it."

"What's the big deal?"

"I don't know. I'm going to try to get out of it with Presby."

They entered his office and Wayne pulled up a chair. They weren't the first to connect to the conference call.

"Hello?" someone called out.

"This is Wayne and Porter."

"Kyle and Sean in Boston. No one else so far."

"Hey, Wayne? Did you hear the one about the widow and widower getting it on?"

"No, Sean, I haven't. I'm still recovering from last week's levity." Sean was good for a sick joke before every conference call.

Kyle tried to intercept Sean. "You can't tell that joke! What if Sandy comes on in the middle?"

"Maybe she'll learn something. See, there's this widow and widower who are friends in the home, ya know, the old folks' home…"

"Yes, I get that."

"…they are platonic friends from the time when their spouses were still living. Anyway, after a while, they begin to be more romantic and physical with each other until the widower, Willard, gets up the nerve to make his move."

"How old are these two?" Porter asked.

"Oh, eighty something. So, the widow, Mildred…" Sean started to chuckle, "…is in Willard's apartment and he starts to grope her…"

"An eighty year-old 'gropes'?"

"He's a really randy eighty, you know? So Mildred's getting all lubed up and they start tearing their clothes off. Mildred is starting to worry and tries to slow Willard down. Thing is, his hearing aid fell out due to the struggle with their clothes and he can't hear Mildred saying 'Wait! Wait!' She finally screams 'WILLARD! WAIT! I HAVE ACUTE ANGINA! I HAVE ACUTE ANGINA!' He hears that and says…" Sean, as usual, was having trouble getting the punch line out. "…and says…'Good! Because your tits are ugly!'"

Sean's cackles filled the phone line. Wayne laughed as well but Porter's face was a blank.

"I don't get it. What's so funny about angina?"

"Dude," Sean said, "Female body part? It rhymes with 'angina'?"

Porter thought for a moment, which made Wayne laugh all the more.

Just then a bah-beep and "Hello? This is Sandy and Mackenzie in Philadelphia."

"Damn, you missed my joke!"

"I doubt I missed anything, you sick bastard," Sandy said.

Everyone exchanged other pleasantries about the weather, the crummy skiing and continuing analysis of Super Bowl XXXII from the week before.

"Oh, Miss, excuuuse me, *Mizzz* Politically Correct in Philly; I have a message from the White House, please hold for the President," Sean began.

Oh, this is going to be bad, Sims-Acheson thought.

"Ah did not have sexual relations with that woman, Miss Lewinski," Sean drawled before dissolving into hysterics.

"Listen, you pig. The only thing he did wrong was to lower himself to throw down with an intern…"

"Oh, so do you now believe that it happened?"

"Who cares? As I said, he shouldn't have needed to do it with an intern. He could have had me for the asking. Doing it with the leader of the free world? What a rush!"

"Please. That's pathetic. I don't suppose perjury matters to you, does it?"

"That's definitely not proven. Some stupid bitch making recordings…"

Dah-ding. "Good morning everyone. Ken Presby here. How are we today?"

Presby, oblivious to the conversation, took roll. "We're still missing Atlanta."

"Not entirely. This is Julia," Julia Berkowski said. "I haven't seen Gary in the office yet. He's likely tied up in ugly traffic on 400."

Then another beep on the line and the telltale sound of cell phone static and interference came on the line.

"This is Gary – skreeeetch – I'm – skeeech – in traf – skreeech – on this – skreeeech – highway. I – skreeetch – hear – skreeetch…"

"Gary, hang up." Presby said, with an "I'm tired of this crap from you" tone. Sean and Kyle rolled their eyes at each other.

" – skreeeetch – k. Bye. I'll try – skreeetch…" And he was gone.

"Let's hope Gary can get back on with us but we need to move on. Folks, it's the start of the second month of the quarter and, as usual, we didn't bring much home in the first month. I want to go over the accounts you are going to commit to closing this month. Identify for me what actions you need from me or someone else in management to close these deals. Al, let's start with you. Where's your commit of $750,000 going to come from?"

"I've got a solid handle on NSA for $100k – basically another server – $50k Starter Kit at DOD and the wild card is our 'government customer' for anywhere from a Starter Kit to $300k for deployment. Mark has been focused on them almost full time to resolve some issues on Solaris."

The "government customer" was a secret intelligence agency. Moskowitz and Fisher both had to have top secret clearances to do business with them.

"What issues on Solaris?" Presby had never sold to the Federal Government and was a little nervous about this deal.

"They have some security extensions built into the operating system which we need to deal with in our installation script," Moskowitz chimed in. "It's a slow process because they tell us specific things to put into our code, but our engineers can't test it. We have to give it back to the agency and they test it and tell us if it worked or not."

"Doesn't sound promising, Al. You really want to commit to this deal?" Presby asked.

Al responded with his trademark gravel-voiced "No praaaablem!"

"Well, I trust you, Al, but please give me some elaboration." Everyone on the line laughed.

"What are you clowns laughing about? I've got assurances that if it is only this installation issue holding things up, we will get the PO."

"Okay, I'll take your word for it."

"Wayne, what's up with you? You scored with $300k this week! Headquarters thanks you! Now, I need another 3 to 400k out of your patch."

Of course you do. "Not to worry, Ken. Found out late Friday that Lehman will be adding servers, at least two more by the end of the month so that's about $150k right there. PensAndClips is already paying dividends."

"NO KIDDING! That's great! You've done quite a turnaround there."

"Well, credit needs to go to Porter, his SE buddies and the guys from PS. Also, I couldn't have calmed down George Melani without the firm commitment from Engler to set things right."

"Yeah, great, at the expense of *my* prospects," interrupted Kyle. "Ken, I know it's not my turn, but seeing $250k pissed away because features got pushed back to fix Potential is not doing my Number or my reputation any good at places like Fidelity."

"Kyle, let's take that offline. I'm working on some quota relief. You ought to stop for a moment and consider where our reputation would be if it got around that we screwed our customers or were less than scrupulously honest. Both Engler and O'Rourke are totally committed to everyone's success, most certainly the customer's. Everyone will need that backing sometime."

"Still doesn't help my commission check for *this* quarter," Kyle muttered.

"Continue Wayne, where can we get another few hundred thousand?"

"It looks good at some of the other old Gatto accounts, Merrill, Independent Life, Bakery Express, Sampson Logistics and Citibank. Delivering the mainframe stuff will allow them all to pull the trigger. It's my understanding that it is still on track for production release on the 17th of March, right? "

"Yes," David Young replied. "Oh, that reminds me; the SEs will have rollout training for version 3.0 from February 24th through the 26th. Travel days are Monday and Friday that week."

"And it's being held, where?" Murphy asked.

"In the HQ training room."

"More importantly, where are we staying?"

"The Sofitel. As usual, email me with roommates and rooms will be booked for you. Use the agency for your flight arrangements."

"Ugh," several SEs were heard to say.

"Sorry for the tangent, Ken."

Presby returned to Wayne's forecast. "Wayne, you have, let's see, 50, 50, 75 and 50 respectively…"

"Might be able to tweak some more …"

"… so that's about $225k. We need to squeeze more. After all, we have to make up for Kyle's losses."

"Ken, that's not fair…" Kyle protested.

"I didn't mean it as some fault of yours. Chill, will you? Wayne, this is great. You've got to find some more, though."

It's never enough, Wayne thought.

"I'll get it somewhere."

Suddenly, an out of breath voice came on the line.

"I …. I'm here!" Gary Reaper had finally arrived at his office in Perimeter Center.

"Catch your breath Gary. We'll get to you."

Presby continued with Kyle who, even after bemoaning the loss of $275k, still committed to $300k to the surprise of everyone, including his SE, Sean. Gary Reaper reported his standard $50,000 commit replete with all the caveats about his "depressed patch" and seized on the few days of Julia's time in New York as an excuse for his pathetic performance.

"So, that about covers it. Anything else?"

"Yes," Wayne said. "Porter and I have two big RFIs to do over the next two weeks. Does anyone have anything they could contribute, like other responses you've given?"

"Yes," David Young called out. "I keep a repository of RFIs. I'll email a pointer to the network location. Also, I have a few cycles so let's divide the thing up."

"That's great! Now, Ken, one is for Manley Brothers and I have to say that it is a waste of time. They aren't –"

"Wayne, we have to do it."

"Why? I'm telling you that there is no business…"

"Wayne, we have to *do* it."

"But…"

"Wayne, let's take it offline."

"I guess…" Wayne said, wondering what the mystery was.

"So, if that's it, let's go sell! Beat VibraWeb!"

"Later," Wayne replied.

Wayne hung up the phone, disgusted. It rang almost immediately.

"Angelis here."

"Wayne, this is Ken. Look, about the Manley RFI, I can't explain yet but it's coming down from Engler. We have to play ball on this."

"Ken, they sent this thing to, like, forty vendors. There aren't more than a dozen who are credible in EAI and that's a stretch."

"I know. But when you find out, you'll understand."

"Can we skip the mystery theater, Ken. We have this Azalea RFI and it is Q1 business. Manley isn't."

"Wayne, do it."

"Okay."

"Great! Let's go sell!"

"Later," Wayne replied as the phone went dead.

"So, what do we do?" Porter asked. "Do we have to reschedule some calls?"

"No. I can't put off prospecting for a lame RFI; excuse me, *two* lame RFIs. We will have to suck it up and get the damn things done."

***

Tom Gatto knew what was coming even before his office phone rang. It was George Means with his Monday morning browbeating for revenue. With resignation, Gatto reached for his office phone.

"Tom Gatto, may I help you?" he answered, still hoping it might be a prospect.

"Means. You ready?" he said with his usual brusqueness. "I'm in DC and need to get to some calls so let's move it."

"I have my forecast right here."

"So, your Number is $700k. You have $200k in. Where's the other $500k?"

"Well, first, when did my Number go up $100k?"

"Just now."

"George, how can you arbitrarily raise Numbers in the second month of a quarter?"

"'Cause we need the revenue. Move on."

Gatto scanned his forecast to find another 100k. *Maybe a couple of developer kits at SensaDyne and Fellows Trust.*

"There's the deployment license for $80,000 at FlamingArrow.com…"

"What the hell *is* FlamingArrow, anyway? I've been meaning to ask you."

"It's a retail web site for Indian goods…"

"… woo-woo or dot-dot," he asked, tapping his forehead.

You're such a class act, George. "They sell native American Indian goods, think Navaho."

"What's it doing in New York?"

"It's run by a group setting up shop in Silicon Alley. Pretty well funded. Anyway, they're starting from scratch and buying a lot of packaged applications which all have to work together."

"Fat bear it!"

Gatto reviewed another six accounts, interrupted a few times with Means yelling "Fat bear it!" His new commit total was $925k, including the Developer Kits he conjured up.

"Not bad. And your pipeline going forward is still pretty strong. But with Thomas' pipe to work with, I would have thought you could have fat-beared some more deals earlier in the quarter."

"George, it takes some time to get acclimated…"

"Poor excuse. I'll expect more in Q2."

"The other thing, George, is that all of the prospects in Thomas' pipeline were big accounts. He was in at the project level or dealing with approval committees; that type of stuff. Long sales cycles. There's no way to fat bear any of those so I'm pushing those out to Q4. Also, many of those prospects have pretty high expectations set by Thomas with respect to how they would do business with VibraWeb, lots of SE time, for instance."

"Understood. I don't want you bogged down in some stupid bakeoff. But at the same time, keep involved. It would be nice to get some big name annuity accounts. Hager and Singh are starting to see receivables moving up and they think it's because we keep bringing in business from these dot-com startups. They aren't paying net-30 like real companies do. What's the deal at Azalea?"

"They issued the RFI so the process has started. I met with the CIO, Miller. He's insane." Gatto described the sword play.

"Hell, I don't care if he gives you a vasectomy, get the deal. We can't let InUnison get this one. We need the *name.* Do you want Hager to call on them?"

Oh, God no! "Maybe later, George. It's very early in the cycle."

"Well, you must bring it in."

"But, George! There may not be any Q1 business…"

"Bring…it…in. Anything else, Gatto?"

"Nope." Gatto was anxious to get back on the phone with prospects.

"We'll talk again on Thursday. You should have some of these closed by then."

***

Means heard Gatto hang up but stayed on the line.

"That fucker didn't seem to fucking get it," Simon Hager said.

"Simon, you do this to me all the time. 'Get so-and-so on the fucking line. I want to hear his status'. All it does is distract them from the business. Of course they're going to be cranky."

"Listen, I want these fuckers to stay on their toes. I know they wouldn't do a fucking thing if I didn't keep reminding them to do their fucking job."

Well, if you *have to be so involved, what do you need me for?* Means wanted to ask but knew better not to.

"Let's call that fucker Hull in Boston. Haven't heard a fucking thing from him for a while."

"We called him last Wednesday, remember?"

"That was fucking eons ago. I want to know why he hasn't fucking closed fucking Fleet yet."

Means dutifully dialed the number.

***

After the conference call, Wayne checked the clock. Almost 8:30 as Porter finished his second bagel.

"Porter, we have about an hour before we have to leave for our appointments. Let's go over these RFIs and figure out how to split up the sections. I also want to call Sam Racker so that he can go to Gibson armed and dangerous."

He picked up the Azalea RFI, turning to the table of contents. "I can handle the company information. It's all about stuff like when the company was founded, how is it funded, bios of the founders. The rest, I'm sorry to say, gets into the technical weeds and I can't add much value to completing that stuff. I know that's going to be a lot. Oh, we are Y2K compliant, right?"

"I guess so. We have four digit years. What else matters?" Porter said. "And I agree. This is a lot of work. I'll hold Young to his offer of helping. What worries me is that we can't respond to many of these questions."

"Just say YES! Give me an example."

Porter turned the pages of the document to the Message Architecture section. "Here's one:

> **Which middleware products and standards are supported by Adapters? This question is distinct from using third party middleware products as a native transport layer that was asked above. Examples of interest include: Tuxedo, MQSeries, CORBA, MessageQ, MSMQ'.**

"Now, maybe if I could understand the question I could answer it, but the whole point of InUnison is that you don't have to worry about those things."

"That's the kind of trap VibraWeb is laying for us. It's actually a weakness of their product but they are promoting it as a strength. Look, the key to these responses is to find some way to say 'yes', plausibly of course."

Porter gave Wayne a skeptical look. "So, is that another euphemism for faking it?"

"Remember 'spin', my friend. So for that question you just say 'yes' and don't elaborate. At least they aren't asking for a lot of description. That's where we would get into trouble."

"How can I say 'yes' when we don't have connectors for all that stuff?"

"Simple. We offer the Connector Development Kit. The customer, their consultants or we can write a custom connector for them."

"And you said you couldn't answer these."

"Even a dumb sales rep can get lucky sometimes."

"All right, tough guy, how about this one? As you know, people were bitching at the kickoff that we don't do data transformation. So how do you answer this one?

> **'What is the transformation map definition user interface/authoring environment? Does your product enable information providers to specify a subset of fields or sub-**

> **components from within a specified message type which they intend to distribute?'**

"Last time I checked, we have no such environment and you can't just say 'yes' because we can turn numbers into characters. I don't know what that second part is talking about, but it's practically lifted verbatim from the VibraWeb literature."

Wayne rubbed his chin. "What about that Rules Agent that's coming out?"

"That's a stretch. The RA allows for logic to be applied to a message before it is delivered."

"Well, couldn't that logic do transformations?"

"Like I said, that's a stretch."

"But you could do it, right? And the Agent has a user interface, right?"

"Yes, but…"

"Then the answer is 'yes'!" Wayne was very proud of himself.

Porter didn't approve but realized he didn't have a choice. "This is going to be painful."

"Look, it's likely that they won't even care about this document. Miller only put it out to delay Norm."

Wayne pulled his prospect folder from his briefcase and waved it at Porter.

"Porter, my boy, get your track shoes on. I have been filling up our schedule for the next couple of weeks. I'm happy to report that I've ruthlessly qualified opportunities at ADP, Johnson and Johnson, various divisions of AT&T. They are all anxious to meet with us and most importantly have funded projects. All, and I mean *all* of the PensAndClips clients are lining up. I wish I could have Craig Mansfield's baby. If we close a representative sample of our meetings with starter kits, my Number is in the bag. Azalea might as well get pushed to next quarter. Then all those starter packs get turned into server deals, and voila, I've made my Q2 Number and then some. I knew the business was out there. Now, back to Azalea and this RFI. Let's call Mr. Rosenzweig and see if you can get in there this week."

I wish I could focus like you, Porter thought. He wasn't confident he could mentally master details like Wayne could.

Wayne picked up the phone only to hear the quick beeps indicating a message. "Let me check this message, first." His eyes lit up as he listened to his message.

"Porter, it's Sam Racker from Azalea. He called during the conference call. He says that Carlton will be in the New York office tomorrow and Wednesday. He wants to meet tomorrow morning." Wayne deleted the message and hung up. "Outstanding. This should work out," he said, checking his schedule. "He wants to meet first thing in the morning, seven-thirty. Do you mind getting in earlier than we planned?"

"Nope. We still have a full day in Manhattan, right?"

"Yes. This is goodness. We can walk right over from Water Street to One Liberty. Let me call him back. All he has to do is sell Gibson on our, ah, 'suggestions'." He called Racker's line and got Connie Sanchez who confirmed the time and place.

"Where were we?" he asked as he hung up. "Right, Mordecai. What was that number again?"

Wayne dialed as Porter gave him the number again.

"This is Mordecai."

"Good morning, Mordi. This is Wayne Angelis and Porter Mitchell of InUnison. We met at the show, remember?"

"Yes, I do. What can I do for you?"

"We had a couple of questions about the RFI. Do you have a minute?"

"Yes, what do you have?"

"So, you were pretty sneaky about this document. You didn't mention it at the show."

Mordecai laughed. "I didn't know about it either, frankly. Stewart, you know, Stewart Miller, kind of assigned it to me. To be honest, well, I'm not supposed to say, but we got that from Miller's cousin who works at VibraWeb. It was drafted by Flanderson. I simply removed specific references to Flanderson and VibraWeb."

I knew it! Wayne thought, nodding to Porter who rolled his eyes. "That explains a lot, Mordi. And I need to protest at least a little since it makes it seem like a waste of our time if this is wired for VibraWeb."

"I know." He stood up to check who might be within earshot of his cubicle. "Look, do the best you can. You know and I know that Stewart doesn't give a damn about this thing but if you blow it off he'll win."

Wayne gave a thumbs up to Porter. "I appreciate your candor, Mordecai. We have no intention of blowing it off. As you know we already have the controller's project going on and we don't want to jeopardize it."

"Um, you should be aware that I'm also in charge of doing a pilot with VibraWeb."

Wayne's face darkened. "I wasn't aware of that but I guess I shouldn't be surprised. It doesn't seem fair."

"Depends on your perspective, I guess. Norm Johnson wasn't exactly advertising for bids, was he? Anyway, someone named Sweeney is coming over this afternoon to start working with me. He's the rep's SE."

"Who is the rep?" Wayne asked, suspecting the answer.

"A guy named Tom Gatto. He's an arrogant asshole. Miller ordered me to work with him on getting the pilot going. I mean, I'm supposed to be the lead on this and this Gatto asshole starts ordering me around. Pisses me off."

"I'm sorry to hear that, Mordi. Is there anything I can do to help?

"Don't think so. I shouldn't be talking to you right now."

"We're asking for some RFI clarification. You *are* the contact."

"True. So what other questions do you have?"

"Porter is here with me and he has some questions. Porter?"

What? "Wayne, I don't have any questions," he whispered.

"Come up with something…"

"Okay, let me get my notes." Porter ruffled through the RFI and found a couple of questions to ask.

"Yes, in the section on security…we do a lot more than what you ask for. Can we add descriptions of our content-based security scheme?"

"You can add whatever you want. In fact, as I said at the show, your security stuff blows away VibraWeb's." Mordi dropped to a whisper. "You guys should add more about the broker queues as well. VibraWeb doesn't have queues, you know."

"Yes, we know," Porter whispered, then realized that *he* didn't have to whisper. Wayne started to laugh at Porter and moved away from the phone. "Any other suggestions?" he asked in full volume.

Porter and Mordecai went back and forth a bit until Wayne cut them off.

"Sorry to break in but Porter and I have an appointment. Thanks for your help, Mordecai. Let us know what we can do to help. Later."

Wayne hung up and turned to Porter.

"We need to get you into Rosenzweig's shorts."

"Excuse me!"

"Figuratively speaking. You need to develop a closer relationship with that guy to see what's going on in IT. Since he is managing this RFI process that gives us an excuse."

"I don't see why some data security guy in IT is so important," Porter said, shaking his head and reaching for his coffee mug.

"All right, let me lay it out for you." He started to draw an organization chart on his white board. "Gibson is the big kahuna now, the decision maker. His influencers are Miller, Racker and now Carlton," he said, drawing boxes under Gibson's name for all the players. "Now, we won't win Miller over, but…" he drew another box under Miller's, "…we need some G2 in the enemy camp and someone who can possibly discredit Miller and that is this Rozensweig guy." He circled Mordi's box for emphasis.

Porter laughed. "So, I guess I'll try to get into his shorts."

"Good man!" Wayne said, looking once again at his chart, tapping his chin with a marker.

"Spencer, Spencer…"

"What about him?"

"We don't have a clear-cut champion here. Maybe Carlton..."

"What about Norm and Racker?"

"They are kind of neutralized. Racker isn't really technical and Gibson won't simply take his word, certainly not over Miller's. Norm's credibility is in the toilet now. No, we are in dire need of a champion and the best candidate here is Carlton. I'll need to get into *his* shorts."

***

"You son…of…a…bitch!

"Pardon me? Who is this?" Tom Gatto asked.

"This is Stewart Miller at Azalea. So, are you a rattler or a cobra?"

"Stewart, I don't know what you're –"

"You went over my head, you motherfucker! You'll never get a cent out of me now. You set foot in here again and I'll cut your head off!"

Gatto had flashbacks to the sword display. "Stewart, I assure you that I haven't had any contact with anyone else at Azalea. My SE has been in contact with Mordecai and that's it. I have no idea what you are talking about!"

"Maybe you haven't but your lackey at Flanderson did. And I'm supposed to believe you knew nothing about that?"

"I swear that I didn't know. Who was it?"

"Some slickster named Larry Liu. He's buddies with Gibson and now I have to play ball with the Controller's group. He bragged about how VibraWeb and his consultants, of course, were going to work miracles. I could have stopped Racker in his tracks but now…"

Gee Larry, it might have been nice if you had told me. "Stewart, again, I swear I didn't know anything about it. Yes, I know Larry but haven't talked to him in weeks. Well, yes, we met at the trade show but that was before I knew anything about your project."

"I don't believe you. But unfortunately I have to spare you for now. We have to duplicate what that wimp Norm Johnson is doing for financial reporting. You need to get me some more help. We don't have time to learn this shit."

For free, no doubt. "Stewart, I'll get you whatever you need. My SE can help scope the job…" *I hope,* "…and we will get professional services in there ASAP, I assure you."

"You sure as hell will. Call me tomorrow with the plan," Miller said, finishing the conversation with a phone slam.

Gatto had to pull the phone away from his ear. *Well, Larry; you got me into this so you're going to supply the talent.*

***

The next day, Wayne and Porter stepped off the elevator near Racker's office. The increasingly friendly Connie Sanchez showed them into Racker's office and took the usual coffee requests. Racker had not arrived yet so Porter and Wayne sat down by the conference table, killing time by looking out the window.

"I'm still amazed at the transformation down here at the Seaport," Wayne commented.

"What was it before? All the time I worked at the bank, we never came down here."

"It was all broken down warehouses. Now, its all shops and trendy restaurants. With your appetite, I would have expected you to know all these establishments."

"Not if I was paying," Porter scoffed.

Connie reappeared with the coffee and another gentleman.

"Good morning, I'm Spencer Carlton."

"Very pleased to meet you. I'm Wayne Angelis and this is the smart guy on the team, Porter Mitchell."

Carlton made himself at home, tossing his overcoat onto a spare chair. They shook hands and traded business cards as Sanchez returned with another coffee for Carlton. "Oh, let me hang this *properly*," she said.

"Oh, thanks. So where are we going for dinner tonight?" Spencer asked Wayne. "I'm holding you to your offer, you know."

"Well, this is kind of short notice, but I'll be happy to accommodate. I was thinking Mesa Grill. Where are you staying?"

"Over at the Millennium. We have a corporate rate there."

"Nice. So are you up to date on this soap opera here?" Wayne asked.

"Yes, Ralph Gibson called me for help. He wants me to manage this pilot, or 'bakeoff', as he calls it. Also, Racker called me after the meeting with Gibson. He's finally recognizing that Miller is out to ruin his life. Gibson and Miller are like this though," he said, holding up his crossed fingers.

"So, are you saying we shouldn't bother?"

"Oh, no. It's just that neither Racker nor Johnson realized what they were up against. That's why Norm's naïve attempt at keeping his project quiet would have worked against him. He should have reached out."

Carlton continued. "I have a project plan ready to go here," he said, patting his briefcase. "It highlights how we can do cross-functional reporting and includes cost savings analysis. Racker may need some resources from InUnison and Miller will need VibraWeb expertise."

"VibraWeb will bring in Flanderson Consulting," Wayne said. "Is that really what you want?"

"That'll be up to Miller, I guess. It's out of my control. It's my job to provide both pieces of the pilot with access to Insurance data. I'm not to interfere with how you or VibraWeb do the job."

"As for InUnison resources, you got them," Wayne said. "We have some Pro Services people right here in New York and we can have Julia Berkowski in Atlanta contribute, not to mention Mr. Mitchell here."

Porter's head whipped around. *Oh, really? What was that about over committing, Wayne?*

"Now, Spencer, I hear that there's no love lost between you and Miller. Why does Gibson think you will be so impartial?"

"I think I have a lot of credibility with senior management up here. Gibson recognizes that I've built an advanced organization that produces results. I've already led several cross-functional projects so I have the track record to do this. My organization's success *is* getting noticed and questions are getting raised about why Stewart won't evolve. Of course, if I stumble, Miller will be all over me like a cheap suit."

"So you have no ambitions?"

"Like what?"

"Like Miller's job."

"Perhaps when the time is right," Carlton said, averting his eyes. "I'm still working hard to build the Atlanta operations. I couldn't care less about taking his job right now."

"I'll take your word for it," Wayne said, not really meaning it. "But I have some requirements, too."

"Such as?"

Wayne pulled Miller's RFI from his briefcase and slid it across the table. "Miller put out this RFI which was written by VibraWeb. It isn't going to highlight our strengths or, of course, their weaknesses. I want to level the playing field. I want a requirement added for at least three Financial Services references and a visit to our headquarters for a briefing on our financials. VibraWeb doesn't have squat for references and our viability is way better."

"You're sure about that?"

"Very."

Carlton pondered that. He had done some research on both InUnison and VibraWeb and concluded that they would both be dipping into the VC well again soon. "I'll take *your* word for that. The HQ visit is a good idea. Gibson loves a good boondoggle."

"That's great. Think Racker will approve?"

"Definitely," Carlton said. "He's desperate to get this bake-off going. If this doesn't work and he ends up having to kiss Miller's ring, he might not make CFO."

"I guess all we need is for Racker to show up and bless this."

Chapter 13 Track Meet

"I'm here to see Tom Gatto with VibraWeb."

"And your name?"

"Larry Liu, Flanderson Consulting."

The receptionist dialed Gatto's number. After Miller's tirade the day before, Gatto summoned Larry to his office to get their story straight and formulate a joint strategy.

She hung up the phone and looked at Liu. "He'll be right out."

"Thank you." Larry sat down on the black leather sofa next to the receptionist desk. He set down his briefcase on the hardwood floor, and before he could extract his *New York Times*, Gatto came around the corner.

"Larry, good morning," he said, reaching to shake Larry's hand.

"Nice place you have here, Tom."

"That's what I thought when I stared," Tom replied, looking around at the substantial amount of glass and natural beech adorning the lobby walls. "But my sales manager is like a human hemorrhoid when he's here. I'd as soon work from home. Come on back to my office."

He led Liu down one hall, left into another and then right.

"I hope you have a map; I'm never going to find my way out of here."

"It's meant to be an intelligence test, like rats in a maze. Coffee?" Gatto asked as they walked past the kitchen.

Gatto pulled two foam cups from the cabinet above the coffee machine.

"So, you sounded a little pissed at me on your message last week. Something wrong?" Liu asked, dumping a second pack of sugar into his coffee.

Gatto stirred some creamer into his coffee. "Well, I'm happy and pissed all at the same time, Larry." He threw his stirring straw into the trash and continued down yet another hall to his office.

"You didn't tell me that you were going to go after Azalea," Gatto said. "I'm certainly happy to see you in there but I'd have liked to have some coordination. I was in to see the CIO and was managing them pretty well. Now, though, he thinks we are going over his head to the CFO."

"Honest, Tom, it was a serendipitous meeting. We were hosting a breakfast briefing for top clients – or potential top clients like Azalea – and I happened to be at the same table with Gibson. He was bitching about how his board was on him about financial reporting and that he had this new controller who was all 'piss and vinegar' about doing system integration. One thing led to another."

"Well, I wasn't going to put a whole lot into this thing because I'm not confident about the CIO's reliability. He could be using us to sandbag the controller and his InUnison project – which is fine, of course; keep those bastards busy – but now the CFO has set us up to do a bakeoff involving some subsidiary in Atlanta. Worst of all, my management has this on their radar screen so they are putting pressure on to fat bear the deal which is out of the question."

"Fat bear?"

"Never mind. I'm more interested in what you told Gibson."

"Hey, all I did was answer the man's questions," Liu said, holding his hands up. "I can't help it if I'm a good salesman."

"Okay, Mr. Salesman, you're going to help me, right?"

"What do you need?"

"Bodies. You know we can't match up in a foot race with InUnison. We're going to have to code around a bunch of things."

"How many bodies?"

"Three or four for two to three weeks in both New York and Atlanta."

"Nine to twelve man weeks? Are you nuts? I don't have talent like that sitting on the bench!"

"Hey, weren't you telling me not long ago that you really wanted to get into Azalea? Well?"

"I'll give you two bodies."

"Experienced with our software?"

"Fact is no one is yet. We are waiting for engagements to staff."

"Well, here's an engagement." Gatto's eyes bore into Liu.

Liu frowned. He realized that he had to get some consultants trained on VibraWeb or his prize partnership would fail just as it began.

"Isn't there any money for this?" Liu practically begged Gatto.

"Not up front. The only good thing here is that now that the CFO is involved, there will have to be results and maybe, maybe, we can pull some coin."

"Better be serious coin," Liu snorted. "It's going to be very hard to justify doing this pro bono. I'll have to hide this somehow." *Shit, there go my billable hours.*

"Get them onsite ASAP. I'm working with this guy," he wrote out Mordecai's name and number on a note pad. "He's expecting your call."

"Gee, thanks."

"So what else do you have for me?"

Ingrate. Couldn't you at least say "thanks"? Liu thought as he pulled out his notebook. "I'm targeting several opportunities…" He pulled a summary sheet and handed it to Gatto.

"Hmmm, I like these names." Gatto smiled as he considered which ones he could fat bear for the quarter.

***

Power walking as usual, Wayne led Porter across Water Street and up Maiden Lane, heading to their next meeting, Smithton Finance in One Liberty Plaza, Porter's old stomping grounds. They paused for the light at Broadway, crossed, and walked up the two blocks to One Liberty.

"Feels a little strange going into this building again," Porter said.

"It's not like we are going to visit your old bank. Focus on Smithton."

"What's the agenda?"

"Standard. I do the company overview, hand it off to you for technical architecture and demo. I want to close on a Starter Kit."

"Do they have a project?" Porter asked as the elevator doors closed.

"Please! It's ruthlessly qualified! I wouldn't waste our time otherwise."

"Oh, of *course.*"

The receptionist on the thirty-fourth floor led them to a conference room and Porter immediately began to set up the laptops. A few minutes passed and two men and two women entered, armed with notebooks.

"Hi, I'm Wendy Frankfurt, Vice-president of Systems Infrastructure. Are you Wayne?" she asked Porter.

"Hi. No, I'm Porter Mitchell, Systems Engineer."

"I'm Wayne. Pleased to meet you. And you are?" he asked, turning to one of the others.

"Max Allred, Architect."

"Phil Axelrod, Analyst."

"Mary Tsang, Analyst."

"So, Wendy, is this everyone?"

"Yes, we should get started."

Porter finished getting the laptops networked together and connected to the projector. He nodded to Wayne that all was well.

Wayne moved to the front of the room and opened the presentation.

"InUnison was founded in 1995 by William Engler who is a pioneer in the packaged integration market. He's been well known in Silicon Valley for over fifteen years at places like IBM and Sun Microsystems where he spearheaded their object-oriented work, including the submission of their work to the CORBA specification…"

He advanced to the financial facts slide.

"Here you can see that we have strong financial backing from some of the biggest names in the venture capital community. We are very healthy financially."

"So, you're not public yet?" Wendy asked.

"No, but we certainly hope to be in the near future."

"It makes it tough to judge your viability without public disclosure."

"We will be happy to detail our finances at the appropriate time." *Like when you sign a seven figure deal.* "Next, I'd like to turn the podium over to the smart guy of the team, Porter Mitchell."

"Thanks, Wayne." *That line is becoming tiresome, Wayne.* "As I go along, please feel free to ask questions. I'd like this to be as 'give and take' as we can."

There was not even a nod from the four audience members.

Porter presented his InUnison Seven Layer Pyramid architecture slides. There were no questions and Porter began to worry about Mary Tsang, whose face never changed from a blank stare. Max's posture with his arms folded across his chest did not alter either. Only Wendy asked questions.

"Now, I'd like to move on to the sizzle of the presentation, the demo," Porter said with a smile, hoping to get some reaction. He was positive that his two-machine demo would get some rise out of this lackluster group.

He showed on his laptop how the InUnison tools created messages and used Wayne's to display results and message data. Everything worked perfectly. Porter was especially proud of the system monitor, which showed the messages graphically as they moved through the system. Each message was a green ball in the graphical window which moved from the message broker to the client application on Wayne's machine. He looked up, expecting to see wide eyes of amazement.

"So, any questions?"

He looked at Wendy, who looked at her team. Max still hadn't moved, Phil was tapping his notebook with his pen and Mary was showing symptoms of a narcoleptic episode.

Wendy continued to wait for questions for what seemed to be forever, so Wayne stepped in to rescue Porter.

"Wendy, that's our pitch," he said. "Where do we go from here? You indicated on the phone that you were starting up an integration project."

"That's right, Wayne, and this looks perfect for it. Our project, Customer Service Consolidation, or CSC, is only now getting started. You indicated that we could get set up with a package deal?"

"Yes, the Starter Kit which gives you five developer seats, the message broker and two connectors."

"Great, put that in writing and I'll send it up to Purchasing. Oh, someone has the room reserved so we need to vacate." She turned to her team. "So, no questions? Clear as mud, right?"

Mary shrugged, Phil nodded and Max maintained his blank stare.

"It's a wrap, then." Max, Mary and Phil picked up their notebooks and left. Wendy stayed behind as Porter packed up their machines.

"That was a very good demo, Porter. Did you have to code much for that?" Wendy asked.

"Oh, there wasn't any code. I should have emphasized that." Porter chastised himself for not doing so earlier. It was, of course, a key attribute of InUnison's software.

"Wouldn't have mattered with this bunch," she said, hooking her thumb. "I'm new here and inherited those stiffs. They think that they are going to sit in their cubicles and maintain a few lines of code a day. They hate to learn new things."

"I know the type. I used to work at Security National here and–"

"Sorry to interrupt," Wayne said, "but we have to be going. I'll have that paperwork to you tomorrow."

"Great," Wendy said. "Porter, I assume you will be our technical contact?"

"Yes, though we do have Customer Support as well."

"Porter can always be your first line support, especially as you get ramped up," Wayne said.

"We'll certainly need that. Max is going to be the point person on this project and he needs all the help he can get."

Wendy showed Porter and Wayne to the elevator and left them with one more goodbye handshake.

Porter shook his head as they entered the elevator.

"Boy, I thought that demo was pretty cool but it didn't go over well, did it?"

"It was fine," Wayne said. "It really didn't matter anyway since Wendy was already bought in."

"And your point is?"

"She had to send a message to her team."

"And why did you interrupt me? I was getting a little rapport with her about the bank."

"You were starting to focus on yourself. Remember, it's all about *them.* She doesn't need to know about your bank experience."

"Doesn't seem fair. I thought we should form a partnership with the customer."

"We don't have to get so personal."

"Oh, but talking *golf* isn't getting personal."

"Of course not! So you know your follow-ups?" Wayne asked, writing off Porter's question as rhetorical. He continued to lead Porter up Broadway to get the Uptown subway at the Fulton Street station.

"No, but I bet you're going to tell me."

"Yes, schedule a visit with Max to get the software installed and get him up and running. And I mean soon, like by Friday."

"But they haven't bought yet!"

"They will, especially after we push them a bit. I'm not going to leave this to Wendy."

A sickening realization hit Porter as they walked along Broadway. "Wait a minute, Friday is the only day this week we don't have sales calls. When am I going to get those RFI's done?"

"There are twenty-four hours in a day, Porter," Wayne said, leading Porter down the steps to the train. "Use them. On to the next conquest!"

***

"Excellent! Told you it wasn't hard," Julia said. Her student had just successfully completed an example project using InUnison's software. She had spent the last two days helping to install the software on the Azalea Insurance servers and acting as onsite trainer for the software developers assigned to the integration pilot.

"Wow. This is great stuff, Julia," her student, Ted Hall, said. "I can jump right in now and get our piece of this pilot going. Those New York guys won't know what hit them."

"Then you know enough to be dangerous, Ted?"

"Armed and very dangerous. Thanks, Julia."

"Super. I need to check in with Spencer Carlton with a progress report."

"Remind him about my raise."

"Will do."

Julia left the server lab and walked up a flight of stairs to Carlton's floor, pausing on the landing to adjust the red scrunchy tying back her blonde mane.

Exiting the stairwell she turned left down a row of cubicles to a stand-alone office near the elevator lobby.

"Hi, I'm Julia from InUnison Software," she told the receptionist. "Mr. Carlton asked me to stop by before leaving."

The receptionist stood up and stuck her head in the office.

"Spencer, Julia from InUnison is here to see you."

Carlton appeared at the door. "Thanks for stopping, Julia. Come on in."

Julia shook his hand as Spencer offered her a chair in front of his desk.

"So, how did your training go?"

"Very well, Spencer. You have some very quick studies on your team. They are off and running."

"Yes, I'm very proud of the team here. Even so, are there any potholes I need to look out for?"

"I don't think so, at least not technically. I think your only potholes will be political."

"Tell me something I don't already know," Spencer said, shaking his head. "When this started, I thought I could be the honest broker between Racker and

Miller but I'm already getting courted and flamed at the same time by both sides. I'm going to have to be a lot more proactive to protect my standing. I'm now the guarantor of success in this pilot and I'm not sure which combatant in New York is on my side."

"I don't know either of those players but I'm very impressed with Porter and Wayne from our side," Julia said. "Wayne is a very refreshing change from his predecessor and Porter has over a year's experience with InUnison."

"Yes, I know; he worked with Norm Johnson. Norm doesn't seem too happy with him though. He still resents my involvement, I think."

"He should know his place."

Spencer raised an eyebrow. "Compassionate, aren't you?"

"Not with people who put themselves above their company."

"Now, that's a little harsh," Spencer said. "He thought he was doing the right thing. In fact, Racker insisted on the covert strategy."

"Perhaps. But he was heading to snatch defeat from the jaws of victory."

My! She's tough. "I hope you have more confidence in me."

"From what I've seen the last two days, I certainly do."

"Well, thanks. Hey, I don't want to keep you. Thanks for the update. Will you be back soon?"

"Yes, I'll be checking in and they have my phone numbers."

She started to get up to leave and Spencer walked around his desk to escort her to the door.

"Uh, one other thing, Julia?" he asked before opening the door.

"Yes?"

"Uh, care to have dinner with me sometime?"

She was usually prepared for an advance like this. It was always some software engineering guy who was the last type on Earth she would be attracted to. Carlton, though, was a senior executive, very handsome and definitely not a geek. Her first impulse this time was to scream "YES" and jump into his arms. What inhibited her, though, was a picture on his credenza.

"Well, you've caught me off guard, Spencer. I, well, how to say this, aren't you married?"

"Married? What gave you that idea? I've always been wedded to my job."

Julia pointed to the picture.

"Oh, I see. No, that's my sister and my two nieces. That's funny; it never occurred to me how that might be interpreted. So, now that we cleared that up…"

Julia looked away from Spencer's face, feeling her face blush.

"Spencer, I'd really like that…"

"But?"

"But, I really think I should take a rain check until this pilot is over. If it appeared that we were, well…"

Damn. "You're right, of course. But I hope you aren't giving me a tactful brush-off."

Julia looked directly into his eyes. "Not at all, Spencer. It'll be more incentive to get this pilot done."

"I agree."

They shook hands and Julia left, with an added spring in her step.

***

The following week, Wayne was still in "the zone", skipping any small talk as he met Porter in the parking lot of some nameless – at least to Porter – prospect.

"Did you get that Manley RFI done yet?" Wayne asked Porter. "You know it's due this Friday, the thirteenth. And how did it go at Smithton with Max?"

"I was up until one last night working on *both* RFI's, damn it. I finished Azalea. I'm making progress on Manley but I'm not getting much help. Young sent me some other responses but none of them have questions like these clowns from Manley came up with."

"Remember, just say 'yes'."

"You ought to be answering some of these questions, smart guy."

"Wrong. I'm just a dumb rep."

"Dumb like a fox. And as far as Max the Wonder Dog, he blew me off. He left me a message Friday morning which I luckily heard before I got too far. He told me he didn't have a server machine ready. He never answers his phone and doesn't return messages. Actually it's not only Max. Thanks to our flurry of sales meetings, I'm getting all kinds of calls now. I feel like I ought to have this cell phone surgically attached to my ear."

"Get a headset like mine."

"I was really being facetious. I guess I'll take the phone calls over these sales meetings. Every one lately has been dull, with lifeless faces staring at me. If they ask questions it is usually showing off."

"Hey, Mr. Cranky, try to put a smile on your face. This is only the first day of another week's worth of sales calls so suck it up. Weren't you happy about the Johnson and Johnson guy Thursday? At least he asked good questions."

"Yeah and my answer to most was 'I'll have to get back to you on that.' I still think that he was showing off for his boss."

"Don't sweat it but don't forget to follow up on those questions. It's important that we don't let that stuff drop through the cracks. You'll get the hang of things."

Porter frowned, his shoulders drooping as they walked across the parking lot.

"At least we don't have to baby-sit Azalea for a while since PS is in there," Wayne said. "Spencer seems to be in charge now and I'll check on him every couple of days. By the way, the Azalea HQ visit is set for the first week of March."

"First week of March? I'm out there for training the week before. Am I going to have to stay there for two weeks? The airfare will be astronomical if I do two roundtrips."

"What, you can't put the company's financial welfare ahead of your personal interests? How selfish!"

Porter missed Wayne's sarcasm as usual. "That's asking a lot with a young baby at home."

Wayne smiled and shook his head at his partner's never-ending gullibility.

They entered the lobby of the building and looked for the elevator, which was tucked into a dark corner.

"Who are these people again?" Porter asked as they waited.

"Randall Electric. Try to focus, will you? They are a distributor of electrical parts and have to integrate their customer service software, something called Clarify and the mainframe. Should be a lay-up for you."

"Who's in the meeting?"

"The Director of Customer Service Systems, her boss, the VP and her technical right-hand man. Oh, and a possible partner for us, a guy named George Orlando." The elevator finally opened and they entered. "I talked to him. Kind of a goofball but seemed motivated to work with us."

They entered the offices and a receptionist took them to a conference room where the attendees were already waiting. Porter set up both of their laptops as Wayne chatted up the director and her boss, an avid golfer. Wayne reprised his opinion of Westchester Golf Links while Porter set up. Finally, Wayne opened the presentation.

"InUnison was founded in 1995 by William Engler who is a pioneer in the packaged integration market, well known in Silicon Valley for…"

So, how many can I put to sleep today? Porter asked himself as he looked at the blank faces in the room. *Ten sales calls in three days. All the follow-up. Another dozen next week. The RFIs. I'll never get caught up.*

And he never would.

***

"MEANS!"

Gatto returned the phone to his ear.

"Tom Gatto, George."

"FAT BEAR! How the hell are you? Got some more POs for me?"

"Could be. I'm working on several of these application service providers but I think that we need some new pricing for them."

"What's an application service whatchacallit?"

Really with it, aren't you, George? He explained what an ASP does.

"The thing is that they are essentially renting our software to their clients like they do SAP or PeopleSoft. If we use our standard licensing structure, they have to buy a server license for every customer. That makes us prohibitively expensive. I see their point. I can close all of these ASPs if we can be creative on the pricing."

"Now, you're disappointing me. I might have to take your Fat Bear title away. We can't take the time to redo pricing. Find someone else to sell to."

"George, I can sell into these guys. We need to…"

"No way. It's the current pricing or nothing."

"But George, it isn't complicated…"

"No way. So what's happening at Azalea? Close it yet?"

"George, as I've told you, there is no business there this quarter."

"I'm definitely pulling your Fat Bear title. Do you want Hager to convince you about Azalea's visibility?"

"No thanks." *And I don't give a shit about my title.* "There's been a complication. They are insisting on reference customers in Financial Services. Also, InUnison is hosting a visit to HQ and Marcus is hearing that InUnison already has their pilot done."

"Great! An HQ visit! We can have them in Santa Clara as well. Khaybar loves to take customers to dinner."

You aren't listening as usual, George. "Who do I use as references?"

"Call Scott Shepherd in Chicago. He'll help you out."

"So, he has some customers out there?"

"Call him. And forget about the ASPs."

He hung up on Gatto.

***

Wayne and Porter exited their third sales call of the day, walking in a light drizzle to Wayne's car.

"That guy gave me the creeps, Wayne."

"Who?" Wayne asked as they exited the Pioneer Industrial Payments Systems – PIPS for short – building in Roseland, New Jersey.

"That Bibolini guy."

"Biboli. What about him?"

"He looked like Freddie Mercury from Queen and his voice reminded me of that slime ball in those Bogart movies, you know who I mean, that short greasy guy?"

"Peter Lorre."

"Yeah, him. Remember him in Casablanca? '*Reeeek, Reeeek, save meee, Reeeek!*' ."

"Freddie Mercury, I like that! 'We are the champions, we *are* the champions'…" he sang.

"Please stop. I always hated Queen."

"Sorry. Anyway, I thought it was the thin mustache that gave him that kind of slick look. You better get used to him, though; we're going to get a project there and his team is going to get the contract."

"That technical guy, Bill, was pretty smart, why can't he run the project?"

Wayne unlocked his car and tossed his bag onto the back seat. "Porter, didn't you notice that Sylvia really didn't have much control of the meeting? Her boss, Pearson, is the real driver here and Freddie Mercury is a golfing buddy," Wayne said, adopting Biboli's new nickname.

"I didn't notice that. Is that what you were talking about as I was setting up?"

"No, Freddie told me on the phone," Wayne said. "It was his way of saying who is in charge here without actually saying so. I don't care; it's going on the forecast for this quarter. On to Magna Insurance. You have the directions, navigator?"

"I suppose that's all I'm good for."

"No, you give great demo!"

"How can you tell? I'd love to do one of these presentations and not have anyone passing out. It's kind of a downer. Isn't there anyone out there who gets excited about our stuff?"

"You're asking a lot," Wayne joked, not realizing the depth of Porter's anguish.

Wayne pulled his Saab out of the parking lot and headed for I-280. From there they curled around to I-80 East to get to Magna Insurance.

On the way, Porter checked his messages.

"You have…fifteen new messages."

"God Wayne! Fifteen messages! See what I mean?"

"Only fifteen? I get at least thirty a day. Speaking of which, I need to get on the phone while we drive, so pipe down."

Porter decided to do the same.

"Hi, Porter. This is Max with Smithton. Hey, I have a machine here which is running Windows NT 3.0. Can we use that? Let me know." Porter deleted the message.

"Now see, Wayne? I've told Max several times we need NT 4.0 and he keeps coming back with the wrong thing."

Wayne was lost in his own message queue and didn't respond. Porter moved on.

"Porter, this is Mary Creeble at Zephyr Machines. I got your number from your corporate office that you are a rep in the area. We have some questions about InUnison. Please call…" Porter jotted down the name and number and deleted the message.

"Porter, this is Max. Ignore my previous message. I don't have that machine available. Bye."

Porter continued through the next five messages. They were all prospect calls needing some technical support.

"Porter, this is Larry at Empire Supply. We can't install this software. If it's this hard maybe we don't really want to use the software. Call soon."

He went through the rest of the messages and decided that he'd better call back the Empire Supply guy.

"Hello, this is Porter with InUnison. You left a message about an installation problem?"

"Yes," Larry said. "I put in the CD and nothing happens."

"Um, you did what?"

"I took the CD out of its sleeve, put it in my CD-ROM drive and closed it.

Nothing happened."

"Well, it doesn't just start. You have to double click on the Installer icon," *Like it says in the manual.*

"That's stupid. It should start when you shove the CD in like most software."

"I don't know why we didn't do it that way, but if you double-click–"

"But you agree that it's stupid, right? Why should you make extra work for me?"

"I'm sorry, Larry. I'll definitely pass along your suggestion."

"I'll never understand why you software companies can't think like users. Thanks. I'll call if I need more help."

Porter dejectedly closed his phone. It rang almost immediately.

"This is Porter."

"Hi, Porter, this is Max at Smithton. I found a Windows 3.1 machine. Will that work?"

Sigh. "No, we need NT 4.0 or later."

"That's going to be tough."

"You must have an NT machine somewhere."

"I don't know. We don't normally use NT. Why can't you guys use Windows?"

"We need the server capabilities of NT."

"I know, can't we borrow a machine from *you*?"

You've got to be kidding. "Sorry, I don't have access to any machines."

"Figures. You expect *me* to have one though."

"I'm sorry."

"I don't know why Wendy always has to do this stuff that needs exotic machines. Nothing wrong with what we've got. I guess I'll keep looking. Thanks. Bye."

Porter closed his phone again.

The timing was tight but they made it in time for their one o'clock appointment. Porter set up the laptops as Wayne talked golf with a couple of the attendees. Finally, Wayne opened the presentation.

"InUnison was founded in 1995 by William Engler who is a pioneer in the packaged integration market, well known in Silicon Valley for…"

***

The next morning, a worn down Porter entered the Azalea offices, exhausted from another late night working on the Manley Brothers RFI, getting it finished in time to submit that day.

"Hello, Porter. Back to visit with us? Boy, you look like hell."

"Gee thanks, Connie. Have to keep Norm in line," Porter said as he shuffled passed Consuelo's desk on his way back to the cubicle of Brewster McNaughton. Wayne had decided that it was time to check on the progress of their pilot and, more importantly, the competing pilot under Mordecai Rosenzweig.

"Mornin' Porter," Brewster said.

"You don't look good, Brewster. Too much happy hour yesterday?"

"God, Thursdays are party days with these people, especially when they have a round of promotions. We had several people make VP so they bought last night. And boy, did they buy."

"Well, not to rush you but I have little time here so what's the status?"

Brewster swiveled to his computer. "We really have this thing nailed. That Carlton guy is a wiz and he has some good people down there. Julia has been helping as well."

Porter laughed. "Not that she really needed to be there. Gary Reaper down there has been hounding her to stay close to Carlton so that he can say he deserves a cut of any deal."

Brewster showed Porter all of the work that had been done to consolidate data from the insurance subsidiary into the corporate wide financial reports. He ran a set of reports with a click of the mouse.

"Simple."

"Excellent! Wayne will be pleased. What do you know about the IT team?"

"Very little. As you might expect, they aren't mixing with us."

"Mind if I use your phone? I want to see Mordecai if possible."

"Have at it."

Porter dialed the extension. "Hi, Mordi. It's Porter Mitchell with InUnison. I'm visiting with Brewster here and since I'm in the building, I figured that I'd stop by."

"You shouldn't be calling me."

"Well, I thought –"

"Look, meet me in the coffee shop. I can't talk here."

"I'll be right down." He hung up, perplexed.

"What's wrong?" Brewster asked.

"I don't know. He wouldn't talk. He wants to meet me in the coffee shop."

"Ooooo, cloak and dagger stuff."

"I better go. Thanks for the overview. You guys rock."

Porter paid departing respects to Connie as he passed and took the elevator down to the lobby. He turned into the coffee shop but didn't immediately see Rosenzweig.

"Psst. Porter. Over here."

Porter spun around to see Mordecai at a corner table away from the windows.

"Hi, how are you?"

"Sick and tired, that's what."

"Why?"

"I've got all these Flanderson consultants hacking code and that creepy Marcus Sweeney from VibraWeb is always looking over my shoulder. He doesn't even *do* anything but eat donuts. Miller keeps asking for status updates."

"Are they accomplishing anything? Norm's team is almost done."

"Yes, that's what I've been hearing."

"From who? Brewster said he hasn't talked at all about their results."

"Spencer Carlton. He's almost teasing us by dropping little hints about what he's seen. The consultants are matching the functionality. They are programming a lot more, though."

"But our way should obviously be better, right?"

Mordi looked at Porter with a raised eyebrow.

"Don't be so sure. All it takes is for Miller to say he accomplished the same feat. You guys had better find a way to do it better."

How can that be, Porter wondered. *Doesn't productivity matter?*

"You mentioned Carlton. Has he been helping the consultants?"

"Definitely. He's been great to work with. Answers questions, gives access. We couldn't do it without him."

Damn. I guess he wasn't kidding about not playing favorites.

***

The third week of February found Porter almost at the end of his patience. He felt punch drunk from the previous weeks of numerous presentations and beatings from interrogators. Few of their meetings yielded prospects excited about InUnison let alone any strong sales opportunities. Porter couldn't understand how Wayne kept his own seemingly inexhaustible energy amid all the rejection. Wayne reminded Porter after every sales call that rejection was motivation. Porter wasn't seeing it that way.

"So, thank you for your attention," Wayne said to his audience. "InUnison looks forward to doing business with Phillips Foods."

"I have one more question," a systems administrator named Mario said.

Porter sighed, loud enough for everyone to hear, horrifying Wayne. Luckily, it seemed lost on Mario.

"I don't want to seem negative…"

But of course you do, you worm, Porter thought, narrowing his eyes, again to Wayne's growing apprehension.

"…but I don't see how this helps me. If anything, tying all the systems together creates a big headache for me. You're going to have to prove that your security –"

"So, I guess you weren't impressed that the National Security Agency uses our system?" Porter said, leaning across the table. "Isn't that secure enough?"

"What Porter means is that we can work with you. I'm confident we can meet your security requirements. Again, thanks for your attention."

Porter grunted.

There was an uncomfortably quiet pause until the audience got up to leave. The host, one Catherine Knoll, raised an eyebrow in Wayne's direction. "Yes, thanks for coming. I'll be in touch about next steps, Wayne."

Wayne knew he'd never hear from her again.

Out in the parking lot, Wayne chased down Porter before he could get to the car.

"Hey! What the hell is wrong with you? If you can't control your emotions –"

"Fuck you!" Porter said, freezing Wayne in his tracks. He wondered if Porter was under the influence or something. He had seen the pressure rising all week as they visited prospect after prospect, few of which registered any real understanding of what InUnison was all about. Those that did had gone out of their way to beat the hell out of Porter on the technical merits.

"Why, tell me why, are we wasting our time? These people are fucking morons from planet Idiot. All the meetings this week had some jerk trying to piss me off, asking any arcane question popping in his mind."

Wayne wanted to laugh, but knew Porter wasn't in the mood for mockery.

"Hey, I've been there. I feel your pain."

"It isn't funny."

Wayne realized he needed to take drastic action.

"I know what we need to do: hit a few buckets of balls. Smack a few balls and the world's problems get smacked with them. I know an indoor range near here. Let's go!"

"Golf? You know I haven't played since college."

"Heathen! We better get you back in the swing of things. We're going to do a lot of business on the links come springtime."

Porter sighed as he didn't have a choice, dependent as he was on Wayne for transportation that day.

True to his word, Wayne pulled into a Hacker's Helper behind which was a bubble covering a driving range. "Not quite like a big outdoor range, but it'll do," he said, popping open his trunk.

"What, you always have your clubs?" Porter asked.

"You never know when you might get a quick nine in."

"In February?"

"It's been known to happen."

He selected a Ping fairway wood for himself and handed a Callaway "Big Bertha" driver to Porter.

Porter felt very uncomfortable as his first few hits dribbled off the tee.

"Just swing comfortably," Wayne said, launching a perfect hit. After a few more he started his therapy session.

"Why is it that you propeller heads take this so personally? Look, what did you expect? It's a little known law of nature, but in every meeting of five or more people, at least one is going to be a butthead. That doesn't mean that the other four agree with the butthead. I know to avoid him. You need to adopt a glass half full attitude, my friend. Concentrate on the ball."

Porter shanked a ball to the left, but at least it flew more than twenty yards.

"Wayne, tell me that we will eventually work with a smart customer again."

"I guarantee it! Look, we are going to win Azalea, and those guys are smart, well, except for IT, but you know what I mean. Don't worry, we'll make our

Number."

"I don't give a rat's ass about the Number!"

That heresy made Wayne hook one.

"Making the Number from accounts like Phillips makes me feel dirty. They aren't worthy."

Now Wayne's bile started to back up. *What the hell did he just say??*

"Listen," Wayne said, pointing his driver at Porter. "Get this through that elitist skull of yours; one, we can't survive on smart, early-adopter customers. There aren't enough of them. Two – and I know I'm indulging your religious zealotry here – has it occurred to you that these people aren't atheists? They just have to switch to our denomination. Third," he said, going nose to nose now, "I'm not going to put my livelihood at risk by having to work with someone whose head isn't in the game. You need to decide if you're up to this job or if you'd rather go sit in a corner sucking your thumb!" He turned to tee up another ball.

"That's not fair, Wayne. I expected the market to be, I don't know, rewarding, grateful."

Whack! Wayne nailed another perfect drive.

My God, he can't let it go. "Hey, don't you remember PensAndClips, Merrill, Sampson, hell, even Melani at Potential? They are all *very* grateful. Buddy, don't crash on me now. I need you! You need to understand that the one great account makes up for the ten stupid ones. Hit some more balls."

Porter sliced his next attempt, his distance improving.

"Okay, look," Wayne continued. "I know I've run you ragged this month but it had to be. We are new in this territory and had to make a name for ourselves. We lost ground in January and had to make up for it. It won't always be this bad. Porter, you are about the best SE I've worked with. Your knowledge of the product and your presentation skills are top notch. Your poise – except for this afternoon – is great. I know how annoying these prospects can be. Try to focus on the five percent we win."

"If you say so," Porter said, looking away.

"You'll be out in Redwood City with your SE brethren next week. Talk to them. You'll get recharged and be ready to change the world again!"

Porter finally straightened his swing out, admiring a fine drive.

"I hope so," Porter said. "Wayne, I appreciate your patience with me. I know most other reps would have written me off by now. But I don't know how much more of this rejection I can take."

***

Entering the Azalea Insurance office building, Julia asked, "Gary, you really don't have to be here, do you? I'm only checking in with the developers."

"I have to, uh, see Spencer about some things."

Julia signed herself into the reception log and handed the pen to Reaper.

"What 'things', Gary? You've been here with me the last three visits and only sat around."

"It's my responsibility to manage the business relationship."

"I thought that was Wayne's responsibility."

"I'm helping."

Sure you are.

The receptionist buzzed them in through the security door and they took the elevator to the fifth floor test lab.

"So is Spencer expecting you?" Julia asked, once in the elevator.

"I left him a message."

"He's pretty busy, you know."

"He always seems to find time to stop by to see you," Reaper said, with a sly smile.

She hid her own smile from Reaper, not wanting to give him the satisfaction of knowing that she liked Carlton's attention. He was positively a Renaissance man. At their status meetings, he usually talked more about art, architecture and music than the details of the pilot. She finally admitted to herself that she was smitten. He reminded her of a serious college boyfriend, an art major who was also technologically savvy. He was the first man to gain her "respect".

"He's very concerned about this pilot so he's been staying close to it."

"Staying close to you, I'd say."

The elevator doors opened and Reaper stepped out first. Julia stopped him outside the car.

"What are you trying to say, Gary?"

"It's obvious he's only there because he wants to be around you."

"Your imagination is spinning out of control. Gary, he's one of the most professional managers I've seen."

"I don't know why you're getting mad at me. After all, if he's attracted to you, it could give us an edge. I think you should, you know…"

"Should *what*?"

"You know…" Reaper repeated, this time thrusting his hips forward and backward. "…the horizontal tango."

Berkowski could only stare at Reaper.

"Now, Julia," Gary said, stepping back from her. "Don't deny the attraction. I've seen you checking him out. I'm saying we could use it to our advantage here. When I was at Sybase –"

"Stop right there, mister! You *have* to be the sickest bastard…I should get you fired for suggesting something like that, or maybe I should perform a John Wayne Bobbitt," Julia hissed, inches from Reaper's face.

"Oh, c'mon, I was *kidding*," he said, recoiling.

"Like hell you were," she said, marching off to the lab. "I have work to do before going to California. Sick, knuckle-dragging Cro-Magnon."

Chapter 14 "Interesting"

"May I help you, Monsieur?"

"Yes, Mitchell; Porter Mitchell checking in."

Porter checked in three hours late to the Sofitel, desperate for a juicy cheeseburger and a tall, cold one.

Reaching the sixth floor, he double-checked his room number written on the key folder and turned to the left for room 621. As he put the card key in the door, he could hear the television. *Ah, Sean's already hacked into the TV.*

He entered and there was Sean Murphy, wearing only boxer shorts, watching a movie. He was relieved that it was a comedy, not *Nasty Nurses III or* some other adult entertainment classic.

"Porter, good to see you arrived. I'm dying to eat. You hungry?"

"Starving."

"We don't have much choice since neither of us has a car. We'll have to go downstairs to the snooty Baccarat," he said, holding his nose. "Or settle for some appetizers at the bar."

In a flash, Murphy was fully dressed in the Silicon Valley uniform: blue jeans and black mock turtleneck, decorated with the InUnison logo. A quick review of the restaurant menu drove them to the bar. "Fuckin' bullshit food. I hate this place," Sean muttered as they wandered into the lounge area.

"Let's sit at the end of the bar so we can see who comes in," Murphy suggested. "Other SEs should be trickling in shortly."

"Are these things drunken brawls like the kickoff?"

Sean chuckled. "No, we're all too cheap. Not that we can't put away the beer, mind you. Now, if Young shows up, all bets are off since we can get him to pay. O'Rourke always waves his expense reports through."

"Young is definitely a cool guy. He really pitched in on our RFIs. I don't think that I could have finished them in time."

"He isn't good for anything else," Sean said. "He can't demo anymore since he got the Management Lobotomy. They don't call him the Sand Man for nothing. Ten minutes in front of a customer and it's bam!" Sean slapped his hand on the bar, startling Porter and the bartender. "They do a face plant out of boredom," Murphy said, laughing hysterically.

Porter smiled and shook his head. "You're nuts."

"No, *your* nuts," Sean countered, pointing at Porter's crotch and still laughing.

They ordered some calamari and chicken filets. "That'll be good for a start. So, what's been happening with you? I don't hear from you anymore and you've missed a few of the conference calls."

"Sean, I have had the busiest month of my life. Once Azalea was off doing the pilot stuff, I didn't have a lot of involvement and figured I could catch my breath. Wayne had other ideas. I lost count at twenty-five sales calls in less than three weeks. It's so repetitive, I'm dreaming about demos. Wayne always says the same thing: 'InUnison was founded in 1995 by William Engler who blah, blah, blah…' I can't stand it anymore."

"That's usually what the first month of the quarter is like. Then you baby-sit the good prospects for a month and close them the last month. Simple."

"Yeah, right. I think Wayne is compressing two months into one. I was looking forward to this training to get me off the treadmill. I don't know how Wayne keeps track of all this activity. I can't keep up with the phone calls and emails asking for support or asking some stupid question that's answered in the manual."

"RTFM."

"What?"

"Standard response to stupidity and laziness: Read The Fucking Manual."

"Right," Porter said, raising his beer glass. "Customers aren't very smart, are they?"

Sean looked at his watch. "Let's see, you've been on board for less than two months. I think that might be a record for a newbie to start calling customers stupid. Congratulations, you've graduated! Next stop, Cynics Anonymous! After a few days with nobody around but SEs, you'll be enrolled."

"Wayne said I'd be recharged after a week with SEs."

"Dream on."

"Why won't customers take responsibility for themselves?" Porter asked.

"They have an opportunity to improve themselves and their companies, really be productive and they act like it's such a burden to – gasp! – learn something new. This guy at Best Mechanical actually told me that if he was more productive, it would undo ten years of, quote, 'management conditioning'. What's up with that?"

"Eat your calamari. You'll feel better. Porter, you need to realize that we are simply trying to sell software, not change the world."

"But our software *can* change the world, Sean! I've *seen* what it can do, hell, I've *done* it."

Sean turned away from Porter and looked out at the pool. "Nothing changes the world. Customers will always be stupid and we'll force feed our software down their throats. Eat your fucking calamari and shut up."

Porter was offended by Sean's verbal spanking. He selected a nice tight curl of calamari and dipped it into sauce.

"Sorry I'm so cranky, Sean. It's been a long flight at the end of a long month."

"Chill, will ya?" Sean was still looking out at the pool and the inlet beyond. For once he seemed at a loss for words.

"Finally! Some friendly faces," Wiley Nelson said. "That flight from Chicago was a bitch. Couldn't get upgraded…Anchor Steam, please," he said to the passing bartender who seemed annoyed at the request.

"You remember Porter Mitchell, right?" Sean asked, waving a tentacle in Porter's direction.

Porter mopped the grease off of his fingers and shook Wiley's hand.

"Sure do," Nelson said. "I hear you're using UBS Warburg as a reference."

"Yes, Wayne has been working with Gustavson on it. While we have some good New York references, UBS is the best."

"I wish we had something in the pipeline to duplicate that feat."

"I thought I sensed testosterone around here," Julia said, sneaking up behind Sean. Her roommate, Mackenzie Jeffords, was with her.

"I could use some testosterone," Mackenzie said. The men raised a collective eyebrow. "No, not what you think, you animals. I needed a break from my sales partner, the Philly Femi-nazi."

Sean grunted and shook his head.

Wiley played host summoning the bartender, now more attentive as the group grew larger. "Gin and tonic, and a chard, right Julia?" She nodded and turned to Porter.

"So, things seem to be progressing at Azalea. Carlton has been great to work with."

"A little too good, if you ask me. Rosenzweig raves about how he's been helping the VibraWeb teams. Wayne and I hoped he'd be on our side, at least covertly."

"Now, Porter, look at it from his perspective. He *has* to be impartial. He's going to do the right thing."

"So, you've gotten to know him that well already?" Sean said, winking at Porter.

"Don't go there, Sean. I already had it out with Reaper. He thought I should get up close and personal with Spencer. I told him to kiss off."

"Sorry. I was only teasing, Julia. Bad joke, I guess." Sean knew where the limits were with Julia.

"So, any hiccups in New York?"

"Not on our side," Porter said. "I still have a few guilt pangs about how things played out for Norm Johnson though."

"Porter, he's in a great situation. Yeah, his ego is bruised but he's a great project manager. He's not a political player. Thanks," she said as the bartender handed her a glass of wine. "Thank God Reaper isn't making any waves. As usual, though, he'll get some credit for stuff he didn't really do. Enough about him; how are you doing?"

"I'm kind of overwhelmed right now…"

"Don't start on that again," Murphy said. "He's doing the 'adjustment', Julia."

"Oh. Yes, it's tough to go from a project focus to a 'just get it done' mode. Let me guess; you think everything should be cut and dried, right?"

"Noooo," Porter said, looking into his empty beer glass. "I'd like to finish something. Things go on and on and on…yes, I'll have another."

"Haven't we had this discussion before, Porter?" Julia said. "Any given activity with a customer may diminish but it doesn't go away. There's always another deal to be had. Well, I take that back. If you're Tom Gatto, customers are finished after he rapes them. Obviously, he isn't wanted back. Be thankful we don't practice such slam-bam-thank-you-ma'am tactics."

More SEs were filing in: Shirley Kudrey from the Bay Area, Ron Defazio from Los Angeles – fit and tanned as ever – Chris Majors, a new SE in Denver, Mark Moskowitz from Washington and Alan Crawford from Dallas with another new SE. The group spilled into the lounge seating area and attracted another server.

Porter and Sean kept up a steady business of appetizers and drafts with the bartender. He was an expatriate Frenchman – naturally – named Francois who was looking forward to his homeland hosting the World Cup soccer tournament that summer.

"Aw, that soccer's for pansies," Sean said. "Good for insomnia I guess…"

"Football, Monsieur, not *soccer…*"

"Yeah, whatever. You only like that game because it's the only game in your town. Now, *baseball,* that's a game."

"How can you say football is slow and boring, and then talk about how baseball is exciting in the same breath?"

"At least in baseball, you know nothing will happen until the ball is pitched. In soccer, oh, *fooootballlll,* you blink at the wrong moment and you miss the one good play for the game. Up and down, up and down. The only good thing is when the Italian women flash their hooters. Another Anchor, please." He shoved his beer glass to the gutter in the bar.

"Oui, Monsieur. You don't know what you're missing."

"Sure I do. Total boredom."

"Hey, Murphy," Moskowitz called out. "Get over here. We need your insight."

Sean took his newly refilled beer and waddled over to the group of five SEs gathered around a coffee table. "So what do you need me for?"

"I bet we go IPO this Fall. The signs all point to it," Moskowitz said.

"There's no way," Wiley countered. "We aren't anywhere near profitability."

Moskowitz rapped his knuckles on Nelsen's head. "Get it through that thick skull of yours. Nooobody cares. Just show sales growth."

"He's right," Sean said. "We need to show a good quarter and we are off to IPO-land." He floated his hand into the air in a drunken but elegant wave.

"I hope so," Jeffords said. "I've been here over a year. I'd like to see some payback."

You greedy little tart, Sean wanted to say. *I'm going on three years. Talk about being handcuffed.*

Porter ambled over to join the group. He was introduced to the new SEs and re-introduced to the veterans from the kickoff.

"Porter," Sean said, "we were debating our chances for IPO this year. What do you have to say?"

"I…I don't know. I haven't been thinking about it."

The entire group was speechless. Wiley raised an eyebrow and scanned the group before turning back to Porter. "You're not *thinking* about it?"

"Well, I…"

"He still thinks he's going to 'change the world'," Sean slurred.

"Oh, one of those," Moskowitz said. The new SEs were looking back and forth wondering if *they* were "one of those".

The waitress brought the latest round and Sean told her to bring another.

"Sean, please," Julia protested. "Not for me, thanks."

"They are so slow around here you have to think ahead," Sean said.

The waitress now felt put upon. "Who wants what?"

"Like I said," Sean babbled, "Gimme another draft."

A few of the others ordered drinks. Porter wandered back to the bar. Julia followed him.

"Porter, is everything all right?"

"Yes, girding myself for a rough night. Sean will be puking or something."

"I doubt it. He's experienced. Don't take all that stuff we talked about over there too seriously. A lot of it is posturing because it makes us all feel so, well, sophisticated."

Porter set his empty glass down, waving off the bartender who wanted to regain a customer.

"Julia, I don't get this obsession with an IPO. Don't we have to prove something first?"

"Of course, we do. I think we are. But for those of us on the front lines, well, we all have our own motivations. Sean's right, Wiley's right, Moskowitz is right. You're right. Don't let it eat you up." She grabbed a handful of peanut mix from the bowl on the bar.

"I'm not contributing."

"What are you talking about? Wayne is number one right now, even better than The Swede. He's going to blow out his Number. You don't do that without quality SE work. What could be better?"

Porter closed his eyes and leaned his head back.

"I'd like to feel that I'm making a difference."

Julia stared at Porter, perplexed. She still didn't know what he was talking about. He opened his eyes, looked at her and left the bar.

***

"Hi, Scott. This is Tom Gatto in New York."

"Hi. Oh, you're the guy who took over for Thomas, right?"

"Right. Anyway, I'm in the middle of a bitch of an account, Azalea Financial. Ever hear of them?"

"Yes, big mother. What's it got to do with me?"

"I'm told that you can help me with reference customers. Who do you have?"

"Who do you need?"

"Financial Services customers who are using VibraWeb."

"Well, there's UBS Warburg, ABN Amro…"

"Really? I didn't know we could use them. I'm willing to bet that InUnison will use UBS. They are a marquee account for them."

"Well, then UBS it is. Should balance out the other guys."

"How come they aren't listed on our web site?"

"That would be pretty brazen, don't you think, even by VibraWeb standards? I tell the prospects that they are very quiet about what they are doing so as to not alert a competitor, it's very strategic, yadda, yadda."

"Can we set up conference calls for this week?"

"Let me check my calendar. I'm pretty flexible so pick your days."

"Let's shoot for Thursday morning."

"Works fine. I'll set it up on our conference call service."

"Great. Let me know once you confirm with UBS and Amro."

"Oh, that's funny! Bye, Tom," Shepherd said, laughing as he hung up.

Gatto wrinkled his brow and stared at the phone for a few seconds, wondering what was so funny.

***

The SEs congregated near the Sofitel registration desk for their rides to InUnison headquarters, grumbling about how the company was too cheap to provide more rental cars and individual hotel rooms. David Young, Mark Moskowitz and Wiley Nelson were the designated drivers and all three rented mini-vans, standard Hertz rental white.

Porter was gnawing on a French pastry and reviewing the *Wall Street Journal*, looking up periodically for Sean. As the vans pulled up to the door, Murphy emerged from the elevator bank and sauntered down the hall.

"Thanks for steaming up the bathroom, Porter. It really puts the curl in my hair, what's left of it that is," Sean said, pulling a few strands across his bald spot.

"You're welcome. You deserved it after your drunken snoring last night."

"I didn't reveal any secrets, did I? I don't suppose I got lucky with Mackenzie?"

"Let's get going folks," Young urged his flock. The SEs lifted their briefcases and computer bags and shuffled silently to the vans.

"Seven thirty is too damn early," Ron Defazio said. "I wouldn't even go surfing at this time of day."

The vans formed a parade down Twin Dolphin Drive in Redwood Shores toward the onramp for US 101. The offices were located in an office park at the end of a peninsula more noted for its bright red and orange salt evaporation ponds than as an incubator of technology companies. Legend had it that many a deal was negotiated by high-tech executives taking a stroll around the giant salt mound located at the opening of the bay inlet.

The entourage spilled onto the parking lot and wandered through the glass doors of the two-floor white stucco and glass building. This being his first visit to the headquarters, Porter simply followed everyone else. Nelson led the pack past the staircase through another pair of glass doors. Beyond was a long aisle of cubicles flanked by short hallways of offices. Nelson turned right inside the doors into the first hallway. The training room was at the end of the hall, inside of which were rows of narrow tables in two-by-two arrangement with one aisle down the middle. There was a lecture stand in front and a projector hanging from the ceiling.

"Who's running the first session this morning?" Sean asked.

"Jimmy Scales," Young replied.

"Oh, an engineer is lowering himself to mix with the field people," Sean said.

"Training isn't trained yet. In fact, they will be sitting in on these sessions. Jimmy's the lead on the core software so we'll be getting it right from the source," Young said to Porter, then turned to Sean. "Try to be on good behavior."

"I'll behave when they check their arrogance at the door."

"What's he so arrogant about?" Porter asked, sipping his coffee and biting into a danish.

"Well, you know, they are smarter than any of us and of course know better than the field about how to sell software. Just once I'd like to make them come on some sales calls and see what it takes to sell their crap," Sean replied.

"Careful what you wish for," Wiley interjected. "They would call a customer stupid or worse."

"Well, they *are* stupid, right Porter?" Sean said with a wink. "Of course, I wouldn't tell that to their faces. When I'm with a customer..." he very solemnly put his hand over his heart, "...each and every one is the second coming of Einstein – or at least Bill Gates."

"Good morning everyone!" In bounced a very short, thin man with a long, brown pony tail that dropped past his shoulder blades. "I see some familiar faces; Murphy, always a pleasure to see you."

"Yeah, likewise, Scales. Did you finally fix that performance bug? BankBoston is still pissed off about having to reboot every other day."

"What bug? I don't recall...oh, right. Are they still using that unapproved configuration?"

"No, and they never were. They have bursts of activity that the broker never seems to recover from."

"Interesting. Perhaps we can talk offline about that," Scales said, turning his back on Sean so that he could connect his laptop to the projector cable. Sean gave Scales the finger.

After checking that the projector was indeed displaying his PowerPoint slides, he turned to face his still milling audience.

"Now, I see some unfamiliar faces." Scales approached Porter. "Hi, I'm Jimmy Scales, lead engineer for the messaging platform."

"I'm Porter Mitchell, SE in New York."

"Ah, the *famous* Porter Mitchell," Scales said, dripping with sarcasm.

"What am I famous for?"

"Being with the company for less than a month and single-handedly rearranging our engineering priorities. I hope disrupting the entire engineering schedule to get that stupid mainframe connector out is going to bring in big revenue. Haven't heard the bell being rung much lately."

"Really I didn't –"

"Lay off, Jimmy," Young said, standing to tower over the diminutive engineer. "You should know better than that."

"Oh, just kidding; you know that, Dave. Pleased to meet you, Porter." Scales moved on to greet some of the other new SEs.

Porter stared at his back.

"Don't sweat that, Porter," Young said. "I'd take it as a badge of honor that you pushed Engineering to do the right thing by your customers."

"But such resentment..."

"Not really resentment. Engineering still thinks that they should be driving the company, instead of the market. Their ego is bruised every time Engler has to tell them to do certain things because, gee, it will maximize revenue."

"Let's get started," Scales said, bounding back to the front of the room. "We have a lot to cover so I'd appreciate your cooperation, and pay special attention to the time when we are on breaks. I know you always sprint for the phones on breaks and then get lost in the socializations. So let's go over today's agenda..."

"Socializations, my ass," Sean whispered to Porter. "I'm paying your Santa Cruz mortgage, you creep."

Scales went through the list of topics, pointing out when someone else from Engineering would be coming in to talk. He then launched into an overview of the new release.

Porter tried to pay attention to the substance of the lecture but became more and more convinced that Scales was trying to intimidate him. Scales repeatedly glowered at Porter in between slides.

Bring it on, pal.

***

The fax machine in Wayne's office came to life, interrupting his email writing. He rolled his chair over to the machine. *This should be Merrill Lynch for a couple more servers.* He took the first page off the bin as the second page started. *Hmmm, it's Sampson Logistics for another developer pack. They are so spooky. Well, I'll always take another $50k.*

Wayne checked that everything was in order and forwarded the fax to headquarters Sales Operations Department, which was one person, Michelle Williams. Michelle handled all orders, forecasts and, most important for the reps, commission calculations. She was one person the reps took care not to annoy.

He rolled back to his desk to look up Mike Giuliano's number at Sampson.

He dialed and then shook his head as the call clicked over to voice mail.

"Mike, this is Wayne at InUnison. Received the order, thank you very much. I would like to know where we stand on the enterprise agreement. You do realize that the proposal – and therefore the discount – expires at the end of the month? Please call me at your earliest convenience," he said, then added after hanging up, "I may need that deal."

***

Back at InUnison headquarters, the training class was getting restless as the wall clock clicked towards twelve-thirty. Scales had allowed them one morning break and nature wasn't simply calling, it was screaming in the bodies of the caffeine-loaded SEs. Adding to the impatience of the group, the training coordinator had appeared at the door to signal that lunch was set up outside the room. Scales was not done, however.

"Now, a couple more things before we break for lunch…"

"My bladder is going to explode if he doesn't shut up," Sean whispered to Porter.

"Race to the urinal?"

"…Now, one last broker enhancement concerns the addition of another lower level of logging mode for administrative messages. This can be turned on dynamically at run time by the systems administrator…"

Murphy leaned over to Porter. "We've only been asking for that for the last two dot releases."

Porter wasn't paying much attention to Sean. The question about logging jogged his memory about a question Sergio at Merrill Lynch once asked. He raised his hand.

"Yes?"

"One of my customers wants to programmatically determine, perhaps using the Rule Agent, which messages get logged. Does this enhancement enable that?"

"No," Scales said. "Why would you want to do that?"

"Well, the customer is Merrill Lynch and they'd like a finer grain of control other than all or nothing. They'd like it to be content-based so that depending on, let's say, the value of a field in the message, the agent could change the logging level of the message."

"Interesting. There would be some performance degradation to the broker…"

"How? It would be done outside the broker by either our agent or a custom one done by the customer."

"Interesting. I don't know why a customer would want to do that."

I thought I just explained why. "Let me go a little deeper then. There are a lot of messages that involve a single trade. They want to prioritize delivery failures higher than others. Then their exception handler can deal with them faster."

"Interesting. Seems like an obscure case."

"I have a customer who has the same request," Wiley said.

"So do I," Jeffords said. "I put in the enhancement request form months ago. Can't you tell us when it's going into development? How tough can it be?"

"Interesting. Well, we need to move on…"

"Hey!" Sean snapped. "Don't give us that 'interesting' shit. Answer the question!"

A chill went through the room. Scales was now glaring at both Sean and Porter.

"I'll look into it. Maybe you should simply recruit Mitchell for enhancement requests from now on. He seems to be in charge of priorities these days."

You arrogant bastard! Porter steamed.

"Well, I guess that's it. Lunch is served."

Porter wanted to challenge Scales but his bladder instructed otherwise. He and Murphy raced to the restroom.

"So, Sean, what was up with the 'interesting' thing?" he asked over the urinal divider.

"When an engineer – or some other smartass – responds with 'interesting' it means 'I think I'm far superior to you and also think your question is stupid but I don't know how to answer you without proving what an arrogant putz I really am.'"

Porter and Murphy zipped up and went to the sink. "And what about that cheap shot at the end?"

"Congratulations, Porter. You are now on their radar."

"Yeah, their targeting radar. Why is it such an imposition to try to do what the market is asking for?"

"Why is Clinton still president?"

They returned for lunch as fast as they had bolted for the bathroom. They picked up paper plates and studied the food on the table.

Porter looked at Sean, who was shaking his head.

"Are we too late?" Porter asked. "All I see are appetizers," he said, referring to the tray of bagels, platter of thinly sliced salmon and tub of cream cheese.

"Porter, I'm afraid this *is* lunch; lox and bagels."

Porter frowned and put the plate back on the stack. "I guess I'll have a bagel." *I'm going to starve if I stay here much longer. I'd be better off on death row.*

"Where's Porter Mitchell?" Young called out.

"Right here," Porter answered. *Here it comes, the "try to get along" speech.*

"Porter, come with me will you?"

Thinking it might be his last meal, he stuffed another bagel into his pocket.

Young led him up the stairs to the boardroom. There was a huge table with seating for at least twenty people. Multiple demo computers lined the windows which overlooked Building 2 and the marina beyond. The inside wall was all glass except for two wooden doors at either end. Venetian blinds lined the glass and were currently open to permit seeing into the room. Young closed the door.

"Porter, I hate to do this but we need someone to demo the mainframe connectivity to a special group this afternoon."

"Who is it?"

"I can't tell you. Engler might tell you but…"

"*Engler* is going to be here?"

"Ah, yes. Don't worry, he's cool."

"Dave, I don't know anything about this setup," Porter said, looking at the demo systems. He envisioned taking down the whole network, ruining the demos for the headquarters marketing staff.

"We can drop your laptop onto the network and you can do your usual rap. You've used our mainframe system remotely before, right?"

"Sure, but…"

"Phil Lansing will be here in a minute to help…"

"DAVE! This is really sudden!" Porter said, shaking his head.

"Don't freak on me. Look, I'm not supposed to tell you but it's a group of potential VC investors. Now I've told you too much."

"From where?"

"Manley Brothers."

"MANLEY! Oh, SHIT! They hate us!"

"Quiet, Porter! You only have to give them the basics. It won't be a technical group. The venture capital people are totally separate."

Porter paced, gathering his thoughts. "Hey, what about Tony from Engineering? He's great at this stuff. I've used him on conference calls."

"You put an *engineer* in contact, *direct* contact, with a customer? One of *our software* engineers? Are you nuts?"

"I'm hearing that a lot, lately. Anyway, he did great! The customers really liked him."

"Oh, God! Don't *ever* do that *again.* Geesh! You can't control them. They'll either do the 'interesting' thing or tell the customer the truth about something." Porter gave him a "you didn't really mean what you just said?" face.

"You know what I mean. I'll see if Tony can be backup but you're going to have to do the demo. Engler just told me they landed at SFO from New York and will be here in less than an hour. Get your gear and set it up over here, near where the projector cable is."

Porter scampered down the stairs to gather his laptop.

***

The hour was passing quickly as Porter tested his network connection for the fourth or fifth time to confirm it was still there. *God help me if I screw this up.* He also repeatedly ran through his example which used data helpfully borrowed from Potential Investing. Everything seemed to be in place.

"Porter?" A heavily freckled face with red hair had appeared through the doorway.

"That's me."

"Hi, I'm Tony; Tony Tibbetts."

"Hey, damn glad to meet you!"

"Likewise. It's nice to put a face to a name. You have quite a reputation around here."

"Oh, yeah. Scales was giving me shit during training for supposedly rearranging his life or something."

"Well, they don't have the guts to take it out on O'Rourke or Engler so I guess you're the target. If it helps any, I'm considered a Benedict Arnold now in Engineering for helping Sales. 'What? Help the company get revenue? That's just not done!'"

"You're not serious."

"Pretty close to the truth. But that's only the top managers. You should know that you're a hero with the rank and file. You'd be surprised how much the engineers want to put out not only a quality product but a useful one as well. Get to know as many of us as you can. They'd love to hear more from the field about how customers are using our products. Brinks and Scales filter it too much. So I hear we have some secret visitors coming in. Need any help with setup?"

"I don't think so."

"Cool. Can I see what you do? I get pulled into demos all the time now. Everyone else seems to be afraid of the word 'mainframe'. I try to tell them it's simply another computer."

"I know what you mean."

Tibbetts pulled up a high-backed, black leather chair and sat down to watch Porter's demo on the projection screen. Porter sped through the demo, rather nervous that his demo might offend the creator of the product.

"That's impressive, Porter. We should duplicate that out here. That kind of real world demo goes over really well. Why are you laughing?"

"Well, I shouldn't say this but I was scolded for letting an engineer actually talk to my customers. You seem pretty savvy about demos and such."

"Most of these boners in Engineering should be locked in and have pizzas slid under the door. Human contact is not their thing. On the other hand, I had to do lots of demos in my last job. I was down the road here with another startup. We didn't have any field technical talent so I got recruited to do demos. Maybe I'll be an SE some day when I get tired of hacking code."

"It's nice to be able to develop things you don't have to live with after the fact."

"You did development?"

"Yes, for a bank. My team got outsourced to EDS."

"Ouch! That sucks. So, what can I do for this gig?"

"Maybe fill in the blanks if they ask detailed questions."

"I think I can handle that."

Just then David Young returned to the boardroom.

"Porter, you ready? Oh, hi Tony," he said, out of breath from running up the stairs. "They're here."

"Yeah, everything looks good."

"Great! We still have some time. There's a tray of sandwiches outside for our visitors."

"Real food? Can I have some?"

"It's on the counter outside that door," Young said, pointing across the room.

Porter couldn't get to the sandwich tray fast enough.

He selected beef and turkey sandwiches, slathered mustard on the beef, mayonnaise on the turkey, grabbing a handful of potato chips and a Coke on the way back to the boardroom.

Before long, Engler and O'Rourke entered with their plates.

"Hi! Are you Porter?" Engler asked. "I'm Bill Engler."

That's great, Porter, stuff your face in front of the CEO.

"Yes, I know," Porter said. "Pleased to meet you."

"I'm sorry we had to pull you out of training but our guests wanted to see a real world example of the mainframe connector in use. What we have out here is, well, lame."

"I don't mind. I'll demo anytime as long as I'm well fed," Porter said, holding up his beef sandwich.

"Let me guess, they had lox and bagels for training. That's not a meal where I come from."

"I take it you're not from Silicon Valley?"

"Indiana. We know how to eat in Indiana."

O'Rourke stepped forward with a sheet of paper. "My thanks as well, Porter. Here's our agenda. Your demo comes after the corporate, financial and technical overviews, essentially at the end." He looked around to see that the Manley group was at the far end of the table. "Now, Porter," he said in a whisper with his back to the guests, "we are going to be talking about some sensitive financial numbers. I hope I can trust you to keep them to yourself."

Gulp. "Yes, certainly. I understand."

"We are close to getting these guys to lead our third round of VC, which should be our last until IPO, hopefully next year."

Next year? There are going to be some bummed out people, Porter thought.

One of the Manley people approached Porter's end of the table. He was a tall gentleman in a navy, light wool suit with requisite investment banker power red tie. He had just enough gray hair at the temples to reinforce the high finance impression.

"Hi, I'm Rob Bailey," he said to O'Rourke. "I don't think we have met yet."

Porter wondered why that name was familiar to him.

"Niles O'Rourke, VP of Sales and Business Development."

"And you are?" he asked, turning to Porter.

"Porter Mitchell, New York Systems Engineer."

"Oh, do you know Wayne Angelis?" Bailey asked.

"He's my sales partner. Oh, now I remember. He called you about getting into Manley. We were kinda beat up in that first meeting."

Bailey laughed. "Yes, I'm sorry about that. I kind of threw you guys to the wolves. I needed to do that so we could gain some inside credibility for the investment. You *did* do the RFI, right?" Bailey asked.

"Yes, all forty pages of it."

"Good man!" He turned to discuss some things in hushed tones with Engler and O'Rourke, guiding them away from Porter.

Porter and Tony checked, again, that all network connections were up and running. O'Rourke and Engler returned to the front of the room as the five Manley representatives distributed themselves around the table.

Engler led off with a generic welcome, a few well received jokes about parasitic investment bankers, and kicked off the corporate overview. Bailey had heard this pitch before but a couple of the other Manley analysts had not had the pleasure. Bailey focused on his long overdue lunch instead.

Engler was about halfway through his overview when the CFO, Jay Antoniazzi, and the VP of Engineering, Samantha Brinks, slipped into the room through the back door. They both circled around to Porter's side of the table, taking seats on Porter's right. Brinks, taking the seat next to Porter, leaned over.

"Hi, I'm Samantha Brinks. You are?" she whispered, extending her hand.

"Porter Mitchell, New York SE." He extended his hand but Brinks hastily withdrew hers and her friendly face transformed into a nasty scowl.

"Oh," was all she said.

Engler wrapped up his presentation and introduced Antoniazzi to give the financial overview. Bailey had seen this as well so he snuck out the door with his cell phone.

Porter was fascinated by the financial report. The CFO laid out the cash on hand, the hiring forecast, the sales forecast – Porter thought that there were too many New York companies on the highlight list for his liking – and the burn rate. He did some quick math in his head.

Shit! We only have three months of cash!

"So," interrupted a Manley analyst, "you have about ninety days cash at your current burn, assuming the sales pipeline delivers, is that correct?"

"Yes," the CFO replied, confidently.

"Not bad."

Not BAD? We're going under in three months!

"As you saw in our hiring projections," Antoniazzi continued, "we are aggressively adding to the direct sales force which will grow the revenue side significantly."

"Now, I wasn't born yesterday," another analyst interjected. "You can't expect that reps will be productive quickly enough to affect this short term burn."

"Actually, yes."

Porter's eyes opened wide. *You can't be serious!*

"For instance we have more business in New York City and New Jersey than we can cover with the existing team…"

Porter saw O'Rourke shooting a glance at him.

"…so we are allocating two reps and a systems engineer to work under our very successful rep there."

Bailey had retaken his seat. "And I know him well. He's one of the best. He's working with our middleware group already."

What do you mean "working with"? Porter shot him a skeptical glance which was returned with a grin.

"God help him," one of the analysts said, sending the Manley team into guffaws.

"What other New York accounts are you working?" Bailey asked Porter.

"Our big targets are Sampson Logistics, First New York, Azalea Financial..."

"Azalea? Didn't our stellar Financial Services analyst downgrade them recently?" the Manley banker asked.

"Yes," Bailey replied. "Mr. Arrogance, Jim Grabin, effectively torpedoed a big commercial paper deal we had going with them. Put their stock in the toilet, of course. I was supposed to golf with the CEO at a meeting in Florida a couple of weeks ago. Now, he won't even take my calls. But enough about our dirty laundry. Azalea would be a great account for you. Good luck."

Antoniazzi turned the session over to Brinks to present the technology. About fifteen minutes into her presentation – which was full of all sorts of block diagrams and technical schematics – jet lag was obviously setting in. The Manley analysts were either fidgeting or downright drowsy. One guy wasn't even hiding his boredom as he propped his head up with his hand and closed his eyes. Even O'Rourke was nodding off.

Oh, this is great, Porter thought. *They are going to sleep through my demo, just like normal prospects.*

Brinks mercifully ended her presentation with gratuitous thanks from Bailey.

O'Rourke stood up, apparently refreshed from his nap.

"To wrap up our afternoon, we have our top SE…"

Excuse me?

"…from New York to show you the power of our connectivity to mainframes, which I believe is something of keen interest. This is Porter Mitchell." He presented Porter with his open palm.

As Porter rose to reconnect his laptop to the projector, Tibbetts gave him thumbs up, while Brinks gave him a severe scowl of disapproval for his show of support. Bailey had the mask-like smile of a used car salesman. The rest of the audience was expressionless, a scene Porter was now all too familiar with.

"Hi, as Niles said, I'm Porter Mitchell, Systems Engineer from New York. I've been asked to provide a demo of our mainframe capabilities using an actual example from one of our customers."

"Not a competitor, I hope," the analyst shouted.

"Well, I can't divulge the customer," Porter replied with a smile. "But it is in Financial Services. So, let me quickly set the stage for what is going on here…"

He described what was running on his machine, the scenario for the example transactions he would be showing and then dove into the demo. To Porter's surprise, the Manley group was very attentive and asked some probing questions, as well as made some snide remarks about competitive products they had seen. The banter put Porter at ease and made the demo an easy exercise.

"So, that's it for the demo. Are there any more questions?"

"Yes," the older analyst said, raising his pen. "Did you do this demo for our middleware group?"

"No. I didn't have this demo done for that meeting. Actually, we didn't get to a demo anyway."

"Let me guess. The showoffs asked too many questions and you ran out of time."

"Uh, that's about right."

"Did you do that stupid RFI?"

I like this guy. "Yes."

"You must be a saint," the analyst said, turning to his colleagues. "It was such total BS; I'd have sent it back wrapped around a pipe bomb."

"Enough internal sniping," Bailey said. "Porter; that was a great demo. Thank you."

Bill Engler rose to field a few more questions about product direction and the meeting wrapped up. O'Rourke led the Manley team to the lobby. Porter was still in the boardroom collecting his gear when O'Rourke returned.

"Porter; thanks again. I know it's tough to get thrown into a situation like that. How are things going for you? I keep hearing good things from Presby and Young about what's going on in New York."

"February has been busy, but in a good way. I could use some help. I'm not very good at time management in this crazy environment. I can't seem to stay on top of all the customer follow-up and phone calls."

O'Rourke shook his head. "There is no such thing as time management in software sales. You get up in the morning, put on track shoes and try to keep up with the race. Hey, how's the recruiting coming? You heard us commit with Manley to accelerated sales hiring. You did want to be a manager, right?"

"I can't seem to manage myself right now."

"Don't be so hard on yourself. You'll find the groove."

"As far as recruiting, I haven't heard anything from Young about that. I know that Wayne hasn't been impressed with the resumes he's seen."

"I'll have to talk to those guys because we need to fill those slots ASAP."

"You mind if I ask a couple of financial questions?"

"As long as you don't mind if I don't answer…just kidding."

"I kinda freaked about the three months of cash. Isn't that, well, a crisis?"

"One week of cash would be a crisis. Three months is an eternity in this business. Seriously, these Manley guys and a couple other Sand Hill Road VCs are sitting on a pile of cash that needs to be put to work. The money we are talking about amounts to about fourteen months at our current burn. Also, if you recall from Antoniazzi's charts, we figure that revenue should triple this year which will slow the burn rate as we approach breakeven."

"I see. Thanks, I appreciate you sharing that. I was ready to run screaming for the exit."

"Don't. We need you more than ever. Hey, I have to run. Thanks again." O'Rourke shook Porter's hand and left the room.

Porter finished packing up his briefcase and, realizing that it was time for the SE training to wrap up as well, raced down to the lobby in time to catch the last white mini-van.

***

"Hey where'd you disappear to this afternoon?" Sean asked Porter as he entered their room.

"I was recruited to do a demo of the mainframe connector for a group of invest…um…a group Engler was meeting with."

"Drop your stuff. I'm going with Wiley and Julia to Chevy's. You want to come?"

"What's Chevy's?"

"It's Mexican. Chain Mexican, but decent."

Porter plopped his case on his bed and they were out the door.

"So who was the group again?" Sean asked as they waited for the elevator.

"I'm not supposed to say."

"Oh, wait. There was greeting sign in the lobby, Manley Brothers, right?"

"Yes. I guess if there was a sign, I can confirm it."

"Actually there wasn't but rumor had it that Manley was in to talk IPO. Everyone's psyched. Were you there for the whole meeting?"

"Yes, it was pretty interesting."

"So, when are we going IPO?"

"Sean, I'm really not supposed to talk…"

"It's this Fall, right?" Sean asked, already very excited about the prospect of his vested shares being valuable. "Look at the valuations companies are getting these days! If we don't go out this year, who knows what could happen. I figure we could at least triple the offering price then…where are you?" Sean hadn't noticed that Porter was standing a few steps behind him, looking at his shoes. "What's the matter, Porter?"

"Look Sean, I'm really not supposed to talk about this but Manley wasn't here to talk about IPO." Sean froze for a moment then his face broke into a grin.

"Don't tease me that way, boy. This is serious business we're talking about. Anyway, as I was saying –"

"Sean, there's no IPO this year."

Sean looked at Porter expecting a "gotcha" or something to come out of his mouth. "You're not kidding, are you?"

"No. They were here to talk about the next round of financing."

"Shit." Sean had to lean against the wall of the lobby newsstand. "If we do another funding round, definitely kiss the IPO goodbye this year."

"Please don't tell anyone else about this. I can't have O'Rourke and Engler thinking I can't be trusted."

"That's a laugh. Those guys are notoriously loose lipped. Especially Engler. He's always telling prospects about product features we haven't announced yet. So what else can you tell me?"

"Only that O'Rourke told me that the new investments would carry us to IPO about fourteen months out. That's not so long, right?" Porter was hoping to cheer up Sean with that.

Sean closed his eyes and sighed. "Fourteen months. Damn. I'm going to need some margaritas to deal with this."

Chapter 15 Points of Reference

Sean was still asleep as Porter rolled out of bed the next morning ahead of his 5:30 alarm. He staggered to the bathroom to brush his teeth, hoping that the multiple margaritas at Chevy's weren't registering on his face like they were in his brain.

Ugh. You look terrible. There's too much drinking in this job.

He quickly brushed his teeth and dressed in workout shorts, T-shirt and Yankees baseball cap. He dug his notebook and cell phone out of his briefcase and went down to the lobby to check in with Wayne.

"Wayne Angelis."

"Hey Wayne, Porter here."

"Good morning! How's the training?"

"Well, the instructor was one of the engineering managers. When he found out who I was, he started giving me grief because of the product release changes we supposedly forced on them last month."

Wayne laughed. "I bet we're both on their shit list."

"Then I missed all afternoon because I got pulled in to do a demo for Engler."

"Who was there?"

"Your buddy, Rob Bailey, and three of his VC analysts."

"You're kidding! He's VC now? What were they doing there? What, are we doing another round of funding?" *And why wasn't I told that a prospect from my patch was in HQ?*

"They may lead the next financing round..." Porter said. He gave a blow-by-blow description of the event.

"Three months' cash? Is that what they said?"

"Wayne, O'Rourke doesn't think it's a big deal and he says that the VCs are all but signed up. What do you think?"

"Cash is certainly king for a startup, the more the better. But Engler and Antoniazzi seem to manage it pretty well. As long as they have the venture firms lined up." *Please, Lord, tell me I'm not Bill Murray in* Groundhog Day*?* he thought. His mind flashed back to his last two startup experiences.

"Thanks, Wayne. That's reassuring. I was worried they were only blowing sunshine. Oh, one other detail: O'Rourke mentioned to them about hiring some reps and putting them under you. The analysts were skeptical that there would be a short-term revenue effect."

"And I suppose Engler and O'Rourke committed to it."

"Pretty much."

"Never fails, my boy. I can't wait to see what my new quota will be once we hire. I haven't seen any decent resumes so far, though. So, let's talk about Azalea."

"Okay."

"I talked to Racker yesterday and he told me they are set to go out to HQ next week. Unfortunately, Miller scheduled a visit to VibraWeb as well. Our meeting is in the morning and then they head down to Santa Clara for VibraWeb. You know what you can do for me? Can you make the rounds with everyone who is speaking?"

"Can you refresh my memory about who is presenting?" Porter asked.

"Yes, Engler kicks things off, then Antoniazzi talks about financial viability things. He's followed by Brinks. After Brinks is Marketing. That about covers it. Make sure that they know we need to demo some future product. Kincaid told me he'd get Lansing, but I don't want to leave that to chance."

"Will do. Anything else?"

"Yes. Now that you are tight with management..."

"Oh, right..."

"...see if you can get O'Rourke and Engler to authorize a limo for the Azalea people. It was routine to do that for customers at my previous companies, particularly in New York. Engler balked at doing it; saying something like it just isn't done in Silicon Valley. If that's the case, then all the more reason to do something to differentiate ourselves. I think they're being cheap."

"I doubt that I, Porter Mitchell, will be able to overcome that."

"You disappoint me. Confirm those speakers then. Since we don't have anyone out there to coordinate HQ visits, I'm a little paranoid that they will forget about us."

"Speaking of Azalea, the Manley guys got pretty excited seeing their name on the prospect list. They said they are the kind of 'crossing the chasm' account they'd really like to see us get."

"Great, I really need more pressure. I still don't think we can close them in March, except for maybe some developer seats. And the way things are going, I won't need them for my Number. I'd as soon apply them to Q2."

"I heard the bell ringing yesterday for your orders."

"Those spooks at Sampson Logistics faxed in a surprise PO and Potential is adding a couple more servers. Melani said to say 'hi'. He wants to know when you can visit."

"When hell freezes over. I don't care if he is being nice to us now. He's a jerk."

"A jerk with a budget. Please humor me and stop in there soon."

"What about Sampson Logistics?"

"Oh, that guy is still missing in action. He's not returning my phone calls so I'm doubtful about that account. But if they keep sending these mystery POs, I don't care if he never calls me back. Still, it was a good thing I low-balled them on my forecast."

"Anything else? My breakfast alarm is going off."

"No, I don't think so, Porter. I'm writing up the reference documents and waiting to hear from Lehman about using them. I'm giving Azalea four names: Potential, Merrill, and Lehman. The Swede is lining up his guy at UBS to talk to them Friday on a conference call. I don't know who VibraWeb will choose but I know they don't have four, and certainly not a UBS."

"I really gotta eat, Wayne."

"Later."

Porter hung up, intending to return to his room for a shower. As he entered the elevator his phone rang.

"This is Porter."

"So, you're alive. I've been worried sick," Brenda said.

Porter winced as he stepped off the elevator. He hadn't called home since arriving in California.

"I'm sorry, honey. I've been involved in things since the moment I got here. We had training, I got pulled into a meeting, then we went directly to dinner and by the time I got back it would have been about two in the morning for you."

"Damn it, Porter! Can't you at least make a quick call during a break or something? We haven't talked in almost two days! What happened to the 'I hate being away' Porter?"

That started the guilt trip. He wondered himself where that guy went. Another part of the life transformation, he concluded. "I'm sorry. I'll do better."

She wasn't ready to let up yet. "And the whole last month, we haven't seen much of you…"

"It's been busy, yes…"

"…you lock yourself in that office of yours until late at night…"

"I had to get those RFIs done and it was the only time…"

"…I don't want to be a single mom, you know."

Porter didn't know what else he could say. "I know. I'll try to do better."

"So," she said quietly, apparently done venting. "How are your meetings going?"

"Pretty well…" he said, giving Brenda the same review of the day as he gave to Wayne. "How's Stephanie?"

"Fine. She's starting to get mobile which adds a whole dimension to my stress level. I can't leave her alone on the floor anymore…"

Porter was still in the hall outside of the elevator, listening to Brenda and gazing out the windows, distracted by the private planes taking off over the hotel from the San Carlos private airport. *Should I remind her that I'm turning right around and coming back out here next Monday?*

Brenda stopped talking after exhausting her supply of activities of the last two days.

"Babe, again, I'm really sorry for not calling."

"I'm over it, but don't do that to me again."

"I promise. Next week, I'll make sure I call when I'm back –"

"Oh, *damn* you! I forgot you're going back there! Listen, buster, you make *damn* sure you call. I'll start dialing your cell phone every half hour if you don't."

"Please don't. I'll call."

"I love you. Hope the training goes well."

"Love ya. Give Stephanie a kiss for me."

***

"Now, that was much better training, don't you think, Porter?" Julia asked as they left for their lunch break.

"At least I didn't have to endure that Scales guy giving me the evil eye all morning. Phil seems like a much friendlier person. Excuse me; I have to grab him before he leaves."

Porter skipped up the side aisle of the training room to intercept the Product Marketing Director, Phil Lansing.

"Phil?"

"Yes?" Lansing replied, turning around abruptly in the doorway.

"I'm Porter Mitchell. That was a great session this morning. Will you be back this afternoon?"

"Porter, I'm glad to meet you at last," he said, shaking Porter's hand. "Yes, I'll be doing part of this afternoon's session."

"Wayne wanted me to touch base with everyone who is meeting with Azalea next week. Kincaid mentioned that he might be delegating some of his presentation to you."

"Oh, yes. We've got a new demo of the user dashboard concept we are working on for later in the year. It's pretty wizzy."

"That sounds great. We want to talk a little bit about future direction and having something to show lends credibility that it isn't slideware."

"Hey, I was going to run out for a sandwich. Want to come?"

Porter checked his watch. "If it's quick. I need to check in with the other presenters."

"Real quick. I was going to shoot over to Jack-in-the-Box."

Burgers! Yes! "I'm with you."

Lansing led Porter to his Toyota Celica in the front parking lot. The restaurant was less than five minutes away on the other side of US 101.

"Ever been to a Jack-in-the-Box, Porter?"

"No, but I've heard about them."

"Ultimate cheeseburger. I highly recommend it. Let's do the drive-up window. Then we can go back and talk in the office. It sounds paranoid but around here you never know who is sitting next to you. Could be a competitor. I was working at Borland and having lunch in a burrito place and this guy sitting right behind me is spilling the beans on what Symantec is doing with their Java tools. Needless to say, I started taking notes." Porter fished for some money to hand to Phil.

"I'll get this one. You can buy when I'm in New York."

"Are you coming soon?"

"We're going to do seminars in some major cities in April, highlighting the new release."

"Cool. Let me know if you need help."

Lansing handed the food over to Porter and thanked the attendant. He pulled into traffic and circled back to the office. Lansing's office was in the rear InUnison building and he had a great view of the marina beyond.

"Nice view. Didn't know that was even there," Porter said.

"I lucked out," Phil replied. "Some others face the other way toward the parking lot." They both attacked their burgers. "So, Tony Tibbetts tells me that you did a kickass demo yesterday. Can we get our hands on it?"

"Of course! I was going to email the pieces to Tony."

"Great! Copy me as well." Phil said. He stopped to reach for a clump of fries. "We can't have too many demos."

"I think I got lucky on the mainframe one. I'm still learning to do demos. I've had some nasty experiences." *I love this burger!* Porter thought as he slowed his chewing, leaned back and closed his eyes to fully appreciate the greasy experience.

"Pretty good, huh?" Phil asked. "So, I heard the bell ringing again yesterday courtesy of your partner. He's firing on all cylinders, isn't he?"

"Thank God. We had a bitch of a January trying to catch up. I thought he was going to kill himself once or twice. He was telling me this morning that he thinks he has his Number for the quarter locked up."

"With Azalea?"

"Without."

"Amazing. Well, the thing is, and I'm not telling you something you don't already know, but O'Rourke and Engler are counting on Azalea to nail down the funding with Manley."

"I got that distinct impression yesterday. Wayne isn't confident he can close it in March; the CIO is trying to get us thrown out."

Lansing put his sandwich down. "Porter, can you catch the door there?" Porter closed the door behind him. "That's not good news. I'm hearing that we might not get the funding without a new big name, one which isn't an early adopter. We used to have Security National but –"

"Yes, I know. I worked there."

"You did? Oh, now I understand. Anyway, that's where the pressure is coming from."

"O'Rourke told me it was no big deal that we only have three months cash…"

Lansing's eyes got huge. "*Is that all?* So, the rumor is true."

"Look, Phil, it sounded like you already knew this. O'Rourke didn't think that it was a big deal anyway."

Phil was dumbfounded, staring off toward the sail boats. "No, I didn't know about the cash situation. Holy shit."

"Please, Phil, they said it wasn't a problem. Even Wayne wasn't concerned."

"Don't worry, Porter. I won't be the one to yell 'FIRE'."

Porter gathered up his wrappers and bag, tossing them into the trash. "Sorry to eat and run. Thanks for lunch. Phil?" Lansing was back to staring out the window.

"Phil? *Phil??*"

"Oh, yes, you're welcome, Porter," Lansing said, without looking up at Porter.

***

While Porter retreated to his training, Tom Gatto was at Azalea, setting up his second conference call of the day. He wished the conference room was bigger, or that at least Stewart Miller wore a less offensive cologne. He and the four Azalea representatives were cheek to jowl around a tiny table with a phone on it.

"Okay, I think everyone is on. From VibraWeb we have myself, Tom Gatto, New York and Scott Shepherd in Chicago. Scott, can you introduce our esteemed guest from UBS?"

"Certainly," Shepherd said. "Sitting in my office here is Nigel Ferguson, Director, Equities Systems. He is originally from UBS in the UK but has been here in Chicago forming a new systems subsidiary, called UBS Equities Systems, to support internal equities activities. Eventually, UBS will be offering its stock trading systems expertise to its broad customer base."

"Hallow," Nigel said in a thick Scottish accent.

"And, if each of you from Azalea seated with me in the conference room could introduce yourselves."

"Stewart Miller, CIO," he said, leaning back in his chair, arms folded on his chest.

"Spencer Carlton, CIO of the Azalea Insurance subsidiary in Atlanta."

"Norm Johnson, Director of Financial Information."

"Mordecai Rosenzweig, Director, Data Security."

"Thank you," Gatto said. "We had hoped to have Ralph Gibson, the Azalea CFO, here as well, but he is on vacation."

"Nigel, first of all, thank you very much for taking the time to talk to Azalea about how you are using VibraWeb. The format for this meeting is pretty straightforward. The Azalea team has some standard questions they'd like to ask and Mordecai will handle those. The other folks will chime in as necessary. Mordi, the floor is yours."

"Good morning, Nigel. First, could you describe the project you have undertaken with VibraWeb? We'd be interested in such details as what applications are being integrated, transaction rates, security issues, that sort of thing."

"We consolidated several equity trading areas. Unfortunately, the systems these groups were using were all different. We were not going to be able to simply flip the Frankenstein switch and go to a new system. We needed a bridge, so to speak, to tie the apps together until we could implement a whole new system."

"Why couldn't you wait for the new system?" Miller asked. "It seems stupid to reorganize without a system in place."

"Who asked that question?" Nigel queried.

"I did, I'm the CIO," Miller replied.

"I don't know how things work in your shop but when the trading people say reorganize, that's what we do. As the system support team, we are called on to make it work."

"Sounds backward to me," Stewart sniffed. Carlton rolled his eyes, as did Norm.

"As I was saying, we had several systems to integrate. We have successfully used VibraWeb to handle data messaging and transformation between the applications."

"How many traders are there, and what is the transaction rate?" Norm asked cutting to the chase.

"I'm afraid I can't give you specifics. That information is proprietary."

Naturally, and how convenient, Norm thought.

"Suffice to say," Nigel continued, "the transactions are in the hundreds of thousands and each transaction generates multiple messages in the system."

Carlton was still skeptical but decided to let it go. "So you haven't had any issues with performance or reliability at those transaction levels?"

"None at all."

"One of the knocks about VibraWeb," Norm began, "is that they cannot guarantee delivery of the messages since they don't do queuing. Don't you need that level of support for something as sensitive as trading?" Porter had planted the question with Norm.

"We use a relational database for persistent storage."

"Which one?" Rosenzweig asked.

"Oracle."

"Did you have to connect to mainframes?" Carlton asked.

Ferguson laughed. "Those boat anchors? We don't use them. Only big Sun and HP servers."

Gatto flinched at the mainframe comment. *Please don't piss off my prospect any more.*

Mordecai asked about the development process at UBS, how long it took their people to be trained on VibraWeb and how quickly they could be productive. He ended by asking about security in their environment.

"Sure, sure," Nigel said. "We obviously must have everything encrypted and access lists for certain types of trades."

"That's all I had," Rosenzweig said.

"I have another question," Norm said. Miller let out a sigh.

"Yes?"

"We are looking at using InUnison on this project and they also have UBS as a customer. Are you familiar with the InUnison project?"

"We looked at them. Very immature technology."

"But it's been adopted as a standard within UBS, correct?"

"Only in a very small area."

"Fixed Income is not a small area."

"A very small area within Fixed Income. I assure you that we are setting the standard for UBS. I have commitments all the way up the management ladder because ultimately our subsidiary will be touching everything. I would question InUnison's honesty if they are portraying themselves as a UBS standard."

Miller sat up in his chair. "I certainly question their honesty," he said, raising an eyebrow at Norm. Norm returned the gesture.

"UBS is a big company. Lots of things go on that even internal parties don't know about," Spencer said. "We all try to inflate our importance and influence when talking about our responsibilities, right, Stewart?"

If I had my sword right now…

Gatto could sense the meeting starting to deteriorate. "I hate to close the meeting, but Mr. Ferguson needs to get back to his regular duties. Thank you, Nigel. Again, we appreciate your time."

"My pleasure. Good luck to you all. Before I go, you couldn't find a better company to work with than VibraWeb. They've done a superb job with us, especially my friend Scott Shepherd."

"Oh, Nigel, I'm blushing," Shepherd said.

That's enough of that! "Thank you for your time, Nigel," Gatto said, reaching to hang up the speaker phone.

"So, those calls went well, I think. You should have some valuable feedback on those two success stories."

"Tom," Carlton said, raising his pen. "I meant to ask why UBS isn't listed as a customer on your website."

"According to Scott in Chicago, UBS tries to keep a low profile and very rarely allows a vendor to formally use their name or logo in their marketing materials. This new business unit is pretty covert right now."

"UBS is on InUnison's homepage."

Damn you. "I suppose UBS might be interested in knowing that. They wouldn't appreciate it. So, are we all set for the visit to Santa Clara next week? My HQ staff is really psyched to host you."

Miller snorted and left the conference room, followed closely by Rosenzweig.

Gatto turned to Norm and Spencer. "Thank you for coming. Pleasure meeting you at last."

"Likewise," Carlton said, shaking Gatto's hand.

Norm shook hands without saying a word and left with Carlton.

***

The next day, the corps of SEs gathered at the white vans for one more early morning trip to HQ for training. Mackenzie sat down in the rear seat with Julia and waited for Young, their designated driver.

"Why the long face, Mackenzie? You have hardly said a word today."

Mackenzie looked around to see that no one was coming.

"Well, haven't you heard? InUnison is running out of cash. There's going to be layoffs."

"No, I didn't know. Who did you hear that from?"

"I overheard Phil Lansing talking on his phone to someone, a recruiter, I think. It must be serious if he's bailing out."

"I think you heard wrong. I know we have plenty of cash and more is on the way."

"From who? Are we being acquired?"

"Look, I'm not supposed to know but remember Porter was missing from training the other day? He was doing a demo for Manley Brothers who is going to lead the next funding round."

"Not the IPO?"

"No. Supposedly it will be our last round before IPO next year."

"*Next* year?" Jeffords said, slumping in her seat. "I can't wait that long. Did Porter tell you about Manley?"

"No. Sean Murphy," she lied. "Porter was sworn to secrecy."

"How did Sean find out?"

Oh, shit. I can't tell her Porter told him now. "He overheard O'Rourke talking to one of the Manley people. He was saying that the funding was a 'done deal'."

"Well I wish I'd have known that before. I sent my resume to a recruiter."

You stupid… "What did you do that for?"

"Hey, I took a big risk coming here! I can't take the chance it blows up."

"It isn't going to blow up, for Pete's sake. Manley wouldn't be this interested if it was shaky."

"I hope you're right." She intended to keep her eyes and ears open, though.

***

Spencer was chatting with Mordecai after the UBS conference call when Stewart came by.

"Spencer, glad to see you're still here."

"I'll be here for a while, Stewart."

"Well, come into my office."

Don't order me around, Stewart, he thought, following Stewart to his office anyway.

"So, what did you think about that call?" Miller asked.

"I found that Nigel guy a little cocky."

"Agreed. He wouldn't survive a day in this environment. But what did you think about his InUnison comments?"

"Typical vendor-on-vendor sniping."

"You don't think that Angelis was lying about VibraWeb not having any financial customers? Both of the ABN Amro and UBS engineers were impressive. I'm very comfortable with them."

"That remains to be seen, Stewart. Yes, it gives me pause but let's see what transpires. You can't argue with the results Johnson's team has achieved."

"It's no better than what we've done down here."

"C'mon, Stewart. You had to have a team from Flanderson to accomplish anything."

"Doesn't matter. By default, my organization should be doing the project. We matched the results and that's that."

"They did it a lot cheaper. What, are you going to allow Flanderson to camp out here forever?

"Of course not. After all, *I'm* not the one who brought them in. Gibson did. We'll get our people trained and those consultants will be out of here in the blink of an eye."

"If the decision is to be made on a sound business standpoint, with cost justification, InUnison is the better choice," Spencer countered.

"So the business about whether they are exaggerating their financial services prowess doesn't matter?"

"Of course it matters," Spencer said. "I am disturbed by what that guy had to say but it may only be internal bickering. We'll see what this other UBS guy in Chicago has to say."

***

Gatto was striding down Liberty Street toward the World Trade Center, triumphant in his handling of the two reference calls. He dialed Scott Shepherd in Chicago as he walked.

"Shepherd here."

"Scott, Tom Gatto calling. I wanted to say 'thanks a bunch' for those great calls. I had no idea we had such great references. I do wish he hadn't antagonized Miller about the mainframes stuff though. I'm starting to win him over."

"The dinosaur deserved it. Anyway, I've made a little sideline for myself doing references."

"I owe you. Come to New York and I'll host an evening you won't forget."

"Very funny, but Hager takes care of that."

"Excuse me?" Gatto stopped in his tracks walking by Five World Trade. "What does Hager have to do with it?"

"Hey, do you think it's easy to stage these things? I happen to do it better than anyone else."

"What's so special about scheduling a customer to meet with a prospect?"

Shepherd started laughing again. "You really are a jokester, aren't you? I'm surprised. The G2 on you from my friends in New York had you as a totally serious, take-no-prisoners kind of rep."

"I am. Anyway, thanks again for the reference help."

"Any customer, any time. That's my motto."

***

It was Friday and the InUnison sales team was waiting in Stewart's conference room for the pilot team to arrive. Wayne strummed his fingers on the table as Porter sipped coffee hoping caffeine would overcome the effects of his red-eye flight from the SE training.

"This is our hour, Porter."

"What do you mean?"

"You can't do any better than UBS as a reference. VibraWeb doesn't have anything like it. This could win it for us. Going to Merrill this afternoon is going to be icing on the cake."

Miller and Rosenzweig breezed into the room. "Good morning!" He looked at his watch. "Well, it's ten-thirty-three. Where's Carlton and Johnson?"

"Right here, Stewart," Spencer answered. "Sorry we are, gee, three minutes late."

"Let's get on the phone and hopefully Bill Gustavson and his UBS guy are on," Wayne said.

He dialed into the InUnison conference service and entered his session number. In seconds, they heard voices on the phone.

"Hi, Bill? This is Wayne in New York."

"Good morning, Wayne. Yes, this is Bill and sitting here with me is Isaac Borisov with the UBS Fixed Income group."

Wayne introduced the attendees.

"Mordecai will lead the discussion so I'll turn things over to him."

"Thanks, Wayne."

"Excuse me."

"Yes, Stewart?" Mordecai asked.

"Isaac?"

"Yes, I'm listening."

"Are you familiar with UBS Equities Systems?"

"Hmmm, no. Should I be?"

"I believe so. They are combining several equities areas into one subsidiary. Sounds like a big deal to me, one that you'd know about."

Wayne looked at Spencer for some sign about what Miller was up to. Carlton simply gave him a raised eyebrow.

"Well," Isaac said, "I am in Fixed Income and don't keep up with everything that is going on but I was in a corporate steering committee meeting recently and there wasn't a peep about some new equities subsidiary."

"Now," Miller continued, "how much of a 'standard' is InUnison at UBS?"

Wayne looked at Carlton again for some explanation.

"Fixed Income has standardized on InUnison and has proposed InUnison as a corporate standard. We have some homegrown middleware which is currently the so-called standard but everyone knows it can't keep up."

"All of Fixed Income, huh?" Stewart challenged.

"Yes. Should there be some other part of Fixed Income?" Isaac was becoming annoyed. "What is up with this guy, Bill?" he whispered to The Swede.

"Did you approve of placing the UBS logo on InUnison's home page?"

"Excuse me a moment," Borisov said, putting the phone on mute. "Bill, is that logo still on the website?"

"I don't know. I haven't looked lately." Gustavson spun around to his machine and brought up the InUnison website. Borisov could see it from where he sat.

"God damn it, Bill! You *have* to get that off of there! I got reamed out by Corporate Communications about that." He took the phone off mute.

"Sorry for that. I wanted to check the site. I did indeed approve that, but mistakenly. Use of the logo has to be approved at the corporate level and is very tough to get. I didn't realize how seriously they took this issue. I assumed that if we were a serious customer, it was okay to put the name and logo out there without an explicit endorsement. My PR people freaked out and have asked InUnison *several times…*" Borisov shot a reproaching look at The Swede, "…to remove it. Vendors are permitted to put our name in an alphabetized list and that's all, without full review."

"Aha! So, they were right yesterday!" Miller said, smirking at Johnson.

Wayne turned to his host. "Who said what yesterday?"

"We had our UBS call with VibraWeb yesterday –"

"What, a *reference* call?" Wayne asked. "UBS isn't a customer of VibraWeb."

"You seem to be misinformed, Angelis," Miller said.

"I'm sure they have VibraWeb in some lab somewhere but Isaac has InUnison in production. It's not some tire-kicking exercise."

"Well, this guy, what was his name, Mordi?"

"Nigel Ferguson. From the UK," Rosenzweig said.

"Right, Nigel was his name. He has standardized on VibraWeb for equity trading."

"Equity trading, huh?" Boris said. "I'd be surprised. That's the second biggest volume activity in the company. Only foreign exchange does more. They would have done an insane amount of analysis, taken months to do it and I would have heard about it in Steering Committee. You have a steering committee there at Azalea, right?"

"Yes, and its name is Stewart Miller," Miller shot back.

Oooh, I'm soooo impressed, you pompous bastard, Borisov thought. "We did a side-by-side with VibraWeb last year and InUnison was clearly better on almost all dimensions."

Wayne broke in, hoping they would stop measuring each others' manhood. "I'd like to return to Mordecai's questions, if possible."

"This is a waste of my time. Bunch of liars," Miller said. He got up and left.

"Mordecai," Carlton said. "Let's continue." He looked at Wayne, pursed his lips and shook his head.

Mordi started with the same questions he had asked ABN and UBS previously. Carlton also posed his queries, as did Norm.

Wayne was now detached from the proceedings, trying to mentally figure out what had happened.

How could VibraWeb have the balls to use them? he thought. S*hit…and the logo thing…The Swede is going to kill me for embarrassing his customer.*

He snapped out of his thoughts when he heard Spencer thanking Isaac for his help.

"Thank you from us as well, Isaac," Wayne said. "I apologize for letting the meeting get off track a bit there. Bill, I'll touch base with you in a few minutes."

"Yes, please do, Wayne," Gustavson said, clearly unhappy.

He closed the call and there was a long silence in the room. Rosenzweig decided he was done and left after saying a subtle goodbye.

"I need to get back upstairs," Norm said. "I'll meet you at Merrill at one o'clock."

"You're welcome to join us for lunch," Wayne offered.

Norm looked at him and Porter. "No thanks." He left.

"Spencer, where the hell did that crap come from?"

"Like Miller said, it was from our call with VibraWeb and their UBS guy yesterday."

"Couldn't you have given me a heads up? I would have been prepared."

Carlton smiled weakly and shook his head again. "To be honest, Wayne, I don't know what to believe. I *do* have to be impartial on this. Gibson and

Racker have their spotlights on this and I'm essentially running it now because they know that Miller doesn't want Racker to win and vice versa. I have two stories to consider."

"I'm telling you, UBS is not a customer of VibraWeb!" He slapped the table. "We kicked their ass there last year!"

Carlton got up. "I'm going to pass on that lunch as well. I'll see you at Merrill. I'll try to get Stewart there."

Only Wayne and a sleep-deprived Porter remained in the room, too bewildered to think. Anticipating that Porter's mind was on lunch, Wayne said, "Are you up for lunch at St. Charlie's? It's on the way to Merrill Lynch. Or are you going to bail on me as well?"

"No way do I bail on my professor. You're going to have to explain what happened here. I don't get it."

They both got up to get their coats.

"It's simple. The gloves are off."

Chapter 16 Dead Animals

"Tom Gatto," he answered, knowing it was time once again for his Monday morning beating. This would be especially brutal, as it was the first Monday of the last month of the quarter. He was in his room at the Santa Clara Marriott, having flown out early for the Azalea meeting at VibraWeb headquarters. He a little woozy from parties with his Silicon Valley friends – including some romps with a new conquest, the insatiable Natasha – and didn't really appreciate the 5:00 a.m. wake-up call on his cell phone.

"Means. Let's have it, Fat Bear."

"As you know, I've been focused on this headquarters visit by Azalea –"

"I didn't see any POs last week. This is now March and the last month of the quarter."

"George, I can read a calendar. I'm already at my Number for the quarter, so chill."

"Chill? How'd you like to have a new Number to motivate you? Oh, and don't forget Azalea."

Asshole. "Look, George, why do you keep bugging me about Azalea even though it is still a long shot?"

"It's a must, Fat Bear. We need the name. Look, I heard that the reference calls were slam dunks."

"Even so, I'm on record that Azalea is still no better than fifty-fifty. The CIO will throw us overboard if it suits him."

"Well, why the fuck aren't you going over his fucking head?"

"George, calm down."

"This isn't George. It's Hager."

"When did you come on, Simon?" Gatto asked.

"I've been on the whole fucking time. You close Azalea or you're fucking fired. It's that fucking simple."

"But I've made my Number! How can you –"

"I don't fucking care. We need the fucking name."

"How can you give me shit when I'm blowing out my Number?"

"Because you aren't fucking doing what we're fucking asking you to fucking do.'

"Look, damn it –"

"FUCKING CLOSE THE FUCKING DEAL! I WANT THEIR FUCKING MONEY!"

"But –"

"CLOSE THE FUCKING DEAL! WHAT DON'T YOU UNDERSTAND?"

You can kiss my ass. "I certainly do understand, Simon. Would you like me to go over the agenda for the HQ visit now, or when I come into the office?"

"I don't fucking care about the fucking agenda."

"Well, Simon, I do have one request of you."

"What the fuck is that?"

"Can you watch your language? I don't think that Azalea will appreciate the f-bomb every other word."

"YOU FUCKING INSUBORDINATE FUCKING BASTARD! I ought to fire your ass for that –"

"Simon," Means said. "He's right and you know it."

That's a first! Gatto was shocked that Means stood up for him.

"There's nothing wrong with my fucking language."

"Think about it, Simon," Means said. "You know it pissed off a number of accounts last year."

"They're all a bunch of pussies. Fucking customers."

"So, what about the rest of your forecast?" Means asked, deciding that it was time to move on.

These people are truly insane, Gatto thought as he spread his forecast over the bed while Natasha worked on his shoulders.

***

Porter and Wayne met at the United Airlines counter at Newark Airport for their flight out to Redwood City. Wayne, being in United's top frequent flyer level, hoped to be able to promote Porter to first class with him.

"Good morning," the cheerful United ticket agent said, motioning Wayne from the queue.

Wayne stepped up with Porter and handed the agent his electronic ticket receipt. "I'd like to see if we can upgrade my colleague here."

She brought up their reservations on her terminal. "Certainly, Mr. Angelis. The flight is wide open this morning. I can put you two in seats 6A and 6B."

"Great. Thanks!" Porter had not been looking forward to being in the cattle section for the second week in a row.

The agent checked their identification, asked the pointless questions about whether they had packed and kept their luggage close to themselves, and handed over their boarding passes.

"Porter, we aren't going to hang around with the riffraff," Wayne said as they entered the security checkpoint. "We're going into the United Red Carpet Club."

Wayne flashed his membership card at the front desk and showed Porter to the cloak room.

"Let's grab those seats over there," Wayne said, pointing toward the center of the room. "We can spread our stuff out on that table. I'll get us some coffee."

Porter took his and Wayne's briefcases to the table and started up his laptop. It finished booting up as Wayne came back.

"Sorry for the delay. I ran into an old customer. We're going to go see him next week."

"You know everyone, don't you? Nice space here, by the way."

"Joining this was one of the smartest things I've ever done. I can always get out of the insanity out there: baby strollers in the knees, clueless bastards whose goal in life is to get into my way." Wayne sat down next to Porter. "Let's go over our agenda one more time. We can't have any screw-ups. We still have that UBS thing to overcome. I can't believe we didn't know they were in there."

"Yes, Wayne." *For the tenth time.*

***

The Azalea group had spent the American Airlines flight from Kennedy International to San Jose largely without conversation. Ralph Gibson resolved to spend dinner at Palo Alto's MacArthur Park trying to strike up meaningful discussions between the competing pairs of Racker and Johnson, and Miller and Rosenzweig. The best he could come up with was to get Mordecai to talk a bit about his experiences at the National Security Agency, which practically bored everyone to tears. While he gave up trying to be the facilitator after the main courses were served, Gibson was going to make one more stab at bringing the groups together via drinks. Gibson hoped Carlton – arriving late and missing the dinner – had finally checked into the hotel so that he could possibly serve as the glue between Racker and Miller.

As he led the entourage back to the hotel, he turned to the group.

"Oh, I love coming out to Silicon Valley. You can practically *feel* the growth out here. I'm really excited about our meetings tomorrow."

Gibson and Miller entered the lobby of the Sheraton Palo Alto and waited for the laggards. While they were waiting, Spencer appeared with his bags.

"Hello. Sorry I'm late. My flight from Atlanta was delayed. This flying around lately is driving me nuts; Atlanta, New York, Atlanta, SFO... Yes, the name's Carlton, Spencer Carlton," he said to the receptionist. "I take it you guys are returning from dinner?"

"Yes," Gibson said. "Sorry you missed it."

"I'll tell you what. Let me drop my bags in the room and I'll buy a couple rounds. How's that?"

"You're on," Gibson said.

Carlton got his key and wheeled his luggage out through the pool area to his room.

"Who's up for some nightcaps?" Gibson asked. "Carlton is buying."

"I'm really kind of tired," Miller said.

Gibson wouldn't have it and he gave Stewart a raised eyebrow.

"Oh all right, Ralph."

"Great! Why don't you all go into the bar out back by the pool? I'll be right there. I need to visit the little boys' room."

The two pairs stopped at the bar to order drinks. Miller and Rosenzweig took their beers over to a table while Racker and Johnson stayed at the bar.

"Norm, I'm nervous about these meetings," Racker said. "I hope Angelis is up to the task. We can't have any more surprises like the UBS fiasco."

"Sam, the VibraWeb work for the pilot was smoke and mirrors. Angelis has assured me that UBS isn't a customer of theirs."

"So, what did that Gatto guy do, fake it? C'mon. InUnison better not screw up tomorrow or we'll be slaves to Miller, VibraWeb or both."

Across the lounge, Miller and Rosenzweig nursed their drafts.

"Mordi, those two didn't know who they were dealing with. They thought that they could waltz right into Azalea and take over. Well, I'm here to tell ya that it ain't gonna happen. I've got Gibson right where I need him; he's in my corner. Racker'll get pissed and leave or something."

"What about Carlton? Isn't he going to have a say in this?"

Miller took a big gulp of beer. "Unfortunately, yes. But I think he's as suspicious of those InUnison clowns as anyone. You didn't see him sticking up for them at that conference call, did ya?"

"No, I guess not."

"That UBS thing clipped their wings, yessir."

Ralph Gibson appeared in the bar, glanced at the continued separation of his staff, and sighed. He went to the bar to order a Chivas Regal.

"Guys, why can't we even tolerate a few drinks together? After I get my scotch can't we move over with Stewart and…and…"

"Mordecai," Norm said.

"Yes, Mordecai."

"Ralph, I'll repeat that I can't work with Miller; he's an anachronism at best and a self-dealing operator at worst." Racker said.

Here we go again, Ralph thought as he sipped his drink. "He's doing what he thinks is best for the company. I don't question his motives."

"Hmmmph," was all Sam could say.

Gibson took his drink over to Stewart and Mordecai.

Spencer found Norm and Sam still at the bar and ordered a Glenlivet.

"Good evening, Sam, Norm."

"Hi, Spencer," Sam said, staring over at the table to see if he could interpret the conversation.

Norm came straight to the point with Carlton. "So, Spencer, who are you going to side with on this?"

"That's a little premature, Norm. We need to hear from both sides tomorrow."

"C'mon, Spencer. You know InUnison is the best company to work with."

"That's what I thought before last week."

"Even if Angelis was mistaken about UBS, it doesn't make him dishonest. He's always been straight with me."

"Look, guys, I'm in the middle on this and –"

"I trust Wayne, too," Racker said. "He's one of the few reps I've dealt with who follows up on his promises. Frankly, I'm surprised at you, Spencer. You know that when I make CFO, Miller's the first to get the heave ho. I'll need a replacement."

"Very subtle, Sam. I thought bribery was beneath you. I think Angelis is on the up and up as well but he could merely be incompetent. But do you really expect me to put my career on the line on the word of a *sales rep?* What if Miller wins? What will you do then? It's my independence on the line as well. Would you stick around knowing you'd have to keep Miller?"

Racker didn't have an immediate response, belying his concern over the possibility that Gibson could choose Miller.

"I thought so." Spencer took his drink over to the table.

"C'mon, Norm. I guess we have to do the politically correct thing. Smile on the way over."

***

Porter walked through the lobby of the Hotel Sofitel, on his way out for a morning jog. The receptionist gave him a friendly *Bonjour!* as he passed.

He turned right once outside the hotel, then right onto Twin Dolphin Drive. As it was six in the morning, there was negligible traffic and a hint of sunrise over the hills across the bay to his right. As he continued, he arrived at the intersection with Oracle Parkway beyond which were the three imposing Oracle towers, with yet another one under construction. As he jogged around those round towers, it occurred to him that they didn't exist ten years prior. In fact, little of the development was there five years prior, let alone ten years. Even so, this area was mature compared with other Silicon Valley towns such as Sunnyvale, Mountain View and Santa Clara where cranes above new office buildings were the most prominent architectural feature. He paused to catch his breath and think about the delirious pace of growth and change which he was now part of.

He gazed up at the main tower with the letters ORACLE mounted near the top. *Could InUnison some day grow to have such a striking headquarters building?* he asked himself. *That would be so cool…*

He jogged around the complex a few times before walking back along Twin Dolphin Drive to cool down. He entered the Sofitel as Wayne happened to be leaving the gift shop with his morning newspapers.

"Good morning, Porter. How was the run?"

"Great. The weather is awesome out here."

"Give me a call when you're ready for breakfast," Wayne said on the way to the elevator. "I'd like to go down to the office as soon as we can so we can get set up and run through the meeting plans one more time."

"I just need to shower and call home. Promised Brenda I'd sing a song to Stephanie this morning."

Porter pushed the five button and Wayne pressed six. "Wayne, you know that there is such a thing as too much preparation. I'm having nightmares about this meeting."

"I know, I know. I can't blow this. It's visible all the way up to the board of directors. I could be at five times my Number but still be labeled a loser if we blow Azalea."

The elevator stopped at Porter's floor. "Look, we are as prepared as we can be. There isn't anything else to do."

"Maybe. But get ready quickly," he added through the closing elevator doors.

***

The InUnison offices were eerily quiet at seven-thirty when Porter and Wayne tried the lobby door. The door was still locked and the ceiling lights were off. Luckily, an early morning customer support engineer who happened by let them in.

"You know the way to the boardroom, right?" Wayne asked Porter as he held the door.

"It's right up the stairs," Porter said, directing Wayne with his briefcase.

Wayne followed Porter up the staircase and past the black leather sofas flanking the broad hallway leading to the boardroom. Everything was as it had been the week before when Porter did his demo for Manley Brothers, and he immediately started to set up his laptop and test the projector.

"The usual coffee, Porter?"

"Yes, and they should have bagels down there. Grab one for me. Don't forget the cream cheese."

Wayne went back down the stairs to the kitchen. He paused to take it in.

He admired the granite counters, Viking all-stainless refrigerator with wine cellar, Capresso espresso machine, Peet's Coffee… *only in California,* he thought. *No, only in Silicon Valley. And we thought InUnison was cheap.*

As Wayne filled a coffee mug for Porter, Bill Engler came in and said "good morning", looking at Wayne as if wondering whether he should know Wayne and embarrassed that he didn't. Wayne decided to help him out.

"Good morning, Bill. I don't think that we've met face-to-face yet. I'm Wayne Angelis."

"Oh, wonderful! I was hoping that you'd be here early. I want to review the agenda for the meeting today."

Oh, no. Please don't say you are going to change things at the last minute.

"Fine. Porter is setting up in the boardroom. Shall we go up there?"

"Yes, that's fine," Engler said, doctoring his coffee with sugar and cream.

"So, Wayne, you've been ringing the bell with frequency," Engler said as they left the kitchen and turned right up the stairs. "It must feel good to be off to a fast start."

"Definitely, when you consider the hole I had to climb out of."

"I hope we met your needs in that area."

"Yes, after a fashion." Wayne wasn't going to let him off the hook totally.

They entered the boardroom where Porter was displaying his demo onto the screen in the front of the room.

"Good morning, Porter," Engler said. "Good to see you again. Are we in for another stellar demo today?"

"Actually, no. They've already seen everything I can show them. We're counting on Phil Lansing to wow them with some future stuff."

"Yes, Phil will do a good job on that. Now, Wayne, Antoniazzi will be going over our financial picture with them."

"Are you going to disclose the next round of funding from Manley?" Wayne asked.

Porter winced and Engler frowned. "I guess there are no secrets around here, are there? Yes, we will talk a bit about that, but no names. Manley doesn't want that just yet."

Since he had Engler talking, Wayne decided to broach the cash issue.

"Bill, I don't think we can talk about the fact that we only have three months of cash. They might not put it into the proper perspective. Miller especially will be risk averse."

"Really? I think it's a great story for us. In theory at the current burn, and, let me be clear, no additional revenue over plan, we have three months. But, thanks to you and The Swede, we should be above plan by about twenty percent. So you do the math. I would think that Azalea would be impressed with that performance. The first quarter is usually soft. This can only enhance our valuation."

"We're twenty percent above plan? I had no idea."

"Yes, and it's very frustrating. We *are* accelerating the next round of financing but we are trying to be prudent. People aren't recognizing that fact or the fact that our expense controls are cutting the burn rate further. Everyone seems to be adopting a glass-half-empty attitude when we should be very proud. We are on very solid ground." He shook his head and let out a long sigh.

Just then, O'Rourke stuck his head in. "Hi, Wayne. Azalea's here. Are we ready?"

Wayne glanced at Porter who gave him a thumbs up. "Yes, we are. I hope you all are, as well. We can't falter on this."

"We are well aware of that, Wayne," O'Rourke said.

Wayne left to escort Azalea to the boardroom.

"Good morning," Wayne said, shaking hands all around. "Please follow me; I'll show the way."

Wayne led them up to the boardroom and the small kitchen area outside the room where bagels, danish and coffee were now available. Racker and Johnson took advantage of the food while Gibson and Carlton found places around the table. Spencer realized that Gibson had not yet met Porter and introduced him.

"Ralph, this is Porter Mitchell. He has been very helpful, indeed, instrumental in our use of InUnison."

"Pleased to meet you," Gibson said, shaking Porter's hand. He looked around at the room and the view out toward the second building. "Fine facility you have here. I wish our boardroom had at least a couple of windows. Of course, we wouldn't have the views you have here in Silicon Valley."

"Well, help yourself to some danish and coffee," Wayne urged. "We need to get started if we are to stay on schedule. It's almost nine o'clock."

Miller gave him a snort, dumped his briefcase on a chair and exited the room. He stepped up to the bagel tray, ignoring Racker and Johnson.

Racker looked at Johnson and smiled weakly. "Good morning, Stewart," he said.

"Morning," Miller answered while examining a cinnamon-raisin bagel. He picked up his plate and a napkin, and returned to his seat without saying another word to Racker.

Porter, who hadn't left his laptop since arriving, realized that he had better visit the restroom before the meeting started. On his way out, he noticed Racker and Johnson.

"Hi, Norm. I hope you're looking forward to our briefing; we have a lot of new information to go over," he said, attempting to be cheerful. Johnson disappointed him.

"Oh, right, Mitchell. I'm really looking forward to spending a whole day being in the same room with Miller, oh, not to mention dinner."

"Dinner?"

"VibraWeb is hosting dinner. Their CEO is going to be there. I don't suppose you have a special lunch for us."

"Uh, I don't know what is being brought in. I'm sure it will be fine," Porter replied, hoping that it wasn't going to be lox and bagels. "Excuse me." He ran down the stairs to the restroom.

"Norm," Racker said. "Will you get the chip off your shoulder? Let's try to help them in this meeting. It's the best chance we have to convince Gibson."

"Pardon me," Norm said, "but if finishing the pilot faster, better and with fewer resources doesn't matter, nothing in this meeting will."

"We should get started so that we stay on schedule," Wayne began. "First, thank you all for coming." He clicked the wireless mouse to advance his presentation to the meeting agenda. "You can see that we have a full morning for you. First, we have our founder and CEO, Bill Engler, who will give a 'State of InUnison' message. Then," he continued, pointing to the next agenda item, "Jay Antoniazzi, Chief Financial Officer, will review our funding and other financial information. After Jay, our Vice-President of Engineering, Samantha Brinks will talk about her organization and a little bit about product direction. I say 'a little' because that topic will be handled in more detail by Phil Lansing, Director of Product Marketing who will be up after Samantha. Finally, we will have a roundtable discussion during lunch, with all presenters, to discuss our formal proposal. I understand that you will need to depart by two o'clock."

"Actually a bit earlier," Gibson said. "The limo picks us up at our hotel at that time."

"Limo?"

"Yes," Gibson chuckled. "Your competitor is sending a limo for us."

"Well, that was nice of them." Wayne shot a quick "I told you so" glance toward O'Rourke and Engler who avoided looking at him. "Now, I'll turn things over to our CEO. Bill?"

Engler got up as Wayne shifted PowerPoint to his presentation.

"I'll add my welcome to Wayne's. We are very, *very*, interested in having Azalea Financial as a marquee customer." He talked in his customary near whisper, the audience obediently drawing closer. "I assure you that we are here to address any and all questions about the company so that you can make a fully informed decision."

Engler presented his standard History of Bill Engler and History of InUnison. He also presented a market overview of Enterprise Application Integration, using Gartner Group's chart to show how InUnison was close to the "upper right" quadrant signifying both market and technical leadership.

Miller leaned over to Gibson, who was nodding to show his comprehension. "Ralph, there isn't a high tech company in the country who isn't in that stupid quadrant when they show it to customers," he whispered. "Doesn't mean squat."

Engler drilled down into the organization chart of the company then showed them the plan for growth over the next four quarters.

"That's quite an aggressive plan," Gibson said. "How are you funding that growth? Revenue?"

"Yes, revenue is a big piece of it but there is more. I'd like to leave that to Jay's talk, though."

"Certainly," Gibson said.

Engler continued with some other organizational information and wrapped up his thirty minutes on a personal note.

"Gentlemen, I know how hard it is for you to make these kinds of decisions. You hear a lot of the same claims from all the vendors and hear all the same assurances from everyone. We try to back up our claims with actions," he said, smacking the back of his right hand into his left. "You've done a pilot and have Mr. Johnson here who has extensive, successful experience with our products. I should think that success speaks for itself. I assure you that we will be totally open with information today. We want Azalea as a satisfied customer for the long term…" He paused to look each of the Azalea people in the eye, noting Miller's skeptical posture of arms folded on chest. "…not only for this one contract."

"Any questions?" Wayne asked.

Gibson took a silent poll by looking at each of his colleagues. He shook his head.

"Then I'll turn the discussion over to Jay Antoniazzi, our CFO. Jay?"

Antoniazzi approached the computer as Porter double checked that his presentation was ready.

"Good morning. Before I start, have you all signed the non-disclosure agreement? As I'm sure you are aware, I will be discussing matters which private companies like InUnison normally do not need to disclose. Naturally, we want that to be left here in this room."

"Yes, we faxed those forms back last week," Spencer said.

"Thank you. Now, to start off," Jay said, advancing his presentation. "We have had two rounds of funding totaling twenty-seven million dollars. The first round, as you can see, was led by Superior Venture Partners. That allowed us to staff engineering and begin work on the product. As Bill mentioned, he was able to secure the core team of talent he had worked with in the past and they were able to hit the ground running in early 1995." He clicked to the next slide. "Round two in mid-1996 saw Superior increase its investment and other firms such as Broadscape became investors. The key use of that money was two-fold: continue to acquire technical talent and create the direct sales force, starting in Washington, New York, Boston, Chicago and the Bay Area. In 1997 we added Philadelphia, Atlanta, Dallas, Denver and LA."

"I assume that those VCs sit on your board," Gibson asked.

"Yes, I'll be coming to that in a couple slides."

Antoniazzi continued with the financial history on the next few slides, emphasizing the conservative nature of InUnison's growth plans and its ability to keep expenses in line.

"Now, for 1998, the numbers look like this." He advanced to the next slide which showed a line chart of revenue and expenses for the year, conveniently converging toward the end of the year. "You can see that our revenue plan is significantly higher for this year and in support of that we will be aggressively hiring for the field sales force."

Miller sat up. "What was the revenue plan for 1997 again?"

"Fifteen million."

"And the results?"

"Fifteen point five."

"And you're still not making money?"

"No. We will be profitable in 1999."

"So, you're asking us to bet on a company that is losing money and isn't public yet," Miller snorted, and returned to his detached posture.

"That's a good point, Stewart. When will you go public?" Gibson asked.

"We really can't talk about that now. Suffice to say, it won't be this year."

"So are you self-funding or will there be another VC round?" Carlton asked.

"We are in negotiations right now for another round of financing. We anticipate closure by Q2."

Antoniazzi finished his last few slides describing other hiring plans and expense items. Wayne stood up and approached the front of the room.

"So, I think we could use a brief, and I underscore brief, bio-break. When we come back, our focus will turn to our product plans."

They all stood at once and made their way down to the restroom.

"Porter," Wayne called out. "Can you let Brinks and Lansing know that we are ready for them?"

Porter had a moment of panic when he couldn't locate either speaker but was relieved to see them both already in the boardroom when he returned. Lansing was about finished setting up for his demo.

"Hi, Phil. Samantha," Porter said.

"Hi, Porter. Good to see you again," Lansing replied.

Brinks ignored Porter.

Wayne peeked into the room. "Figures. No one has come back yet. We need to get going, so I'll go corral the troops. Oh, hi. I'm Wayne Angelis. You must be Samantha."

"Yes," was all she said, spurning Wayne's hand.

"I'm Phil Lansing, Wayne. Pleased to meet you."

"As I said, I'll go gather the audience. You ready to go?"

"Yes," Phil said.

Wayne found most of the group lounging on the sofas in the hallway.

"Folks, we'd like to get started again." Gibson led Miller and Rosenzweig back to the room. Wayne looked down the stairs, spotting Racker and Johnson in the first floor hallway. "Sam, Norm, we're ready to start again." They started up the stairs so Wayne returned to the boardroom.

Wayne rejoined the meeting and introduced Brinks.

"It's my pleasure to introduce our Director of Engineering, Samantha Brinks."

Brinks narrowed her eyes and stood up. "That's Vice-President of Engineering, Wayne."

"What did I say? Oh, Director. My apologies, Samantha."

Brinks' presentation was slide after slide of organization charts – past, present and future. She droned on about how the teams were aligned product-wise. Her description of the product engineering life-cycle was more than ten slides long, with the slides on her quality assurance testing process equally detailed.

Wayne leaned over to Porter. "Porter, you *did* tell her she only has thirty minutes, right? She's killing us here. Look at Spencer. He can't even fake like he's paying attention."

"As you may recall, she wouldn't talk to me last week. You may have to give her the hook."

Wayne thought that Brinks was finished when she asked for questions about the product development process but was disappointed.

"Now, my next section deals with how Engineering gathers marketing information at design time."

Wayne felt that he had to step in as she was now pushing forty minutes. "Samantha, my apologies, but we are pushing the clock here. I know you weren't here but Bill touched on some of this already."

Brinks' normally pale face became noticeably flushed. "Wayne, this is an important part of my organization's responsibility…"

O'Rourke came to Wayne's rescue. "Yes, we acknowledge that, Samantha, but we have to move along. Thank you!"

Brinks quickly gathered her notes, gave O'Rourke and Wayne one more nasty look, and left the room.

"Next up is Phil Lansing, our Director of Product Marketing," Wayne said. "He will be showing you some coming attractions in our product line."

To Wayne's relief, Phil put on an incredible demo of the new development environment, showing vast improvement in the speed of developing and deploying InUnison applications. He built several transactions using numerous databases and, of course, the mainframe, in less than thirty minutes.

"That's amazing!" Gibson said.

"And the security enhancements are very impressive," the heretofore silent Rosenzweig offered.

"You still think you need Flanderson, Stewart?" Racker asked.

"It's all fine and good here in this controlled environment," Miller scoffed.

Spencer was silent, but Wayne could tell that he was thinking.

"Spencer, you look like you have a question."

"No, not a question. I was thinking about how much more quickly the pilot would have gone with this version of the tools. Stewart, you have to concede that –"

"I don't have to concede squat," Miller said.

"Thank you, Phil," Wayne said. "That wraps up the formal part of our agenda. Looking at the time, we have less than forty-five minutes left. If it's all right with you, I'd like to skip the roundtable in order to have plenty of time to go over our proposal."

Gibson quickly polled his colleagues and replied, "That's fine, Wayne."

The receptionist stuck her head in the room. "Lunch is here."

"Great! Let's get a sandwich, beverage and reconvene here. I have copies of our proposal to go over."

While they filled their plates, Wayne placed a copy of the proposal at each chair. Once everyone was back in the room, Wayne stepped through the structure of the deal. He was disappointed that no one asked questions.

"So, can I infer that the lack of questions means we can sign today?" Wayne said, attempting to inject some humor.

"Humph," Miller said.

"Well, Wayne, this isn't as generous as *some* deals I've seen from InUnison," Spencer said, winking at Wayne.

"Looks like a fine proposal," Gibson said. "Obviously, we can't simply pass judgment on this today. Besides, we will still have to decide if InUnison is our technology of choice."

"Of course, Ralph."

"I don't see any Professional Services on this," Miller said. "How much are you going to screw us on that?"

"Because you already have significant expertise in-house in the form of Norm's team, we didn't want to include that in this contract. We do have a separate schedule of PS fees should you want to leverage our resources. You will note that we are throwing in training for free."

"Big deal."

Racker felt compelled to counter Miller. "Beats having an army of consultants, Ralph."

"Good point, Sam," Gibson said, nodding in agreement. He checked his watch. "Okay, we've got to go. Thank you all for a wonderful briefing. You have a solid company here. I'm sure we can do business in the future, if not right now."

What does that mean? Wayne thought.

They all exchanged handshakes with O'Rourke and Engler, and Wayne escorted them to the lobby.

***

The caravan of three Azalea cars pulled into the Sheraton lot at approximately the same time. Spencer was the first to walk through the side door to the lobby. Through the front door, he could see a gleaming white stretch limousine waiting. He approached the driver, who was finishing a cigarette while standing next to the limo.

"Hi, is this for Azalea Financial?"

"Yes. You're going to, uh," he double-checked his paperwork, "VibraWeb on Scott Boulevard in Santa Clara?"

"Right. The rest of the group should be along shortly."

"My name's Damien. Help yourself to the bar if you like," Damien said, opening the back door for Carlton.

Carlton leaned into the car. Mounted along the left side was a fully stocked liquor cabinet with ice bucket and another cooler with beer and mixers. *That's the last thing I need,* he thought. He shook his head and stepped away from the limo.

"Thanks, but nothing for me right now. I'll go into the lobby and track down my colleagues."

He walked back into the lobby, just as Norm came down the side hallway from the restroom.

"Is everyone assembled, Norm? The limo is here."

"So I see," Norm said, glancing out the front door. "Racker, Miller and Rosenzweig are in the restroom. Gibson had to run up to his room for some reason." Johnson paused to see if anyone else was coming. "So, I thought they did a good job this morning."

"Yes, I was very impressed with Engler. He has such a compelling way about him. That demo blew me away. They have some great stuff in the pipeline. Now, Brinks gave me the willies."

"Can't be perfect. Her team is putting out great stuff, though."

Finally, Gibson and the others were ready to go. Carlton led them to the limo. Damien introduced himself, again pointing out the libations in the limo.

"Great!" Miller said. "I could use a brewski." He reached for an Anchor Steam in the cooler. Johnson opened a Coke while Gibson unscrewed a bottle of water.

"Everyone here?" Damien asked.

"Yes, let's get going," Gibson replied.

Stewart had already drained his beer and popped open a new bottle. "Now, this is style!"

"So I was impressed with InUnison. Any comments?" Gibson asked.

Spencer spoke up. "Yes, Norm and I were chatting before we left. They are definitely pushing the envelope on the technology."

Miller waved his beer bottle at them. "Of course you'd like them. That flashy demo was right up your alley."

"Weren't you impressed at all, Stewart?" Sam asked.

"Not real world," was all Miller could say.

"So, look at how green everything is out here. Beautiful," Gibson said, hoping to lighten the mood.

The trip came to a near halt as they entered Mountain View on 101.

"The radio reported an accident up ahead," Damien offered.

"Fine with me," Miller said. "As long as the beer holds out."

Sam could only shake his head. *Wait until I'm CFO, you slug.*

***

"Wayne!" O'Rourke called out to Angelis from the end of the hallway where his office was located. Wayne was schmoozing with the sales operations coordinator.

"Sorry, got to go I guess," Wayne said. "Thanks for the heads-up on the PensAndClips calculations."

"Hey! I want your comp check to be correct. That royalty structure complicates things."

Wayne crossed the hallway to where O'Rourke was standing.

"I want to get you, Mitchell and Engler together to discuss next steps with Azalea," O'Rourke called out. "Engler is free right now so let's camp out in his office. Oh, there's Porter. Porter, in here," O'Rourke called out, motioning to Porter as they walked into Engler's office.

"Bill's assistant, Sharon, says he'll be right back," O'Rourke said, sitting down on one of the conference table chairs. "I have to say that the meeting went well, but I was disappointed in the non-reaction to the proposal."

"They didn't want to start negotiating right there," Wayne said.

"I'm sure. Here comes Bill."

"Sorry to keep you guys waiting," Engler said. He pulled out the last remaining chair around the table and sat down. "Are you two sticking around or flying right back?"

"We're on the two-thirty back to Newark so we need to get going shortly," Wayne responded.

"I won't keep you. So, what did we accomplish this morning?"

"I think we did well, Bill," Wayne said. "Your opening remarks went over very well and the demo definitely caught their attention."

"What about the proposal? They didn't seem to have much reaction to it."

"I know. I prepped Carlton for it but I don't know if he talked to the others about it before the meeting."

"I don't think he did," Porter said. "Norm didn't know anything about it."

"Should we have given it to them last week?" Engler asked.

"I thought about it, but I didn't want it to fall into VibraWeb's hands."

"Right. Well, Wayne, what other feedback do you have for me? We're trying to do these HQ meetings better than we have in the past. I think that the field is a little shy about bringing customers out here."

"I don't know about that. The key is to provide information, particularly the 'vision thing', and demo product that they haven't seen in the field. We did that today and it really gives us credibility. There was certainly a lot of steak there. We could use some more sizzle, though."

"Bill, I have to be honest," O'Rourke said. "Brinks needs a makeover."

"Niles, don't –"

"They were ready to run for the exits, Bill! I've sat through a dozen prospect visits and she does the same damn thing every time. She shows those org charts out the wazoo with the result that she bores the audience to tears. And those tents she wears…Dumbo would look better dressed."

"Now, don't get personal. I'll figure out how to tactfully suggest some things to her, or maybe find someone else from engineering to put in front of customers."

"That would be great, Bill. Now, Wayne, what else do you need from us to nail this down?"

"I'll let you know but their decision will hinge on what they think of VibraWeb and whether Gibson will go against Miller. I know we went a long way with Carlton. He felt exposed after the reference controversy and was wavering."

"Don't worry, Wayne," Engler assured. "There's nothing VibraWeb has over us."

***

The limo finally pulled into the VibraWeb parking lot more than half an hour late due to a nasty three-car pileup on 101. Having processed his beers, Miller was desperate for a restroom while the others were now a little cranky, limo comfort notwithstanding.

"Let's get this over with," Racker said.

"Sam, be fair," Gibson said. "We need to be objective here. We gave InUnison our attention. These folks will deserve the same consideration."

Inside the lobby, a huge sign about fifteen feet long, "Welcome, Azalea Financial!" was stretched across the lobby wall. The receptionist called the Vice-President of Marketing, Eugene Kaczynski, who was hosting the meeting. Tom Gatto greeted them first since he had been hanging around the lobby as the minutes ticked by.

"Hi! Welcome! Stewart, Mordecai; good to see you again."

He turned to the others who were coming through the door.

"Please follow me to our audio-visual center. Gene will meet us there."

Gatto led them down the hallway to a dark, windowless room. After fumbling for the light switch for a few seconds, he found the proper knob and the room lit up, revealing itself to be more theater than meeting room. There were four tiers of high-backed reclining chairs upholstered in burgundy leather. The walls were covered in soft, thick beige fabric while the floor carpeting was a dark green with a dot pattern matching the burgundy of the chairs. All the fabric and carpeting rendered the room completely noiseless.

The entire front wall was one huge rear projection screen, in front of which was a raised floor creating a stage. Gatto strode across the stage to a podium where he had his laptop set up. He toggled the video output to the projection system and the front wall came to life with another welcome message complete with Azalea's logo.

"Goodness!" Gibson said. "Look at this place."

"Are we here for a movie premier? Where's the popcorn?" Miller joked.

"Please fill in from the front," Gatto said, motioning toward the first row of easy chairs.

Norm and Sam looked at each other, shrugged and took seats in the second row. Miller, Rosenzweig and Gibson sat in the front row while Spencer remained in the back, deciding between Coke, Sprite or bottled water iced down in a large bin by the door.

"Hello. I'm Gene, VP of Marketing," Kaczynski said, as he entered the room and spotted Carlton.

"Spencer Carlton, Azalea Insurance."

"Is everyone here? We have a lot to go over this afternoon."

"Yes, we are all here. Let me introduce you around."

Kaczynski and Carlton descended the steps along the right side of the room. Spencer introduced each participant in turn and took a seat in the third row by himself.

"Great to meet you all! I am the host for your visit. We've developed a great, multi-media presentation, or should I say *presentations*, to introduce you to our fine company." He clicked ahead to an agenda slide.

"So, we will start with a corporate background video to introduce you to our executive team, then –"

"Aren't any of the executives going to be here?" Racker asked.

"You will meet our CEO and CTO at dinner. Now then –"

"And the CFO?" Racker asked. "We'd like to explore your financials."

"Unfortunately our CFO position is open at the moment." Singh fired him for being a little too forthcoming with the board. "Dr. Singh will be able to address any of those questions, however. Now, continuing, after the corporate background, we will have a product overview followed by a great demo of our forthcoming Business Process Modeler. Let's get started!"

Racker slouched in his chair. *We aren't going to get any information here. This is a waste.*

Kaczynski gave Gatto – who had drifted to the back of the room – a nod and he shut off the lights. The screen switched from the agenda to black. Suddenly the VibraWeb red logo appeared full screen synchronized with a blast of music straight out of the *Star Wars* theme. In fact, the display was a recreation of the opening from those movies. The logo receded and the crawl of words began.

> **"It's the start of the new millennium and the information technology departments of the Global 2000 corporations are under attack by hostile software forces. These forces are multiplying and IT needs a savior to make them all work together. The CIOs' cries for help reach across the galaxy and are heard by..."**

The crescendo of trumpets and cymbals became almost deafening as the screen was once more filled with the VibraWeb logo.

"...**VIBRAWEB**...WEB...web...web."

The graphics flew so suddenly that nearly everyone in attendance drew back from the screen. Gatto, having been warned about the video, merely shook his head.

The video left the *Star Wars* theme behind and began a frenetic drum solo, with short video clips and still shots, flashing on and off, synchronized with the strong downbeats. The pictures were of VibraWeb employees working hard at their desks and presumably playing hard at pool and table soccer in the company game room. Each employee was broadly smiling.

The drumming quieted, and a video of CEO Dr. Khaybar Singh, began. Attired in black silk dress shirt and slacks, he had his back to the camera, looking out his office window. He turned abruptly as if the viewer had stepped into his office, interrupting his daydream.

> **"Welcome to VibraWeb. I know that you will come away with an appreciation for our company and our great products. We are driven to build the best integration software in the industry."**

He moved to his desk and sat down on its corner.

> **"Now, sit back and enjoy the briefing. Excuse me; I have to get back to making great software."**

He grinned at the camera as he faded to black.

A narrator began an overview of the company's history, starting with the story of Dr. Singh's poor childhood in Bombay – complete with pictures of him playing in what looked like an open street sewer – his "escape" from poverty to the United States, his rise through CalTech and early career at Hewlett-Packard where he met and worked closely with his CTO, Chin Tsai, himself a refugee of sorts from China.

The video continued to profile key executives and engineers, all of whom seemed to have had it tough on the way up life's ladder. Even Simon Hager was depicted as being from a broken home and having to care for his younger brother while his dad was in jail for beating his mother, who was in and out of drug rehabilitation in the early Seventies.

That explains a lot, Gatto thought. *Assuming it's true…*

Gibson leaned back and motioned for Racker. "These people certainly seem to have character, don't you think?"

"Yes, Ralph." *This is bullshit.*

The presentation shifted gears and a new face appeared.

> **"Hello, I'm Joel Scofield, Director of Product Marketing and I'll be giving you an in-depth tour of our products and a key new product, our Business Process Modeler which we feel will revolutionize the integration process. So, let's dive in!"**

The camera followed him to a computer screen. After about thirty minutes of alternating between what was happening on the computer screen and views of Scofield smiling, Norm leaned over to Racker.

"How are we supposed to ask questions, Sam? Is numb nuts up there going to be able to answer, you think?

"Duh, Norm; this is all arranged precisely to avoid questions."

"Oh." Norm turned around to look at Carlton who simply shrugged and turned up his palms.

The demo continued for another thirty minutes, by which time Miller was sound asleep, his head bobbing periodically back and forth.

> **"Now, I'm going to warn you," Scofield said from the screen. "This next demo will *KNOCK* your socks off!"**

His emphasis on "knock" woke Miller up.

> **"This is your ticket to vast productivity gains; the VibraWeb Business Process Modeler. Our BPM allows you to graphically model your business transaction and work flows. The win for you is improved time-to-value of services and products, better risk management and of course higher productivity. Let me show you how it works…"**

The view on the screen was now the full screen from the computer and showed a white workspace with a column of icons and shapes along the left, the "tool palette" he called it.

> **"I'm going to use a hypothetical, but realistic example of a long distance telephone company who is rolling out a new service package. We are going to play the role of a business analyst and model the necessary data flows between applications – such as credit authorization, network provisioning, billing, etc. – define what messages have to go where and simulate that flow as we go along. Using VibraWeb, that analyst need not know the internals of those applications, simply how they have to interact."**

He began dragging and dropping little boxes from his tool palette onto his electronic workspace. The boxes represented systems which this new service would have to use or update. He started to draw lines between the boxes which dramatically snapped together with clicking sound effects. As boxes became connected, another window would pop up on the screen – with its own swoosh sound effect. He typed in names for items of data which would pass between the applications.

He continued for some time building this process model, complete with some decision nodes in between the connecting lines. These nodes would determine which path to take depending on criteria such as "is the customer credit worthy?" If "yes" then provision the system, if "no" send rejection letter."

Miller was losing consciousness again even as Gibson was on the edge of his seat. Even Johnson and Racker were paying close attention. Carlton was jotting down several questions.

Scofield proudly finished his demo, leaving the simulated messages – represented as little envelopes – flowing around the screen.

> **"So, I know you will see how revolutionary this product is. Your analysts will be happy, your IT people will be happy and, tee hee, your top and bottom line will be most happy. Thank you and enjoy the rest of your visit."**

Scofield faded out and Dr. Singh reappeared, still sitting on the corner of his desk.

> **"We hope you've enjoyed your briefing. I can't wait to be able to count you among the dozens of satisfied VibraWeb customers. So long for now."**

He got up and returned to his desk chair, facing his computer. The *Star Wars* music returned as did the VibraWeb logo, this time starting as if in the distance, growing until it filled the screen and then vanished as if passing through the screening room. It swooshed as it did, with a whispered voice saying "VibraWeb", the "web" echoing through the surround speaker system.

Kaczynski stepped back to the podium as Gatto raised the lights.

"I can see you're impressed. Let's see, it's almost five o'clock and dinner is set for six. Your limo will take you to dinner."

"I have a couple of questions," Spencer called out.

"Shoot."

"After you do all that great graphical modeling, does the Process Modeler then configure the core VibraWeb system based on what the business analyst puts in?"

"Hmm, I think so. That's a technical question. You should ask Dr. Singh at dinner."

"We have an hour. Can't you get someone in here to answer a few technical questions?"

"Dr. Singh can address that at dinner."

"And he will address the financials as well, right?" Racker asked.

"Certainly," the VP of Marketing said with a smile.

"Another question," Racker said. "How come you didn't put any customer testimonials in the video? I would have thought that you'd want to show some projects or something. I would have used UBS Warburg, for instance."

"Good point, Sam," Gibson said.

"UBS Warburg?" Kaczynski looked at Gatto in the back of the room. *Answer the question, you putz!*

"Well, you heard the reason on the conference call, right? They are very tight about their endorsements," Gatto offered.

"But no customers whatsoever? Not even quotes? Seems strange."

"Well, what can I say?" Kaczynski said. "I apologize for running off, but I'm already late for a five o'clock staff meeting. I'll leave you in the good hands of Bill here."

"It's Tom, Gene," Gatto said.

"Oh, sorry. Right, Tom. We're growing so fast I can't keep track of all these new faces! Goodbye! Pleasure meeting you all!

He scampered up the steps and out the door.

"Hey, Gene!" Gatto called after him as he chased him down the hallway. "You can't blow out like this! What the hell am I supposed to do? They're going to have a lot of questions. And what about that modeler question?"

Kaczynski didn't stop so Gatto chased him down, and pulled him to a stop. "You've gotta give me some ammo here, Gene."

"Look, are you dense or what? If there were answers, don't you think I'd give them? That stupid modeler is nothing but eye candy. It doesn't really do jack shit. Singh thinks it will sell software, though. Now, is that the answer you want to give them?"

"Of course not, but, Jesus, how can we make such a big deal about it if it's crap?"

"It's very pretty crap. But as far as a real tool, you could do a better job with Visio."

"So, the answer to Carlton's question about configuring the messaging system is no?"

"Correct. It's a cool drawing tool and that's about it."

"But, again, why are we making such a big deal about this then? I don't get it."

"No, you don't. Look, you must know by now that the core product is almost useless without a lot of services –"

"Yes, I know all too well."

"Singh and Tsai decided that they'd whip up some tool to configure the system. Unfortunately, the messaging configurations are so distributed that no centralized tool can deal with it. They already had a software team working on this before they figured out it wouldn't work. So they rationalized that they could get some marketing value out of it anyway. And we are. You saw how a couple of those guys were sporting serious wood."

"Is everything this company says bullshit? There isn't a single thing in that presentation I can back up."

"Now, you're getting it! Hey, I have to go. Good luck!" He spun around and marched off down the hall. He turned around to yell one suggestion, laughing as he did. "Hey, maybe you can get an engineer to talk to them. They might even tell them the truth!"

"Oh, shit."

***

Gatto decided to leave the Azalea people alone. He couldn't face any questions for which he knew the answers would be wrong. He waited until about five forty-five to return, figuring that he would simply have to tell them that it was time to go to dinner.

Dinner. How do I control that? he wondered. *God only knows what Singh or Tsai might tell them.*

He returned to the screening room.

"Sorry to leave you so long. I thought we had some technical people lined up to chat but apparently my signals got crossed.

"That's fine," Gibson said to Gatto's relief. "Dr. Singh can handle our questions at dinner." Carlton gave a snort.

"Your driver knows where you are going. I'll be along shortly with Drs. Singh and Tsai, and our VP of Sales, Simon Hager. Get a head start at the bar, of course!"

"Don't have to ask me twice," Miller said.

The Azalea team piled back into their limo and their driver departed for Bombay Maharaja, an Indian restaurant in Sunnyvale. Miller started his happy hour in the limo by taking advantage of the still fully stocked beer cooler.

"That was an amazing presentation," Gibson said. "And that Process Modeler; I've never seen anything like it. That should really help things with some of our processes, right?"

"Yes, the graphics were certainly impressive, Ralph," Carlton admitted. "But I'd like my question answered."

"Well, we'll have to find out at dinner, won't we?" Gibson said.

"Carlton," Miller sputtered, beer foam covering his upper lip. "You don't get what they're doing."

"Oh, and you do, Stewart?"

"One thing I know is that the VibraWeb presentations were a hell of a lot more interesting than InUnison. What a snoozer that was."

Right, Stewart. You're an expert on snoozing, Spencer thought.

Miller had to down his beer quickly, as they pulled up to the restaurant in less than fifteen minutes. Damien opened the doors and the six spilled out in front of a doorway which looked like it was straight from the Taj Mahal – gleaming white with graceful curves rolling upwards to a pointed dome. A blue-turbaned, Indian maître d' greeted them.

"Welcome to Maharajah. Your host has arranged for a private room. Please allow me to guide you."

He led them through a maze of scrollwork black screens which separated the tables in the main dining room. Subtle sitar music could be heard in the background.

The private room had similar screens mounted on the walls with candles flickering in transparent red shades mounted between the panels. An enormous, round table with a large lazy Susan was set in the middle of the room.

"Good evening, my friends!" Dr. Khaybar Singh called out as he arrived with Dr. Chin Tsai. Singh wore his usual all-black silk shirt and slacks while Tsai was clad in rumpled beige cotton slacks and dusty blue oxford shirt. He peered out from round, black-framed glasses. Last to arrive were Gatto and Hager. Gatto made another plea for Hager to watch his vocabulary. Hager promised to try.

After drinks were distributed, Singh tapped his glass with a spoon to get everyone's attention.

"Again, welcome to Silicon Valley! I hope you were pleased and informed by our presentation this afternoon. I look forward to getting to know you better during dinner. May this be the beginning of a very productive and mutually beneficial relationship," he said, raising his glass.

"Here, here!" Gibson shouted.

"Ralph," Racker whispered, "don't get *too* excited here."

"C'mon, I'm only being courteous to our host. Indians are very charming, aren't they?"

The group engaged in idle chit chat over another round of drinks and appetizers. Singh was engaged in conversation with Miller and Rosenzweig – saying "interesting" and stroking his beard a lot – while Norm and Sam talked golf with Hager and Gatto.

"I get out every couple of weeks Spring to Fall," Racker said. "Can't get my handicap below fifteen."

"Fu…damn handicaps. Who f..frickin cares?" Hager said. "I play for the fu..fat payouts from the suckers at the club. Yes, another scotch, please."

Gatto knew that after a couple more scotches, Hager was going to start carpet f-bombing.

"So, Simon. What's good at this restaurant?" Racker asked, looking over a menu.

"I don't know. I don't come to these fuck…frikkin weird restaurants."

"I have to admit that I'm not that experienced myself. Maybe these venison chops, or wild boar with mango turmeric sauce…"

"Wild boar?" Johnson asked. "Is that a kind of pig?"

Chin Tsai was alone picking through the spinach cakes, rampuri tikki and seekh kabob. Spencer saw an opportunity and sidled up to Dr. Tsai.

"Very impressive product presentation today, Dr. Tsai," he said, examining the appetizer tray. *Hmmm, did someone already eat all the meat items?*

"Thank you. I'm sorry, I've forgotten your name," Tsai said with a hint of an Asian accent.

"Spencer Carlton, CIO of Azalea Insurance. Insurance is a subsidiary acquired a couple of years ago. I'm based in Atlanta."

"Ah, very good. I love Buckhead."

"Yes, I'm very fond of some restaurants there as well. I have a couple of questions, technical in nature, which couldn't be addressed in the meeting."

"Yes?"

"First, the Process Modeler."

"Yes! You like that?"

"It certainly has some great graphics. When is it being released?"

"We don't have a firm release date yet but should be next quarter. There are no dependencies with the rest of our product suite."

"I'm curious. There was nothing in the demo about using the tool to configure the core messaging system. That must be in the plans."

"Oh, certainly," Chin said, glancing over at Singh.

"In the first release?"

"Oh, excuse me. Khaybar is motioning for me."

Carlton looked over as Tsai scurried away, noticing that Singh's back had been to them the whole time.

Damn it, I still can't get a straight answer.

Gatto saw a chance to talk one-on-one with Carlton and crossed the room.

"So, Spencer. How was our presentation?"

"Very slick. You must have a very good marketing department."

"Yes, they are very professional."

"Now, Tom, I'm still trying to get an answer about the process modeler."

"Weren't you talking to Dr. Tsai? Didn't you ask him?"

"Yes and he practically broke out into a cold sweat. He ran away without answering me."

He took Gatto further into the front corner of the room.

"Look, Tom, I'll be straight with you. I think the whole afternoon was bullshit and I think that cool modeler is especially bullshit. Now, you wowed the unwashed in the crowd like our CFO but I'm going to be the swing vote here. Be honest with me for once. Is the thing real or bullshit?"

That's an easy choice, my friend, Gatto thought quickly.

"Spencer, of course it's real. We wouldn't make such a big deal about it if it wasn't. Now, I promise that before you leave tonight you will get an answer out of either Dr. Singh or Dr. Tsai."

"I'd better. Otherwise, my recommendation is going to go to InUnison. They may be boring, but at least I think they're playing straight with us."

I don't doubt that for a minute, those pansies, Gatto thought.

The server stepped up to Singh and whispered into his ear. Singh then broke off from his conversation to ask everyone to take their seats. The server handed a single menu to Dr. Singh, seated to Gatto's left. Gatto leaned over to his CEO.

"Khaybar –"

"*Doctor* Singh, please."

"Yes, Dr. Singh. Aren't the rest of us getting menus?"

"No, I'm ordering for the group.

Racker was sitting on the opposite side of Singh from Gatto and overheard. He leaned over to Norm on his left.

"Just a heads up. Singh is ordering for everyone."

"Might as well. I didn't recognize a whole lot on the menu anyway."

"Excuse me," Singh said. "I'm taking the liberty of ordering several dishes for the table. We can sample them all." The server readied his notebook for the order.

"Everyone will start with the turmeric vinaigrette salad, then we will all share baingan bharta, chana masala, aloo gobhi, oh, better make that two orders of the baingan bharta." He laid the menu down and leaned back in his chair in triumph.

"I don't recognize any of those things," Rosenzweig said to Gibson sitting to his left next to Gatto.

"I think the masala is pasta," Gibson speculated.

"No, that would be *mar*sala."

"Oh."

Gatto saw the panic in their faces, except for Miller who was into double digits on his beer bottle consumption. He opened the menu to see what exactly Singh had ordered. *Eggplant, garbanzo beans, potatoes with cumin. Shit.* He leaned over to Singh again.

"Dr. Singh, I understand and respect your vegan beliefs," he whispered. "But shouldn't we have at least one meat dish for our guests?"

Singh's eyes met Gatto's and narrowed to slits. Without turning to the table he asked in a commanding voice, "Anyone here want to eat dead animals?"

Initially, no one moved. Then a hand slowly went up.

"I'd like a nice thick slab of bloody prime rib if you got it," Stewart said, giggling. "Oh, and don't forget the au jus! It isn't the same without that." He raised his beer bottle for emphasis.

All heads turned to Miller and then back to Singh. There was a very awkward silence as Singh stared at Miller for a moment.

"No, my friend; there is no prime rib. But I think that you *will* enjoy my choices."

Singh ordered red and white wines as the group returned to idle but tense chit chat.

Well, one good thing, you asshole, Gatto thought, as he looked at Singh. *After that, they won't ask any more questions.*

***

The United flight to Newark landed a bit late at 11:05 PM. Wayne had once again come through on the upgrade for Porter, who was very grateful.

"I'm going to travel with you whenever I go out west. There's no going back to coach after this trip."

"My pleasure, Porter. Although you aren't very good company when you sleep for so much of the flight."

"Hey, I was awake for the meals."

The Captain signaled the typical two bells telling the passengers that it was safe to stand and gather their belongings. Porter was first to their overhead bin and handed down Wayne's overnight bag, then retrieved his own.

"So, what are you going to do with all your free time the rest of the week? You should be thanking me that I didn't schedule a bunch of sales calls."

"Yes, thank you. My wife in particular thanks you. She's kept a stiff upper lip the last two weeks with me being in California but I know she hates it."

"Well, the rest of the month should be quieter for you. I'm going to try to schedule calls but there's the usual last-month-of-the-quarter paper chase, in particular this Azalea stuff. I'm almost hoping that they come right out and say that they can't make a decision this month. Oh, and I have interviews with rep candidates for New Jersey."

"That ought to be interesting."

They walked through the cabin door and up the jet way to the gate lounge.

Wayne checked his watch.

"I guess it's too late for a nightcap."

"Definitely. I'd be crucified at home if was any later than I already am."

"Let's talk tomorrow."

***

"Well, that dinner sucked," Miller said. The curry had cut into his beer buzz and he resented it.

"I think that it's pretty damn arrogant to force people to eat things because they have certain habits," Norm said. *Oh no, I just agreed with Miller!*

"Gentlemen, I was very impressed with our host," Gibson said. "A little culinary exploration is a good thing. Now, let's get down to business while the day is still fresh in our minds."

Gibson led his team to a corner table in the Sheraton lounge after ordering a round of after-dinner drinks. "So, who wants to start? Stewart?"

"There's no doubt in my mind, food preferences aside, that VibraWeb is clearly the superior company. They were much more professional."

Racker and Johnson both slumped in their seats.

"Stewart," Racker said. "What was more professional about their presentation?"

"What, you don't know? That video, that modeler. That's great stuff. InUnison was booorrring."

"VibraWeb was all sizzle and no steak…literally. We couldn't ask any questions," Sam countered. "And where was the financial information?"

"Now, I'm not concerned about that. Flanderson no doubt vetted them on that," Gibson said.

Oh, you are so damn naïve, Sam thought.

Norm weighed in. "Look, I didn't learn anything today that alters my strong belief that InUnison is the most productive system out there for integration."

"That modeler looks pretty productive," Gibson said.

"I don't see the productivity of merely drawing pretty boxes," Carlton said. "Gatto swears it's real, but I didn't see it."

"You're not making any sense," Miller said. "And speaking of finances, InUnison must be desperate if they have to beg for more investors."

"You don't know what you're talking about," Racker said. "That's how these companies get funded. Believe me; they aren't going to have to beg."

Racker, Miller and Johnson started arguing, and Gibson realized that a civil discussion with that group wasn't going to work. He motioned for Spencer to follow him to the bar.

"Those guys are hopeless. How do I resolve this?" he asked Carlton.

"I'll be honest with you, Ralph. I lean toward InUnison. They've been much more forthcoming. I'd still like some answers from VibraWeb. Talk about arrogant. Geesh. I don't know if I can do business with them."

Gibson looked over at the now animated discussion between Racker and

Miller, fearing that Azalea would lose one of them and he would be blamed.

"Spencer, I trust your judgment. I *need* your word that you can give me an honest appraisal here."

"Absolutely, Ralph."

Chapter 17 Raising the Dead

Gatto impatiently tapped a pen on the desk in his room at the Marriott, cell phone firmly in place on this left ear. *Damn. I can't get anyone today. Don't they know I have to close business this month? No, idiot, of course they know.* He let the voicemail greeting finish and left his fourth message of the day, this time with the purchasing agent at Morgan Stanley. He was also frustrated with the outcome of the Azalea visit the previous day and knew he would obsess over it during the flight back to New York. Means would be all over him.

"Hey, keep it down. I'm still trying to sleep," Suzy Kestral said, as she covered her head with the covers.

"Not surprised, after the marathon you put me through last night. How does Niles O'Rourke keep up with you?"

"Very funny. Like I would throw down with that middle aged, anal retentive lounge lizard. Of course, if it makes you jealous…"

He was about to parry that when his phone rang.

"Tom Gatto."

"So, is it closed yet?" George Means asked.

So much for waiting until New York.

"Is what closed? I'm working on a dozen deals," Gatto said.

"Azalea, of course. Wasn't the production great?"

"Oh, right, George. Lots of give and take. Look, that 'production' as you call it blew the business for us. They didn't get any questions answered."

"Like what?"

"Like our financial position."

"We're a private company. We don't have to tell anybody jack."

"InUnison apparently did."

"It shows how desperate they are."

Or more confident, maybe. Shit, I'd *like to know where* we *stand,* Gatto thought. "And the Process Modeler? It's total horseshit."

"It looks great, though."

"Yeah, well, it didn't impress Spencer Carlton who happens to be the swing vote now."

"I don't like the way this conversation is going. I'm hearing a lot of excuses. Close the deal."

"I'm going to certainly try but I need something tangible to push us over the top. I'm not hopeful."

"Remember, your job is on the line for this. Either close the deal or be sure InUnison doesn't."

"Sure, George." He gave the phone his raised, right middle finger as he heard Means hang up on him. *How could I torch InUnison? It's preposterous,* he thought.

"Oh, that was nice," Suzy said. "You always flip off the phone?"

Gatto glanced at his companion, the bed covers falling away from her body as she sat up. "Only when the caller is a pain in the ass."

"Well, why don't you come over here and I'll take care of any pains in your ass." She pulled the covers back to let him rejoin her.

"That's one thing I can count on when I'm with you," Gatto whispered into her ear. They started to cuddle but Gatto remembered that he had to make a note about an account. He abruptly got up from the bed and went to his briefcase.

Suzy wasn't pleased. "You fucking sales reps. You're always thinking about the next buck. You know, I'm not exactly ugly. How can you stop and leave like that? Need some Viagra or something?"

"No, the best stimulation for me is the sound of a PO on the fax machine."

"Bastard! You're as bad as my boss; can't tear himself away from his stupid forecasts."

"That's because he's too stupid to understand…" He interrupted himself and turned to her. *Forecasts? InUnison's forecasts!* He smiled, grinned actually, at the havoc he imagined he could wreak in Angelis' accounts. "Hey, I'm sorry sweetie. I got carried away with end of quarter stuff."

He jumped back under the covers, cradling Suzy's body in his, nibbling her neck and ears.

"So, what would I need to do to get a glance at those nasty forecasts?"

Suzy turned with a sparkle in her eye, flicking her tongue at Gatto.
Is that all? "With pleasure, darling."

***

The Azalea team also had returned on an early morning flight the day after the meetings. Except for Racker and Johnson, there was little conversation among the Azalea representatives. Upon disembarking at Kennedy International in New York, Gibson asked Spencer to meet with him the following morning. Spencer noted that his CFO brooded for the entire flight and was clearly anguished about his impending decision. He made sure to be on time.

"Good morning, Spencer. Thanks for coming in early."

"What's on your mind, Ralph?"

"I need to make a final decision here on this integration software. I realize now that I'm totally confused. This computer business used to be so simple. I could say, 'leave it to Stewart'. Now, though, I'm worried that Stewart may not be up to the task anymore, either. I'm getting increasing rumbles from the troops about the inadequacy of our systems."

It's about time, Ralph, Carlton wanted to say.

"Both companies succeeded in my view, but, boy, do I have a political dilemma here between Racker and Miller. Whoever loses might resign over it. Mr. CEO, Masters, would be pissed about it either way; he brought in Racker to replace me when I retire but Miller has such a reputation around here."

The door is opening, Spencer, his inner voice said. *Maybe a little shove…*

"Ralph, I stand by my comments about InUnison. They have proven to be the more efficient platform to work on. It may be personalities but they are a much better company to do business with as well. VibraWeb is very professional…" he said, choking on his words, "…but not as forthcoming with information. This will be a long-term relationship and there has to be a high level of trust. We aren't buying some shrinkwrap computer game here. This will eventually touch everything in Azalea's business and potentially our business partners."

"I see," Gibson said, not really comprehending. He leaned back in his desk chair, stroked his chin and looked at the ceiling, hoping for some divine inspiration. "Fine. Let's get moving with InUnison. I'll have to talk to Stewart. Let me be clear, this is tentative but I know we have to get the whole contract process going if we are going to close this by the end of the month and get the good terms from InUnison. Make it clear to them that if there's any hiccup, we might change our mind."

"Certainly, Ralph. I'll get started right away." Carlton glanced at the calendar on Gibson's wall. "It's only March 5th. We have plenty of time."

"You never know once the lawyers get involved."

Carlton stood to leave, but thought that he had better try to be noble.

"Ralph, Stewart is a pro. He'll get over this."

"Nice try, Spencer, but I know you don't get along with him either. This process has opened my eyes somewhat to the fact that time is passing him by."

Like a bullet train, Ralph. "I'll keep you apprised of progress." He picked up his coat and left Gibson's office for his temporary space down the hall.

Gibson returned to his desk, picking up the phone for the call he dreaded making.

***

Carlton closed his office door and looked up Wayne's phone number in his PDA.

"Wayne Angelis."

"Good morning, Wayne. Spencer Carlton here. I have some good news for you."

"Oh, yeah?"

"Gibson has given InUnison his tentative, and I want to underscore tentative, nod."

"Outstanding! I wasn't expecting a decision this soon after the HQ visit."

"He wants me to get going on the contract. Now, I warn you, our purchasing process is very anal so be ready."

"But you realize that our proposal is good only through this month. We can only bend over for so long. I'm almost embarrassed at how we are dropping trou for you guys."

"Nice posturing – no pun intended. We are very aware of the time constraints and I'm sure we can make this happen. Once I find out who on our end will handle this I'll be in touch."

"What's Miller's reaction?"

"I don't know. Gibson wanted to break it to him gently. This could really push him out the door."

"That would be good for you, right?"

"There you go again."

"Please. You can deny it all you like, but as I said early in this enterprise, you'd have to be considered to replace Miller."

"Gee, I never thought about it. That's my story and I'm sticking to it," Spencer replied with as straight a voice as possible.

"Anything you say, Spencer. I'll get my end moving. Later," Wayne said.

Yes! This means a blowout quarter! he said to himself as he took a victory lap around his office. *Number? What Number?*

The first person he called with the good news was Porter.

"Porter! We got it!"

"Got what?"

"Azalea, knucklehead!"

"No way!" he shouted as he stood up from his desk chair. "How big?"

"The proposal is for one-point-four mil plus maintenance. We'll have to talk about professional services."

"Is that all up front?"

"Could be, but I doubt it. They'll negotiate something over several quarters. They can't absorb it all in one drink. I'd say, oh, half a mil this quarter maybe."

"Way cool."

"That would put me around seventy-five percent of my whole year, what with the other stuff that should come in. Hey, we still have a lot of work to do, a lot of paper to chase but huge kudos to you for your dogged work. Couldn't have done it without you."

"You're welcome."

"Great, then, back to work. Later."

***

Miller sat in front of Gibson's desk, looking at the floor and shaking his head.

He finally spoke without lifting his head. "So when should my last day be, Ralph?"

"Stop it, Stewart. This isn't about you."

"Oh no? Everyone around here has been sticking it to me for a while now. I don't have any authority any more but I sure as hell still have the responsibility. I'm tired of this shit."

"Stewart, the environment has changed. We can't have one person responsible for our computers anymore. First of all, technology isn't foreign to these new managers. They view it as a core part of their business units to run and therefore their responsibility. Continuing to centralize everything is viewed as inefficient."

"So you're saying I'm *inefficient*? Obviously, I don't have your confidence any more. I might as well check out."

"No, Stewart, you certainly still have my confidence. You have to accept the new reality of having to be more of a service organization. Now, as far as this integration project, it came down to Sam and Carlton having more confidence and trust in InUnison than VibraWeb. Even Rosenzweig was more impressed with them."

Traitor! You'll never get out of data security, you Benedict Arnold. "Oh, some low level termite like Mordi has more say than I do?"

"No, but you were the only one who continued to hold out. It looks spiteful."

Miller wanted to say all kinds of things about who was more spiteful but thought better of it.

The two were silent for an uncomfortably long time. Gibson finally decided that the meeting should come to an end.

"Stewart, let me be clear. We value you as highly as we ever have. This is only one decision out of many."

"Yeah, like Oracle Financials, Peoplesoft…other stuff that got rammed down my throat."

"Stewart…"

Miller turned and stormed out of Gibson's office and returned to his own, slamming the door behind him.

Bastards! I've had it with them! Let them dissolve into chaos around here. What do I care? I've been here over twenty-five years and they're going to toss me aside. Well, I'm going with my head high, damn it. Like a Marine.

He sat down and fished Gatto's business card out of his file and dialed the number.

"This is Tom. I'm out of the office today. Please leave a message or call me on my mobile phone, 917-555-2020."

Miller punched the receiver button and dialed the cell phone number.

"Tom Gatto."

"Stewart Miller here. They're giving the business to InUnison. Aren't you back here yet?"

"Flew back yesterday. How'd Gibson decide so fast?"

"That pantywaist from Atlanta must have cornered him. Hardly gave me any chance to give him my arguments."

Maybe if you had held off on the brewskis the other night you might have had a better chance. "So is that that?"

"No way. You're a shifty little sneak. Can't you get some dirt on InUnison?"

"Stewart, I have to work on business I can close." *And hope it's enough to save my job.*

"Damn it! I need to blow this thing up!"

"Stewart, I'll see what I can find out but don't hold your breath."

***

Friday morning, Gatto was jarred awake at 6:30 a.m. by the ring of his cell phone. That could mean only one thing.

"Means, here! I haven't seen any POs come across yet. What's the holdup? I would have expected at least that FlamingAss.com would come through."

"It's FlamingArrow.com, George…" Gatto corrected, still rubbing his eyes.

"Whatever. You aren't one of those guys who waits until the 31st are you?"

"I guess you've forgotten about my decent January start?" Gatto said.

"Ancient history. So, what's your status?" Means demanded.

"FlamingArrow has a PO on their CFO's desk. Fellows Trust has the contract in legal. They are pretty much taking our paper so I don't anticipate any delay."

"Dates, man, give me DATES!"

"FlamingArrow, today; Fellows next week."

"Well, I guess that *is* progress but it isn't enough." Means said. "Good bye."

Geesh, if you'd quit taking up my time with these phone calls…. he hung up.

"Seems fucking light to me, Means," Hager said. Means had linked the Evil One in as usual. "And what's he been doing on fucking Azalea?"

"Azalea is history, Simon. Get over it."

"If he doesn't make his fucking Number –"

"He already has, Simon."

"We ought to raise his fucking Number then, so he can't make it and I can fire his fucking ass. Kind of a fucking double-secret Number."

"Goodbye, Simon."

***

Wayne was staying very close to his fax machine that sunny Friday morning. He had been assured that Lehman had their approvals in hand and that Fabozzi should be sending his in from Merrill any minute. His office phone rang.

"Wayne Angelis."

"Wayne, this is George Melani, how are you today?"

"Fine, George. Have any good news for me?"

"Well, yes and no. The PO is still in purchasing. They have some issue with the maintenance fee. I really don't have any time to deal with the bureaucrats. I'd rather you call them directly and work it out. I don't really get this administrative stuff."

Wayne opened the Potential file – it was on top of his desk as were all the other Q1 hot files – to search for the purchasing manager's name.

"Ah, should I call this Mike Willard? The 18% of list is pretty standard."

"Yes, he's the guy. You may have to educate him about things. Or he's trying to justify his existence by giving you a hard time."

"You taught him all you know, right?" Wayne teased.

"Hey, how many times do I have to say I'm sorry? Porter's been so great to have around that he's renewed my faith in humanity, well, a little slice of humanity. I owe you guys, big time. I'm still grinding my axe for the Sun rep, though."

Good thing I'm not that poor bastard, Wayne thought.

"George, I'll give Willard a call right now."

"Hey, I'll transfer you." The phone beeped a couple of times and then rang four times. That could mean only one thing…

"Hi, you've reached Mike Willard's voice mail. Leave a message. I'll call back."

"This is Wayne Angelis of InUnison Software. I understand that you have some questions about our PO. Please call me at 914-555-8422 and we'll straighten it out."

***

"Hello, this is Wayne Angelis."

"This is Mike Willard at Potential Investing. You left a message."

"Oh, thanks for returning my call so quickly. I understand that there is some confusion about the maintenance fee."

"There's no confusion. What is this 18% of list for maintenance? It's outrageous."

Wayne pinched the bridge of his nose. *This shouldn't be happening…*

"It's pretty much industry standard, 18% of list per year for software updates, patches and phone technical support. After all, this is simply an additional server purchase on top of the original deal which had upgrades and maintenance for one year at 18% of list."

"I don't know who approved that but we are expecting 15% of net. That's what our other vendors are giving us."

Wayne didn't believe that for a second. He could believe that some hard up rep might shave a few percentage points, but the Support manager would have his head if it was based on net price instead of list.

"Mike, would you mind sharing one of those agreements with me? I could pass it through our legal and see if we have some flexibility," Wayne said, calling Willard's bluff.

"Of course not. That's privileged information."

"You realize that you risk delaying George Melani's project if we have to renegotiate this piece?" Wayne asked, hoping that this purchasing bureaucrat knew of Melani's temper.

The sudden silence on the other end of the line confirmed that Willard did indeed.

"Who--whose project did you say?" a now shaken Willard asked.

"George Melani. You might need to call him. As you know –"

"Oh, my mistake! Heh, I thought this was a different project. Of *course* it's 18% of net, oh, excuse me *list*. Sorry for the misunderstanding."

"So, when can I see the order?"

"Shortly. Nice to talk to you." Willard abruptly hung up.

Wayne's fax machine came to life less than ten minutes later.

***

Porter sat at his home office desk, feverishly punching the keys on his laptop. He was programming a new demo and was in "the zone", not wanting to stop while his creative juices were flowing.

"Wow. This is amazing. You've been in your office for three straight days!"

"It's kind of boring," Porter said, not appreciating the interruption.

"So, you can't be happy, can you? You complained about how much running around you were doing a month ago."

"I guess this business goes at two speeds: zero or Mach 2. Right now, Wayne is focused on getting the orders, so we aren't doing much prospecting. I'm babysitting a couple of accounts, making sure they don't have any technical issues that would get in the way of the purchase order."

"Doesn't sound tough."

"It is when the customer is stupid or lazy, like those creeps at Manley."

"You shouldn't talk that way, Porter. They are the ones paying you."

"Manley isn't, the cheap bastards. I wish that there were more smart customers like Merrill or PensAndClips. Even those Russians at Sampson Logistics were smart. They never have to call for help."

"Fine, let's move to Moscow."

"Nyet."

***

Two weeks passed as all sales teams accelerated the paper chase, putting pressure on external purchasing and internal order processing bureaucrats. In his office, Gatto checked off two more items from his list of calls for the day and reached for his phone for the next call. It rang and he answered it instead.

"Good morning, Tom. My name is Phyllis Majors. I'm principal in the Majors Group here in Bedminster. We are a placement firm specializing in sales and pre-sales technical people in the Northeast. I was given your name as the manager for VibraWeb in New York. Is that correct?"

"That's correct," Gatto said, not wanting to devalue her perceptions with the truth that he was only a rep for VibraWeb in New York.

"I have a strong candidate for Systems Engineer. May I fax over the resume?"

"To be honest, I don't have headcount right now. I expect to get some shortly." *Or maybe I can replace that stiff I have for an SE.* "Can you give me the Cliff's Notes version?"

"Yes. She's been an SE for five years, done a little engineering before that."

"What companies?"

"Her current company is InUnison…"

"You realize that they are a direct competitor."

"Really? Didn't know that. I'll check on the non-compete then."

Typical. Didn't do any research.

"I'm pretty sure their SEs had to sign," Gatto said. *I, of course, didn't,* he thought, recalling how gullible the InUnison management had been. "Just curious; why is she leaving? I hear that they are doing well."

"Something about their financial predicament."

"Their *what*?" Gatto was now all ears.

"She says that they will be out of cash in a matter of weeks. VCs are turning them down for more investment and she's worried about layoffs. She wants to get a jump on things. Oh, do you guys need a marketing guy? I got a resume of a guy from InUnison as well. Unlike the SE, he didn't give a reason but when you start to see paper coming from one company, it usually means something is up."

"Very interesting. Thanks. Actually, fax that resume to me here in the office."

He gave her the number and said goodbye.

***

"I have about had it with these lawyers!" Wayne shouted at Ken Presby. "The Azalea guys are waiting for the language changes. Do you realize that it's the twentieth of March?"

"No way! Gee, how'd that creep up on me?" Presby said.

"Not funny."

"Look, I don't have control over these things so I'll kick it up to Niles..." *As usual,* Wayne thought. "…he'll put some pressure on these lawyers."

Wayne hung up the phone and rubbed his eyes. He could feel the old stress headache rising in his temples. The phone, however, would not rest.

"Hello, this is Wayne."

"Wayne, Harry Matthews."

"Got any candidates for me?"

"That's what I like about you Wayne; skip the guy talk and get right to the point. Someone piss in your corn flakes today or something?"

"You know I have only a couple of weeks left in the quarter. You'd be cranky too. What makes you so chipper?

"Business has never been better. Demand for sales reps and especially SEs is at an all time high and going higher. I'm actually able to get twenty-five percent on my placements. How about your business?"

"I'm doing well business-wise, but there are the usual roadblocks like lawyers in these deals."

"Okee dokee, Wayne. Well, I've got a resume here you might be interested in. A William Thomas. He's currently between jobs. His last one was at, let me see, oh, right, VibraWeb."

"No kidding? What patch?"

"New York."

"Well, how can he go to a competitor?"

"You're looking for Jersey, right?"

"Yeah."

"His non-compete specifies Manhattan. He says he can sell in Jersey."

"Fax it over, then. Can't be any worse than the corpses others have sent me."

"I don't know him personally but some acquaintances vouch for him."

"See if you can set something up for a week from Thursday," he said, glancing at his calendar. "That's the twenty-sixth. I'll be in the city that day. See if he can do lunch at the Marriott Marquis."

"You are in such a rut. Can't you find any other place than the Marriott? You always have me set up meetings for you there."

"Home away from home, or at least, it's my home office away from home office."

"I'll set it up with the candidate."

***

"Hello? Is this Mackenzie Jeffords?"

"Yes it is."

"Hello! My name is Jake Malloy. I'm with the placement firm of Malloy and Malloy here in New York. How are you this wonderful day?"

"Fine."

"I understand that you are a Systems Engineer with InUnison. Is that correct?"

"Yes, it is."

"I happen to have a number of openings I'm trying to fill with high tech companies here in the Northeast. Since you were referred to me – and recommended very highly, I might add – I thought I'd see if you might have some interest in making a change. How are things at InUnison?"

"Not going my way. Actually, I am looking to move on."

"Not feeling challenged?"

"Oh, it's not that. I'm, well, confidentially, I'm concerned about the company's viability."

"In what way? Financially?"

"Yes. They are running out of cash. Also, I'm hearing that the next release will be late, which means customers are going to defer purchases."

"Doesn't sound good," Malloy said. "So, can you fax me a resume then? I can start lining up meetings."

"What's your fax number?" she asked.

"917-555-3401."

"Also, please use my cell phone number to call me," Mackenzie added. "It has voice mail."

"Certainly, Mackenzie. Thank you *very* much," Malloy said in closing. *You have made my day.*

***

Wayne dialed the 800 number for the Monday morning pipeline review with Presby and the Eastern sales team. On this fourth Monday of March, Presby would be turning up the heat even higher for end-of-quarter deal closings. With only seven business days left in the quarter, Presby was seventy-five percent of the way to his Number and he was starting to exhibit angst and stress about the other twenty-five percent.

Wayne was only the second rep to connect, though a couple of the SEs were already on. He introduced himself as he was beeped onto the party line.

"Good morning! This is Wayne, who's on so far?"

"Porter here."

"Al Fisher, with Mark in the Tyson's office."

"How's the weather down there?"

"Cold and rainy. Not great. How about New York?"

"Not too bad, dusting of snow."

"Good morning, this is Sam and Kyle in Boston."

Presby, to the surprise of everyone, connected in a bit early this morning.

"Hi, this is Ken, everyone here? Wayne, Kyle, Al, Gary?"

All answered in the affirmative except for Gary Reaper in Atlanta.

"First an announcement. The new release will ship next Friday, the twenty-seventh."

"You're positive about that?" Al Fisher asked. "I was hearing some rumblings from the SEs about a delay."

"There was a delay in the hard copy manuals. They have the electronic versions on the CDs so we decided to ship anyway. The VCs need to see that we can keep to our release commits as well as our revenue commits. Let's make the rounds. Kyle?"

Each rep ran through the list of deals they were chasing paperwork for. As usual, it would all come down to the last few days. Headquarters would be ready to take the orders, slap shipping labels on the CDs and get them out the door right up to midnight.

"Folks, let's wrap up. You know the Numbers; you know why we have to hit the Numbers. Yes, the quarter is looking good for us in the East and Central but the West Coast team is sucking wind. I really want this team to break out, big time. We have the talent …" *except you, Reaper,* he wanted to say "… so let's get out there! Let's go sell! Beat VibraWeb!"

"Ken, can you stay on for a minute?" Reaper asked, having finally connected.

Presby would have none of it today. "Gary, I'll have to call you back later. I have to get on another call with O'Rourke," he lied.

***

Wayne hurried out of the huge subway station at Times Square, squinting as his eyes tried to adjust to the bright sunshine on Broadway. He glanced at his mobile phone – a habit now firmly ingrained in his subconscious – and noticed the message indicator. He dialed his voice mailbox and punched in his pin. There was one message.

"Hi, Wayne. It's Spencer Carlton. Wanted to let you know that the contract and PO are on Gibson's desk for signature. Actually, I gave it to Connie Sanchez to bird dog and that's better than having it on his desk. She'll fax it to you as soon as he gets in and signs. Call me if you need anything else. Oh, and thanks to whoever kicked your lawyers into gear. Talk to you."

"Thank God!" Wayne said. He hit the delete key and checked the date on his watch. *March twenty-six. Not bad. Hell, there's still almost four business days left in the quarter. I can relax now.*

No way, Wayne, he scolded himself as he speed dialed his wife.

"Helen, can you do me a favor?"

"Maybe."

"Can you check the fax machine periodically? I should be getting a fax from Azalea shortly and would really like to know that it got there."

"I'll be around all day," Helen replied, sighing.

"Thanks a bunch! Later."

***

Miller had his feet up on his desk as he perused his weekly *Computerworld*, focusing on the executive position ads. Since Gibson had made the InUnison decision, he was spending a lot of time considering his future and was having a great deal of difficulty coming to terms with it.

These positions are all bullshit. All of them would be a step down, he thought as he tossed the trade rag onto his desk blotter. He reached for his mug and started for the coffee machine but was interrupted by his telephone.

"Miller."

"Good morning, Mr. Miller. My name is Jake Malloy with Malloy and Malloy Search. I understand that Azalea has lots of new initiatives going on in information technology and I have a lot of talent I'd like to place. In fact, I just got the resume of an engineer from a software startup."

"What company?"

"An EAI company, InUnison. Are you familiar with them?"

"Unfortunately, yes. It looks like we may need some InUnison experience around here soon." *Damn it!*

"Really?" Malloy was silent for several seconds.

"Malloy? Are you still there?" Miller asked.

"Yes I am. This puts me in an awkward position."

"Look, I don't have all day. Tell me about the candidate."

"Well, that's what's difficult. My candidate found out that InUnison is close to running out of cash. Worse, their release will be late. That would doom their quarter and any VC money along with it. Might even put them out of business. She's nervous that she could get laid off. Also I talked to a marketing guy in Redwood City who confirmed the whole thing as well. They're in deep shit."

"You're serious?" *They lied to us at the meeting! Damn!* "Fax that resume over immediately!"

***

Miller tried calling Gibson, but got voice mail. He decided that he'd better track him down personally.

He sprinted to the elevator, shocking everyone in the computer center who witnessed it since Stewart disdained physical exertion. He paced frantically while waiting for the elevator to reach the datacenter. Still out of breath by the time the elevator stopped on the twenty-sixth floor, he walked as briskly as he could to Gibson's office. Gibson was at his desk and on the phone.

"Ralph! This is urgent!"

"I'll call you right back, Barry," Ralph said to his caller. "Where's the fire, Stewart?"

"InUnison is going under," Miller said, his chest heaving as he tried to regain his breath. "They lied to us about their financials and they can't get their new release out either. There won't be any new VC money for them. I'm telling you, they're toast! You didn't sign that PO did you?"

"How did you find out?"

"A recruiter called me about a candidate who works at InUnison but wants out," Miller said truthfully, then decided to embellish it some. "Also, my industry sources, a couple of them, confirmed the situation. Where's the PO?"

"Oh, no! I signed it and gave it back to Connie to fax!"

This time Miller had a competitor. He and Gibson sprinted through cubicles to the copy room where the fax machine sat.

"CONNIE! STOP THE FAX!" Gibson yelled when he thought he was in range.

Consuelo thought she heard her name and peeked out of the room to see the two middle-aged executives hurtling toward her. Heads were popping up from the cubicles to see what the commotion was about.

"Ralph?"

"Did you fax that PO yet?"

"It just started. Looks like it just finished the cover page."

"STOP IT NOW!"

"You don't have to yell, Ralph!" Sanchez turned and looked at the machine. "But I don't know *how* to stop it."

The signature page was already moving into the scanner.

"Damn it!" Gibson said. "Isn't there a button or something to stop it?"

"Here," Miller shoved Connie aside and unplugged the power cord. "When all else fails…" Stewart said, holding the plug up in the air.

Connie stood there paralyzed, offended by Miller's shove.

"Good thinking, Stewart. Now, let's go back to the office and talk this through. Let's find Carlton. He's still in New York. Connie, hang onto that document."

"Geesh, you'd think the sky was falling," she said as she exited, hip checking Miller back into the wall.

***

All was quiet at the Marriott Marquis while Wayne waited for Bill Thomas to show for their lunch appointment. He settled into a lounge chair opposite the restaurant and pulled Thomas' resume out of his briefcase to review one more time.

His phone rang. "This is Wayne."

"Wayne, this is Stan Fabozzi at Merrill Lynch. Is there something you want to tell me?"

Uh oh. I've heard that curt tone from you before. "Not that I can think of, Stan."

"Don't you want to update me on the status of this month's release?"

"Nothing has changed to my knowledge. Oh, wait. We *are* dropping hard manuals. Is that important to you?"

"So, it's still going to ship this month, right?"

"Yes. My manager confirmed that this past Monday. Do you have a concern?

"And how's business? You guys still liquid?"

"Yes, the quarter looks good. We're talking to some new VC. What's this all about, Stan?"

"A few minutes ago, I got off the phone with some headhunter named Jake Malloy. He called about a candidate, one of your SEs. Supposedly she's leaving because you're running out of money and the release will be delayed. This isn't going to be a replay of last quarter is it?"

Thank God he said the SE was a "she". At least it isn't Porter. "Stan, on my honor, we are in very good shape. Do you have a number for this Malloy guy? I'd like to call him."

Fabozzi gave Wayne the 800 number Malloy left with him. "Look, Wayne, you've been good to us this quarter but, please, no surprises."

"None from me, Stan. I'll get to the bottom of this."

He hung up and dialed the 800 number. "We're sorry. But the number you have dialed is not in service," the recorded message said. "Please recheck the number and try again."

Strange, he thought. *Maybe I didn't get it right from Fabozzi.*

His phone rang again.

"Wayne, it's Porter. I'm over at PensAndClips, you know, helping configure the beta of the new software. Did Mansfield call you yet? He's pretty pissed."

"About what? No, he hasn't called." *What now?*

"He got a call from some headhunter – Malloy I think his name was – who wanted to know if he had any openings for an engineer. It turns out the candidate has InUnison experience which prompted interest from Mansfield."

"Let me guess; he told him she was an InUnison SE and that we are going out of business."

"Essentially, yes. We aren't, are we?"

"We might if this guy keeps calling our customers. He called Fabozzi. I tried the number for this Malloy but it doesn't exist."

"Shit. What are we going to do?"

"Well, tell Mansfield it's all bullshit and that I'll stop by this afternoon to clear the air." He saw a young man in a gray, pinstripe business suit waiting by the restaurant entrance, scanning the lounge. "I think my lunch date is here. I have to go. Later," Wayne said, as he stood and motioned to the man he hoped was Bill Thomas.

"Hello," Wayne said, approaching his guest. "Are you looking for Wayne Angelis?"

"Yes, I'm Bill Thomas. Pleased to meet you. So, closing business I hope?" he said, pointing to the phone.

"Not exactly. I have a recruiter calling my customers and making them nervous. I'm getting a big PO today, though."

"That's good to hear. The quarter has been good?"

"Yes, I had a rough start but it came around."

"Have you been seeing competition from my old company?"

"Surprisingly little, though they made some waves at this big account I'm closing."

"You mind me asking who that is?"

Wayne thought for a moment. "I suppose not. It's Azalea Financial. You know them?"

"Yes. They would have been on my radar this year. Congratulations!"

"Thanks. I think our references in Financial Services here put us on top. VibraWeb didn't have any here in New York."

"Well, none that would step up for them. I did sell *some* software last year, after all. But we always pissed them off eventually. That's one of the reasons I left. They treated everyone like dirt, reps and customers alike. Repeatable business was non-existent."

"Well, they came up with ABN Amro and UBS, both in Chicago."

"UBS? When did they get business from them? I busted my ass to win them last year. Gatto really turned them off and I thought I had it made until your guy in Chicago blew them away."

Wayne started to laugh. "Want to hear something ironic? Tom Gatto is now working your old patch for VibraWeb."

"You don't say? That *is* funny. Anyway, UBS told me that they were standardizing on InUnison, corporate-wide."

"Supposedly, there's some equities department in Chicago using VibraWeb. They had the contact there participate in a conference call with the Azalea people."

"Not face-to-face?"

"No."

Now it was Thomas' turn to start laughing. "Doctor Reference."

"Pardon me?"

"Look, I know positively that VibraWeb had no deals with UBS or ABN while I was selling for them and I haven't heard anything new from my spies there. They are still out there chasing quick business. I'm surprised they went after Azalea. It's too big. Anyway, I bet they went to Doctor Reference." He started to laugh again.

"Doctor *Reference*?" Wayne asked again.

"Yes, aka, Scott Shepherd. He's a rep in Chicago. Whenever we needed a reference, we were supposed to go to him."

"He's the only one with references? That's pathetic."

Thomas leaned in for effect. "Wayne, he *was* the reference. Scott and his SE. Get it?"

Wayne didn't get it right away. Then his right eyebrow went up and his jaw dropped. "You're kidding."

"Nope."

"They faked the references? You have *got* to be shitting me."

Thomas nodded and reclined back in his chair, letting the revelation take full effect.

"They faked the references," Wayne repeated. "That's…in my entire career, I've never heard of such a thing."

"Now, to be clear, I never took advantage of Scott's, uh, services. I couldn't be so blatantly dishonest. But management put a lot of pressure on when a prospect insisted on references."

"Well, at least it didn't work at Azalea. We won the business. In fact, the PO may be spooling off of my fax as we speak."

Wayne's phone rang and he looked at the caller's number. "Excuse me, this is my wife. Hi, honey."

"Well, you started to get a fax from Azalea but it didn't finish. Pretty much got the cover sheet and part of page two which looks like a purchase order."

"Damn. I'll have to call them to retransmit. Thanks."

Shit. "Sorry for the interruption. I have to call Azalea."

"I know how it is at quarter end. I was surprised that you would schedule an interview for this week."

"We need to staff up fast," Wayne said, dialing Sanchez's phone number. "I can't wait... Hi, Connie. It's Wayne Angelis with InUnison."

"Yes, what can I do for you?"

"Your fax didn't come all the way through. Sorry for the imposition but could you resend?"

"I can't do that, Wayne."

"Why not?" he asked, as a creeping dread started to come over him.

"Gibson told me not to resend it. When I started to send it, Ralph and *Steeewwwooort* came flying into the copy room like madmen and pulled the plug on the machine."

"Why did they do that?"

"They didn't tell me but they are in Gibson's office with Spencer Carlton now. No, wait, the meeting is breaking up."

"Can I talk to Spencer?"

Connie put her hand over the mouthpiece but Wayne could still hear her muffled voice.

"Hey, Spencer? Can you take a call from Wayne Angelis? Oh. Wayne?"

"Yes?"

"He said, and I quote, 'you bet your ass I'll take his call'. I'll transfer you."

"Thanks, Connie." Wayne was now on the edge of his chair, phone in his left hand and the fingers of this right hand supporting his face.

"Wayne? What kind of bullshit have you been feeding us?"

"Spencer, let me guess; you guys got a call from some recruiter named Malloy."

"Miller did and he's totally bullshit about this. He's got Gibson all wound up now to the extent that he's re-examining the VibraWeb proposal, calling that Flanderson guy, Larry Liu, and I don't know what to believe."

"There's no truth to it, trust me –"

"Wayne, you know what 'trust me' means in this business? 'Fuck you', that's what. I didn't realize that this was going to be a career threatening decision. I backed you and now Miller has Gibson looking at me sideways."

"Spencer, please! It isn't true! You've got to believe me!"

"You better figure something out and fast."

"I'll get Engler in here –"

"Why? He's not going to have much credibility with Miller or Gibson now."

"HE DIDN'T LIE!" Wayne yelled, causing a few heads to turn in the lounge. Bill Thomas was still sitting across from him, looking around the lounge himself and hoping no one thought that he was the source of the outburst. "Spencer, I'll tell you who's lying. I found out that VibraWeb faked the references."

"Wayne, you can't deflect this by making stuff up about the competition."

"I can't explain it now but it's true! Look, I'll figure something out and let you know tomorrow. You have to believe me!"

"Do it. I don't want to wake up working for Miller."

Wayne dropped his phone and could only stare into the distance.

"Uh, Wayne? I assume the interview is over," Thomas said.

Wayne couldn't speak. He nodded instead. Thomas started to get up as Wayne regained his voice.

"Who is trying to ruin my life? I have a recruiter calling around blowing up my deals, including Azalea."

"Don't underestimate how low VibraWeb can go. They'll do anything to win a deal or keep the competition from getting a deal. Sort of a scorched earth tactic."

"Or a scorched Wayne…" He started to recover and his brain cleared a bit.

"Well, I'll have to bring in the heavy weapons myself," Wayne said, gathering his things together. "Bill, I apologize but I've got to circle the wagons."

"I totally understand. Let me know if I can help in some way."

"Thanks for the offer. I'll let you know when we can reconvene here, assuming you're still interested after this fiasco."

"I'm definitely still interested. Give me a call."

They shook hands and Thomas walked past the registration desk to the elevators.

Wayne pulled out his notebook and started a list of people he needed to call. *Presby and O'Rourke; Porter? No, I'll see him at PandC; Melani; who else?*

He was interrupted by his phone.

"This is Wayne."

"Wayne, this is Neil Shiff at Lehman. I got off the phone with some headhunter…"

Ah, shit.

***

Tom Gatto's phone rang and he reflexively reached for the receiver.

"Means! What's the situation?"

Why do I not pay better attention to caller ID? Gatto asked himself.

"Yes, George? What can I do for you?"

"Any movement on Azalea?"

Gatto had to think quickly. He didn't want to tell him *exactly* what was going on.

"I'm working on it. Apparently there's some scuttlebutt about InUnison being in a cash crunch and people exiting. Miller, the CIO at Azalea, is trying to use that to blow up the deal."

"How does that help us?"

"Can't hurt us."

"There's not much time –"

"No shit, George. As I've told you before, I *can* read a calendar."

"Then tell me what the date will be on Monday."

"March thirtieth."

"Good, because that happens to be the date of your next forecast review."

"George, you know that I'll be sitting in my office by the phone and fax. Don't expect to go on sales calls."

"Can't we get in to see Azalea?"

"No, George, it's out of my hands. Miller will either work his miracle or he won't. And just because he gets InUnison kicked out doesn't mean we would automatically get the business."

"Now see, there you go again with the negativity. I don't like the way this conversation is going."

"I'm managing expectations."

"Well, *manage* to be in your office early on Monday. I'll be there by eight."

***

Wayne's left foot tapped impatiently as the grimy, decrepit, freight elevator rose excruciatingly slowly to the PensAndClips offices. He was anxious about what kind of reception he would get from Craig Mansfield.

"Craig, how are you?" Wayne asked as he finally emerged from the freight elevator.

"What's going on, Wayne? That Malloy guy shook me up."

"Someone is trying to sabotage my quarter. Look, I swear to you that we are in fine shape. Is Porter still here?"

"Yes, I'll go get him for you."

Mansfield disappeared back toward their computer lab and Wayne wandered to the front of the office where the conference table was, his mind still churning on his predicament.

"Wayne, I was hoping you'd get here," Porter said, walking briskly to the conference table. "I got three calls this afternoon asking about our alleged cash crisis. What's going on here?"

"Let's sit down."

Mansfield started to walk away, assuming Wayne needed some privacy.

"Craig, please stay. I want you to hear what's going on. I may need your help."

Wayne stood and walked to the front windows.

"Someone out there is trying to sabotage my quarter by spreading rumors to my prospects. Shit, it's almost as if he has my forecast. He says he's a recruiter representing an SE from InUnison who is trying to get out of the company before we lay her off."

"Is it only happening in your territory?" Mansfield asked.

"I talked to a couple other reps and they haven't heard a peep. The Swede – he's our rep in Chicago – is closing the quarter strong. Al Fisher in DC; he had 'no praaaablems' as usual."

"It's a female?" Porter asked.

"Female what?"

"SE."

"Oh, yes, that's what Carlton told me at Azalea."

"To my knowledge there are only three women in the SE corps: Julia, Mackenzie and Shirley. Shirley is in the Bay Area so I doubt that she would call an East Coast recruiter, right? I'd be crushed if it was Julia."

"Let's call her. Mind if we use the speaker phone, Craig?"

"Be my guest."

Wayne dialed her mobile number.

"Hello, this is Julia. May I help you?"

"You certainly might, Julia. It's Wayne in New York."

"Wayne! Good to hear from you. Did we get Azalea yet?"

"Not quite. That's one reason I'm calling. Um, I need to ask a personal question."

"No, I'm not augmented."

"Augmented? What are you…oh. Very funny." He held his hands out in front of his chest to describe Julia for Mansfield who put his hand on his mouth to stifle a laugh.

"Wayne, behave," Porter whispered.

"I heard that. Is that Porter?"

"Ah, yes. Sorry, I forgot to mention that he is here. We are on the speaker phone at PensAndClips. Craig Mansfield is here as well."

"*Wayne!* What is this, *Candid Camera* or something? I make an intimate joke about myself and you have a *customer* listening?"

"Pleased to meet you, Julia," Mansfield said.

"Likewise, I guess. So, is this call just to humiliate me?"

"No, Julia," Wayne replied. "There's a recruiter calling my prospects claiming to represent an InUnison SE looking for a job. It's a female SE. Please tell me it isn't you."

"Stupid bitch."

"Pardon?"

"Mackenzie. She heard some rumor that we were running out of cash and told me that she called a headhunter. I told her she had bad information and that we were just moving up the next round of financing. She must not have waved off the headhunter.

"She never should have joined a startup since she's such a worry wart," Julia continued. "She doesn't understand how we are funded and that there are regular infusions of capital until we go public. She'll believe every negative thing that comes out."

"Did she tell you who she called?"

"Hmmm. No. Want me to find out? She'd tell me, especially when I lay a guilt trip on her for causing all this trouble."

"Let me know what you find out. Later."

Wayne punched the end button.

"Well, now we know where this started. Damn it. Oh, Craig, did Malloy give you a phone number for him?"

"Yes, an 800 number. I have it right here in my notes," he said, pointing to his notebook. Wayne reached across for Mansfield's notebook. It was the same number he got from Fabozzi.

"It doesn't exist. I tried calling it and it's not in service."

"Wait," Mansfield said, fishing for his cell phone and flipping through his incoming call list. "Right, now I remember. The caller ID for the call was one of the new 917 area code numbers. You don't see too many of them yet."

Wayne wasn't paying close attention to Mansfield. "I know; I'll call Harry. He's one of my best recruiters. Maybe he knows him."

Wayne checked for Harry's number and dialed.

"Hi, Harry, Wayne Angelis."

"I was hoping you'd call. How'd the interview go with Thomas?"

"Well, I'll get into that later. I'm really calling to see if you know a recruiter named Malloy, Jake Malloy."

"Yes, I knew him. He had one of the oldest firms on the island. He was like our elder statesman."

"*Was*?"

"Yes, he passed away a couple years ago. His firm was sold to Half because of inheritance taxes. We picked up a couple of guys from the firm."

"Well, he must have risen from the dead. Someone named Jake Malloy is calling all of my prospects and passing nasty rumors."

"Wayne, he's tits up. I went to the funeral."

"You wouldn't happen to remember what his number was?"

"I still have it in my Rolodex. I don't throw anything away, especially phone numbers. Hold on."

They could hear him flipping through some cards. "Here it is. 800-555-7866."

"Yes, that's it. Thanks, Harry."

"So, what about Thomas?"

"We met but the shit hit the fan and I had to put him off. I'll call to reschedule."

"Don't wait long. It's a seller's market and he's going to be hot."

"Of course, Harry. Bye. Convinced now, Craig?"

"I guess. Unless you staged all this."

"Please. Oh, speaking of 'staging', Porter, I found out that VibraWeb faked their references. Remember the confusion about UBS?"

"Of course. But you can't be serious. I know I'm naïve but, please."

"It's a dog-eat-dog world out there." Then he remembered Bill Thomas' parting warning about not underestimating VibraWeb. He looked up at Porter and then Mansfield, a suspicion growing in his head.

"Craig, what was that 917 number?"

"917-555-3400"

Wayne dialed the number.

"This is Tom Gatto with VibraWeb. Leave a message." He hung up immediately.

"Gatto."

"What, he's 'Malloy'?" Porter asked.

"Has to be, or he's orchestrating this."

"Jesus," Mansfield said. "How low can the guy go?"

Wayne turned to the computer sitting on the window ledge. "Craig, mind if I browse for a moment?"

"Be my guest, again."

Wayne brought up Internet Explorer and entered the URL for the AltaVista search site. Once there he entered "Jake Malloy New York". He got dozens of entries back and quickly scanned through a few pages worth of hits until he found the one he was hoping for and clicked on it.

"What are you looking for?" Mansfield asked, now looking over his shoulder.

"Obituary. And here it is." He read the article from the New York Times. "This is all I need." He clicked on the printer icon to print the document and Mansfield went to retrieve it from the printer in the back of the office.

"At least we can refute the source, right?" Porter asked.

"Yes, I can calm down most of the prospects. But Azalea..."

Wayne got up and strolled by the windows again. "Miller could still use this to blow us up. Who knows, he might even be part of the plot. But how do I prove that it's Gatto? And if I can, will it matter with Azalea?" He sat back down and started to despair.

"How can it not matter? We're clearly the best solution."

"Porter, when are you going to accept that technology is the least of their considerations?"

"But this cash thing isn't true!"

"Ah, yes it is, Porter, sort of. That stupid bitch in Philly did in fact put herself on the market and didn't have the common sense to keep internal information, even mistaken internal info, to herself." Wayne cracked a smile thinking about it.

"What's so funny?"

"It's actually kind of brilliant what he's doing. Even if he were caught he has plausible deniability."

"How so? Tell me you wouldn't do something like this."

"Oh please, Porter. Grow up! If a piece of information like that fell into my lap I'd use it in a heartbeat. I'd pass the tidbit along, absolutely. Somehow, he got access to my prospect and customer list. He might have known a few of the existing customers from when he was in this job but not so many of the prospects."

"But raising someone from the dead?"

Mansfield returned with a copy of the obituary. "So, what's next Wayne?"

"First, I fax this to all those people who got calls so they can move forward with their deals. Azalea, well, I don't know."

Wayne returned to the windows. "You have to admire the originality. I guess I don't have the imagination to scheme like this. Damn. I'm going to have to raise the ante. What's the saying, 'he pulls a knife, you draw a gun'?" Wayne paused to gaze out the window, hoping to concoct a retaliation scheme. "God, he's fucking brilliant. Not only could he blow us up, he might get the Azalea deal himself. Genius."

"I don't believe you! He's an asshole!"

"Some of the most brilliant people are assholes" Wayne said, still looking out on 21st Street. "It's like I'm Patton and he's Rommel. Old George admired Rommel's strategic thinking and boldness. It didn't stop him from kicking Rommel's ass across Africa and it won't stop me from kicking Gatto's ass across Manhattan. He will not get away with this unanswered!"

"Wayne, I don't think this is the right way to go," Porter said, alarmed at the growing rage within Wayne.

Wayne ignored Porter. He had now convinced himself to return fire. Numerous devious ideas came to him and one in particular gelled in his mind. He turned from the window with an evil grin.

"I know! He's always going after dot-coms. Craig, you know the Silicon Alley community. Isn't there some association we can use to spread some dirt about Gatto? We could get pictures doctored up. Maybe showing him with known hookers or something. Maybe, Gatto at a gay club? He'd freak at that, the gigolo."

"Brilliant!" Mansfield said. "The president of the trade association is –"

Porter was horrified. "Wayne! This is 'mutually assured destruction' not sales strategy! How does destroying Gatto help you achieve your Number?"

Wayne tried to come up with an answer. Destruction of Gatto was certainly his goal. He wanted to go on the offensive, not simply react. Porter was being naïve, he'd understand later. Gatto must die!

Mansfield, disappointed that he allowed himself to be caught up in the plotting, spoke up first. "He's right, you know."

A simple statement but it had the effect of a slap across the face.

Wayne was all of a sudden ashamed of himself. He never wanted Porter to see his repressed, primal killer instinct, a side of him he had worked hard to purge since his early uncontrolled days in sales, days which included his time with Realtime and Tom Gatto. "Damn. He's done it to me again."

Porter exhaled in relief. "What do you mean, 'again'?" he asked.

Wayne knew he needed the therapy of unburdening his soul. He hoped his tale wouldn't destroy his relationship with Porter, though.

"We were both working Manhattan for Realtime Analytics – we sold advanced financial account management software – and the territories were not well defined. We scrambled to work an account before the other could. Management liked the so-called 'competitive' atmosphere; thought it was macho.

"Anyway, we were constantly stepping on each others' toes. Gatto never took any loss of an account well and constantly harped to our manager about my 'poaching'. It was incredibly embarrassing. I had prospects sign and date what amounted to an affidavit at the first meeting to prove when I called on them. It didn't matter. Gatto could always come up with some other criteria for why an account was his. He started to get personal as well. After a while, Gatto wore me down and I started to give his crap right back, trying to sabotage his deals, attack him personally. He succeeded in dragging me right into the gutter with him and he's doing it to me again."

Wayne stepped back to the conference table and sat down.

"The final battle came at Providential Securities, the huge brokerage up on Park Avenue."

"'Huge' is an understatement," Mansfield chimed in.

"Right. Somehow, Gatto found out I was meeting with the Director of IT at Providential and he schedules a meeting just before mine with the head of the brokerage department, the guy who owns the customer relationships. Neither of us put the account on our forecast for weeks so as to not tip the other off, but he knew I was in there and laid – in a manner of speaking – a trap for me.

"Finally, one day, the IT director calls my manager to tell him that they only wanted to deal with Gatto. She told him that Gatto was much more professional to work with. Now, my manager wasn't a gullible guy. He knew something smelled about this and checks into things with the brokerage guy. He didn't know anything about my involvement but inquired into what the IT director was doing. He found out that Gatto was the woman's new boyfriend. Her office colleagues claimed they were throwing down on her office sofa during evenings."

"Oh, my god!" Mansfield said. Porter could only stare, open-mouthed at Wayne.

"This was too much even for my scum bag manager –"

"I should hope so! Seducing a prospect!" Porter said.

Wayne laughed. "Oh, he didn't mind that. It was a favorite tactic of his as well. No, I gave him an ultimatum: Gatto or me. I was doing twice the business Gatto was, so it was a no-brainer who to fire."

Wayne's cell phone rang.

"Angelis."

"Rob Bailey. Wayne, what the *hell* is going on?"

Wayne collapsed into a chair. "Rob, don't tell me a guy named Malloy called you."

"No, but there's rumors all over Wall Street that you guys are history. Man, this is my *ass* we're talking about. We were supposed to close the VC deal today. Now it's on hold pending review."

Oh shit! Now we might really go under.

"Now, Rob, look at it this way: if you invest, we have no liquidity emergency."

"Very funny. There's talk of Manley suing your CEO's ass for fraud and misrepresentation. What is the deal?"

Wayne, as calmly as he could, recounted his day for Bailey.

"So you see, Rob, this is a lot of BS thrown up by VibraWeb."

"Can you prove it?"

"I can prove the fake reference thing. The rest…well…"

"What about Azalea? We based our decision on you getting that. I thought that everything was signed."

"It was but then this so-called recruiter called from the grave. I can fix it."

Bailey was silent for an uncomfortably long time.

"Rob," Wayne said. "I *can* fix it. The truth shall set us free."

"Nothing personal, but I can't take that for granted. My job's on the line." Bailey paused again. "I'm going to work something."

"What?"

"You do your thing; I'm going to do mine. I'll be in touch."

"Later."

Wayne looked at Porter. "Thanks for snapping me back to reality. I would have blown the quarter trying to get back at Gatto. Sometimes, the competition can get the better of me. I promise to keep it under control."

"Hey, I wanted to cut his nuts off, too! Wayne, I totally trust you. You've taught me the sales game and been patient. I owe you a lot. I doubt many other reps would have been so nurturing."

"Thanks. Let's go for a cold brew. I have to figure out what to do. One thing for certain, Porter; there will be a 'Come to Jesus' meeting on Monday with those Azalea clowns."

***

Julia pulled her Nissan Maxima up to Carbo's Café in the trendy Buckhead section of Atlanta. The valet opened her door, handing her a claim check for the car. She was grateful to not have to find her own parking on a busy Friday night.

She stepped into the bar area, scanning the room for Spencer. He spotted her before she saw him, picked up his change and stepped away from the bar to approach Julia. He approached, wearing a rather formfitting, argyle V-neck gray sweater and pleated khakis. His blue eyes, focused on her, caused some flutters in Julia's stomach. *I don't recall Brosnan wearing that but…I hope I'm doing the right thing here,* she thought, as she felt her cheeks flush.

"Thanks so much for meeting me tonight. I know we are breaking our 'agreement'."

"Well, I'll take you at your word that this is a business meeting."

"I promise."

She had no intention of holding him to it. Quite the contrary.

"I thought you were in New York this week."

"Yes, but I had business to deal with down here today and flew back last night. I'll be going back Sunday night."

"Is this going back and forth getting to you yet?"

"Yes. I'll be glad when this integration decision is made and I can stay here in Atlanta. I don't think Gibson's ever heard of conference calls; he keeps summoning me to New York."

He led her to the dining room where the maître d' checked Spencer's name off his list, selected some menus and seated them in a corner table for two.

"Have you been here before, Julia?"

"No. To be honest I don't come into Buckhead much any more. It's overrun with Georgia Tech people and always seems crowded."

"Oh, I'm sorry. I guess we could have gone somewhere else."

"No, I didn't mean that the way it sounded." *Damn, now you've insulted him already.* "I apologize. I used to love coming into the area. It's, I don't know, changed a little. So, what do you recommend?"

"Well, it's true gluttony but I love Carbo's Classic Carpetbagger."

Julia searched the menu. "Oh, my, you're right. 'Filet pocketed with a mini lobster tail with lobster cream sauce'," she said, closing the menu and setting it aside. "Looks great. I'll take one!"

Their server took their orders and disappeared.

"So, Spencer, what did you want to talk about?"

"Julia, I've closely watched you work with my team on the pilot…"

Oh, no, here comes the job offer…

"…and I've come to trust your judgment and certainly your integrity. It's been a very refreshing experience to see you so dedicated to InUnison while maintaining total professionalism even when your competition is working in the next room. I can't think of too many other vendors who could do that.

"Well, I'm very flattered. Thank you," Julia said.

Spencer took a sip of his pinot. "I need some reassurance, Julia, that it isn't only you; that it's InUnison's values as well."

"So, you're a little spooked by the financial rumors?" Julia said, disappointed that he hadn't extended a job offer.

"Yes. I'm feeling exposed here. Christ, this was supposed to be a straightforward pilot but it's now a battle to the death between Miller and Racker. I was simply supposed to be the impartial observer."

"You knew at some point that you would have to weigh in."

"Right, but I figured that it would be an obvious choice in the end and even Miller would recognize it. I'm ashamed to admit that I underestimated his survival reflex. Now, I'm as much the enemy as Racker."

It was Julia's turn to sample the wine. "So now you're second guessing yourself? What happened to that self-confident Carlton swagger?" *'James Bond' wouldn't be so tentative.*

"I've been working very hard to build an information organization here which provides a real service to Azalea Insurance. I've reached out to department heads to tell them that we should be viewed as a service organization to them, not some arrogant ivory tower telling them how to run their business…"

"The anti-Miller…"

"…yes, but most importantly, doing it by example. I thought that Gibson was starting to recognize that when he appointed me to do this pilot. Now, I'm not sure he trusts me after the financials issue blew up yesterday."

"Spencer, you're dancing here. What is really your concern? I don't see what's changed."

Spencer leaned forward and looked directly at his dinner guest. "Look me in the eye, and tell me InUnison is not going down the tubes."

"You don't really believe that crap? C'mon!"

"What am I supposed to believe? It's a classic 'he said, she said'."

"I'm amazed, Spencer. Is your opinion of the industry so bad that you can't believe that any company can be on the up and up?"

"Frankly, yes, it is that bad, and I don't believe that you are so naïve to not know the shitty state of affairs in the industry. People are making career decisions when they choose software and the vendors don't care about that at all. They know their products won't fulfill their promises or flat out doesn't work."

"*Riiiight*, and everyone in IT is pure as the driven snow. You know that for every shady vendor, there's some IT flunky who knows he's wasting his company's money and does so because it means job security fixing the mess. No, I'm not naïve. But I'm at InUnison because we *do* fulfill our commitments and we *do* put out a quality product. The industry isn't nearly as bad as you make it out to be. I know plenty of other companies like InUnison. It's cliché but a few bad apples…"

"So there's nothing to the rumors?"

"No, unless we lose business because of them. Let's face it; we are a startup and liquidity will always be a concern."

Spencer leaned back in his chair, studying his wine. "I appreciate your candor. I guess we'll see what happens on Monday."

"Monday?"

"Wayne Angelis asked Gibson for a meeting to straighten things out."

"Who's going to be there?"

"Obviously, everyone involved in the pilot from Azalea. I spoke to Wayne earlier and he said Engler was flying in. He alluded to bringing in some 'witnesses'. He wouldn't tell me anything more."

"Bill will do whatever it takes to clear up this situation up. He takes his reputation very seriously."

"I have no doubts about that, Julia. It's a necessary condition but perhaps not sufficient."

They talked more about the pilot project and continued to debate the state of the industry. On several topics, Spencer had to simply agree to disagree despite Julia's withering logic.

Their main course served, they began to savor the beef and lobster.

"This is excellent, Spencer. Thanks for suggesting it."

"You're welcome," he responded. "Now, can we put business aside for the rest of the meal?"

"You promised," Julia teased. Seeing his hurt, puppy dog look, though, she realized he took her seriously. "I think we've solved enough of the industry's problems. I release you from your commitment." Julia said with a wave of her hand. Their eyes locked on each other as she reached across the table to stroke his hand with the tips of her fingers. Her whole body was alive and alert to any sensation. "I really respect you, Spencer."

She took his hand in hers, gently squeezed and leaned further forward.

"So, how far is your house from here?"

"Uh…not far…" Spencer mumbled.

***

Rob Bailey was in his World Financial Center office overlooking Battery Park. He regularly worked into the evening and then enjoyed the wealth of dining and drinking establishments of lower Manhattan. It provided an opportunity to run into other financial executives and gather some intelligence for Manley Brothers.

As he packed his briefcase with study material for the weekend, his boss appeared.

"Hey, Rob! Glad to see you're still here. I have some good news for you."

"What's that?"

"Our slick CEO worked his magic. It's all done and should be announced on Monday, pre-market."

"Should I ask how he did this?"

"Well, I know he was on the phone with Masters, Azalea's CEO, for a long time and Masters talked to Engler at InUnison for even longer."

"So, Angelis is going to close Azalea?"

"It's taken care of."

"How?"

"You don't want to know."

"That's what I thought," Bailey murmured.

Chapter 18 Come to Jesus

Wayne fidgeted as he waited in the lobby of the Millennium Hotel, watching *Squawk Box* on the CNBC cable channel. Both Porter and his CEO were late, eroding his patience. The next story on the TV piqued his interest.

"Let's go now to the 'Faber Report' and…the Brain, David Faber."

"Thanks, Mark," Faber said, the screen split between himself and the show host, Mark Haines. As Faber started to talk, Haines' head slid off the screen to the left and Faber's took over. "There's an interesting upgrade from our old friend Jim Grabin at Manley Brothers this morning. He is upgrading Azalea Financial from 'underperform, underweight, sell' to 'overperform, equalweight, hold'. Now, what makes this interesting–"

"That's an upgrade?" Faber's partner, Joe "Kahuna" Kernen interrupted. "How can you tell?"

Faber chuckled. "Hey, I'm reading the release. What makes this interesting is that about four months ago, he downgraded the stock, questioning the financial management of the company. I did some quick research and found no new news on Azalea so I can't tell what Grabin is acting on here. He merely says that there have been improvements over the past quarter."

"So, are we awarding a Lame-o on this?" the Kahuna asked.

"This clearly needs *some* award," Haines weighed in.

"How about 'End of the Quarter Clean Sweep Award'," Faber offered. "Maybe Manley is doing some business here. I have it on good authority that Manley lost a big chunk of business when Grabin downgraded Azalea. This might be a redo."

"Now, David," Kernen said. "You *really* don't think they are breaching that *impregnable* Chinese wall between investment banking and research, do you?"

"You're so cynical, Joe," Faber replied with a wink. "In other news…"

So, good for Azalea, Wayne thought.

Porter hurried through the plaza of the World Trade Center to meet Wayne. He had mindlessly walked to the Marriott World Trade since that's where he usually met Wayne. It took about five minutes of sitting in the lobby before it dawned on him that he was in the wrong place. As he entered the Millennium, Porter spotted Wayne standing in the lobby and looking at his watch.

"Wayne, sorry. I pulled a brain fart and went to the Marriott."

"No problemo. I'm more nervous about Engler. He's checked in but I can't get through on his phone. We have to get going."

"I wish we would have had more time to talk on Friday. What am I supposed to do here?"

"Nothing. Try to look intimidating."

"Oh, I've been practicing that at home with Stephanie."

"That's good! I don't hear sarcasm from you enough. You'll get this sales stuff any day now."

"Speaking of sarcasm…"

Wayne walked over to the house phone to try his CEO's room again. This time Engler picked up.

"Bill, we have to get going. I've been trying you for twenty minutes."

"Sorry. I was leaving a bunch of voicemails. This trip came up so suddenly that I needed to leave some instructions with people I was supposed to see today. Anyway, I'll be right down."

Wayne hung up and gave Porter thumbs up.

"So, did you figure out how we are going to prove that Gatto is behind this dead recruiter?" Porter asked.

"I'm afraid not. There's nothing to trace back to Gatto, except that phone call to Mansfield and that doesn't mean squat. I'm going to have to rely on Engler's reputation for integrity."

"Do we only have Engler?"

"No. I made some withdrawals from the favor bank and briefed Spencer on Friday, hoping he would step up for us. He was pretty negative, though."

Engler finally appeared in the lobby and found the New York sales team.

"Is this weather forecast for real? How can it be in the eighties in March? I brought a heavy coat."

"It's been a wacky year weather-wise," Wayne said. "Warm winter, very little snow. The skiing was pretty crummy."

"So, what do you want me to do here?

"Be totally upfront with these folks."

"I always have been."

"I know, but the only thing that will save the day is to clearly demonstrate our good faith to the CFO, Ralph Gibson. Remember him?"

Engler grunted. "Yes, he was the Tweedle Dee to the CIO's Tweedle Dum."

"Now see, Bill, you have to purge that from your brain. If we don't win him over, we're done."

"I'll behave." His sandy beard closed over pursed lips.

They exited the hotel turning right to walk the length of Fulton Street, which was bustling as usual with shopkeepers putting out tables of their wares, hoping the warm weather would increase traffic.

Connie Sanchez greeted the InUnison trio as they stepped off the elevator.

"Good morning, Wayne. I'll show you to the conference room. Your other guests are here as well. I have them waiting in a spare office next to the meeting room like we discussed on Friday."

"That's great, Connie. I appreciate the help."

"Anything I can do to help you screw that Miller swine is all right by me."

She ushered Wayne, Porter and Engler first to the spare office where Engler was introduced around and Wayne briefed his witnesses on expectations. As they left that office, they bumped into Spencer Carlton just arriving.

"Good morning, Wayne! What a wonderful day!"

Wayne wasn't prepared for such a jovial greeting from Spencer after their tense conversation on Friday.

"Well, you're in a much better mood than when we talked on Friday. Did you get laid over the weekend?" Wayne joked.

Spencer grinned from ear to ear and skipped into the conference room. "Good morning, everyone! Marvelous day, isn't it?"

Porter looked quizzically at Wayne. "He got laid," Wayne said, with a twinge of jealousy.

"Julia will be disappointed," Porter said, knowing of her attraction to her "Pierce Brosnan". On the contrary, Julia was anything *but* disappointed. She had, in fact, spent the entire weekend wearing one of Spencer's Georgia Bulldog sweatshirts, and little else.

"Good morning!" Wayne said, entering the meeting. "I hope everyone had a good weekend. You all remember our CEO, Bill Engler, right?"

Miller, Gibson, and Racker all nodded their heads.

"First of all, thank you for coming on such short notice. We really need to clear the air here on some issues."

"There's nothing to clear up," Miller said, assuming his smug, slouching posture. "You guys are in financial trouble and we don't want to become dependent on a dying company."

Wayne maintained his calm outward composure and pressed on.

"Now, Stewart, let me dispel one thing right off the bat. That recruiter who called you?"

"Yes, Jake Malloy."

"Are you aware that he's dead?"

Miller sat straight up. "What? Did he get hit by a bus over the weekend or something?" he said, laughing and looking around, expecting to see others appreciating his joke. None did.

"No. He died of a heart attack two years ago. Here's his obituary." Wayne distributed copies of the article.

"There must be more than one Jake Malloy."

"Not that we can find. Did you try that 800 number he gave you?"

"No."

"It's Malloy's old number which is now disconnected. Gentlemen, someone has been posing as Jake Malloy and spent most of Thursday calling my prospects, spreading a lie about InUnison's viability."

"Wait a minute. He faxed me a resume. Some woman named Mackenzie. Was that faked too?"

"Jeffords??" Engler whispered to Porter sitting on his right. Porter nodded.

"She's toast," the CEO whispered.

"You can't be serious," Gibson said. "That would be pretty low even for software sales rep standards."

"No, unfortunately the resume is real," Wayne said. "We may be small but there is a lively rumor mill at InUnison, particularly when it comes to financial matters. This young lady got spooked and went to some recruiter. But not to this Jake Malloy, obviously."

"She's toast," Engler hissed again.

"With respect to your question, Ralph, I'm reluctant to name anyone because I don't have irrefutable proof. I would hate, *hate* to engage in any character assassination."

Gag.

Wayne continued. "I'd rather that we focus – for the moment at least – on any lingering viability questions. To that end, I've invited Bill Engler here."

"What about our viability is in question?" Engler asked. "I thought we addressed all that in our meeting at the beginning of the month."

"We didn't hear about your cash position," Miller challenged, pointing his finger at Engler.

"You didn't ask," Engler said.

"That's a good point, Stewart," Gibson said. "Perhaps you could enlighten us, Mr. Engler."

"Our cash position right now is a little over four million."

"And your burn rate?"

"About one-four per month."

"That's not even three months!" Miller said. "See Ralph they are –"

Gibson raised his hand, cutting off Stewart before he took over the floor.

"If memory serves, your revenue plan was seventy for the year, ramping quarter to quarter. Is that correct?"

"Yes, the quarterly plans are ten, fourteen, nineteen, twenty-seven," Engler replied.

"And if memory serves as well, you were on plan for this quarter?"

"Yes, but not now. We are looking to do twelve to thirteen."

"Really? That's fantastic!"

"But Wayne's Number is in jeopardy because of this sabotage effort. He could do two mil himself otherwise."

In your dreams, Bill, Wayne thought.

"So, you conceivably added at least two more months to your cash position?"

"Yes, at minimum. Our pipeline for the second quarter is looking very strong and don't forget the new VC money."

Gibson looked up at the ceiling as he digested the information. "This goes a long way to satisfying me."

"Not for me, Ralph," Miller said. "I think we need and wait to see what happens with them. They could be just telling us this stuff. Our deal is a big piece of their quarter. That's the only reason they care so much."

Sam Racker finally spoke up. "Stewart, stop being so obstinate. We never did get this kind of information from VibraWeb."

"Well, you didn't *ask*," he said, smirking at Engler who showed no reaction.

"The hell we didn't!" Racker said. "We specifically asked that it be presented at their corporate briefing. Instead we got *Star Wars* redux." He turned to Gibson. "I'm satisfied, Ralph."

Miller wasn't finished. "Ralph, we didn't need this kind of information from VibraWeb because of the Flanderson partnership. They wouldn't have done that deal if VibraWeb wasn't sound."

Carlton snorted. "Please, Stewart."

"No, that's a good point," Gibson said. "Larry Liu told me that."

Racker and Carlton looked at each other, shrugged and gave up.

Now you've forced me to go nuclear, Wayne thought.

"Stewart, as I said, I had hoped that our financial disclosures would resolve things but as you have attacked our integrity, I feel compelled to respond. You seem to have faith in Tom Gatto. I'm going to prove to you that it is misplaced."

He stepped from the room to the spare office next door and ushered in George Melani, Craig Mansfield and Bill Thomas. Melani had his signature satin shirt, open to his sternum, his ponytail secured with three rubber bands. Mansfield had at least found a pressed white shirt and flowery blue tie to go with his ripped jeans while Thomas was wearing the classic blue bank interview suit.

"Stewart, were you aware that Tom Gatto used to sell for InUnison?"

"No. So what?"

"I have here two of his former customers: George Melani, Director of Strategic Systems at Potential Investing and Craig Mansfield, CTO and co-founder of PensAndClips.com."

"Oh, great, a day trader and a 'new economy' guy," Miller said. "Nice hair, by the way." *The Marines would eat you for lunch, you hippie.*

Melani's eyes narrowed and Wayne gave him a calming hand on his shoulder.

"George, would you mind briefing my Azalea friends on your experience with Tom Gatto?"

"With pleasure. We bought InUnison late last year primarily to be able to integrate with customer mainframes. The connector was supposed to be released by December but was delayed. Tom Gatto didn't tell us. In fact, he lied to my face about its availability and then falsified the contract to exclude it." He was still standing but was leaning his huge frame on the table. His eyes were locked on Miller. "Wayne here had to clean up the mess. Most important, Mr. Engler actually changed his release schedule to accommodate our needs. I've never seen a software company care so much about its commitments, even ones that shouldn't have been made. Mr. Engler and Wayne are tops in my book. So is Porter Mitchell."

"My story is pretty much the same," Craig Mansfield said. "We needed the same connector and, yes, InUnison backed us up one hundred percent. In addition, they gave us very good partnership terms once Wayne took over. We are totally dependent on them and we are comfortable with that."

"Sounds to me," Miller said, slouching in his seat again, "that there is a lack of contract discipline with you guys. Of course a rep would take advantage of that."

"Look, damn it –"

"Easy, big guy," Wayne said, hoping to plug the volcano.

"Ralph, we already went through the reference dance before. This is more of the same."

"Stewart, this Gatto man tried to screw these people," Racker said. "How can you stand by him?"

"He's being a rep. That's why you need people like me to keep them in line."

"Speaking of references," Wayne interjected in order to regain control of the meeting. "This is William Thomas, formerly of VibraWeb. He sold for them until January. Tom Gatto took over his territory.

"Do you remember that we didn't think that UBS Warburg was a customer of VibraWeb?"

"Yes," Gibson said.

Bill Thomas spoke up. "It was faked. VibraWeb has no reference customers because they always piss them off. They fake references all the time."

"Now I've heard it all," Miller said, throwing up his hands. "So how did they fake that call? He knew a lot about UBS."

"It was staged by the Chicago rep and his systems engineer. His nickname is Doctor Reference. Of course he knows about UBS and ABN Amro; he's been trying to sell into them for a couple of years."

"And how did you come to meet Wayne?" Miller asked.

"I was having an interview with him."

"Oh, *now* I see it clearly. Ralph, this guy is trying to kiss Angelis' ass to get a job."

"Good point, Stewart."

"Look, Ralph, this is bullshit," Miller continued, emboldened. "They are tearing apart Gatto who isn't here to defend himself."

"Let's get him on the phone," Carlton suggested. He reached for the speaker phone in the middle of the table. "Know his number?"

"Not off the top of my head. I'll have to run down to my desk."

"Fine," Gibson said. "We need a break anyway."

Miller walked to the elevator to retrieve the number while the other Azalea people went to refill coffee mugs.

"Wayne, I really have to get back to the office," Melani said. "If you need any more help, I know this guy named Guido who could take care of that dude."

"I don't think that will be necessary, George. Thanks anyway."

Porter approached Wayne. "We don't seem to be making much headway here. Miller's attitude is stall, stall, stall."

"I know. I was hoping to provoke him to do something stupid but he isn't taking the bait. I don't know whether calling Gatto will help or not. He'll deny it all and it's his word against ours."

Engler had been listening to this exchange. "Wayne, are all CIOs out here like Miller? Maybe we are better off without him."

"Welcome to my world, Bill. Thankfully, there are an increasing number of CIOs who are more enlightened than Miller but that's the hand I've been dealt here."

"You're a saint. I wanted to rip him a new one. He essentially called me a liar in there."

Miller returned to the conference room where Carlton and Mansfield were still waiting and gave Spencer Gatto's phone number.

Wayne, with Gibson right on his heels, returned to the conference room.

"Do we have Gatto on the phone?" Gibson asked.

"Yes. He's in his office with his regional manager."

"Now, I don't want this to be a circus. Wayne, you will only speak when spoken to. Otherwise, I'll have to ask you and Mr. Engler to step outside."

"I totally understand," Wayne said.

Uptown in Five Penn Plaza, Tom Gatto was indeed in his office with George Means, wondering what this call was all about.

"Good morning. This is Ralph Gibson at Azalea Financial. How are you today?"

"Fine."

"I have Stewart Miller, Spencer Carlton and Sam Racker here with me, as well as Wayne Angelis and Bill Engler from InUnison Software."

Gatto hit mute. "They brought Engler in. We must have them on the run; they're pulling out all the stops." He took the phone off mute.

"Good morning, Angelis. How's the quarter shaping up? Did you steal enough business from the other reps to make your Number?"

Wayne glowered and started to reply but Gibson intercepted him.

"Now, Tom, I'm going to tell you what I told Wayne; this won't be a circus. I'll dismiss you if you aren't civil."

F' you! "My apologies."

"As you know, we are trying to come to a consensus on the direction we want to go with respect to software integration. Some, uh, questions have arisen and we'd like to get some clarity from you."

"What questions?"

"Are you certain that UBS Warburg is a customer of yours?"

"Yes, absolutely. You were there for the conference call."

Means started to snigger.

"Well, we have an accusation that the UBS personnel on that call were actually VibraWeb reps or SEs."

Means had to cover his mouth at this point.

"That's quite an accusation. I assure you…excuse me for a second. I have a call on the other line," Gatto said, muting the phone. "What the hell are you laughing about?"

"I wonder how they found out. This is a first."

"What are you talking about?"

"Shepherd must be losing his touch."

Gatto could only stammer as the reality sank in. "You mean it *was...*?"

"What? You didn't know?"

"OF COURSE NOT! NO ONE TOLD ME!"

Means was totally out of control now.

"George! What do I tell them?"

"I don't give a damn! This is too funny! We even faked you out."

"Shit, George. How was I supposed to know?" He took a moment to compose himself. "George, in the future please remember that I generally like to know the truth about my lies." He took the phone off mute. "Sorry about that. End of quarter business you know. So, we were discussing the conference call with UBS –"

"And ABN," Carlton added.

"Well, I'm a little *insulted.* This is my integrity being questioned here. I wouldn't do such a thing as fake a reference."

Means had regained his self-control. "And I assure you that he'd be summarily fired if he did such a thing," he said into the speaker.

"See?" Miller said. "He's a stand up guy."

"This is Sam Racker. There were also charges made by some of your former clients at InUnison about altering contracts and misrepresenting release details."

Damn you, Angelis. "And who might they be?"

"Potential Investing and PensAndClips.com," Racker said.

"We had a few misunderstandings, that's all. In fact, I was given bad info from my management at the time. It wasn't my fault but I had to take the heat for it. It's one of the reasons I left. They tried to stick me with the blame."

"Sounds reasonable," Miller said. "Reps are always the last to know things."

"Good point, Stewart," Gibson said.

You lying sack of… Engler was practically biting his tongue in half.

Miller's obstruction and Gatto's dissembling cleared away any lingering doubts for Spencer. He was now firmly on InUnison's side and took to the offensive, armed with the details from his Friday conversation with Wayne.

"This is Spencer Carlton. Do you know a recruiter named Jake Malloy?"

Uh oh. "Yes, I do."

"Have you talked to him lately?"

Shit. He knows. "No," Gatto prudently replied. "He passed away a couple of years ago."

"Funny, because someone using his name has been calling the InUnison prospects and spreading a rumor that they are not a viable company."

"Yes, I've heard that as well. It's sad." He winked at Means who now had a confused look on his face.

"Now, who would stand to gain from killing InUnison's deals?"

"Well, I suppose I might. But Azalea is really the only deal where we are competing."

"So you weren't behind the calls?" Carlton asked.

"Of course not! I have deals to close. I don't have time for such shenanigans." He grinned and nodded to Means. George, finally comprehending the truth, gave Gatto two thumbs up.

"Last question. Did you call Craig Mansfield last Thursday around one o'clock?"

All eyes in the conference room locked onto Spencer.

"What the…?" Miller mouthed.

"I don't recall calling him."

"Your phone number was on his caller ID…"

Damn that caller ID!

"…and he could only recall that it was around the time that this dead recruiter called him from the afterlife."

"Oh, wait a minute. Yes, I did call him. He didn't answer though. It went right to voice mail and I didn't leave a message."

"What were you calling about?"

"I don't think that's any of your business."

Carlton gave up. "That's all I had. Thank you."

"While Tom is still on the line, I want to ask Engler about the release stuff," Miller demanded.

"Proceed, Stewart," Gibson said.

"About the release confusion at the end of last year – did every rep know that the release was going to be late?"

Damn you! "There was some miscommunication –"

"There! You see? That's what Tom said!"

"As I was starting to say, yes, there was some confusion but for some reason, only Tom Gatto seemed to get it wrong. He clearly, and intentionally, misled his customers. You only met two of them. There were at least seven customers who were misled. Even so, we did right by them. Unlike the competition, I want all of our customers to be referenceable. As I said in my closing remarks at the HQ meeting, I know the commitment and leap of faith it takes for customers like yourself to choose technology from a new company like ours. One false move and..." he snapped his fingers, "…our reputation is history. I'm proud of these guys," he said, motioning to Porter and Wayne. "They have rebuilt our reputation here in New York. I can't believe you don't clearly see our value and determination to make Azalea successful."

Miller started to respond, but Engler held up his hand.

"I'm not finished, sir. You have questioned my veracity and that of my sales team. I had hoped that our testimonials here today would convince you of our integrity. I have never misled anyone. If anything, I'm too forthcoming. Why? Because, again, unlike the competition, this isn't some get-rich-quick scheme. I want to build an enduring, billion dollar software company and that takes successful, repeat customers. It means being a partner with our customers, not an adversary or worse, a parasite. It means standing behind our commitments.

"I've tried my best to hire people whose attitude and moral compasses are in alignment with mine. I'm not perfect, witness Mr. Gatto. But Wayne and Porter certainly match my profile.

"Make no mistake, people. We *will* make you successful. I'd rather tank my company making you successful than take your money and see you fail."

Carlton and Racker were nodding slowly and turned to Gibson.

"Nice speech," Miller said. "The best I can say about your company is that it has good intentions."

"You're an idiot!"

All heads turned to Porter. "Yes, I'm talking to you!" he shouted, pointing a finger at Miller. "You called my CEO a liar, the rest of us incompetent at best and that's *totally unacceptable!* Mr. Engler is, hell, all the managers at InUnison are some of the most upfront, decent people I've ever worked for.

"InUnison can solve your integration issues and that means dollars to your bottom line. We *proved* it but you don't give a damn about your company's finances. This is you protecting turf at the cost of your company's efficiency!"

Wayne debated; *I should stop him, but what the hell?*

Carlton turned so that neither Miller nor Gibson could see him fighting to stifle his laugh. At the other end of the phone line, Gatto had to mute the phone once again, lest they all hear his and Means' snickers.

Miller smiled at Porter and broke the silence. "So what's your point?"

"*YOU ASSHOLE!*"

Now there was no hesitation. Both Engler and Wayne jumped up to grab Porter before he could hurdle the table.

"*I'VE HAD IT WITH YOU POMPOUS IT BASTARDS!*"

They wrestled Porter out the door.

"MY GRANDMOTHER KNOWS MORE ABOUT SOFTWARE…"

"Porter, chill," Wayne told him as he gently but firmly pushed him out the door.

"…*AND SHE'S DEAD!*"

Wayne successfully guided Porter into the spare office.

"We should hire that kid," Means said. "He still actually cares about this shit."

"I've had it!" Porter said as Engler closed the door.

"I think you made that perfectly clear," Engler said.

"I joined this company to spread the word about InUnison, about how we could make their businesses and lives better. I expected customers to appreciate what we offered. Instead, all I got were lazy idiots or obstructionists like Miller. He pushed me over the edge."

Porter's knees buckled and he collapsed into a chair by the window.

"Shit. I'm sorry. Am I going to be fired?" he asked.

"No," Engler chuckled. "O'Rourke will most likely give you a bonus. Based on that example of blunt honesty, though, you should be in Engineering not Sales. But don't get in the habit of calling senior executives 'assholes'. I'd save it for special occasions."

"So, are you all right here, alone?" Wayne asked.

"Yeah," Porter said, burying his face in his hands. "I don't believe I did that."

Wayne and Engler returned to the meeting.

"Well," Gibson said, raising his eyebrows. "I can't make a real distinction here between these two companies…"

Miller and Racker started to talk but, again, Gibson held the floor. "…but I have a solution." His eyes swept the room. "I talked to Larry Liu from Flanderson Consulting yesterday…"

Spencer groaned, Miller rolled his eyes and Racker shook his head.

"…and he says that since we have essentially a draw in this competition we could use both…"

"Bravo, Larry!" Gatto whispered. "Always playing an angle."

"BUT RALPH!" Spencer shouted, louder than he planned. "They don't work together and Liu doesn't know jack about InUnison! Besides, it makes no freaking sense to have to integrate the integration systems."

"Well, now we see your true colors, don't we?" Miller countered. "I never believed that you were impartial."

"C'mon, Ralph. Liu wants the consulting money," Racker said.

"But this is a great solution," Gibson begged, visibly disappointed that his brilliant compromise was met with such rejection. "It's a hedge in case one of these companies fails."

Just then the door to the conference room opened and Leonard Masters, Azalea CEO entered. A classic "gray-templed businessman", he was a very large, but fit, man, and filled the doorway.

"Having a party here, Ralph?"

"Not exactly, Leo. We're trying to resolve this integration impasse."

He introduced himself around. "Pleased to meet you face-to-face, Bill," he said when he got to Bill Engler. Wayne looked at Engler who smiled and nodded.

"Well, I'm here to straighten this out. If I understand the issues, we were all set to award the contract to InUnison, right?"

"Correct," Spencer said. "They proved to be the better solution."

"So, you say," Stewart countered.

Masters turned to him and narrowed his eyes. "You, Miller, should be quiet." He turned back to Gibson. "And things got confused over some BS about InUnison going under or something."

Oh, oh. This isn't good, Gatto thought.

"Yes, that's correct, Leo. But I have a solution…"

"So do I. I can clear this all up. I have it on good authority that Manley Brothers is investing heavily in InUnison. There is nothing to the rumors about financial insolvency. I talked at length with Mr. Engler here last Friday and he disclosed that Manley was their lead investor for this round…"

"And you're taking his word?" Stewart asked.

"Shut up, you Neanderthal! I confirmed it with my counterpart at Manley late Friday."

"I didn't think you were a big fan of Manley Brothers, Leo," Gibson said.

"Business relationships flow and ebb, Ralph," Masters said with a grin.

"The stock upgrade…" Wayne murmured to Engler who smiled a little broader. "I'll be damned."

"So, InUnison gets the business?" Miller asked, standing up and leaning toward his CEO.

"Yes. You got a problem with that?"

"I'll resign before that happens!"

"Fine. Have your office cleaned out by noon, along with those stupid mugs. I'm tired of hearing about how our systems are twenty years behind. Spencer, congratulations. You are now CIO."

Stewart, looking like he had been run through with his samurai sword, turned and left the room.

Gatto and Means simply shrugged. "*C'est la vie,*" Means said. "Hard to compete against that."

"Excuse me?" Gatto said into the phone.

"Yes?" Gibson answered.

"It doesn't sound like you need us on the line anymore. Let us know if we can be of assistance in the future." He hung up.

They all got up to go.

"Ralph, Sam, Spencer. I need you to stay for a few more minutes," Masters said.

"Wayne, stick around," Spencer said. "I'll get you that PO." The InUnison team retreated to the spare office next door where Porter waited.

"Ralph, this thing got totally out of control," Masters said. "And Sam, I hold you partially responsible. That renegade squad you started…all that did was piss off Miller. Spencer will take over from now on."

Sam started to defend himself but Masters raised his hand. "I know better than anyone that we should have shoved Miller out a long time ago. Anyway, Ralph, I think it's time to schedule your retirement party."

"After this experience, Leo, I'm all for it."

***

Next door, Wayne and Bill briefed Porter on the outcome of the meeting. He was thrilled that InUnison won the deal, and especially to learn that his outburst hadn't done any damage.

"Bill, one piece is still missing," Wayne said. "How did Masters get Manley to upgrade the stock? That sounds, well, a little shady. And why didn't you tell me about it going into the meeting?"

"I know *noth*-ing," Engler said, doing his best Sergeant Shultz imitation.

"Oh, please."

"No, really! All I know is that Bailey called me to say that they were going to put a good word in for us with Masters. I know better than to ask for the specifics. Anyway, before I know it, Masters calls me and grills me about our finances. He's one sharp CEO. I told him about this meeting but I wasn't sure what, if anything, he might do. I didn't want to raise expectations with you."

"I guess we don't want to look the gift horse in the mouth either."

"Nope. I know how it might look but we got our money and none of us did anything but answer some questions truthfully."

I wouldn't mind knowing what was in it for Grabin, though, Wayne wondered.

***

The very next morning, the Manley analyst, Jim Grabin, sat with his wife and three-year-old daughter, Uptown on 92nd Street, waiting for their interview. Before long, a very prim, gray haired woman approached from an adjacent office.

"Good morning! Mr. and Mrs. Grabin I presume? I'm Ms. Longsworth, Dean of the Wee Wee Preschool. And this must be the precious Ashley Grabin. Oh, she's adorable! Please come in."

The Grabins all trooped into Ms. Longsworth's office and settled into chairs.

"Well, now, first my apologies for the mishandling of your application. I'm appalled that we overlooked your qualifications. It was so nice to hear from Mr. Masters yesterday. He spoke so highly of you! It isn't often that one of our directors gets this involved in such matters as admission. He's such a busy man, being CEO at Azalea and such."

***

Later that same day, March 31st, the sales adversaries leaned back in their respective desk chairs, miles apart, reviewing their forecasts and results.

Not a bad quarter, Wayne thought. But what a close call.

Not a bad quarter, Gatto thought. Especially since I inherited that lame pipeline. Could have really blown out the Number if Azalea...oh well.

Gatto was about to turn out the light in his office and thought better of it.

I need to celebrate this, he thought as he fished out his Pilot. "Let's see…ah, Cindi! I hope you still wear that dental floss for underwear." He dialed and made arrangements for his evening entertainment.

***

Porter came home a little after seven; too late for dinner with Brenda and Stephanie, but Brenda had saved some homemade macaroni and cheese, one of his favorites.

"The mac and cheese is still in the oven," she said. Stephanie squirmed at her right breast.

He wasted no time filling a plate and sitting down at the kitchen table. He was happy to enjoy his dinner in solitude.

He finished, cleaned up his plate and started the dishwasher.

"So, you seem a hell of a lot better than yesterday," Brenda said as he entered the living room with his beer.

"Yes, we got the order from Azalea." He went on to explain what had transpired including the twist that, technically, the deal went through Atlanta now that Spencer Carlton was the new CIO. By the generally accepted sales compensation rules, Grim Reaper could claim a larger share of the deal. Reaper was already lobbying sales management.

"I'm sure that Wayne will get his full compensation. It only seems fair."

"Doubtful, Brenda. He'll have to fight for that."

"But he, and you, did all the work."

"How naïve," he said, acting as if he'd been in the business for years.

"Oh, really?" Brenda lifted a now sated little girl from her chest.

"Sorry, I didn't mean it that way."

"Here, she needs to be burped and I have to go to the bathroom."

He held his grinning six-month-old in both hands as his wife positioned a diaper on his shoulder.

"The really good news is," he called out to Brenda as he positioned Stephanie at his shoulder, tapping her back. *Don't do it, little girl,* "we made..."

Stephanie gave a little grunt and out came a stream of milk onto Porter's shoulder, totally missing the diaper.

"…our Number."

***

Gatto met Cindi at the Grammercy Tavern and immediately ordered a very expensive Cabernet Sauvignon.

"So, you seem lively, Tom. You must have big expectations tonight," Cindi said, as her fingertips played with Gatto's chest hair peeking above his open shirt.

"No more than usual," Gatto replied. "It's so boring though, making your Number quarter after quarter."

He pulled her to him and planted a lingering, sensual kiss.

"A preview of coming attractions," Gatto said, reaching for his wine.

***

In Scarsdale, Wayne Angelis finished faxing some straggler purchase orders to corporate operations before Helen entered with two martinis.

"Since I knew that it was the end of the quarter, I figured we would be having either a celebration or you'd need to drown your sorrows."

"Thank you, my dear! It is the former! Those last few POs pushed me way over the top of my Number!"

"I'm happy to hear that. What a quarter, huh?" Helen asked, with enthusiasm, tallying up her own winnings.

Wayne shut down his computer and was about to turn off the fax machine when it came to life again.

"Now, who is faxing you something at nine-thirty at night?" Helen asked with irritation.

They both looked at the cover page as it emerged.

"Oh, my. It's from Sampson Logistics. It can't be…"

He read the note on the cover page:

"Wayne, sorry for the late submission," Giuliano wrote. "I only got final budget approval this afternoon. I hope all is in order and that we can still get the discount for the quarter."

The second page printed and was ejected. Wayne scanned the page and saw the bottom line.

"Holy shit! Five hundred fifty-five thousand! And that's just for one quarter!" He checked his watch again. "I have to fax this out right away. What a bonus!"

He stacked the purchase order into the reader slot on his fax machine and was about to hit SEND when he paused.

"Why did you stop? Get it out there so we can start our celebration," Helen said, waving the martinis. Having closed the condo purchase, she wanted to pitch her next project, a new deck with hot tub.

"I don't need it for *this* quarter. If I wait until tomorrow, then I'll be well on my way to my Q2 Number…*hey!*"

She shoved Wayne aside and hit SEND.

"You and your Number."